The Silence

The Silence

Chris Westwood

PIATKUS

First published in Great Britain in 1993 by
Judy Piatkus (Publishers) Ltd of
5 Windmill Street, London W1

**The moral right of the author
has been asserted**

*A catalogue record for this book is available
from the British Library*

ISBN 0 7499 0195 0

Phototypeset in 11/12pt Compugraphic Times by
Action Typesetting Limited, Gloucester
Printed and bound in Great Britain by
Biddles Ltd, Guildford and Kings Lynn

To Mandy Little —
for just about everything

PART ONE
September Rain

Chapter One

The Centre was one of the few terraced houses still standing on the row. There were four of them in all; two were unoccupied and boarded up, another inhabited by squatters, the remainder of the row having been condemned and pulled down long ago. In hazy late summer, fumes from the motorway flyover and dust from a nearby construction site formed a constant ground smog that caused the Centre and its three companions to waver in the heat. When it rained, the brown dust coating the walls of the houses turned liquid.

Some of the dust had settled inside the Centre. A layer had formed on each window-sill, and on every surface not recently swept clean. Upstairs, where only the bathroom and toilet were used, it was everywhere. In the late evening, motes danced in the columns of light squeezing between the drawn curtains, and the distant rush of motorway traffic became muted, like a stream. In its way the endless sound was lulling, so much so that by midnight Linda Walker had fallen asleep on the couch, thumb still marking her place in the paperback novel she'd been reading.

In the next room, Godfrey's voice rambled on, the words unclear, rising now in a query, falling as he emphasised something deeply felt. This sound was lulling too, like the motorway. Far down in Linda's sub-conscious the muffled voice hummed, a trapped insect trying to escape. She was so far gone that when the phone rang suddenly she came to with a start.

The book fell from her grasp and landed face down, splaying the pages, adding another crease to the weary spine. Linda sat upright, letting the room come into focus. Her sleeping bag was still bound like a Swiss roll at one end of the couch. Directly above a bookcase bowed under the weight of popular paperbacks, an old square rug hung from the wall like a tapestry. To her right, between the books and the door, was an open fireplace, the hearth and grate overflowing with rubber plants. The phone, on the desk by the window, was still ringing. Although she'd set the volume at minimum, it seemed inordinately loud. By the seventh ring she was at the desk, sliding onto the hard-backed chair, reaching for the receiver. As she did so she took a deep, purposeful breath, composing herself.

'Hello,' she said. 'Samaritans, can I help you?'

The *I* was important, the *Help* a key word. The thing was to personalise these first moments quickly, provide the caller with an easy way in. The wrong inflection, a half-hearted or preoccupied tone could lose them forever. So she sat, the receiver pressed to one side of her face, a forefinger tracing a line through the new layer of dust on the desk surface, and waited.

And then, the silence.

Almost every call seemed to begin this way. For some reason she found the first faltering pause, the void, the instant before she heard the voice, far more worrying than anything the caller might tell her. Usually, it meant that whoever was on the line would either be steadying themselves for the emotional outburst that followed or registering her voice, a woman's voice. Sometimes, with sex callers, the sound of a woman was all that was required. Others could only confess to a man, as if to a priest. Always, though, the silence felt to her far longer than it was. A second or two might pass, and it would cross her mind that anyone, anyone at all could be calling, that she could be about to hear the worst thing in the world, something she'd rather not share. And then the caller would clear his or her throat, and Linda would find herself again, and life would go on. The call could take place.

Except that sometimes, as now, the silence continued. She clutched the receiver, still waiting. In the next room Godfrey's voice rose and fell mildly. There were two lines

4

into the Centre and one private line out. As a rule all calls were initially directed to the other room, then diverted here if the first line was busy. Linda cleared her throat. Somewhere on the line was a recognisable sound, much like the rush of motorway traffic. Perhaps the caller was close by, or the sound was merely a nervous intake of breath. Finally she repeated herself, her mouth still parched from sleep.

'Samaritans, can I help you?'

'I don't know that anyone can help,' replied a voice, a woman's, mid or late thirtyish, slightly groggy and slow.

Immediately, before she could check herself, Linda had a crystal-clear picture of an empty room, shabbily furnished, and a lonely, bedraggled woman, wearing only a slip, in an armchair, knees drawn up almost to her chin. Perhaps a cigarette in one hand. Perhaps an empty or half-empty tumbler. A voice could set off so many images.

'I can try. I can try to help,' Linda said. She waited, but the silence prompted her on. 'You can talk to me as freely as you like, you know. This is between the two of us.'

'Nobody knows,' the voice sighed. The short, ragged breaths were close to sobs. Linda waited. 'Nobody knows what I've gone through.'

'But you feel it will help to tell someone?'

'You, you mean? I don't know.'

'Still, you picked up the phone. A lot of people don't get that far. You must have wanted ...' But she was pressing the point. Better to stand back, give the caller time.

'Sometimes it's easier saying what you have to say to someone you don't know.'

'It would be nice if there *were* someone I knew I could tell it to.'

'An understanding friend.'

'Yes, but I don't have that. People who have that don't know how lucky they are.'

'Even close friends can be hard to approach about certain things,' Linda said. 'What's good about our set-up is that we're anonymous. You can say whatever you like − we don't know you and you don't know us. We could pass one another in the street tomorrow without realising.'

'Do you judge people for what they say?' the woman

5

asked in a voice that was somehow altered, sharper, coming down like a whip. 'Do you hold what they tell you against them?'

This was not the typical caller. Most, having found the courage to pick up the phone, wasted no time at all in coming to the point. Here was a woman who wanted to know where she stood before confession, as if this were a matter of profit or loss.

'Everything that passes between us is confidential,' Linda said finally.

'Everything?'

'Absolutely.'

'But you didn't answer my question. About whether or not you make judgements.'

'Me personally? If I do, I can't help it. It's human nature to do that, but I don't attach blame if I can help it. Sometimes we all do things we're unhappy about but have no control over.'

'"Judge ye not,"' the woman's voice began, before breaking into humourless laughter. '"Judge ye not," or something or other. I can't remember the rest, even though I knew it by heart once. Did you ever do anything you were unhappy about?'

This time it was Linda who hesitated. Had the woman phoned for help or to intimidate her? Some callers, a surprising number, contacted the Centre for kicks. Training had prepared her for many eventualities, but occasionally hoaxers could be hard to spot. A man who claimed to be preparing for suicide had once kept Linda engaged on the phone for two traumatic hours before heartily thanking her for her time and inviting her out to dinner. Another caller had rotated between three separate personalities − one week a jilted young business woman; the next a housewife whose husband beat her; the next a lonely bedridden spinster − until one of the daytime Sams had made the connection, noting a turn of phrase, a common reference which linked the three. Oh, they were out there all right: the down at heart, the genuinely desperate. But the twisted and deceitful were out there too, in equal numbers.

Linda glanced at the noticeboard above the desk, to the

6

left of the window. Pinned to it were several memos and colour photographs and the card the other Sams had given her for her thirtieth birthday. Next to this was a colour print of George and herself emerging from church, dusted with confetti, flushed and smiling.

'We've all done things we're unhappy about,' she said. 'Otherwise we'd hardly be human, would we? Making mistakes is how we learn.'

'But sometimes our mistakes are too great to learn from. The only thing to do then is bury them, wipe the slate clean, pretend they never happened.' Again, the homourless laughter, the background of distant noise. 'Will you judge me for what I've done, I wonder?' the woman said.

All at once, Linda wished Godfrey were free to take over, but she could still hear his mumbling next door. There was something − not in the silence between exchanges, but in the woman's voice, the knowing quality of it − that troubled her. She was back to the silence again, the moment before conversation began, and the numbing prospect of what might be revealed.

'Someone is dead because of me,' the caller said.

Linda took another deep breath, transferring the receiver from one hand to the other. She mustn't react. The caller had decided to come clean and mustn't be dissuaded.

'Did you hear what I said?' the woman demanded.

'Yes. But I was waiting for more.'

'You're in luck, then. There's much more.'

'Are you talking about someone you knew? Someone close to you?'

'Someone I knew. Not close to me, though, not in that way. Someone who didn't deserve to live.'

The words were becoming harsher, the voice colder still. There was an edge to it now, vaguely familiar, that Linda wanted desperately not to recognise. She could no longer visualise the woman curled dismally in an armchair. There was no half-empty tumbler. The imagined features were changing, the dishevelled hair rearranging itself.

'Why do you say this person didn't deserve to live?' she wondered.

'Some people don't. They take the joy out of living for

7

others. They only exist to hurt and drag you down with them. They just keep on coming, they push you to the point where you've no choice but to retaliate ... You must have known someone like that yourself, Linda.'

At first she couldn't be sure she'd heard correctly. Her lips moved without sound, unable to form a meaningful reply. The important thing about the system of anonymity was that it protected the person taking the call as well as the caller. If the desolate needed help, the calls must be personalised, but this was too close: too personal. Samaritans were allowed to give out their first names on the phone − it helped build confidence − but tonight she hadn't needed to. The caller already knew her.

'Did you call before?' Linda said conversationally, in spite of her nerves. 'Is that how you knew my name?'

And now there was a new and vast silence, on the line and in her heart. Perhaps this was why she had always feared that moment before the first words were uttered; it was the fear that someone out there knew her, that they had called her, Linda Walker, for a reason. She held her breath. The room was suddenly uncomfortably warm. The connection, the distant traffic, Godfrey next door, all had receded to a dim hiss.

'I know more about you than your name,' the voice said. 'And I'll ask you again, Linda. Do you judge people for what they tell you? Do you really believe we learn from our mistakes?'

But it wasn't a point of contention; Linda understood that only too well. The call had not been made out of desperation or as a cry for help. It had been made, she thought, as the truth slowly dawned on her, despite what they'd agreed all those years ago, huddled together inside the ice house.

'Alison?' she said, and as she spoke the room darkened. One of the few remaining streetlights outside had just gone out with a whisper. 'Alison, is that you?' The speaker's image was suddenly complete: sullen-eyed, raven-haired, fifteen years old. The left ear was pierced and studded, the finger-nails painted blue. 'Ali, we shouldn't be speaking. You know what we said. You're breaking the agreement we made.' It didn't occur to her to ask how Alison had traced her.

'You're right,' the caller's voice said flatly. 'We all know full well what went on and was said. But that was then, and things change.'

They wouldn't be changing without this call, Linda thought angrily. Without this call, the past might have been kept at bay, perhaps eventually forgotten. We were different people back then, she thought, and we made mistakes, as everyone does, and dealt with things as we saw them at the time. It should have been over, but instead the voice on the line was saying, 'Linda, it's beginning again.'

'That's nonsense! You know it is. Why are you doing this?'

'Give me a minute, hear me out. Something has happened to someone we know.'

'Who?'

'Take a look at the day after tomorrow's papers and you'll understand everything.'

'Why not tell me now, since you took the trouble to call?' The rushing traffic felt lodged within Linda's head, thick and relentless as her thoughts. She couldn't be sure anymore that the muffled hum she heard was Godfrey's voice next door. 'You can't break our silence after all this time, after however many years it's been, just to leave me hanging in mid-air. Remember what was agreed. We weren't to involve ourselves in each other's lives again unless it became really necessary.'

'I remember, Linda. Take a look at the papers,' the caller repeated, and hung up.

As she replaced the receiver, Linda noticed her hands shaking. She clutched the front edge of the desk to steady herself, and felt the tremor through the rest of her body. In the darkness beyond the window where the streetlight had gone out, her car was parked. Anyone could be concealed near it, watching, waiting for her to emerge from the Centre. Thankfully it would be first light by the time she came off duty, but for the moment she couldn't see how she was going to get through the night. How could she empathise with others now, hearing their problems, when her own were suddenly so alive and immediate?

Fifteen years, she thought, still seated, unable to budge

9

from the desk. In all that time they had kept the promise, and as if by magic there had been peace. From a distance she'd watched the others succeed and rise – Alison first through provincial newspaper reporting, then magazine journalism; Michael, after years of frustration, through publishing – and as long as they remained strangers it had seemed they could all go on prospering forever in their separate, secret lives. But it had always been on the cards that the spell would break, that one day there would come a familiar voice she had thought she would never hear again. Until now she hadn't been certain why she feared the silence, the brief hesitation before the first word of every call.

She was still at the desk when the phone began ringing again. In the dust on the desk-top she had, without realising, drawn a gallows, a noose, a hanged stick-man. Averting her eyes from it, she took a deep breath and lifted the receiver.

'Samaritans, can I help you?' she said, and waited for whatever came next.

Chapter Two

More than two hundred miles away, in a third floor hotel room overlooking Piccadilly Circus, a telephone receiver was being replaced, then lifted again. Presently, the hotel receptionist answered. The caller cleared his throat, requested an outside line, and dialled.

This time he was through to emergency services.

'Police, please,' he specified. 'No need for an ambulance. Too late for that, I'm afraid.' Within seconds he was speaking to an authoritative-sounding police officer who didn't intimidate him in the least. He let the officer wait for a minute before saying, 'There's been a nasty accident you should know about. Someone got hurt. It won't be easy to identify them. From what I can make out, it could be anybody.' He glanced across at the bed, marvelling at his play on words – anybody, any body – a joke that the officer had evidently missed altogether. 'Yes, that's correct. Whoever did this must be sick, not in their right mind. You really ought to get someone over here now.'

The officer waited, possibly expecting more, then said, 'Could you give me your name and home address, sir?'

'Not really.'

'I see.' There was a lull. 'Then perhaps the address you're calling from.'

'That won't help you,' the caller said firmly. 'This is the first time I've been here and I don't expect to be back.'

'Then I don't really see what we can do, if you're not prepared to help us.' The policeman sounded as though his interest were waning. Perhaps he suspected a hoax, or was taking this disinterested approach to draw him out, tempt him to say something he'd later regret.

The caller took his time. He, not the authorities, was the one in control here. A strange sense of power surged through him, making him dizzy. The french windows were three-quarters open, and he watched the lace curtains billow inwards before the air sucked them out again, towards the balcony and the night.

'Perhaps "accident" isn't the right word,' he decided. 'Whoever did this must have had a strong stomach, is all I can say. It takes me back to the art class at school, reminds me of – '

'Did you say art class?' The officer sounded perplexed.

'Reminds me of how, when I'd drawn something badly and despised it for what it was, I'd scribble it out, take firm hold of my pencil and scratch out what I'd done until you could hardly identify it. You know the feeling. And that's how this looks to me. As if someone was trying to scratch out what was there.' He was leaps and bounds ahead of the policeman now; the voice of authority had gone, was mewling and sighing for want of the proper response.

'Listen,' the caller said. Quickly, he gave the name of the hotel and the street, and hung up.

He stood in front of the dresser in the dimness, resting his fingers lightly on the phone. Next to it was a glass and the small tin of Coke he'd taken from the mini bar before calling. In the dresser's mirror he could see, reflected behind him, the lifeless mess on the bed.

He couldn't make out the details in this light. Not that he needed to, for he knew only too well how precisely the face had been re-drawn, the skin, eyes and tongue removed, the features obliterated. Even the tips of the fingers had been cut off, and when the officer who'd taken the call heard of that, he'd finally get the joke: lacking a face and fingerprints, it really could be any body.

Pouring the Coke into the glass, he stepped on to the balcony and looked down. Even at this hour, the traffic flowed endlessly. The blaze of neon might have been a dream he had woken into. In spite of the busy streets the city air felt cool and fresh, as it never seemed to do in the

12

day. For the first time in weeks – it felt more like months, like years – he was beginning to think clearly.

Of course the police would have no trouble identifying the body – what remained of it. They would only have to check the register, or the personal effects that lay scattered here and there about the room – the passport, the personal address book; all they required was here to see. Would they trust the details and miss the point? The point being that this really could be any body. Only the name on the register downstairs gave this mess on the bed an identity. So he had placed the eyes and the fingertips on the small night-table beside the bed, arranging them casually, like cast-off accessories; a watch, a brooch, earrings. The police could piece together the parts and make their identification, but they really ought to think twice before doing so. What had taken place here tonight was a statement they should not ignore.

For a moment he stood quietly, sucking Coke between his bad teeth, relishing the promise of pain in his mouth. It was said that the fizz he was drinking could erase the rust from an old nail left immersed in it overnight, and that, in time, even the nail itself would vanish. He hadn't put the theory to the test, but he liked the roundness of the idea: one thing overpowering another, thus purifying it. That was why he felt elated now, released and heightened and – he laughed, startled – almost giddy with joy. The adrenalin was flowing, his heart tripping madly. He was the Source, erasing the unworthy with his pencil, scratching it out, re-writing it. In his mind's eye he saw, pencil line by pencil line, the slow formation of a hangman's noose, and the face on the stick-man suspending from it.

Somewhere in the night, in the direction of Westminster, he heard the first weary rise and fall of a police siren. It might or might not have been to do with his call, but it was time he was moving on. Not finishing the drink, he set the glass down on the dresser as he passed through the hotel room. As you make your bed, so you must lie in it, he thought as he left, not looking back but closing the door softly, while the siren rose above the noise of traffic.

13

Chapter Three

Linda was too preoccupied to notice the first drops of rain on the windscreen as she turned left from the main road on to Park View. All the brown identikit houses in the estate had blurred and begun to melt before she thought to switch on the wipers. On the seat beside her was the evening edition of the *Post*, still folded to the story on page two that she'd sat and re-read, aghast, while parked outside the newsagent's. She glanced down anxiously, hoping it would read differently this time, praying she'd been mistaken; preoccupied, she almost overshot her own driveway.

George's Sierra was already inside the double garage. They no longer travelled together to and from the college in Wakefield where they had first met and still taught, for their lecturing hours seldom coincided. She parked the Mini, her pride and joy, picked up her newspaper, and stared out from the garage gloom at the street.

Sweet suburbia. The long, hot summer months had scorched the houses and their allotted squares of desolate lawn until even the slightest breeze turned the air thick with dust. Now the rain, instead of freshening the streets, was marking the pale grey tarmac with grubby smears. It wouldn't have been so bad, Linda thought, fumbling for her keys on the doorstep, if the houses themselves had personality. But this was where the dream led, this was what everyone was striving for, clocking on and off for: the driveway you could overshoot because it looked like all the others, the 1.5 cars and 2.4 kids, the street named Park View from which the view of the park was excluded.

This year's housing development had seen to that.

For several seconds Linda stood, idling her key back and forth in the door, her fingers trembling. She must pull herself together before George saw her; she was in no mood for explaining. And she would be forced to explain, wouldn't she, since neither the news item nor the call she'd taken at Samaritans on Sunday would mean anything to him unless he knew everything else. She took a deep breath and stepped in out of the rain.

George was preparing a ham salad sandwich in the kitchen that seemed like the set of science fiction film. Everything shone, immaculate; George's shirts revolved soundlessly in the automatic washer; a Seiko wall clock ticked off seconds with precision. There was the appetizing smell of percolating coffee. Linda came in behind him, pecking his bearded cheek and giving his shoulder a squeeze. George stiffened and only half-smiled, and at once her spirits sunk further.

'Didn't hear your car,' he said flatly, 'for the rain.'

'You're early,' she said. 'I thought you had tutorials all day today.'

'Thursday. Today's been nothing but pushing paper, knocking the course into shape. The students should do so much work.'

'The first weeks are always like this, you know that. You'll be into your stride before long.'

'We can but hope. How was your day?'

'On the whole, I'd rather've been in Philadelphia.'

This was delivered in her best W.C. Fields, but it fell on stony ground. George nodded and sliced his sandwich into triangular halves, putting the used knife on the drainer. As yet he hadn't looked up. He was subtly but surely avoiding her, in that way he had when he knew he was in the wrong for some reason. Yet he was oddly radiant, with a fused, almost glossy look to his skin: a look she hadn't produced in him since the early days of their marriage, following frenzied lovemaking. But it was something he was keeping to himself, afraid or ashamed to show how elated he was. Then, in a flash, she understood everything.

He wore no tie. His shirt seemed too pristine, too carefully tucked in at the waist for this time of day, as though he

15

hadn't been wearing it long. As he poured himself coffee she wondered how long his car had been sitting out there in the garage, whose house it had been sitting outside an hour or so ago.

Six months ago he had vowed that the affair he'd been having with Sonia, a youthful part-time lecturer in his English department, was over. It had been a brief, physical release for him, and Linda had finally accepted his tears and promises. Now that she thought of it, it occurred to her how like this he had seemed during the first weeks of the affair: distant, yet secretly glowing. A heat rose to her cheeks as she stared down at her feet in their flat canvas shoes, and sensed him turning towards her.

'Linda,' he said.

'Don't say it. Don't tell me. I don't won't to hear, whatever it is,' she said breathlessly. She strode past him, flung open the refrigerator door, plucked out the unfinished bottle of Napa Valley Chardonnay they'd opened for last night's meal, and slammed the door shut. She shot George one brief look before seizing a glass and marching through to the adjoining lounge, where she threw herself into an armchair and shied the *Post* as far away from her as possible.

After a time, George came in and sat on the sofa opposite, watching in silence while she sipped her wine. She forced herself not to look up, not even when he began blowing on his steaming coffee to attract her attention.

'Drinking before dusk, Linda? This isn't like you.'

She held her tongue, though the temptation to let rip was overwhelming. Instead, she gazed sullenly past him to the framed print of Van Gogh's *Sunflowers* above the fireplace. Below this, on the mantelshelf, their wedding photo seemed to accuse her of disloyalty: she looked so happy in George's arms. Perhaps she had overreacted, and should let it go. She only knew that she couldn't face a scene tonight, wouldn't dare trust her emotions after what she'd read in the newspaper. She wondered, briefly, whether she'd misjudged him, whether his flushed appearance had another explanation – good news he was about to share with her – but then she caught his gaze an instant before he looked away, and she knew.

16

'I'm drinking because I feel like it,' she said bitterly. 'Please let me know if I don't have good reason to.'

He sighed. 'Can we discuss this later?'

'Later would suit me just fine. I'd like time to think.'

'I have to be going out soon,' he said.

'Really? And there I was, thinking you were being sensitive for my sake! She must be something special, if you can't spare a moment to talk this through before having to run out and meet her.' She was drinking without tasting, breathing in short little gasps between sips. Her face felt aflame, ready to burst. There was no air in the room. She had the feeling that if he left her alone for a time, it would pass; the threat of tears and histrionics would fade. Just now she felt close to attacking George for all the wrong reasons.

'Tonight,' he said, 'I'm seeing Bob Bailey about the course. It's running our lives at the moment, I swear. We arranged this evening weeks ago.'

'You're so transparent,' she said, and drew her legs up into the chair.

'And you're so wrong.' But there was no conviction in his voice. If he'd only made the effort to lie convincingly, with passion, she might have respected him more than she did this minute.

George made a slurping noise as he sipped his coffee. She was forcing herself not to look at him. Then she heard him fingering his beard, a nervous reflex. Did he believe loitering with intent would prove his innocence? She felt trapped, as if in a waiting room, making desultory conversation with an uncommunicative stranger. How much like children we are sometimes, she thought. How quickly we revert, how driven we are by fear and suspicion. She was educated, married, in her thirtieth year, slumped in an armchair sulking like a moody teenager. Had sulking put an end to her problem fifteen years ago? Of course not, but then again nor had reasoning, nor pleading, so here she was, half a lifetime later, remembering Sunday night's telephone call.

It's beginning again.

Someone is dead because of me ... because of us.

She emptied her glass and refilled it. From where she sat she could see, through the window, a Sierra like George's pulling into an identical double garage across the street. Out climbed Mr Hanson, together with his wife and 2.4 children, hastening indoors from the rain. Out of the corner of her eye she saw George picking up the *Post*, unfolding it, blinking at the headline. For one moment she imagined he was going to ask her about it; but she had never mentioned Alison or the others to him. That was part of the agreement they'd made, to let their secret lie. Besides, the longer she'd been with George, the more distant it became, the harder it had been to explain. He was reading the story and shaking his head, relating none of it to her.

'"Police are today seeking the killer ..."' he mused, clicking his tongue disapprovingly. It was a habit of George's to read aloud selected snatches of newspaper items, as though he could only communicate in brief clicked phrases, sub-headings. This was his way of making conversation when there was nothing else to say. Linda braced herself as he went on.

'"The young woman's body was discovered in her room at ... Brutally stabbed ... Later identified as Alison Lester, a freelance journalist, recently returned from an assignment overseas ... According to a colleague at the monthly magazine *Persona*, Lester was believed to be investigating child prostitution rings in Thailand ... Amongst her personal effects were several used notebooks and interview tapes ... It is not yet known whether there is any connection between Lester's last assignment and her death ..."'

There was more, but Linda already knew the rest. In her car, outside the newsagent's, she had read the words over and over until their meaning sank in. George's voice was measured and unaffected; he might have been announcing the latest share prices. He was doing this, she knew, to fill the awkward silence between them, but he was only making things worse. When he saw the way she was looking at him, he stopped reading.

'Linda, are you all right? Are you going to be all right tonight?' He put down the paper. 'Listen, it isn't too late to cancel this. I can easily call Bob — '

'Don't break your date on my account,' she said coldly.

Two minutes later she heard the front door slam, then the

Sierra's engine starting up. From the armchair she had a clear view of George reversing down the drive and accelerating down the street. He didn't look back. She glared at the wine in her glass, realising she couldn't face drinking any more.

Ironically, she had wanted George out of the house tonight anyway. Even without this new, unexpected complication — whether or not it was Sonia again hardly mattered, she was too numb to care who it was — she might have tried persuading him to go out and leave her alone. Quite what she intended to do with the evening now that it stretched before her, she couldn't decide. What she mustn't do was cloud her head any more than she had already.

She returned the bottle to the kitchen, then forced herself upstairs two steps at a time. In the bathroom she ran a basinful of cold water and stood for a minute, immersing her hands and wrists until they ached. When she palmed the water into her face she felt herself gradually coming to life again.

Had Alison known what was coming when she'd called the Samaritans Sunday night? Then why had there been no fear in her voice? In retrospect she'd sounded smug, even triumphant.

Linda studied herself in the mirror above the hand basin until she went out of focus. Her short-cropped mousey hair looked flattened and lifeless, her grey eyes disorientated. For a long moment her mind felt utterly empty, clear as day. But her heart was racing, her hands clenching tensely, as if her body already knew what had to be done.

There was a telephone extension on the stand at her bedside, and a Wakefield area directory. Cross-legged on the bed, she began turning the pages, frowning as she tried to summon up middle names, married names.

As far as she knew, Alison had stayed based in the area despite a career that had sent her several times across the globe. Her byline had appeared in countless up-market magazines. Here she was, A. Lester, with an address in Horbury. Linda moved her fingernail over the name, the street, the number, and shivered. The occupant would never return. In her mind, Alison would always be fifteen years old, dark-eyed, petulant, vowing to break out and better herself. In time, she'd certainly risen through the ranks, but why had she stayed? Perhaps to show solidarity or strength of character, to signify she hadn't allowed herself to be driven away.

Next she turned to the M's, and remembered that Michael McCourt had been the first to leave the region. She seemed to recall a newspaper interview in which it was stated he'd moved to London. At the time he'd described himself as a rat deserting the north's already sunken ship. That must have been three years ago at least. In any case, Michael had always been one for leaving. Hadn't he once said − it might even have been that last day at the ice house − that there should be a physical distance too; that it wasn't enough to live streets apart, consciously avoiding one another?

She stopped for a minute, wondering how Michael was keeping. In a way, she felt she already knew, having bought and read each of the novels he'd published since his first, six years ago, which at times had seemed like open letters to her and the others. In them, she'd smelt and tasted fragments of her past, wept at memories he'd revived. Pain never died; at best it lay dormant for decades. Through his books, she had kept closely in touch with Michael McCourt's pain all these years, watching him mature. Her memories of him aged fifteen were mostly warm, except towards the end, when everything had fallen apart. Even now, when she conjured up his peach-fuzzy face, the broad boyish smile and unkempt hair, she glowed secretly inside. He had been such a leader in some ways, so insecure in others. She remembered his shyness when alone with her, his strength when the group were together. How badly it turned out for all of us, she thought: not to have grown together, to have shared so little. How wrong, how rotten, how unfair.

Bill Anderson, as far as she knew, had never returned since college. Even before he went, his family were preparing to move east to the coast, where they had bought an all-purpose store at a clifftop camp site. Assuming they still ran the place, or had retired there, Bill shouldn't be impossible to trace.

What about the others? She squeezed her eyes shut in an effort to conjure them up. Strangely, she could always picture the school building with ease. Seen from a distance, a concrete island afloat in an asphalt sea, all uniform grey blocks either two or three floors high. All day long a thin wisp of brown smoke rose from the narrow spire-like chimney above the boiler room. At nights or during holiday periods the deserted complex had a chilling atmosphere, as though no human being had ever set foot there.

Faces were somewhat harder to visualise. Naomi would certainly still be around. She had married young and found work in a factory; like so many others of her age, she had stopped living before she'd started. It was as if vicious, small-town life had grabbed her one day and said, You're mine, and you're staying. Forever.

There was Vincent, of course: Vinnie, whose weight problem was constantly used as a weapon against him by others, even his friends comparing his fleshy breasts to a girl's. When she thought of him now, she saw the quivering mouth, the confusion of sadness and anger which seemed always to boil behind his eyes. She wondered which emotion had finally won. As she returned to the area directory she realised she hadn't a clue about Vinnie's last name, or the name of Naomi's husband. She put the book down by the phone and tried to think.

Five minutes later she was climbing steps to the attic. A skylight set into the slanting roof overlooked cases and cartons of stored bric-a-brac, keepsakes, dust-covered curios. As a child she had dreamed of sleeping and waking in a space like this, high up amongst the low, dark beams, with the stars above her whenever she opened her eyes. She was past all those childhood dreams now, she reminded herself.

In an old hardwood chest, which would one day be stripped, varnished and moved downstairs, were bags of inherited clothes she'd hoarded: her mother's white lace wedding dress and veil; a black, sequined evening dress, also her mother's, which Linda had worn once to a party. There were genuine silk stockings to woo young men with, a beret she couldn't place. Hidden beneath the garments were the papers she wanted, many dating from school and polytechnic. They were packed tightly inside a blue vinyl vanity case. As she began unpacking it, the smell of age filled her nose and mouth. The precise, rounded handwriting she'd

21

used for an essay on Wilfred Owen made her smile. She'd changed so much since then; *made* herself change. She'd had no choice but to leave her old self behind.

Surely somewhere amongst this lot there would be a memo to herself, a scribbled name or number, something to help her begin tracing the others. She didn't stop to wonder how right she was to be doing this; she only knew that she couldn't just wait, as she had waited in the past, for the silence to end. An exercise book she'd used as a diary offered few clues. The entries were very sporadic, in some cases weeks apart, and she couldn't remember having written any of them. Halfway through she stopped at a paragraph where her usual, precise handwriting degenerated to a scrawl.

Today I saw Alison again, and it all came flooding back to me. I was shopping at Lewis's in Leeds, drifting between the clothing departments, when I saw her coming out of the caféteria. I've a feeling she saw me first, and when I looked I saw her eyes brighten and her mouth open as if she were about to speak or call my name. And for a second I reacted the same way, took a step or two towards her. I'd seen her name in a music magazine — some article she'd written — and I wanted to ask her about it. I wanted to ask about many things. She looked good, with bright eyes and clear skin, not at all as I remembered her. Then it dawned on us both — I felt it and saw it in her face at the same time. It was like a light going out. Suddenly I remembered it was three years later, and thought how short a time that was when you got down to it, but we still couldn't get together and laugh and joke about old times and probably never would, never. Then she turned away, we both turned away, and a crowd of shoppers filled the gap between us. When I looked back towards where she'd been standing there was no sign. It was then I knew what it meant to be a stranger to someone you'd shared so much with. We didn't know each other and we never had; that was what we had to pretend. I ran to the nearest toilet and wept.

She could have been weeping while writing this, but for the

life of her, Linda couldn't remember. She couldn't imagine herself poised over the exercise book, pen in hand. Nor could she picture the scene in Lewis's that day. Like all hurtful memories, she'd blotted it out, making a positive effort to forget. From the moment she'd secured her place at polytechnic she'd purposely filled her life to overflowing: studying, working, meeting George, marrying, building upon that life. She hadn't opened the door wide enough to let the past in. Yet now, she thought, there's no preventing it. Because it's forcing the door of its own accord.

She closed the exercise book, feeling lost somewhere between then and now. She'd buried so much of herself back there; they all had. Her head was spinning, and not because of the wine. Above her the skylight was streaming with grubby September rain. She was piling papers back in the case when she heard the phone in her bedroom purring.

Linda picked up the receiver on the run and sat on the bed's edge, breathing hard. When she'd recited the number she waited, and for several beats her heart filled her mouth. Not *that* again, please. Not the endless silence. But the voice on the line, a man's, was hesitant, as uncertain perhaps as her own.

'Linda? Linda *Grayson?*'

She held her breath. 'Walker. It's Walker these days. It used to be Grayson. Who *is* this?'

'I knew you as Grayson. You knew me as lard-arse, I think.' He laughed, but the strain in his voice was apparent. 'Linda, it's Vincent. Vinnie – remember? I've been trying all day to trace you.'

Chapter Four

The address was a tavern in Stanley, on the outskirts of Wakefield. The building was new, with interiors done out to look decades old. As she entered the crowded lounge bar, Linda saw Vinnie rise from a seat in the corner nearest the toilets and nod towards her. He'd clearly been watching the door, awaiting her arrival. She recognised him instantly, wondered whether she'd changed as little in his eyes. Fifteen years had barely touched his pudgy baby face, though the small moustache he'd grown made her think of Oliver Hardy. Which reminded her, as she crossed the sawdusted floor, that his surname was Hartley. When she reached his table he took her hand in his, neither shaking nor squeezing it.

'Hello, Vinnie.'

'Linda. It really is you.'

They sat for minutes, gazing across the table at each other in disbelief. Around them the slur of voices at other tables sounded muffled and distant as a dream. We're really here, she thought. We're breaking the spell, inviting catastrophe.

Vinnie laughed nervously. Folded on the table before him was a newspaper, *The Independent*. Next to it was his empty pint glass and an ashtray filled with dog-ends, one of which still smouldered.

'They do food here, if you're hungry,' he said.

'Not for me, thanks.'

'A drink then?'

She nodded. 'A small one. I'm driving.'

It was too late to ask herself whether she'd done the right

thing by agreeing to meet him. There had been a moment in the car-park outside where she'd imagined turning round, coolly heading back the way she'd come; but even as the thought crossed her mind she was locking the car, strolling towards the tavern lights.

She sat watching Vinnie at the bar. As he leaned across to shout his order, his trousers sagged and his shirt rode up from the small of his back, exposing a broad strip of white flesh. When he returned with the drinks – his a beer, hers a gin and tonic – she said, 'Do you live near here?'

'I – yes. Not far. It's a small place, you wouldn't like it very much. It's not the sort of place you use for entertaining. At the moment it's better for me to meet people outside. Landlord problems, you understand.'

'Are you – do you live alone there, Vinnie?'

'Well, yes.' He looked flustered, his face reddening. 'There's work, you see. Haven't much time for anything else: relationships and such. One day I'll slow down, I suppose.'

'One day we all will. What do you do?'

'Do? Work, you mean? Oh, not much of anything, really.' He was so self-conscious, so ashamed of the way his life had turned out, the inferior thing he'd become. His shirt was straining at the buttons, and rounds of sweat stained his armpits. 'It's sort of a mobile video rental van. A bit like selling ice-creams, really. I go from street to street, cover this whole area as far afield as Outwood and Abbotsbridge. It's a living, I guess.'

Linda was smiling fondly, but Vinnie averted his gaze. A grey coat was draped over the back of his chair and after searching its pockets he tugged out a pack of Dunhills and a matchbook. As he took his first, desperate draw on the cigarette, she thought how much in common he must have with the ones who called her at the Samantans each week; the many good, real people life had pushed too far and hard.

'You didn't smoke before, did you?' she asked.

'None of us did in those days, not even when half the school smoked. We had to make a point of standing out from the crowd.'

'Going against the grain.'

25

'Challenging the order.'

They laughed. He found her eyes again, and beamed through the hurt. 'We were such rebels, weren't we, Linda!'

'Rebels against rebellion!'

'Christ Almighty, I miss us. I miss the way we all were.'

'Don't, Vinnie,' she said calmly. 'It's too painful. Don't let's rake everything up again.'

'But we *are* doing, aren't we, just by being here? You must understand that, otherwise you would've refused to come. When I said we had to talk, you automatically accepted that.'

'I was in the middle of tracking you down when you called,' she admitted.

'There you are, then.' He tapped the newspaper twice. 'You're not the only one who's read the headlines.'

'Are the papers all saying the same thing?'

'The ones I've seen are.' He pushed *The Independent* across the table. Scanning the page three story, she noted again the words: Thailand, investigation, child prostitution. 'They're emphasising different things,' he said. 'This one suggests she might have been killed because she was trying to link her findings to child pornographers in this country. None of the papers are in any doubt that she was killed because of the story she was working on.'

'And what do you think, Vinnie?'

He swallowed hard before answering. 'They're all wide of the mark. Alison was killed for another reason. We all know that, don't we?'

'Isn't there a chance *we're* mistaken, though? That we're interpreting what happened to Alison in the only way we can?'

Vinnie looked at her levelly. 'Is that what you believe, Linda?'

She shook her head slowly. At last she had to put into words what she'd sensed for two days. 'No, I believe we're all in danger, wherever we are. I believe Alison was only the first. There may have been people who wanted her dead, who she meant to expose, but would they have gone about it like this? The reports make it sound as though someone had *fun* putting Alison to death. They weren't just silencing her.'

'Besides, why would the people she was investigating leave all those incriminating notes in her room? *Reams* of notes, for crying out loud. Even interview transcripts.' Vinnie's eyes were wide, aghast. 'Whoever left all that stuff was feeding the newsmen a line. They went for it, too. It's so damn obvious.'

Linda's eyes were on the report in *The Independent*. A stray detail leapt at her from the page, and she re-read it quickly. 'There's a suggestion here that someone called the police from Alison's room on Sunday night, to report the killing, possibly the killer himself. Vinnie, do you realise what that means?'

'What?'

'I might have been the last person Alison spoke to before she died.'

'You *talked* to her?'

'Sunday night, yes. I'd better explain.' For a moment she hovered outside herself, watching someone else's fingers reach casually for Vinnie's cigarettes. She took one, lit it, and coughed lightly. It was only her third or fourth cigarette, ever. Smoke filtered out on her breath as she talked. 'For two hours a week over the last couple of years I've been manning a phone at Sams − the Samaritans − the branch in our old town, Abbotsbridge. You can imagine what that involves. I'm there for anyone who phones needing help, needing to share, to talk out whatever they're going through. It's hard sometimes, but it's something I need to do. And four times a year I'm committed to doing an overnight stint there; eight hours right through till morning. As it happened, that's what I was doing on Sunday night when Alison called.'

'She contacted you *there?*'

'How she knew I'd be there I don't know. Being a Sam isn't something I've ever shouted about. Only a few of my close friends know. At first I didn't recognise her voice at all. Even now, when I re-think what happened, it was more what she said than the way she said it that told me I was speaking to Alison. There was something in her voice I didn't remember. It must have been −' She shrugged and put down her cigarette. 'The situation was so unusual – I was disorientated, half awake. The phone call woke me from a doze. She knew my name, which unsettled me. Then she began asking pointed questions: had I ever done anything I regretted, did I judge others for their mistakes? It's bad enough, if you're manning a help line, to find yourself listening to someone you know, but this was more than that. It was frightening.'

Vinnie had grown unhealthily pale. 'You didn't feel the same fear when I called you tonight?'

'No, I don't believe I did.' She considered for a moment. 'Well I suppose I thought, this is *Vinnie*. I was excited as well as uncertain. Sooner or later I would've tried to call you anyway. But on Sunday, I never said to myself, this is *her*, this is Alison. All I knew was that something was wrong. *She* was wrong. And she told me to watch for the newspapers – *today's* newspapers, Vinnie. She knew that something like this would happen. She was practically forecasting her own death.'

'How, though? How could she know?'

'Perhaps it had already started when she called,' she suggested, then wished she'd held her tongue. Her stomach lurched unpleasantly, taut with nerves. A dull headache threatened. 'Oh God, I don't know, Vinnie. She said it was beginning again and it is, isn't it? We were wrong to think it was over.'

'I never thought it was over,' he said gravely. They drank and sat without speaking for a time, while the noise in the bar washed over them. All the other voices sounded foreign, everyone chanting loudly, simultaneously, in a babble of strange new languages.

At last Vinnie asked if she was ready to leave.

Outside, the main road beyond the well-lit tavern was ominously dark, the streetlights too widely spaced. There was no sign of life, no traffic. 'Get in, I'll drop you at home,' Linda said, hurrying Vinnie to the car. 'I don't know about you, but I'm not so happy about any of us wandering the streets at night now.'

'Yes, I know. If he can trace Alison to some London hotel, he'll have no trouble finding the rest of us.'

28

He, Linda thought, twisting the key in the ignition. The small, innocuous word hung in the air between them like an echo of a shot. It was the first time the threat had been named, made human, and it gave her the shakes. There was another name too – a boy's name – but she couldn't bear to think of that as well. As she pulled out from the car park a bulky black vehicle reared up on her right, headlights flaring, and she was forced to hit the brakes.

'Steady, steady,' Vinnie said quietly. 'We're not finished yet. We've got to learn to keep ourselves together.'

They drove through the dim Stanley streets, Linda following Vinnie's careful directions. 'So what are we going to do?' she asked as they turned along a row of renovated three-storey terraces.

'Keep going along here,' he said, pointing. Then, 'If you feel the time's right, I'll start approaching the others. They'll be aware of what's happened if they've followed the news. In which case I'd say they'll be thinking exactly like us, wondering whether we've any choice but to meet again.'

'And then what?'

'God knows. So far I can't think past the point of seeing everyone again. What we'll do when we're together again I can't imagine, but we can't face what's coming alone.'

'Will you need any help?'

'Not at first. I've a few addresses and numbers to check. Naomi is no problem; I could find her blindfolded. She still lives on the estate where she was born. Tom Quigley is local, too.'

'Tom Quigley!' Linda slapped a palm against her forehead, amazed at herself. 'How could he slip my mind? He was the oddball who did the impressions, the voices, wasn't he? The pastor's son? The Godchild, we called him. How could I ever forget *him*?'

'Tom was never really one of us,' Vinnie said. 'But he was part of what happened, he was there on the day. We could try him and Naomi first, see how they feel about this.'

'And the others?'

'Well, I have a number for Bill. His folks were very helpful. He's married and selling computer peripherals in Derby these days. Michael I don't know about, but I think

I know how to find him. The last I heard, he was somewhere in London. Oh, could you drop me off here? Just on the right. See where my van's parked?'

Linda drew up outside the terraced house. It was early, she thought, for the whole street to be so quiet, with only a distant barking dog for a soundtrack. She waited while Vinnie fiddled through his pockets, finally pressing a small stiff card into her hand. It was too dark to read whatever was printed on it, but he quickly explained, 'My number, for when you need to get in touch. I've a feeling we'll be talking pretty soon.'

'It's good to see you again,' she said. 'I only wish we were able to do this ... differently. Without this dreadful mess.'

'Yes,' Vinnie said, and got out.

All the houses on the row were fronted by low brick walls with wooden gates, and steps leading up to their front doors. Linda waited while Vinnie closed his gate after him, then started up the steps. The top of the flight vanished into a pool of darkness which concealed the entrance. As Vinnie reached his front door, he vanished too. Then, with her window rolled all the way down, she heard his key in the door and his voice calling softly through the dark.

'Goodnight, Linda. And thanks for coming.'

Yes, she thought. It is beginning again. Soon they would be back where they had been fifteen years before. Reunions were meant to be fun: festive, upbeat occasions arranged and attended by old friends. That was how they were meant to be. There was nothing festive about this reunion, though. Alison, oh Alison, she thought wearily, you're bringing us all together again. It was only as she let out the clutch and drove from Vinnie's that the cold underside of that thought dawned on her.

He was the one whose actions were forcing them together again. Alison had merely been his catalyst, his way of doing it. Surely that was why the killing had been high-profile, so right for the media: a journalist horribly murdered while researching a taboo story. It had everything the tabloids desired – the glamorous victim, the hint of secret, for- bidden evils, the bloody violent death. With so many ripe ingredients, the story had to be guaranteed coverage; and so the message had gone out loud and clear, to Linda, to Vinnie, to the rest of the circle. The murder of Alison Lester was a publicity vehicle: nothing less. Perhaps they were all playing right into his hands.

Someone is dead because of me ... because of us, she thought. The darkness inside the car felt almost palpable.

She'd driven another hundred yards or so before realising Vinnie's road was a long, sweeping crescent. Following it forward would eventually return her to the main road, then she could head back to town through Stanley. Her mind was so full as she neared her junction that she almost missed George's car, parked just before it.

Linda slowed, double-checking the number plate in her headlights. There was no doubt about it, the vehicle *was* George's. A sticker in his rear windscreen said politely, PLEASE KEEP YOUR DISTANCE, and she thought with some anger, *touché*.

She stopped alongside the Sierra, wondering what to do next. George's car was up on the kerb outside a terraced house much like Vinnie's, in which only the upstairs lights were on, the curtains drawn. Bob Bailey and his wife, Paula, owned a semi-detached house, several miles away, in Sandal. Sitting there, tapping the steering wheel, she saw herself running up to the door, voice raised, fists flying, ready for the scene of her life; then, more calmly, leaving a cryptic scribbled message pinned beneath George's windscreen wipers.

In the end she did neither. For all she knew, for all she cared this minute, he and Bob were up there at the Wakefield Glee Club headquarters, singing their hearts out. With a crash of gears, she got the Mini moving again, on through the dark towards the main road and whatever lay beyond.

Chapter Five

At six p.m. New York time, Michael McCourt's concentration snapped, and he rose from his work, drawn by sounds of activity elsewhere in the apartment. In the bedroom he found Tessa, with whom he had shared his life and his income for the past eighteen months, half-dressed from the shower and packing a suitase. The case lay open on the bed, and she was tossing in handfuls of clothes at random. When she noticed him watching from the doorway she paused only to shake her head with disdain. She had the kind of temper legends were made of: to Michael her mane of fiery auburn hair had always seemed peculiarly appropriate.

'What does it *look* like I'm doing?' she said when he inquired. 'We've rehearsed this scene so regularly you ought to have it down pat by now.'

He held his tongue while she picked up her Martinez Valero shoes, in case she decided to hurl them at him. She always spoke in terms of rehearsals, scenes, theatrical peaks and troughs. It was a pity she had never made it on the stage, he thought; she could have expressed herself fully there, in full view of the audience she desired.

'Besides,' she said now, 'is this your idea of a life? Holed up in some pokey loft in TriBeCa? Never even speaking to me when I come home from work because you're plugged into that stupid little dreamworld of yours?'

'If that's all you think it is, you've misunderstood me from the start. If you can't live with my work, Tess, how can you live with me?'

'A pertinent question. So do you still need to ask why I'm walking out?'

'Because you're sick of me or sick of this place?'

'Fifty-fifty, I'd say.'

Michael was doing his best not to react in kind. 'This pokey loft, I'll have you know, is costing a fortune in rent. If it was up for grabs, they'd be forming a queue, they'd be fighting in the streets for it. Flavour of the month artists, young pretenders from Wall Street ...'

'Let them queue! Let them fight in the streets. The streets are so goddamn dusty and shabby and anonymous anyway, and the goddamn cast iron buildings are *rusting*, McCourt. Where else on earth would you see such a thing?'

He shook his head slowly, tried to be conciliatory. 'What's good enough for Bob De Niro is good enough for me.'

'Did you say Bob? Jesus, McCourt, spare me the pet first names. Next you'll be saying Bobby!'

'Bobby and I are like that,' he taunted, making a finger and thumb circle. He stood leaning against the door jamb, arms folded, wondering whether this was the last time he would see her in underwear. There was something infinitely depressing, he reflected, when that stage in a relationship was reached where the physical aspect was definitely, unarguably, over.

Tessa glared at him for a moment, then seized a turtleneck sweater fit to strangle it. 'Don't help me,' she said, as though demanding the opposite.

'If you insist.'

She slung one more handful of expensive garments from Saks and Bloomingdales in the suitcase, then turned on him. Her eyes were so wide the pupils were surrounded by white on all sides. 'You bastard, McCourt. Has it fully occurred to you yet what I'm doing here? Going by that wistful expression, I'd hazard a guess not. What's happening is, I'm heading out to the real world where people know a thing or two about living − in the flesh, that is, not just in their heads. I'm walking *out* on your dim little literary world forever, never to darken its fucken doors again.'

'Well, we're both in need of a change,' he said mildly.

'You bet. I'm heading uptown right away.'

'How far uptown? Spanish Harlem, perhaps? Maybe I should warn them you're on your way.'

That so incensed her that she slung in more clothes. Did she ever buy anything other than clothing with the meagre money she earned behind the glass of an off-Broadway ticket booth? Tessa had moved to New York from Wilmington, Delaware, her sights trained squarely on the big time. Like many underachievers, she had found the city's mean streets paved with fool's gold. Anything less than success was punished mercilessly here. Perhaps, finally, frustration at falling short of her own dream had turned her against Michael's fulfilment of his. He could think of no other reason. Certainly he'd been anticipating this final 'scene', as Tessa would have it, for some time. It was as though she'd grown to resent the way his work sold sight unseen these days, the way his name on a title page could guarantee interest while hers at an audition was merely the next on the list.

Leaving Tessa to contemplate a new life without him, Michael returned to his study. Last summer, within months of moving in, she had done the apartment out in strong primary yellows and greens, though he'd had to insist on neutrality for his work space. No visual distractions – sheer minimalism, in fact. The walls were a dull cream, the floorboards varnished darkly. Other than the desk there was no furniture, not even bookshelves. On the VDU, the cursor winked at him halfway down a fresh page of his new children's book, *Out of Sight, Out of Mind*. From the bedroom came the clank of coathangers.

Naturally, writing for children didn't and never would pay the rent in TriBeCa. But Michael could afford to indulge his talents. Like so many other events that had shaped his life, success had taken him as much by surprise as anyone. It had arrived with his first – to date, his only – novel for the adult market, a music business blockbuster much like any other. Partly a sincere attempt to expose the slime behind the scenes, partly a cynical marketing ploy, *Rubber Bullets* had first been mooted, then enthusiastically nurtured by his American agent, Harvey Klein, who had later sold it at auction for a good five figure sum.

34

The novel exuded sleaze. In it, a naive small-town English boy turned twenty-one and moved to London, became slowly defiled as he entered the music industry and rose through its ranks, whoring and manipulating, and so on and so on, until finally he teetered at the zenith of corporate America, fending off mobsters only marginally more corrupt than himself. At heart it was sheer wish-fulfilment fantasy — the familiar rags to riches tale with a moral, but sales were beginning to justify the large advance he'd received, though critics had universally condemned the book. In objective mood, Michael understood why. At times he even wondered where the novel had sprung from, which dark part of himself had created the beast. None of the characters were even remotely likeable or sympathetic. There were explicit scenes of drug abuse and extreme violence. Everyone slept with everyone else, but only for advantage. And they didn't so much make love as get high on cocaine and fuck one another stupid. Not that he'd ever considered sex dirty, but in *Rubber Bullets* he'd succeeded in making it truly depraved. Men ate men, dogs ate dogs, men ate dogs.

All six hundred pages had been grafted out without heart or soul, the critics had argued. It was an empty sensual thrill. Michael couldn't argue with that, but he had tried hard to write it well. Yet for some reason he felt nearer to finding himself whenever he wrote for children: while Harvey was politely hinting at sequels to *Rubber Bullets* he was escaping down the years again, journeying back fifteen years. Now, he closed his eyes for a second and saw, as clearly as if it were before him again, the chalked-out shape of the hanged man.

He switched off the word processor. He wouldn't be able to concentrate on writing anyway, not with Tessa's packing distracting him. Shouldn't he be in there this minute, begging her not to go? But he felt uninspired, at best mildly irritated, as if a fly were angrily circling the study while he tried to compose. A year and six months with the same woman suddenly seemed a tremendously long time. There were moments when it seemed as if they had been here forever, thrusting and parrying. She was still packing furiously when he collected his corduroy jacket on his way from the apartment. He asked her politely to leave the spare key under the mat when she left. She told him to go fuck himself.

Instead, he took the stairs down and came out on East Broadway, from where he took a taxi to Charlie O's on 48th Street. In the days before he moved to London the thought of drinking before nightfall had scarcely crossed Michael's mind. Lately, however, like the tainted hero of *Rubber Bullets*, he paid less attention to the hour than to his need, and at the moment his need was severe. Soon the numbness would pass and he would slowly begin to re-live the good things he'd shared with Tessa; he would begin to feel again, and to hurt. Before that happened, he required a buffer. A beer and a chaser would do the trick.

He had always been at home in this bar, to which Harvey Klein had introduced him soon after Michael came to Manhattan. It was Harvey's customary first stop after work and, true to form, he was already propped on a stool at the bar when Michael entered. Set before him was a measure of bourbon. Easing on to the next stool, Michael ordered two more of the same and a pitcher of Bud.

Harvey looked at him, narrow-eyed. Creases formed at the bridge of his nose. 'Why aren't you writing?' he said.

Michael laughed. Harvey's Brooks Brothers suit and painstakingly combed white hair lent him, during office hours, the dignified appearance of a TV district attorney. It was only after a couple of drinks that the image slipped askew: the eyes turning pink, the hair growing slightly dishevelled, the officious tone softening.

'Like the rest of the world, I occasionally need a break,' Michael said.

'*You* need a break? That's a good one! You should experience what I have to go through each day.'

'You never change, Harvey. You're splendid.'

'Oh, well. The cosmos needs its constants, its fixed points in the firmament.'

'Which is why you can always be found in this bar after work hours.'

'There's good reason for that tonight. What I'm doing is,

I'm stiffening my nerves before venturing home. My apartment's being re-decorated again, and I'm dreading walking in there and finding all my precious belongings in bits. For re-decorating read *reducing, annexing.* Christ knows where my wife comes up with these people.'

'Well, at least you won't be returning to yellow and green walls so loud they make your teeth hurt.'

'This is true.' He watched Michael pouring the beers, froth climbing steadily up the glasses. 'Is everything well with you, Mike, apart from your colour scheme?'

'Sure. Everything's fine.' They exchanged a glance. 'Why shouldn't it be?'

'It's only that I tried calling you before I came down here from the office. Tessa answered. She didn't say very much, only that you'd gone. But she didn't sound good, to be honest.'

'She wouldn't. You'll have interrupted her packing. She's leaving me and heading uptown where the buildings don't rust.'

'She's . . .' Harvey's eyes fluttered; he finished his bourbon quickly and gaped. 'Are you serious? But I thought you two were so . . .'

'We were, once. Not lately. We've been drifting apart for a long time, so slowly I didn't even see it until I woke up one day next to this complete stranger. It isn't her fault, but I think it finally dawned on her what spending her days with an author – this particular author – really meant. The problem seems to be too much living on the page and not enough in real life.'

'Mike, I'm really sorry.'

'Don't worry.' Michael raised a dismissive hand. 'If you'd seen how it's been lately you wouldn't feel sorry but relieved.'

Harvey sighed. 'Is there any truth in that, do you think?'

'In what?'

'That business about your not doing enough living in real life.'

'Well, yes. Don't tell me you haven't heard a writer say that before. Some of us are better equipped to deal with things on the page than in the real world; it's the one time

37

we're able to control all the things that . . .' Michael stopped for a mouthful of beer. 'You don't really want to sit here after work listening to this, do you?'

Harvey shrugged. 'I did wonder, if living in the real world is such a problem, why you moved to New York, of all places. Cities don't come any realer.'

'How should I know? Perhaps I'm – '

'Perhaps you're what?'

Running away, that's what, Michael thought. Perhaps he *was* running away. To him, New York was still *un*real, a landscape of the mind. He had found himself here, and lost himself. Wiping a foam moustache from his lips, he said, 'Incidentally, why were you calling me? Did someone buy a film option or something?'

'Why did I call?' Harvey needed a minute to consider, then snapped his fingers. 'Oh, nothing like that. There was a message from England, someone calling himself Vincent Hartley. Does the name ring a bell?'

Michael bought himself time with a drink before answering. As he swallowed, his throat seemed to contract, and liquid went down the wrong way. He coughed, spraying beer across the bar. While he fought for breath, Harvey slapped his back lightly, smiling apologetically towards the nearest drinkers.

'I'd say the name *does* mean something,' he said, and drew out a slip of paper from an inside jacket pocket. 'He left this number for you to ring.'

'Did he say anything?' Michael managed, the colour slowly returning to his face.

'No. Only that he must speak to you personally, but that it wasn't important. From his manner I would've judged that it was: not that it's any of my business.'

'You judged correctly.'

'You English are so good at playing things down. The stiff upper-lip and all that.'

'That's only for public consumption. On the surface, cool and composed: underneath, screaming bedlam. That's us.'

'That's how it appears to me,' Harvey said. He was studying Michael closely, no longer a business associate so much as the surrogate uncle who had given Michael

38

the guiding hand he needed soon after moving here. They had come to know one another well enough these past three years for Harvey to see what a stir this news had created. 'Seems I caught you on quite a night,' he said placidly. 'Is there anything I can do to help, Mike?'

But Michael was drifting in thought, reaching instinctively for his bourbon. Downing it in one he stared at the small slip of paper Harvey had handed him. There was Vincent's name: below it a Wakefield telephone number. For several seconds he sat digesting this, transfixed, his body frozen. His mouth was open – he might even be speaking, though he had no idea what the words could be. Something had happened for Vinnie to phone. It had once been agreed that everything between them was over forever; that was the only way it would work. And for so long it had seemed to be working for him, at any rate. He'd thrived over here and fortune had smiled on him. More than this, he'd been close to forgetting what he was running from. Until now. There were some things that could never be outdistanced or forgotten. There were some things that refused to let go.

'Harvey, I'm sorry, you'll have to excuse me,' he said, and without looking back slid off the stool and went out from Charlie O's in search of a taxi.

By the time he reached the apartment he was too preoccupied to notice that Tessa was gone. In any case, only by opening the wardrobe door in the bedroom would he have seen a difference. Her only possessions seemed to be clothes; as long as he had known her she had never so much as looked at a book, or exclaimed with delight at a painting. Whether she had claimed and taken anything of significance escaped him now, as he settled at his desk, unfolding the scrap of paper with one hand, lifting the telephone receiver with the other. Beyond his study window the lights were coming on in TriBeCa, and a light rain was falling. Glancing at his watch, he calculated that it must be around midnight in England, a little late to be calling. Nevertheless he tapped out the number and waited.

After so many years he should have been cherishing this

moment, rather than dreading it. But the trans-Atlantic connection came good so quickly he hadn't time to reconsider. On the third or fourth ring, Vinnie answered.

'Michael! Mikey!' His voice was strained but joyous. 'Is it really you? I thought we'd heard the last of you, you damn deserter!'

'Well, here I am. You found me without too much trouble.'

'Went through your publishers over here, who put me in touch with your London agent, who put me in touch with Harvey Klein. He was helpful but wouldn't give out your number.'

'I see.'

'Thanks for getting back to me so soon.'

'Don't mention it, Vinnie.' There was a brief, uncomfortable pause. Light rain caressed the window. This wasn't a call like any other; there was no room for the dizzy, frantic small talk of reunited friends. Ever since that day at the ice house in Parks Wood such a conversation hadn't been possible. At last Michael said, hesitantly, 'Is everything all right over there?'

Vinnie cleared his throat. 'I haven't forgotten our agreement, Mike. I wouldn't have bothered you if ... Do you take any of the English newspapers?'

'Now and then.'

'Have you seen any recently?'

'Not for a week or so, no.'

'If you had, you'd have known what this call was for. Mike, do you remember Linda Grayson?'

'Yes, of course.'

'And Naomi Freeman and Tom Quigley?'

Michael was nodding vigorously as if Vinnie could see. 'Yes, yes, I remember them all, the whole crew. We called ourselves something. The Circle, The Society ... What did we call ourselves, Vinnie?'

'The Brotherhood.'

'That's right.' Michael felt himself wanting to smile, but as ever the memory was a fusion of dark and light, romance and tragedy. In his mind's eye the faces were fully formed, as vivid as snapshots. The Brotherhood had been a team like

40

no other. They had wanted to change the world, once; but, true to form, the world had changed them first.

'And do you remember Alison Lester?'

'Certainly. She was the first to break out, wasn't she?'

'She became a success in her field. Never married. Never moved far from home, even when she could afford to. Mike, do you remember when you said we should never meet or speak again unless – unless the worst happened?'

'Yes, I remember that too.'

'Well, better brace yourself then. Alison was murdered on Sunday evening. That's why we have to talk.'

Michael closed his eyes as all strength left him. A rushing sound whistled through his ears. Alison's darkly concentrated features flashed before him, smiling, laughing. He remembered her ruffling his hair once, throwing an arm about his shoulder to comfort him.

When he failed to reply, Vinnie went on, 'There's a general impression we feel is false – that she was murdered because of a story she was working on. We believe the circumstances were convenient for her killer, set up to fool the authorities.'

'But can you be sure? Sure, I mean, that this has any bearing on us?'

'Reading between the lines in the news reports – there must be restrictions on what they're allowed to print, they don't come right out with it – you can tell she was messed up so badly you couldn't even recognise her. They had to use dental charts and what have you.'

'Jesus Christ.'

'I've been talking to Linda. Linda Walker, she is now. She's married.' He waited, perhaps anticipating a reaction from Michael, then continued, recounting what had happened during Linda's Sunday Samaritans duty. 'We're agreed that the call was the significant thing. Someone made sure that Alison spoke to at least one of us – Linda, as it happened – on the night she died. There was a reason for that, and the reason was to make sure we all knew the press and the police had it wrong. It was to single us out, involve us directly.'

'In other words, if Alison was killed for her story, why would she bother striking up old acquaintances at that particular time? Her mind would have been on other things.'

'It should have been, but she mentioned nothing about her research during the call. Instead she played cryptic games, hinting that someone had died because of her, telling Linda to watch for Tuesday's papers.'

'*Tuesday's*, did you say? Not the following day's?'

'That's correct. Doesn't that strike you as odd?'

'I'm not sure. I – ' Suddenly Michael, trying to order these facts in his mind, realised how dull the swift drink with Harvey had made him. Clarity was slipping, like a moist bar of soap, through his grip. 'What does it mean, Vinnie?'

'That someone knew Alison would be dead soon after that call. The whole thing was being supervised; she was under instruction, maybe even at knifepoint as she talked. A man who might have been the killer telephoned the police within minutes. It was Sunday night, when this happened, remember. It was late.'

'Yes? So? So what does that mean?'

'The obvious, really. The story was too late for the Monday editions. They would all have gone to press by then. But Alison, or whoever was forcing her to make the call, knew that the story would break the next day.'

'But that's impossible! Impossible, I mean, that Alison – the Alison Lester *we* knew – could behave as she did on the phone, knowing that. She was always so hyper, so emotional. How could she hide what was happening to her? Why bother calling at all? Close your eyes for a minute and see if you can imagine her complying. It . . . it just doesn't sound like something she would do, Vin.'

'My feelings entirely. Linda has the same doubts at heart, but for all that she's convinced it was Alison she spoke to. No one else would know what Alison knew, what all of us know.'

'That's not true, Vinnie. There is someone else, and you know it.'

'Yes.' The silence, punctuated by soft-falling rain, slowly extended until it seemed almost physical, a string on the verge of snapping. Then Vinnie said, 'But it couldn't be,

42

could it? We were supposed to have made sure. He couldn't have come back for us, could he?'

In his way, he was pleading for reassurance, a reassurance Michael could not give. To Michael's right, in the second desk drawer down, was a squashed pack of Camels. Though officially he had given up smoking two years ago, he had always kept cigarettes within reach, out of sight and mind, yet there if desperation set in. These were months old. The stale taste that greeted him on lighting one hardly mattered, however. He closed his eyes and waited for the hit.

'Is it raining in England, Vinnie?' he asked, after a time.

'It's raining here. I don't know about the rest of England, but it's raining here. It started five or ten minutes ago. Why?'

'Just wondered. Anyone would think you'd sent the English weather with your call tonight.'

'Doesn't it make you homesick, Mike?'

'Never been homesick in my life,' Michael said. 'But then I've never felt what you'd call at home in my life.' The darkness gathering, he leaned forward and switched on the desktop anglepoise. Around him the creamy room glowed warmly.

'But you'll be coming home, won't you?'

'Home?' He sighed. 'I guess so. Something tells me I have no choice.'

'I thought we might meet first in London,' Vinnie suggested brightly. 'Neutral ground. Give ourselves distance while we decide what to do. I'll make the arrangements at this end.' Vinnie sounded animated now that Michael had agreed to attend. 'We'll choose a comfy hotel, nothing excessive, where we can talk and ... whatever. I'll get back to you as soon as we're sorted.'

Before signing off, they traded more information, Michael volunteering his home number, Vinnie supplying Linda's, in case it was needed. At last Michael said, 'Let's hope and pray we're doing the right thing, Vinnie.'

There was no reply. The connection had been cut, or perhaps Vinnie had hung up, not realising Michael had more

43

to say. Sometimes the silence had seemed endless, indefinite, but it had always been destined to end. And so Michael McCourt felt it end as he put down the phone, fifteen years older but still no wiser, and no longer running away.

Chapter Six

Tom Quigley was proving the only hitch to Vinnie's plans so far. Three times Vinnie had been re-directed to new addresses which Tom had vacated, and this one on the Blackmore estate didn't look any more promising. It was too close to home for one thing, lying as it did to the north of Abbotsbridge, just minutes from Parks Wood. Could Tom have elected to settle here, so near to his memories? If so, he must have been a glutton for punishment. He had never really belonged to the band of outsiders, as Vinnie loved to think of The Brotherhood – he had always been weak, going where pushed, playing follow my leader to protect himself. But for all that he was important to the reunion, both as witness and participant in what had taken place. Even if the years had failed to change Tom and he remained an outsider amongst outsiders, Vinnie wanted him involved.

He slowed the mobile video rental van at an unmarked crossroads, then crawled on, frowning through the fading light to make out house numbers. The Blackmore estate had always been a no-go zone, where problem families were flung together by housing officers lacking foresight. Vinnie remembered avoiding the area as a child, having heard stories of street fights and public slanging matches, a regular feature of Friday and Saturday nights here. Little had been done to improve things since then. The grey, pebble-dashed council houses had a uniformly desolate, uncared-for look, and the road surface was crumbling and potholed. Stray dogs and abandoned cheap plastic toys were everywhere, blocking gateways, littering the road. Close to where Vinnie pulled over, two young boys were prising up a drain-cover with a stick. They stared as he clambered from the van, then went on with their work.

The address he'd been given and its semi-detached twin were like two halves of a split personality. Next door, the softly lit windows were curtained with lace and miniature rose bushes studded the flat, cropped lawn. Vinnie, however, was advancing along a cracked path overgrown with thistles and weeds towards a front door from which much of the paint had been stripped or scratched. In the midst of the tangle of overgrown grass and weeds stood a mouldering armchair. Something in the midst of the chair, either mould or a displaced cushion, might have been a figure poised to rise and greet him. Vinnie laughed nervously, reminding himself how bad the faltering light was for his eyes.

When he knocked at the door he was conscious of the boys looking up from their grate, waiting with him. Did they know something he didn't? If he'd bothered to ask, they might have told him Tom Quigley had moved; he was half-expecting to discover that anyway. He knocked again and listened, but there was no sound from within, and by the time he was back at the van the boys had vanished. Before jumping behind the wheel he hesitated, thinking of enquiring at another house. But this was Sunday evening; everyone would be getting ready to go out, and in any case he'd been driving for hours without success. Tomorrow he would think again about Tom. Tonight he could do with a mental reprieve. Picturing the tavern in Stanley, a glass of his favourite beer before him, he started the engine.

After the Blackmore estate, the road took him abruptly into no-man's land. An entire housing development had been flattened on the outskirts of town, on both sides of the road. To the right, where once had stood rows of small family shops and red brick terraced houses, he saw bulldozers and cranes, abandoned for the weekend: beyond them the skeletal outlines of three derelict factories, their steel-girder structures partially covered by walls of corrugated iron. Further along on the left, facing two fourteen-storey tower blocks, a handful of terraced properties stood defiantly in the middle of nowhere. Hadn't these once formed part of

46

the estate where Michael McCourt had lived? Somewhere amongst the wasteland would be a rubbled plot marking Michael's house. Occasionally Vinnie had visited after school or during holidays, afterwards waiting here on this road for his bus home. If it hadn't been for the disused railway bridge, straight ahead, and the motorway flyover beyond it, he wouldn't have known where he was.

Just ahead, parked in front of the terraces, was a car he thought he recognised. He slowed for a closer view, and made the connection. The vehicle, an old Austin Mini, was Linda Walker's. So this must be where she did her Samaritans stint. He was deliberating whether to pop in and see her when a figure shot out from behind her car.

For an instant the figure, a man, was trapped in the Transit's headlights. He raised his hands, signalling Vinnie to stop. Instinctively, Vinnie accelerated, away from the unknown. Even as he did, he retained a clear image of the man, as he'd once retained the startled gaze of a hare seen too late on a dusky country road, seconds before feeling the van thump the small body aside.

Had the man been loitering there? He'd given the impression of having been crouched by Linda's car, possibly tampering with it. Wouldn't it be wise to turn around and go back, just to be certain? Ahead was the railway bridge, the light at the far end of the gloomy archway just visible. Slowing as he approached it, Vinnie checked his mirror. As he did so, the man's face made sudden sense, and he hit the brakes, stopping the Transit short of the arch.

Tom Quigley was running along the street behind him, still waving both arms in the air. He was wearing a heavy black donkey jacket, blue jeans and cheap trainers that slapped the road surface like rubber flippers. As he drew near, Vinnie saw how haggard he looked, with a thick growth of beard and chapped, patchy skin. He stopped by the van and stood for several seconds, breathing hard, staring at Vinnie without recognition.

Vinnie swallowed hard, unable to believe his luck. Without doubt this was Tom Quigley. Yet something about him — the wild, disorientated eyes, the grubby skin, his ragged breathing — stopped Vinnie short of announcing himself.

'Is there some problem?' he said.

Quigley nodded, open-mouthed. 'Sort of. Mind if I hitch a lift?'

'Not at all. Get in. Where to?'

They were passing beneath the M62 flyover and towards open country when the hitchiker said wearily, 'Just let me off wherever it's convenient.'

'What? All the way out here?'

'No, I mean when we get to Wakefield, if that's where you're heading.' After a thought he added, 'Don't go out of your way, that's all.'

'I won't be. I live there. Whereabouts are you from?'

'Abbotsbridge, would you believe? You must be wondering why I'm hitching away from the place. But I shouldn't ... I don't want to go home at the moment.'

'Are you running from something?'

Vinnie sensed Tom Quigley's gaze settling on him. 'Running? Why do you ask?'

'It's the obvious question to ask. Have you seen yourself in a mirror lately?'

Tom Quigley shrugged and stared out of the window, away to his left. A turning for Parks Wood came and went agnonisingly slowly, the junction still marked with a rustic hardwood arrow.

'In the old days,' Quigley said in a far-away voice, 'some of us used to go there quite often. It was the place to head for after school. Hardly ever came this way, though – by the road. There was an approach through a snicket behind the houses where friends of mine lived.'

'Is it still the same? Can you still reach it that way?'

'Wouldn't know about that. It's been such a long time since ... since we ... That's all in the past now, anyway.'

'I just wondered, since you live there.'

'If living's what you call it. I'm not sure anyone *lives* in Abbotsbridge these days. What brought you over there, if you don't mind my asking?'

'Oh, just visiting an old acquaintance. He wasn't at home.'

Quigley nodded and turned back to face the road, folding his arms neatly. They journeyed without conversing for several miles. The smell of halitosis and stale clothing had begun to permeate the car, and Vinnie discreetly rolled down his window. He could scarcely contain himself. The urge to let slip who he was swelled up like laughter locked in his chest. When the time was right – not now, travelling through the dark – then he would break the news. When Tom agreed to attend the reunion the circle would be complete.

They were on the outskirts of Wakefield, passing the rugby football stand, then a brightly illuminated bowling alley, when Quigley began to grow restless. Leaning forward, he wiped an imaginary smudge from the screen. His breathing was suddenly reedy and thin, drawn through his teeth. He switched on the radio and flicked randomly through the pre-set stations before switching it off again.

'Is everything all right?' Vinnie asked. 'You're so jumpy you're making me feel the same. Is there something you want to get off your chest?'

'I don't know. I don't know. Maybe I do want to talk.' Again, Vinnie felt Quigley's gaze in the dark. 'You're very kind. But it's enough you should do me this favour.'

'No favour. I told you I lived over here.'

'You asked me, before, if I was running from something.' He waited while Vinnie found his lane approaching the main town roundabout. 'The fact is, I was; I still am. Not that hiding or running will make any difference.'

'Is that what you were doing when you flagged me down? Hiding from something?'

Quigley sighed. They were nearing the Kirkgate roundabout and the turn-off for Stanley. 'Hiding from some*one*, to be specific. Are you really sure you want to hear this?'

'Everyone needs someone to confide in.'

'A confessor, you mean. Then perhaps we can find somewhere comfortable. You might not need my gratitude but I can always run to the price of a stiff drink.'

Vinnie smiled. Unusually, he was beginning to relish this scenario: knowing, yet not being known. For so long the prospect of seeing the others again had been a worrying, daunting thing, but suddenly he felt lifted, elated. His work was complete, it was finally going to happen. If they were going to come together again – even though it had taken

Alison's death to make them do it – it should be something to savour. He wanted to see Tom's face in the light when he finally realised whose van he'd been travelling in. He wanted to see the circle joined again. Still smiling, he accelerated uphill past Stanley Royd hospital.

Minutes later he was parking the transit outside his flat in the crescent. 'There's pizza and beer in the fridge, and space on the couch if you decide you want to lie low for tonight. It's entirely up to you but you're welcome. But beware the landlord. I'm behind with the rent, and the bastard hates noise.'

Tom Quigley let out a low, dry whistle and scratched at his beard. 'You certainly know how to treat a weary traveller, Mr ...'

'Vinnie. Just call me Vinnie.'

'Vinnie.' Tom Quigley considered this, but the name seemed not to ring a bell. He added, without irony, 'You certainly are a good Samaritan.'

Which reminded Vinnie, as he reached the front door, key in hand, to phone Linda immediately. She should know that he'd found Tom Quigley; she should also be advised to be on her guard if Tom's fears were justified. It was only now, as the front door swung open and he stepped inside, that he wondered whether he'd been hasty in fleeing Abbotsbridge tonight. His only excuse was the heat of the moment, recognising Tom after fifteen years, forgetting everything else. In the instant he'd registered the face, everything had come together; the threat had diminished. If he'd thought twice while driving away he might have realised the threat was behind them, perhaps lying in wait for Linda.

The thought became a physical tremor that caused him to fumble and drop his keys. Following up the steps, Tom Quigley stooped to collect them. His heavy jacket strained with the effort, so bulky and tight he might have been wearing a surgical corset underneath.

His eyes were narrowed and smiling as he handed over the keys. He aimed a finger at Vinnie, admonishing him. 'Vinnie, you say. Vinnie who? You know, I'm beginning to wonder about you. I'm wondering whether I know you from somewhere.'

50

'Wonder a minute longer,' Vinnie said, leading the way up the darkened stairs to his room on the top floor. Once they were inside he grabbed a lager from the fridge, steering it into Tom's hand and Tom into the living room area. The flat was furnished with the landlord's threadbare hand-me-downs and smelt faintly of the air freshener Vinnie frequently sprayed to ward off the musty hum. Several promotional film posters obscured the peach-coloured walls. Tom was quickly drawn by two shelves of VHS films which Vinnie had bootlegged from the tapes he rented.

'Can you keep yourself company for a minute?' Vinnie said from the doorway. 'I've a phone call to make, then I'll explain everything.'

'*You'll* explain everything? I thought I was supposed to be doing the talking.'

'We both have a lot to discuss, believe me. Just bear with me.'

Before leaving Tom to browse, Vinnie put on a Mary Coughlan record at low volume. From the bedroom he heard the muffled rise and fall of the music as he searched a local directory for the Abbotsbridge Samaritans.

A mellow-voiced male answered, hardly reacting when Vinnie asked for Linda by name. No doubt he'd decided this was a frequent caller with an attachment for one of their volunteers. Linda, however, had gone off-duty fifteen minutes ago. Thanking the man, Vinnie hung up and dialled Linda's home. There was no answer, which hardly surprised him, since she lived as far from Abbotsbridge as he did. He would try again later.

As he put the receiver back on its rest, the volume of the music in the next room increased dramatically. Tom must have turned it up without thinking: he'd better have a word before the landlord went spare. Then Vinnie realised the music was louder only because the adjoining doors had been thrown open. His hand was still on the phone when he noticed Tom Quigley at the bedroom door, slowly unfastening his donkey jacket. There was a soft metallic clink as Quigley progressed from one button to the next.

'Vinnie *Hartley*,' he said through a grin. The rotting, neglected teeth had always been a Quigley trademark. In

51

the midst of his grubby beard, they looked vaguely obscene. Recognition had transformed him after all, but for some reason Vinnie took no pleasure in seeing the change. He'd wanted to watch Tom's face light up, but the glint in the man's eye was knowing, calculating.

'You remember, then,' he said, starting towards the door.

Quigley didn't move a muscle. 'Yes. I remember well enough, lard-arse. I remember only too well.'

For a matter of seconds Vinnie was thrown. The room fell out of focus around him. Tom Quigley's tone was new and alien; the words weren't spoken in fondness. When he took another step forward, expecting Quigley to dodge aside, Quigley stood firm, folding his arms.

Vinnie's mouth was running dry. 'So you know who I am. You were having me on just now, pretending you couldn't place the name. You knew — '

'From the moment you picked me up, sure I did. Did you think you had changed so much?'

'Then you *expected* me to come looking for you. When the news about Alison broke ... You realised that sooner or later we'd be forced back together again.'

'Sure. I knew that would bring everyone running.'

'Well, here we are then.'

'Yes, here we are.'

'So what is it, Tom? What's wrong? Why are you looking at me like that?'

'Go and sit down, Vin,' he said gently.

There couldn't be any mistake; even the beard and the grubby skin couldn't disguise Quigley, the preacher's son. Of course this was fifteen years on and people changed, often markedly. Yet there was something in Quigley's manner now — in his voice, his look, his posture — that Vinnie had seen once before. What shocked him was the knowledge that he hadn't seen it in Quigley.

'Sit down, I said,' Quigley reiterated. 'Go and sit on the bed, Vin, there's a good lad.' As he advanced towards Vinnie, he held his jacket open and spread it wide, like a flasher in action.

Vinnie stumbled back several paces, aghast. He had seen

this done before in comedy skits: salesmen sporting their illicit wares – watches, erotic postcards – inside their coats. Quigley's jacket was unique, however. The lining was laden with instruments of torture – a rack of knives of various lengths, a coil of rope, a miniature hacksaw. With this shining array, anguish and pain could be fine-tuned by degrees, made to sing unreachable notes. As Vinnie felt the bed thump the backs of his knees, he began to weep uncontrollably.

'What are you doing, Tom? Why are you ... Why are you ... Please, Tom, please! – We're supposed to be on the same side.'

'The same side? Jesus Christ! Is that how you still see the world, Vin? Us and them?'

'That's how we were before, and how we still are. It's primitive-sounding, I know. But we were friends. We were – '

'I was never your friend. Never anyone's.'

Mary Coughlan was still singing. All her subtleties were lost in the silence that now filled the room. All notes blurred together, all melodies became a drawl. The bed, with its four brass corner posts, creaked as Vinnie put his weight on it. His overweight body, a burden to him since early childhood, quivered at the shock of his sobs. *Lard-arse. Lard-arse.* Above him, half-dissolved through Vinnie's tears, Quigley still held open the left side of his jacket. With his right hand he was reaching for something.

Vinnie blinked. Moisture streamed down his cheeks.

'What happened to us all that time ago,' he said, 'it must have affected you, Tom. It did something to you. Stopped you from seeing clearly.'

'Oh, but I see clearly enough. My vision is twenty-twenty, brother.' Now, in his right hand, he brandished a whorl of nylon rope. 'Time for you to undress, Vin. Take off those clothes and leave them on a pile by the bed.'

'Tom, *please*! I'm begging you.'

'Just do as you're told, Vin. You ought to be comfortable while we talk. When you're undressed you can tie your feet to these posts here.'

'No. No, I won't. You can't make me do that.'

'Don't whinge, Vin, it makes you sound like a stuck pig. Just be good and do as you're told.'

Vinnie felt his last spark of energy ebb away. At first he could only sit there, wringing his hands, somewhere between fainting and retching. He was distantly aware of his parched tongue trying to retreat down his throat. At the edge of his vision the bedroom furnishings – a dresser, a standing lamp – contorted visibly. Perhaps six paces beyond Quigley, the open doorway beckoned. One second of inspiration was all he needed. Gathering all his strength, Vinnie threw himself to his feet, intending to blunder Tom Quigley aside in his rush for the door.

Once, cornered in the school changing room after gym, he had snatched at the same opportunity. Three older boys had waited until the others dispersed and then turned on him, demanding a private view of his penis and testicles. 'To make sure there's no truth in the rumour you aren't all together down there,' one had smirked. 'Just whip it out and it'll be over in a tick,' said another. Through his fear he remembered how they had stood: several feet apart, two with their arms folded challengingly across their chests, the third with his thrust deep in his trouser pockets. One had made jokes about the size of Vinnie's stomach, saying that nothing below it could grow in the shade. Vinnie sat facing them on a hard wooden bench, the strap of his kit bag wrapped twice around his hand. Away to their right was the cold steel and enamel of the showers, where he was certain they meant to drag him. The echoic drip of water chilled him. It was only as he raised his head and saw the open changing room door that he knew he had a choice. Without warning, he launched himself forward.

As he repeated this, sixteen years later, he was met by the firm thrust of Tom Quigley's outstretched hand, and immediately fell back on the bed.

'Please,' he murmured. Even then he was reaching to untie his shoes and remove them. He couldn't believe he was doing this; but his strength had given out. He had only ever been able to resist through the Brotherhood's collective strength. Without them he was nothing. The doorway was receding into the distance now and his only hope of survival was to do as he was told. Hitching up his buttocks, he dragged off his trousers and let them fall to the floor.

'And the rest, and the rest,' Quigley said wearily. He had taken a sleek, curved hunting knife from his jacket and was cutting the rope into lengths; it sliced through the nylon like butter. Vinnie forced himself not to look, concentrating instead on his shirt-cuffs. His breathing was out of control now, gasping and panting, like a thirsty, excitable dog. Removing his shirt, he blinked away tears and was faced with the pale wedge of his midriff.

'You murdered Alison,' he said. 'She was one of us and you murdered her.'

'Correction. *We* murdered her.' There were now four lengths of rope on the bed. 'Everything we do comes back to us in the end. It all becomes part of us. And everyone has to face judgement for their actions sooner or later. Your time starts now.' Quigley waited until Vinnie had finished squirming from his Y-fronts, then gestured for him to lie down. Vinnie hesitated; Quigley showed him the knife.

An escape was completely out of the question. The bedroom door was miles away, a speck of light on the horizon. Through waterlogged eyes Vinnie had a diffuse grey image of the changing room, the three boys jerking towards him as he flung himself forward. He felt their hands clawing him, sensed a shoulder seam of his coat give softly, then saw, like a vision, the outline of the games master at the threshold.

'Help,' he cried.

'Help,' he murmured sixteen years later. But this time around there was no one to hear.

Everyone needed a confidant – a confessor, as Quigley had put it. Leaning forward to secure his right ankle to the bed-post, Vinnie thought again of Linda Walker and her helpline. By now she would be arriving home safely – safe for now, but only because the threat was here, in this room, at the foot of the bed. She'd be setting her bag down in an armchair, pouring herself a drink, perhaps mulling over next week, when she and the others would travel to London.

'Where will everyone be staying?' Tom Quigley said lightly, reading his mind. 'Somewhere nice? You may as

55

well say. Sooner or later I'm going to know everything. It'll all be assimilated.'

'What do you mean, *assimilated*?' Vinnie's face was awash with snot and saliva. He swiped at his chin with the back of a hand, then edged his left foot towards the other post and grabbed a fresh length of rope. 'You can kill me too – I'll never tell you anything. Dying doesn't worry me, not now.'

'Ah, but death *shouldn't* worry you, Vinnie, my brother. However, I could keep you alive. Think how much worse that could be.' He patted his laden donkey jacket for emphasis. 'Still, the choice is yours. You can either go gracefully or disgracefully, whichever you prefer.'

'You know how to find us, you've already shown that. You don't need my help.'

'But a little goodwill goes a long way.' When Vinnie had finished securing his ankles, he smiled appreciatively and stepped round the bed. 'That's fine, just fine. Now lie back. All the way down. You don't have to say anything, Vin; but remember, I'm under no obligation to make this easy for you.' He added with displeasure, 'Christ, but look at you. There'll be no confusing you with just any body.'

Vinnie blinked fiercely, as if to squeeze out sheer terror from his eyes, while Quigley bound his wrists. There was the faintest clink of metal, then the slowly overpowering smell as his bowel gave way. Above him, Quigley made a face.

'What a sorry lot we are, when you get down to it. How dreadful we are inside. We're vile as children, but we never grow out of it, do we? We're born sick and then spend our lives getting sicker. But look at us – just fucking look at us.' Again, the glint in Tom Quigley's eye: a look that wasn't entirely his, as if someone else were trapped inside him, trying to get out. At the back of Vinnie's mind, almost lost amongst so much confusion and anticipation of pain, was the thought that this man was too literate to be Quigley, too philosophical in his brutality. Hadn't Linda said that Alison, on the phone, was *wrong*, not herself? Tom Quigley was also, somehow, wrong.

'Please,' he managed one last time.

'Listen,' said Quigley, whispering.

56

In the next room the music had stopped. Silence had overtaken the flat. The whole bedroom seemed to pound soundlessly, thick with odour and fear. The traffic outside sounded miles away, a blurred rushing noise soft as a breeze. It was a silence that deepened meaningfully, at least for Vinnie, as Quigley drew out the first surgical blade. The sight of it brought a scream to his throat, a scream large enough to shatter the quiet, which was probably why Quigley opted to remove his tongue first.

PART TWO
On Returning

Chapter Seven

Two years ago, during a brief and intensely physical fling with a petite, blonde divorcee named Mona, a listings magazine editor with a daunting co-operative apartment on the Upper West Side, Michael had made an unusual discovery. Left to himself while she dashed to the shops one late Saturday morning, he had drifted from room to room, horny, agitated that she was taking so long. Bryan Ferry crooned gently through extension speakers in every ornate white room. In the bedroom he took two brief, bored puffs from a joint left over from last night, pressed out the rest in a marble standing ashtray, and casually opened a wardrobe door. Inside he found, bundled between and beneath the prim dresses and smart suits she wore, a complete and varied set of rubberwear. Skirts, tops: even a one-piece resembing a scuba outfit with cut-outs for the breasts.

This had been several weeks before he met Tessa. Later, he vividly remembered standing before the full-length mirror that was set inside the open wardrobe, balancing in his hands the black rubber mask with its zippered back and cut-outs for eyes, nose and mouth. He remembered unzipping it slowly, until it flopped open and empty in his hands. He stroked it, surprised by how cool and smooth it felt, more like leather than rubber, he thought. It was only then that he sensed and heard movement near by, and saw the blurred shape in the mirror.

Behind him, far back in the room, Mona stood watching. Her arms strained under the weight of two bulging Zabar's bags, which at last she set down. She looked flushed and elated from her morning spree, and her hair was lightly tousled. She held his gaze in the reflection as she came slowly up behind him, laying her fingers on his shoulder. 'Why don't you try it for size?' she said.

BA Flight 172 from JFK was forty-five minutes behind schedule somewhere over the Atlantic when this memory came drifting towards Michael through the clouds. Since take-off he'd been plying himself with neat Bushmills malt from a hip flask while perusing the proofs of his last children's book, *Pushover*, which he'd brought to keep his mind occupied.

Several times during the flight he'd had to rush to the washroom and splash cold water in his face to bring himself back to reality. There, in the mirror above the hand-basin, he had seen himself trapped, wild-eyed, like manic John Lithgow in the *Twilight Zone* re-make of *Nightmare at 20,000 Feet*. It could have been the effect of several days of persistent alcohol abuse that recalled the strange and unnatural sensation of wearing the mask. It had felt, he'd thought at the time, like having his skin stretched to fit a far larger face. Worse, after Mona had zipped him up, was the stifling pressure and heat, the feeling of being without air even as he drew breath. Most ludicrous was the image of himself in the full-length mirror, standing ungainly in black mask, white bathrobe and nothing else. Then Mona giggling, covering her mouth.

It was the laughter that set him off, for he'd realised she was laughing at, not with him. Inside the mask he was perspiring, unable to close his eyelids properly. Grappling with the zipper behind his head, he reeled away from the mirror. When the zipper resisted, Mona laughed harder. He remembered being strangely excited, despite the embarrassment. By the time he had prised off the mask, though, her laughter had died and he'd known he was seeing the last of her. He had dressed and left without another word.

For the third or fourth time Michael re-read a passage in *Pushover*, pencil in hand, and understood suddenly why he'd needed to write it. The book had been written for children, yes, but the emotions that fired it were adult.

A thirteen year old boy named Shaun, overweight and reclusive, modelled loosely on Vinnie Hartley, had moved to a new town and school, only to face constant persecution from his peers. There was a viciousness amongst adolescents with which Michael had never come to terms. In one scene, Shaun was left to the group's mercy in a classroom during break. When the last member of staff had gone he had been stripped half-naked and bound to a chair, insulted and jeered at, some of the girls kissing him, making him cry.

It had actually been toned down for the novel, but in real life Michael had looked helplessly on while the scene played itself out for what seemed an age. Witnessing Vinnie's humiliation he'd done nothing: doing what was right had mattered less than avoiding the group's disfavour. Even now, he was trying to exorcise that day: the snorts of derisive laughter and slow applause echoing off the classroom walls. Perhaps his own humiliation − tearing with both hands at a rubber mask that refused to come off − was the reason he'd finally been forced, despite himself, to write *Pushover*.

But he was losing himself in memory again. He sipped whiskey and tried to read on. His face felt tighter than ever. Beside him, the middle-aged Bostonian woman with whom he'd chatted falsely before take-off had fallen asleep holding a book, her head lolling close to his shoulder.

In the story, the boy named Shaun − no longer a pushover − had been given a chance to fight back, gaining friends and respect in the process. One by one, the ringleaders, those who had led the hate campaign against him, were beaten down. The persecutors became the persecuted. In its final chapters, *Pushover* became an elaborate revenge fantasy. Finally, however, the boy faced a bitter victory: he had become the aggressor, the very thing he'd hated and opposed. Persecution didn't destroy him, but changed him for the worse. It had put him in touch with the dark side of himself.

Of course Harvey Klein loved the story, as did his publisher. But only the Brotherhood would understand the novel, understand why it had been written. We're all like that underneath, was the message. There are well kept secrets in every closet. We're all hiding from something, running in fear of something. And beneath the pile of proofs on his lap was the artist's preliminary sketch for the dust jacket, an idea suggested by Michael and approved by the art director: a hanged man and gallows, drawn in chalk on a dusty blackboard. Above this, the title: below, Michael's name.

He was on his way home, returning to the scene of the crime, as all criminals were meant to. Ever since Vinnie Hartley's calls last week he had drunk too much and slept fitfully. He had squeezed out no more than five or six pages of the new book. Tessa had vanished without trace from his apartment and his thoughts; she hadn't left a forwarding address and so, at the weekend, he'd thrown all her mail in the garbage.

The second call from Vinnie was the one that had rattled him. It was to confirm the Brotherhood reunion, to name a time and a place. It's real, he had thought; it's going to happen. Their London hotel, the Heartland, would be large and anonymous but comfortable, Vinnie insisted. There, they could meet and be together, free to reminisce, far enough from home to see clearly what should be done. Whatever that meant – whatever *should* be done – was a matter Michael had managed so far to avoid. Taking one final swig from the flask, emptying it, he turned the artist's sketch on his lap face down. When he looked up, one of the stewardesses was passing his seat. He waved a hand and asked for more whiskey.

Beside him, the Bostonian woman snored faintly, her head nudging his shoulder. For the first time he noticed that her thumb marked a place in the paperback edition of *Rubber Bullets*.

Everything was wavering slightly by the time he reached Customs. All his fellow passengers in the slow, shuffling queue were engaged in muted conversations he couldn't decipher. Perhaps they were discussing his drunkenness; his duty free allowance clinked neatly in a carrier against his right leg, and he wondered whether the alcohol already in his blood meant he should head for the red sector.

In the airport lounge there were anguished cries and groans when an announcement declared that French air traffic controllers were delaying the flight from Paris. Eager-eyed family members searched hopefully for familiar faces, ignoring Michael. The hubbub became a soft-hued dream, spinning in and out of focus around him. He was deliberating whether to travel in style by taxi or head for the Underground instead when a clean-shaven man in a parka stood up from a couch, clutching a board with Michael's name written on it to his chest. He had caught Michael's gaze and was waving even before Michael recognised him.

'Mikey,' he said. 'I don't believe it! Look at you!'

At first Michael blinked, surprised by how much Vinnie had changed. If not quite a rake, he was very much trimmer than Michael remembered. These days he had cheekbones, and wore his clothes rather than strained from them. In a moment the buzz of airport activity filtered out and he was sober again. He lowered his suitcase and met Vinnie's firm handshake.

'Look at *you*,' he replied at last. 'Lard-arse? It can't be. Tell me I'm mistaken.'

'Afraid not. What you see is what you get.'

'Where's the rest of you?'

Vinnie laughed. 'Which reminds me of Ronald Reagan in *King's Row*. Remember when we saw that and howled?' Seizing Michael's suitcase, he started away. 'Hell, you know what dangerous drugs can do to your figure! Seriously though, time moves us all right along, doesn't it? God, it's great to see you, Mikey. I can hardly get over it. This way – the car's just outside. We'll arrive at the hotel together.'

'It's more than I expected, seeing you here,' Michael marvelled, as they stepped outdoors into night-time and began the search for Vinnie's car, a rented Ford. It was parked between two Porsches on the far side of the concourse.

'Well, I checked the airport for your flight, and decided it would be nice to give you a personal welcome. After all, it isn't as if you'd just driven down from Milton Keynes!' Unlocking the driver's side door, Vinnie paused and looked up. 'You didn't have to come home, you know.'

'I realise that.'

'It would've been safer where you were.'

Michael shrugged. 'Distance doesn't make that much difference. It would've caught up with me eventually.'

'But you'd rather be there than here, I'll bet.'

'Yes, I think so.'

'We're glad you made it, anyway. You were always the heart of the circle, Mikey.'

'I don't know about that, Vin.'

'Oh, but you were. Nothing would've been the same without you. It wouldn't be the same without you now.'

Michael collapsed wearily into the car, still clutching his flight bag and duty frees. Vinnie flung the suitcase into the rear. As they sped from the pool of light that was Heathrow, a Boeing 747 climbed steadily above them, and Michael felt his eyes trying to close. Perhaps a taxi would have been better; at least he could have slept through the ride without being rude. But he was obliged to talk now.

'It looks like a long night ahead,' he said.

The new, streamlined Vinnie gave a slow nod. 'A long few days, even.'

'Had the others arrived when you left for the airport?'

'Actually I haven't even checked in yet. I came straight for you. How's that for service? You ought to feel honoured.'

'I do, I do.' Michael smiled faintly and drifted, letting the road and the lights flow towards him. It wasn't until they reached Hammersmith that he thought again about *King's Row*: the rainy Sunday afternoon they had watched it and howled.

He seemed to remember it had been at Alison Lester's house: himself and Bill on the two-seater sofa, Alison and Linda ferrying in peanuts and tins of beer. Ronald Reagan without legs, Robert Cummings clenching his fists and his jaw, the syrupy score rising to a crescendo, and the whole room crying — but tears of laughter. 'Where's the rest of me?' they had chorused on cue, and cracked up.

Michael frowned and touched his brow, where the skin

still felt taut from his drinking, and cast a sideways glance at the silhouette driving him. If the *King's Row* afternoon was still so vivid that Vinnie should mention it, why couldn't he remember him being there?

Chapter Eight

Michael was drifting near to sleep when a jolt of the car disturbed him. His senses returned slowly in disarray. A combination of long flight and dehydration from drink had done its worst, and his mind felt shrouded, too congested for clear thought. Before he understood why, he experienced a flood of both relief and nervous apprehension; then realised Vinnie was parking up. He nosed the windscreen to see outside. They must have arrived. The Brotherhood were perhaps only seconds away.

It took Michael slightly longer to register the darkened sidestreet they were on, the row of unglamorous shop windows, the absence of any hotel signs. 'Where are we?' he wondered, suddenly alert. His tongue felt alien and fungous.

'Earls Court. Hogarth Road, to be exact.'

'I thought the Heartland was in Covent Garden.'

'It is. Always has been. But there's a slight change of plan. This is only a detour.'

'You didn't mention detours at the airport.'

'I didn't think it would make any difference.'

'To what?' Michael swallowed. A long hit of what was in the duty free carrier would help: better still black coffee, sobriety. Ever since the night in Charlie O's when Vinnie's name came uninvited out of the blue he'd been living a drunken dream, warding off the past – and the future. 'What's this about, Vin?'

'Huh?'

'What are we doing in Earls Court?'

'Well, we're − '

'What the fuck are we doing in Earls Court? The group sticks together, you know that as well as I do. We don't even have a plan yet, that we can afford to detour from it.'

'Calm yourself, Mike. Give me a chance to explain. We wouldn't be here if it wasn't important.'

'I don't doubt it's important, but you should have told me.'

'About what? I was letting you sleep.'

'Before, I mean. When we met.'

'I was pleased to see you. I never imagined you'd make an issue of this. In any case we're only visiting, Mikey.'

'Visiting who?'

'Tom Quigley. Remember? One of *us*, brother, one of *us*. What's so terrible about that?'

Michael recoiled as Vinnie touched his shoulder, and was instantly ashamed of his outburst. Having existed so long in a bubble he'd forgotten how to function outside it. No wonder Tessa had left him; his inertia must have driven her away. And now he didn't know now to behave towards Vinnie. Shouldn't he trust him, having travelled so far, having shared the great secret for so long?

Vinnie said, 'You're not the only one who's afraid, you know. It's something we all have in common − sleepless nights and nervous days.'

'Yes, I know. I'm getting us off to a bad start, aren't I?' Vinnie shook his head but said nothing. Michael went on. 'In some ways I still haven't landed yet. Do you realise I haven't set foot in this country for nearly three years? This is all so unreal, closing my eyes for a minute, expecting to open them somewhere else but instead finding − *this*.' He gestured towards the deserted street. 'Why isn't Tom with the others?'

'He's to join us here. We're to collect him and bring him to the Heartland. No more detours, I promise. Shall we go in?'

Michael followed Vinnie from the car towards a white-painted door between two shops. Along the street to their right a black cat snuggled in a haberdasher's doorway, and Michael half-expected Orson Wells to lean forward into the light, smiling enigmatically. Beyond the junction, the traffic rushed along Earls Court Road as the lights changed; nearer, directly beneath their feet, was the rumble of an underground train.

Without knocking, Vinnie tried the door, pushing it firmly. The door swung inwards on silent hinges. The bottom few steps of a staircase were just visible in the gloom. Vinnie glanced in at the dark, then at Michael. He smiled and gestured, and Michael realised he was still clutching the duty free carrier.

'You must be serious about your drink these days, Mike.'

'Deadly serious.'

Vinnie twitched a thumb towards the interior. 'Probably Tom hasn't seen us. Should we go straight up?'

'Unless there's a bell or a buzzer. We could call him down.'

But Vinnie was already indoors, vanishing into the pall of shadows as he strode upstairs. After a moment, Michael followed. As he stepped in off the street, the darkness swept over him, as did the thick, tainted smell of the hall. There was almost no light above, and it was hard to decide where the stairs ended.

'Is Quigley skimping on electricity or what?' he wondered, stumbling upwards.

There was muted laughter from Vinnie, but no reply.

Michael went on. 'It's surprising, don't you think, to find Tom Quigley tucked away here in the heart of London?'

'How's that?'

'He was always such a born yokel; you couldn't imagine him ever leaving home.'

'Sssh! He might hear.'

'What makes you so sure he's up there, Vinnie? Who lives like this, without light?'

'Strange days call for strange measures,' Vinnie's voice echoed from higher up.

'Well, I never saw stranger.'

Nearing the upper steps, Michael could make out an open doorway directly ahead, and through it, rooftops and sky framed by a tall sash window. The sky was impossibly clear and still, as if it had been painted there. Reaching the landing, Michael stopped, facing the framed night. It was then, staring out in a moment of calm, that he knew he'd been had.

'Vinnie?'

There was no answer. For a time the only sound was that of another underground train, its noise gradually gathering, rising steadily up through the structure of the building to fill its empty and silent spaces like a cry.

Michael held his breath. He put his hands to his ears, which only made things worse; the train felt trapped in his skull. For too long the tremor seemed like the threat of something about to happen, the drumroll before the crescendo. Its passing left him alone with his fear and his pounding heart.

'Vinnie?' he repeated, dry-mouthed. He had no sense of Vinnie's nearness; no sense of any living presence in the building. Perhaps his instinct on starting awake in the car had been right after all. This wasn't Tom Quigley's place, and the man who had brought him here was not Vinnie Hartley. If he hadn't been sozzled from the flight he mightn't have been so vulnerable.

But he still had time to get out before it − whatever *it* might be − could happen. At the foot of the stairs the pool of light described the open front door and the street beyond. Michael edged forward, no longer sure of his footing. He'd taken several blind steps across the landing towards the light below, but the problem now was the reverse of when he came up: he couldn't be sure where the stairs began.

Michael threw out a hand, groping for a wall or stair-rail, and froze. It was hard to be sure whether a scent, a sound, or something less tangible made him stop, turn, gasp faintly beneath his breath. All he understood was that he was alone in the presence of something he'd experienced only once before. For half his life he had kept it at bay, but now the dream of survival was over. He shuffled on frantically, feeling for the uppermost step with his foot. His fingertips found purchase, the edge of a wall that felt slippery. The darkness was so complete he was beginning to mistrust even his senses. Then, somewhere off to his left came the rush of activity he'd half-expected.

Roaring towards him out of the black was the smell of death itself.

Stupidly, Michael dodged back, away from the stairs. It would have been safer to throw himself down. Had Vinnie's phone calls to New York been a hoax, part of some elaborate ploy to get him here? How pointless, how foolish, to have resisted returning for so long, only to find himself cornered the minute he got off the plane. Something soundless and quick whispered across his upper left arm, and he let out a cry.

As he flung up his hand to protect himself he felt the same neat swish of air, the same wild surprise at being cut, this time between his third and fourth fingers and down across the palm to the heel of his hand. Would it help to see his attacker? Perhaps a face would make things worse; perhaps that was what he feared most. The weapon flashed past his eyes, just missing. He skipped away neatly, then realised he was being forced back through the open doorway above the stairs, into the blackened room.

Despite the large sash window there wasn't enough light to tell Michael anything. The figure advancing on him was barely a silhouette, but the aura inside the room made him almost glad to be blind. Part of what he smelt was himself, his own open flesh. The sleeve of his coat was drenched, his arm sang musically. Worse, though, was the deeper aroma rising beneath his own, overpowering it: the smell of *old* blood, old soil, of an act of terrible intimacy, and a secret shared for life.

Once, while skimming the pages of a scientific journal during a break from his work, Michael had chanced on the first of a series of articles concerning the senses. That month's was a discussion of smell. This, it was claimed, was our most immediate link with the past, capable of triggering explicit and vivid memories. A whiff of perfume or sun oil − or for that matter a hint of state sweat in a rush-hour commuter train − could instantly conjure up times and places, faces and incidents long forgotten. On so many occasions Michael had strolled past fruit stalls, gutters blocked with stagnant water, driven through open fields and polluted streets, and drifted off in time without provocation.

Total recall could occasionally be an inconvenient thing, but it was always unstoppable.

In the dark room above Hogarth Street the smells of memories were so thick, Michael was gagging. It was all coming back now. Of course it had never been far away. Impossibly, even above the rusty odour of blood, he detected a richness of freshly turned soil and September rain falling. He recalled a moment of sheer terror, shared with the others in open-mouthed silence. He saw eyes widen, a white hand pressed over a mouth, stifling an inevitable scream.

'Sssh,' someone said. 'Be quiet. Hold it down.'

'There there,' said another.

There was the rich, penetrating odour of vomit as someone – perhaps Vinnie – doubled up in a corner: again the refreshing scent of rain gusting into the ice house. All these memories were thicker than blood. Through them Michael could even detect halitosis – and then he returned to himself. What he could smell was the figure's breath in his face.

'Welcome home, Mikey,' a voice said in front of him. The dark blade swished downward again. 'It's so nice to have you back where you belong.'

'Vinnie?' But already he knew it couldn't be Vinnie. The voice was all wrong, for a start. It lacked Vinnie high, slightly petulant quality, constantly on the verge of complaining or whining. This was broader, more guttural. It could have been anyone.

Michael stumbled backwards. Now pinned against the window, he'd run out of both space and time. In the dim light his attacker was sketchily outlined, bulky and featureless, right arm raised for the kill.

'Should've *known* you weren't Vinnie,' Michael protested. 'You couldn't have been. Vinnie never sat through *King's Row* that afternoon. He phoned Alison halfway through the film to apologise for not coming.' Yes, he could practically taste the day now, the rain outside, the peanuts and beer in the warm room, the telephone ringing. In the darkness his senses were almost primordial, uncannily in touch with the past. 'Sure, that's what happened. Vinnie had been doing some odd job or other at home, soldering or wiring, he'd forgotten the time. Then the rain came down, and he phoned to arrange to meet later. Whoever you are, you aren't Vinnie. Your memory of that afternoon isn't his.'

'Then whose do you think it is?' This time, to Michael's astonishment, the voice was pitched higher and lilted, like a girl's. It was only the slightest shift of inflection, but it made all the difference. Alison, he thought; but that was impossible. He'd journeyed home prepared for anything but that. If someone had tricked him into returning, Alison hadn't been part of the ploy. Since that first conversation with Vinnie he'd followed the story avidly in the English newspapers. Alison's death was beyond dispute.

'How should I know whose memory it is?' Michael said. 'You tell me. You're in charge here.'

'The Source is in charge, my brother,' the figure said, and twitched the blade, nicking Michael's left shoulder. 'The hanged man's back from the gallows to settle an old score.'

The thought struck Michael that these could well be almost the last words he would hear. It was such a pitiful scenario. He wouldn't have written it for anyone. Someone had invited him home to die, and it seemed he would do just that, most likely without a face, never to be found. Somewhere between JFK and the Heartland hotel he had vanished without trace. And this after years of fear and uncertainty and waiting. He'd hoped for a better *dénouement* than this.

The killer spoke gently, reassumingly. 'I'm your friend from days gone by, if you want it spelled out. In fact, I am *all* of your friends.'

'Go fuck yourself,' Michael told the assassin's outline. 'Calling yourself a friend is blasphemy after what you did to Alison – '

'And Vinnie. Let's not forget about Vinnie.'

Something turned over in Michael's stomach. For a moment he thought he would be violently sick. In his mind's eye he saw again the face greeting him at the airport: how familiar, yet unfamiliar it had seemed. He blinked away the image as the blade came down, and he tumbled.

The fall was not intentional, but it was the best thing that could have happened. For one thing, it threw the assasin off balance. As Michael hit the floorboards he heard the blade scrape the window pane. Scrambling to his feet he realised he and his assailant had somehow traded positions; Michael was nearer the doorway now. The figure's outline loomed against the window. Against the skyline it was possible to make out the shape of the head, large and mop-haired, the upturned collar of a jacket. Taking careful aim, Michael whiplashed his duty free bag towards it.

The impact rocked the assassin visibly. There was a second of dead calm in which even the sounds of outdoor traffic seemed to recede. Michael heard a thump as the weapon hit the floor. The assassin let out a low, wavering sigh and lifted an unsteady hand to his face. Michael struck out again, this time clenching the neck of the bottle inside his bag. It was a bottle of rare Wild Turkey rye, and he would later regret the noise of shattering glass that greeted the third of fourth blow.

The assassin went down. Michael didn't wait to see if the job was done. He dropped the makeshift blackjack and turned, propelling himself clear of the room. Four strides took him across the landing, a fifth made him airborne. The stairs were no easier to find than before, and he was falling before he knew it. More or less halfway down, he managed to seize a hand-hold, though the stair-rail gave slightly as his full weight rocked it.

Yes, welcome home, Mikey, he thought. Welcome home indeed.

Somewhere above him there were sounds of leaden movement: his host either collapsing completely or forcing himself upright again. Michael didn't wait to find out which. A brief look told him the keys were gone from the car outside. He grabbed his flight bag from the passenger side, abandoned the heavy suitcase, and without pause for breath ran towards Earls Court Road.

Chapter Nine

The Trinidadian taxi driver took one look at the blood darkening Michael's sleeve and screwed up his face. 'What happened to you, mon? Someone carve you up? Someone take all your stuff? You sure you don't want no hospital?'

Michael shook his head and fished out a clean white handkerchief for a tourniquet. 'It isn't as bad as it looks. Just get me where I want to go and I'll take care of it there.' He repeated the address and slumped back in the seat, moaning.

'Just don't mess up my upholstery, mon, is all. This car's my livelihood. I's doing you a favour, driving you all cut up like this.'

'Don't think I won't remember.'

'You sure you don't want no hospital?'

Michael closed his eyes and the driver turned up the Wailers.

Ten surreal minutes later they were drawing up at the Heartland's entrance on Russell Street, Covent Garden. Inside, the hotel was a compromise between snug and anonymous, as Vinnie had promised. The white-walled Art Deco foyer slumbered to a soundtrack of boozy piano music, a loosely improvised 'Smoke Gets in Your Eyes'. In quiet, far-flung corners distinguished older men sat taking coffee and cognac with elegant younger women, presumably secretaries or PAs; it was hard to imagine them as spouses. The girls at reception, all dark trim haircuts and bright red lips, answered the busy telephones curtly in mild French accents.

At last a receptionist whose name, Francine, was printed across her lapel badge came to the desk. She was too self-absorbed and efficient to pay much attention to his injury. As Michael leaned across the counter to sign for his key she said, her voice climbing a musical scale, 'Would you like the house doctor to look at that, sir?' She made this sound like another incidental detail: morning paper, tea and toast, emergency treatment for knife wounds? – all part of the service, sir.

'Thanks, I'll let you know,' Michael said, grateful to be playing this effortlessly. 'Just send up some gauze and cotton wool for now.'

Adjoining the foyer was a spacious, softly-lit piano bar, The gentle live music was coming from there. A slim-hipped, well-dressed woman in her mid or late forties was leaving, arm in arm, with her toy boy. He seemed to be holding her upright, making certain she walked in a straight line. The woman flattened a hand to her forehead and giggled hoarsely. Beyond the bar, at the far end of the foyer, were twin carved oak elevator doors set into an alcove. As the couple reached the alcove a group of three – a man and two women – stepped from one of the elevators and turned towards the bar.

Michael stared after them, heart lurching. His first instinct was to run forward, seize Bill's hand, throw his-arms around Linda and Naomi in turn. Instead, from his place at the reception desk, he watched while Bill ushered the women to a table, then leaned across the bar to order.

He knew these people. Their faces were new versions of those he'd memorised. Even at this distance, he could see how subtly altered they were, in ways he'd taken for granted in himself. Linda was seated facing, Naomi with her back towards him. Both were dressed casually in jeans and sweaters, Linda's sleeves rolled to her elbows as if she meant business. During those last days at high school it would have been impossible to imagine Linda as a mature adult woman. Now the change made so much sense. At fifteen and sixteen she had been very nearly there, like an inspired first draft; at thirty she looked as she'd always been meant to.

'Your key, sir,' the receptionist said, tapping it twice

on the desk. Michael pocketed it without a glance, and moved nearer the piano bar's entrance. The player was now improvising 'Ain't Misbehavin'. Though Michael stood full in the foyer's light, none of the trio noticed him. Bill was preoccupied ordering the drinks; Naomi and Linda were becoming acquainted again. They spoke quietly, with long, fond pauses. There was an air of sadness about the couple as if they had returned from a funeral. Perhaps they had. He *knew* these people. For a time he simply stood and observed, an outsider looking in, fearing that if he blinked they would vanish again.

When he reached his room on the third floor he found the twin beds clinically well made, so perfectly tucked it was hard to believe they'd been slept in before. He pounded the pillows and ruffled the sheets of the bed nearest the window and dumped his flight bag on the other.

The medical supplies were brought to his room ten minutes later and in the white-tiled, antiseptic bathroom he washed and dressed his arm. The cut above the elbow, though bloody, wasn't as deep as he'd feared; the marks across his collar-bone and forearm were more tender, though even less deeply scored. Afterwards he lay on the bed with his eyes shut while the room gyrated slowly about him. His body felt so heavy, he doubted he would ever raise himself again.

When the spinning sensation passed he took a whisky miniature from the Mini bar next to the bed and lay back in the dark. Tomorrow he would pay for all this drinking with a head like thunder, but for now it was necessary to keep reality at one remove. What had happened tonight already seemed less than real: a scene he'd dreamed up for a novel. If not for his wounds he might have believed he'd imagined it all. The most troubling thing − the reason he was blunting his senses with booze again − was the voice, the manner, the look of the man he had met at the airport. Instinctively he'd taken this man for Vinnie. Yet in so many ways he was so far removed from Michael's expectation of Vinnie as to be untrue. Could even fifteen years change someone so much?

Vinnie had always been the victim, never the persecutor. Life seemed to have singled him out for the role, cursing him with a body, a demeanour, that invited punishment. Even if Vinnie had re-invented himself since then he couldn't have lost that look. There were auras about people, like scars, that might fade with time without ever vanishing. Vinnie could never had been anyone but himself, even now. Michael should have realised as much at the airport.

He's gone, he thought, and wherever he is, he's with Alison. So I finally came home to my friends; but my friends weren't at home. I'd kept them waiting too long, and now it's too late.

Michael finished the whisky miniature and lay back, alone with the dark and his heartbeat. Everything seemed to be rushing ahead of him; his pulse, his muddled thoughts, and then a sudden clear memory of footsteps slapping across tarmac, of the subtle beginnings of a stitch in his ribs, with red-faced Vinnie at his side.

They were racing, but not one another. Fifteen years ago the high street in Abbotsbridge had been cluttered with market shoppers on Wednesdays, Fridays and Saturdays. At that time the traders still thought it worthwhile to travel there, before the town began winding itself down. This, a Friday, must have been straight after school, since the stalls were still open and browsers blocked the pavements on both sides of the road. In his Heartland hotel room, Michael closed his eyes but could nevertheless see all . . . smell all. The whisky had triggered ancient memories of an open pub door he and Vinnie were dodging past. There was smoke and drunken laughter trapped inside. Hazy four o'clock sunlight strobed between the canopies above the stalls while slow-moving motorists honked at careless pedestrians.

'Where do we go from here?' Vinnie panted, his face a shade between scarlet and blue.

'Here,' Michael said, and threw himself left, into an alley between two shops. 'Keep moving, Vin, or they'll have you.'

'That's if − ' Vinnie fought for air − 'my heart doesn't give out first. Just hold it a sec, Mike.'

Thankfully the alley was dark enough to conceal them from passers-by. Vinnie lolled forward, hands on knees, head bowed. Amplified by the narrow damp space between the walls of the alley, his breathing sounded painfully near to asthma. 'It they find us they'll murder us,' he said, straightening up, hands nursing his ribs.

'I doubt they'll go that far.'

'Are you saying you want to stay here and find out?'

Michael, however, was already striding towards the light at the far side of the alley. It opened into a small municipal car park, on market days always over-subscribed, beyond which, across a road and over a sagging fence, was a short-cut through the woods towards home. Reaching the car park, Michael looked back.

'Are you coming too, Vin?' he called; and then his heart lurched. Crowding into the alley from the high street were the group he and Vinnie were supposed to be fleeing.

From where he stood in the light, peering back through the alley's dim telescope, he couldn't make out their faces, though their manner told him all he needed to know. As soon as they rounded the corner from the high street they seemed to stiffen, become alert: momentarily they'd given up the chase, but had immediately picked up the scent again.

'Vinnie!' he called, but Vinnie was already running. For a second or two Michael faltered, wondering whether to hang on for Vinnie or save himself; by the time he'd decided Vinnie had already reached and passed him, and the others were only paces away.

As the group swarmed forward something one of them carried – a stick or an iron bar – scraped along a wall in the alley. Michael jumped, turned, and fled across the car park without a backward glance.

Vinnie was already into the road, taking advantage of a gap in the traffic. Michael followed. After the alley daylight seemed unnaturally intense, objects at the fringe of his vision shimmering as if about to explode. All he could hear as he tottered into the road was a growing roar of voices behind him, voices that might or might not have carried his name. It wasn't until he'd half climbed the fence at the edge of Parks Wood that he saw how close the others were – and, chillingly, how jubilant, how elated they seemed.

For a second – it couldn't have been longer than that –

he locked eyes with the ringleader, Sachs. All he saw there was wanton pleasure. What kind of bastard was this, that thrilled to the giving of pain and terror? On Sachs' left stood Tom Quigley, bedenimed, impassive and expressionless as ever. Did he really mean to take part in this? Probably not, but the crowd always swept him along; he hadn't the wherewithal to refuse. The others grinned as they waved their fists or wafted their weapons like batons. For a moment they were stranded where they stood, twenty or thirty feet distant, while traffic surged in both directions. Michael dropped to the turf and took off towards the bridle path that wound into the woods.

Vinnie was slightly ahead, moving with a vigour Michael had never seen him exhibit on the sports field. Of course this was different: perhaps not a life and death matter, but who could really tell where Sachs was concerned?

'Jesus, Michael, God help us both,' Vinnie was panting. His nose and gaping mouth trailed snot and saliva; his eyes were practically blind with tears. 'How did we get into this mess? How did we let it happen? They'll catch us in the woods and do anything they like – anything they bloody well like, because no one will know, no one will see!'

Shut up, just shut up, Michael thought, though he wasn't wasting energy on words. Keep moving, he thought, and overtook Vinnie as the bridle path veered off to their left. Going that way and then making a detour might throw the others off the scent. With luck they would follow the path just far enough to allow Vinnie and Michael a clean getaway.

Michael ducked to his right, onto a vaguely trodden track that wound down through a dense plantation of mature chestnut trees. At this point the light became thicker than that in the alley they'd passed through. The trees had been planted too closely together; at the uppermost reaches they were crushed and distorted, with splintered or crippled limbs. Several boughs seemed to be extending themselves downwards, towards their roots. Others were growing in improvised loops. Nightfall here was a constant. Even if Sachs guessed they had come this way, he'd never be able to spot them.

There were more than two hundred miles and sixteen years between the point where the plantation ended, eventually becoming a scrub of wispy young birch and overgrown, trodden-down bracken, and the room where Michael McCourt lay, drifting between memory and sleep.

Michael turned onto his side, facing the open window, reliving the scene once again. The chase had been only the beginning; the point at which the Brotherhood materialised. In its way it had been an invigorating experience − the threat of violence, the unknown terrain, the first signs of nightfall as Michael and Vinnie emerged from the trees within sight of the bracken.

'Keep moving, Vin,' he remembered saying. 'Another hundred yards and we're home and dry.'

He clenched his eyes so tightly his face felt like something outgrowing his skin. Yes, he thought. That was the day we all began to change. The day that Roy Sachs *forced* us to change. The Brotherhood had happened in the end because there was no other way.

Chapter Ten

Half an hour later, unable to sleep, Michael rose and made coffee from a sachet provided by the hotel. He drank it black without sugar, just hot enough to singe his tongue on the way down. The Mini bar beckoned, but even he had his limits. He decided not to face the others tonight, but wait until morning. By then he might be capable of relating what had happened, if not quite explaining it.

Besides, the memory of that late afternoon in Parks Wood was so strong he felt obliged to give himself up to it, be alone with it. In a sense this was much like summoning up a novel from nothing, or at least from vague, half-remembered experiences, waiting for something to emerge in its own time. Suddenly and without warning it might all make perfect sense, everything dovetailing together neatly. The emergence of a story, like a birth, could be something you knew was coming before knowing precisely what form it would take. Perhaps he needed to come to terms with the past in order to face the reunion tomorrow. Until now he'd tried to avoid looking back. He'd been able to face what had happened only by transforming it into fiction, purging something within himself without naming it. How *did* we get into that mess? he wondered. But he already knew.

Memories beget memories, the past implodes on itself, and while picking a route through Parks Wood he had asked himself much the same question. Beyond the chestnut plantation the sky seemed to frown as evening gathered, but it was much too early for nightfall; a storm was on its way.

'How the fuck *did* we get into this?' Vinnie demanded, not requiring an answer. The answer was easy: we invited it.

It had been a day in June, the summer vacation rushing ever nearer. At times, however, it seemed they would never get there. There were moments where spoken promises stopped the world in its revolution, as when Roy Sachs or one of his sidekicks whispered, 'You're dead. After school.'

Initially the tirade was directed at Vinnie alone. Often the words were less than serious, spoken only for show. What troubled Michael, however, was the sense that the madness in Sachs' eyes was something more than show, that in fact he was capable of everything he promised. What kind of bastard was this?

Two weeks before the end of term, Michael looked up from inspecting his fingernails as his name was called from the English register. Bartholomew, head of the department, uttered each name once only in a voice hard and curt as a cough. Behind him a whiteboard was still scrawled with formulae from a previous lesson: maths or physics, Michael could never be sure which. Out of the silence came distant cries from the sports field. Michael answered Bartholomew's call and glanced with an air of boredom towards the window with its vista of distant greenery and upreaching rugby posts. This was the last lesson of the day, which explained the slouched, world-weary atmosphere in the class. One girl was playing cat's cradle with a palmful of string; another was sneaking a look in her compact, shielded from Bartholomew by her bag. Only one figure between himself and the far window sat upright, attentive; Linda Grayson, whom he really only knew to say hello and goodbye to. When he realised she was staring straight back at him he almost gasped aloud. They both looked away in the same instant, with a similar degree of panic.

At first he thought he'd been hit in the chest; caught in the act of snooping. Could she tell from a look what he thought of her – that he wanted to know her? Could the rest of the class sense the moment, read his thoughts? He felt that all eyes were focused on him. Michael held his breath while Bartholomew went on with the register. Parker, Perryman,

Robertson, Rollins, Russell, Quigley. When he chanced a glance back in Linda's direction she was staring intently at her folded hands on the desk-top, and Bartholomew had stopped at a name on the list.

'Sachs?' he repeated. 'Roy Sachs?'

There was no reply, although Sachs was present. It wasn't Bartholomew's style to repeat himself more than once, and so he waited, and waited. For three or four beats there was silence; then a slight, spontaneous movement as the class turned to stare at the culprit.

Sachs reclined at the back near the window, his feet in Doc Martens on the desk. He was chewing a wad of gum, his jaws working exaggeratedly; his army fatigues were patched with anarchy symbols and names like Crass. Gradually, as more and more faces turned towards him, he began to smile insolently, his gaze, which had fixed on Vinnie Hartley, filled with contempt.

'What are *you* gawking at, hippo gut?'

'Sachs!' Bartholomew's cough sounded more clipped than ever, and his eyes, behind their thick-lensed spectacles, seemed to swell out of all proportion. 'Are you here or not?'

'What do you think, *sir*? What does it look like?' But his sights were still trained on Vinnie. 'Watch yourself, after, that's all,' he said.

This brought a subdued ripple of laughter from those with whom he shared the back row – Quigley, Jimmy Jazz, Nat Fleetwood. Michael returned his attention to the front, managing as he did to catch Linda's eye. She seemed to half-smile without looking his way; perhaps it wasn't intended for him. Bartholomew's tongue swept neatly across his lower lip and he took a long and arduous deep breath. Having coughed two more names he closed the register, and the session began.

Naturally enough, this was the point where memory faltered. It wasn't the stuff of drama, the educational part, and Michael had mentally filed it under O for Oblivion. Not that he'd objected to the novel they were studying, *The Grapes of Wrath*, which he personally adored. But even then he had been galled by Bartholomew's treatment of the book.

Here was a living, breathing work of creation that for one obscure reason or another had to be desecrated, murdered and dissected before it could be understood. For almost an hour Barthlomew mused and read extracts, hinted at Biblical parallels. Even Michael, who had read it from cover to cover, found himself sagging as the lesson progressed. Gradually the cries from the sports field grew louder, and the temptation to gaze towards the window became greater. Towards the end there were feigned snores and yawns from those at the back, and laughter, and then stifled groans as Bartholomew said,

'What I'd like you to do is spend the weekend thinking about all the ways Steinbeck used the gospels as a foundation for his novel. Dig deep into your Bibles − assuming you have access to Bibles − keep them handy as you work through the text. Then, when you've looked at this thoroughly, you will write me a five hundred word essay. Root out the religious symbols, list them, discuss them, explain their significance ...'

It was cold-blooded torture all the way, and left the class numb with shock. When the last bell sounded, only two or three chairs scraped back. The majority remained seated, stunned, unable to move. Bartholomew made a hasty exit.

A minute spun out. At Michael's right hand, Vinnie shook his head and blew air through his teeth while his fingers tore the wrap from a Milky Way. 'Does he really mean it? Do you think he really means it?'

'Of course he does. He always means it,' Alison Lester grieved, dragging herself to her feet, collecting her things. 'He also means it when he threatens detention if the work isn't done in time.'

The rest of the group began, in fits and starts, to disperse. Shouts from the games field had become the shouts of the whole school heading home. 'Those fuckers,' someone scowled behind Michael, 'they've nothing to worry about.'

Michael's first impression was that the comment referred to the rest of the school: those leaving without the burden of homework. He began loading files and exercise books into his Adidas bag while Vinnie, beside him, scraped back his chair and stood up. Immediately Vinnie was pushed forcibly down again, so hard his chair almost toppled. A ripple of fear went round the room, and more chairs were thrust back, more bags swept up. After that the exodus was almost soundless. When Michael looked up he saw Sachs, his hand resting meaningfully on Vinnie's shoulder. Behind them stood the others, Quigley, Fleetwood and Lang, like pale shadows.

'Those fuckers,' Roy Sachs' repeated through a smile. 'They've got what it takes up here – ' He tapped his temple. 'They won't lose any sleep tonight, fretting about their assignments.' His words seemed intended for Michael as well, but it was Vinnie's desk he had perched on. 'Then again, nor will I,' he added, smirking.

At the fringe of his vision Michael saw Linda get up to leave. He couldn't be sure that she looked back, though her movements were slow and measured; she did seem reluctant to desert. When she'd gone Sachs removed from his combat fatigues a crushed pack of Embassys and some matches. Having lit one, he blew the first lungful of smoke towards Vinnie. 'You're good with words, aren't you?'

'Well, I . . . ' Vinnie was visibly straining not to pass the buck towards Michael, not even to look his way. It would have been easy for him to remind Sachs that if he was good, then Michael was considerably better. But that was common knowledge; Sachs wanted Vinnie.

'You could easy knock off an essay like that,' Sachs said. His cropped dyed black hair and high, broad forehead seemed to emphasise his hardness, as did the smoke he exhaled. His whole image, even to the anarchy symbols and cigarette burn marks on one of his wrists, presumably self-inflicted, was contrived for effect. 'You could knock something off like that in your spare time. It ought to be easy for someone like you to do that.'

Michael couldn't resist intervening. Jabbing a thumb towards Quigley he said, 'Maybe he's the one we should be asking about religious symbols. He ought to know more than we do. It's his dad's stock in trade.'

Quigley looked away, ineffectual. Sachs didn't even award Michael's outburst an answer. Leaning forward, he snatched the Milky Way from Vinnie's clutches and lobbed it towards Fleetwood, who forced it wholesale into his mouth, nearly choking himself as he chewed and swallowed. 'Let me put it to you like this,' Sachs went on. 'You're going to write me an essay, lard-arse – or else.' He turned towards Quigley. 'Or else we're going to what? Tell him, Tommo.'

'We're going to make him an offer he can't refuse,' Quigley replied on cue. The intonation, the delivery, the twitch of one eyebrow, the cocked head: all were authentic Brando. The others laughed approvingly. Michael, amazed by Quigley's impression still pitied the poor fool who could only make himself acceptable by performing to order.

'Does he juggle as well? Stand on his hands? Recite the Lord's prayer backwards?' he wondered.

'Shut it, McCourt, or I'll have your insides out!' Sachs fumed. Stubbing out his cigarette on the desk, he returned to Vinnie, palms outspread, fingers extended as if in a plea. 'What you should understand is that you haven't a choice. Thing is, *I'm* not throwing away my precious weekend doing that shit for Bartholomew's sake; I've things to do, Vinnie, people to see. Whereas you ... Well, someone is going to have to do this thing.' He shrugged. 'Simple equation: I thought of you. Decided I'd let you help me out.'

The hangers-on snickered amongst themselves. In the lull that followed Michael heard two female adult voices, the voices of members of staff, increasing in volume as they patrolled the corridor, nearing the classroom. He held his breath. The unwritten law was not to involve the staff, no matter how critical things became. But the voices faded step by slow step and were gone.

'And if –' Vinnie leaned back in his chair as Sachs leaned forward, – 'If I refuse?'

'Then, lard-arse, I'll have Mr Fleetwood grab your right leg, and Mr Jazz will grab your other; and I'll have them both run in opposite directions and split you in two. Is that understood?' His tone remained calm and controlled, but the glimmer in his eyes betrayed his rising anger. When his right hand flashed outwards, skittering Vinnie's chair over, and Vinnie with it, even Tom Quigley jumped, alarmed, to attention.

In toppling backwards, Vinnie struck his shoulders and the crown of his head against the desk behind, which skewed aside slightly as he fell. Michael took to his feet, and at once found himself collapsing involuntarily to the floor. He dropped to his knees before he realised why he'd gone down. The pain shooting upwards from his abdomen to his back, through his kidneys, seemed immense, impossible; that was because Sachs' right foot had connected with his balls.

Vinnie Hartley was close to tears. There was genuine terror in his gaze as he watched and waited for Sachs' next move. Sachs took his time. Emulating some celluloid rebel hero without a cause, he chewed his gum laboriously, clicking his fingers as if keeping a rhythm. Then, through the ache that seemed to be swelling in all parts of his body at once, Michael registered something else: a click that was more than fingers meeting, a sound that drew breath from the others and a whimper from Vinnie.

Sachs moved forward and down in one flourish, clamping Vinnie to the floor with a boot heel. In his right hand he wielded an open flick knife; with his left he seized Vinnie's hair so tightly Michael heard it tear at the roots. When he let go, Vinnie's head lolled against a desk-leg, his mouth open but speechless, his red face contorting around tears.

'Never could stand to see a grown boy cry,' Sachs tutted. Now he had a fistful of sweatshirt, and with one hand was shoving it past Vinnie's gut and chest to his throat while levelling the blade with the other. 'Jesus, look here, boys! Look at the tits on this.' He gave one a rudimentary squeeze, gazing at his sidekicks for approval. 'Lard-arse, I never knew it could be like this. Would you like me to suck them?' And then, in a flash, in a new, hard toneless voice, 'Or would you like me to cut them off? How would it be if I cut something off you: a piece here, a piece there?'

'Sachs ...' Michael tried to protest, but even the effort of speaking was too much to sustain. He could not budge from his knees; his aching testicles were bringing on nausea. Even if he had the strength to fling himself at Sachs there'd be no point; his punishment would be ten times worse. Then, through half-closed eyes, he saw Sachs release Vinnie, fold up the knife and stand up.

'As for you,' he told Michael, 'this don't even fucking concern you. When I want to hear your opinion I'll ask for it. Otherwise – ' he mimed closing his mouth with an imaginary zip – 'do the sensible thing and keep out.' Turning to leave, he couldn't resist one final fling, ruffling Michael's hair almost playfully. 'Make sure the work's done by Monday,' he told Vinnie, before leading the way out.

It took perhaps a minute for Michael to haul himself as far as the nearest chair. Even lowering himself onto it sent another spurt of pain through his system. The white room shimmered. He sat doubled over, straining for breath. Vinnie, sniffing back tears and snot, gradually unfolded himself and drew up another chair. They faced one another blankly, listening to the voices of the departing clan: out the main doors, across the yard, echoing and fading between D Block and E Block. They sounded wild, euphoric. Tom Quigley was doing Sylvester Stallone, presumably at Sachs' request. There was laughter, applause. The brief, violent release had lifted them for the weekend.

Finally Vinnie shook his head. 'One of these days someone's going to have to do something about him,' he said vaguely.

'Yes,' Michael said.

Someone did do something about him, Michael thought, all these years later. But had it been worth it in the end? Had the punishment been out of proportion to the crime? Was it possible that Sachs ...

Shuddering, he shook away the dilemma and went to the door of his room, pondering before opening it. This was no good, he couldn't settle; couldn't even control his thoughts. The coffee had got him moving again. It was late, but he might find the bar still open downstairs, and the others in attendance, and if so all well and good. Suddenly he felt capable of seeing them again. In the elevator, going down,

90

he toyed with the idea of picking up cigarettes, making a conscious effort to start smoking again. After all, did it matter what he did to his body if his soul was already beyond redemption?

Chapter Eleven

At this hour the music in the piano bar was pre-recorded. Apart from one couple slumbering on each other's shoulders, the tables were empty. Still disorientated, Michael was mildly relieved to find himself alone. Presumably the others had retired while he was still cruising through the past. Ordering a double Laphroaig, he seated himself in a corner to contemplate.

The whisky, with its peaty phenolic tang, livened his palate immediately, unlocking yet further closed memories, this time of a long-ago visit to the Western Isles. The brine, the seaweed washed up on the sand and shell beach, the small distillery with its towering pagoda boldly facing the sea. His father had marched him towards it, dragging Michael along for the first conducted tour of the day. With an air of efficient boredom the guide recited historic and technical facts as if sleepwalking through the routine. Finally, Michael had been allowed his first taste of genuine *uisge beathe*: at barrel proof, straight from the cask. At first it had practically knocked him flat, made his eyes water, weakened his knees. For the rest of the day he had wandered in a daze wherever his parents took him, still tasting the lingering dram.

Now, alone in the Heartland, he tasted the islands again. And something more than that: something nearer and more immediate. Memories begat memories, the past turned slowly in on itself. One flashback unveiled another. There had been the same peaty air in Parks Wood the day he and Vinnie had fled from the gang – a pungent odour of last year's leaves trampled underfoot, of old solids becoming liquid, of nature transforming itself. Perhaps for an instant he had remembered the Hebridean isles, the wild winds, the barren expanses of unplundered peat bog, as he stumbled clear of the chestnut trees and towards the bracken. He couldn't know now what had passed through his mind then at every turn, but he clearly remembered Vinnie's cry:

'How did we get into this mess?'

Yes, they had — Michael had — invited trouble. In the end, it was all he could have done. After Sachs and his sidekicks had left the room, he and Vinnie sat watching one another for long minutes. 'One of these days,' Vinnie said, 'someone's going to have to do something about him.'

'Yes,' Michael agreed.

'No. I mean really do something. He can't keep getting away with this.'

'Of course not.'

Vinnie rose, rubbing his eyes, dusting his clothing. 'He thinks every time he needs something doing he's only to come to me, and it ... it just isn't — *fair*.'

Though the ache filled his entire body, Michael managed to stand too. Together they walked from the classroom. 'Isn't this the first time he's asked you to do his work?'

'*Asked* me? Are you joking?'

'Forced you, then. Threatened you.'

'It's the first time he's made such a noise about it, or approached me in front of others.' They crossed the yard towards the sports field, Vinnie watching the ground before his feet. 'But yes, I've done work for him. Who wouldn't? History, maths, even French comprehension, which he knows I'm no great shakes at. Who wouldn't put themselves out, knowing what he might do?'

Michael, appalled, stopped dead in his tracks. 'How long has this being going on?'

'A term or so. Mostly this term. Once or twice before that; he must have known from the start he was on to a good thing.' Vinnie was sniffing again, his voice struggling for control. 'How was I to know it would get out of hand? I only want a quiet life, I only want leaving alone.' His lips were quivering and anger had reddened his cheeks. 'So what choice do I have but compose him his bloody essay and have done with it? In my position what would you do?'

It was just after nine the same evening when the answer presented itself to Michael. Until then he had been straining over a story he meant to submit soon, on spec, to *Fantasy and Science Fiction* magazine. This would later become his first published work, the most accomplished piece he had written. Unable to fix clearly in his mind what he wanted to say he put down his pen, picked up the phone in the kitchen and called Vinnie.

'In your position I'd write it,' he said. 'In fact, Vin, I *will* write the thing.'

'Which thing? You can't mean Roy's essay.'

'Why not? Didn't you tell me you only wanted a quiet life? So here's your chance to have what you want.'

'But Mikey ...' Vinnie sounded at first perplexed, then suspicious. 'What do you have in mind, exactly? You're not going to ... You wouldn't try screwing him up, would you? If you do your worst — I mean hacking out some rubbish that's bound to fetch an E or an F — he'll kill you. The thing about Sachs' is he expects decent grades, nothing too obvious, but enough to keep him from failing. And he isn't stupid. He reads what you do. He'll want to copy it over into his own hand, and he'll know if it's purposely shitty. You didn't ought to take that risk, Mike, you really didn't.'

'So I won't. I'll do my very best, I'll give him a *Grapes of Wrath* analysis to end them all.'

'To be honest, I like the sound of that even less.'

'No matter. Leave everything to me, Vin. Just enjoy your weekend.'

'You'll only stir up more trouble, Mike. Things might be better left the way they are. You ought to think yourself lucky not to be involved.'

'But I *am* involved,' Michael protested, taking care to lower his voice in case his father should overhear. Behind the closed living room door the TV sounded implausibly quiet. He imagined his father turning, straining to hear, his whole body taut with attention. 'If what happened today didn't involve me ... Well, my balls must be five times their natural size, Vin, which believe me isn't half as

94

wonderful as it sounds. If Sachs hasn't ruined me for life I'll be surprised, and what did I do to deserve that? Didn't you say something ought to be done?'

'Hmmm. But saying and doing are two different things. This is worrying, Mikey. You should be aware by now he doesn't know when to stop. It's as if something – something bigger than he is – takes over; he crosses a line and nothing matters anymore. No one can deal with him when he's like that.'

'Yes,' Michael said, remembering all too clearly a scene that in later years he would re-work for *Pushover*: a scene that haunted him still.

It was Sachs who had turned the class against Vinnie that day during their first term at high school. Someone had summoned their group tutor, Nicholson, to an impromptu staff meeting, and Nicholson had foolishly trusted them to take care of themselves. Within minutes, convinced that no one would dare interfere, Sachs and Fleetwood had swooped upon Vinnie Hartley. A ripple of anxiety and awe circulated the room. Michael sat at his desk with downcast eyes and folded hands. When he looked up, tempted by the hoots and howls of the class, he felt himself flushing. Alison was shaking her head in disgust and demanding, 'Isn't someone going to *do* something about this?' Linda's face was masked by both her hands. Bill Anderson might have been absent, or in hiding. In a corner of the room, Vinnie had been forced into a chair, stripped of his shirt and belt, both of which were used to secure his hands behind him. His face was scarlet, his eyes brimming. Several girls – Sachs' acolytes – moved about him, touching his soft white body, flapping their tongues, gasping with feigned pleasure. Just for a second, Michael met Vinnie's gaze, which seemed to be pleading for help from the midst of his hell, and Michael had looked away. Later, reinventing the incident, he had imagined himself protesting, doing something, doing the right thing. But instead he had stared at his folded hands on the desktop, afraid of becoming involved; anything to deflect the spotlight from himself.

'But how much longer is this going to go on?' he asked

the telephone receiver, and at the far end of the connection Vinnie said, tiredly, 'I don't know.'

Michael stared about the cork-tiled kitchen for guidance. The second hand advanced on the clock face, ever nearer his future. A gull was in flight on the World Wildlife Fund calendar. Many others flocked behind it, a confusion of distant grey shapes like fading pencil ticks. 'Maybe you and I aren't the only ones who feel this way,' he said. 'Have you seen their faces lately?'

'Whose faces?'

'Everyone's. All right, perhaps not everyone's. But here and there you can tell what's running through their minds; you can feel something new in the atmosphere.'

'Can you?' Vinnie was attempting to retreat further still. He'd initiated something he now wanted to stop. 'Can't say I've noticed.'

'You have. You just won't admit it.' In the living room, the TV volume increased a notch. There were screams and shouts, a single gunshot. Sensing his parents return to the screen, Michael relaxed. 'The fact is, if *someone* takes a stand against the bastard, others might follow. Anyone can see they're just waiting for someone to set the ball rolling.'

'And if they aren't? If they don't follow? Mikey, excuse me, you sound like a damn vigilante. If this is an idea I put in your head, let me take it all back as of now.'

'Drop dead, Vin! You can't really expect me to believe you haven't entertained the same thoughts.'

'Entertained, yes: but that's about it. Think of me, will you? Can you seriously see me as an avenging angel? Or take yourself: a writer, never a fighter. You're really as much a wimp as I am. I've read your stuff and I know you can make it happen on the page, but, please – '

'Steady on,' Michael said. 'This isn't about taking up arms, just refusing to be walked over. Think of everything he's done to you since the first year.'

'Think of everything he still might do,' Vinnie said.

'All it takes to change something is one step of faith,' Michael said, and Vinnie replied, 'You know, Mike, there's probably something wrong with your brain. In fact now

I'm convinced there is. If I understood you any better I might ...' Vinnie paused, exasperated, the kitchen clock ticking away fifteen more seconds before he continued. 'Michael, do what you have to. Write the bloody essay, take it off my hands. But don't get us all killed in the process, please.'

Even after he'd handed the four finished pages to Roy Sachs, first thing Monday morning, Michael couldn't be sure what had driven him to it. Was he knowingly courting disaster or had a genuine desire to protect Vinnie forced his hand? Either way, Sachs' expression when the essay was set on the desk before him made Michael want to snatch back his handiwork at once. Spencer, their tutor in fifth form, had not yet arrived. At first Sachs just stared at the pages, saying nothing. With narrowed eyes he glanced at Michael, then back at the desk. Away to his left, Tom Quigley belched, to the amusement of others. Leaning back in his chair until its front legs left the ground, Roy Sachs chewed gum, smoothed a hand back through his hair.

'What the fuck's this?' he demanded.

Michael jumped. The air in the room around him seemed to vibrate sympathetically. From somewhere, far detached from himself, he heard his own voice answering.

'It's the piece you asked for, *The Grapes of Wrath*.'

'I know that, McCourt, I'm not fucking blind.' A fire seemed to ignite behind his slitted eyes as he waved a hand towards Vinnie, seated several desks away. 'Thing is, what's it to do with you, and why isn't lard-arse standing where you are explaining this to me?'

'Because he didn't write this.'

'Why?'

'Well, because ...' Michael faltered, sought out the first lie that occurred to him. 'He had to go away for the weekend; and we decided that, rather than let you down, I should step in, do what I could.'

Through the silence that followed he felt the lie trying to accuse him. How empty and unlikely it sounded. The class were watching like one huge and many-eyed face. And his cheeks were burning; surely someone would notice

97

his embarrassment, and expose the lie. Sachs turned a couple of pages, chewed philosophically, said nothing. He didn't seem to be reading so much as relishing his power. Watching him, Michael pocketed and unpocketed his hands, scratched places that didn't itch, folded his arms loosely across his chest. It was all a horrendous mistake, he knew, but too late to rectify. His only option now was to go on with it, play the part. He had done his best. When Sachs finished turning the pages, Michael managed to smile.

'Are you sure this is kosher?' Sachs asked.

'What do you think?' Michael flung up his hands. Having come so far he might as well go the rest of the distance. 'Wait till you look at it closely. Didn't you realise Jim Casey's initials are the same as Jesus Christ's? Or that *twelve* – count em – twelve members of the Joad family set off with him on the road? The disciples, right? There can't be any question. And didn't you know Exodus is practically written across every page, with California standing in for the promised land? Or that Rose of Sharon is the virgin Mary? Or that the vineyards – '

'You know I don't read,' Sachs replied smoothly. 'The question is, can I trust you with this?'

Michael thought, Can a pork chop sprout wings and fly? But he answered sincerely, 'If only I'd paid as much attention to mine as to yours! Then again, all those religious metaphors take it out of you, and I was running out of steam by last night.'

But Sachs remained doubtful. He stared at Tom Quigley, but Tom's face remained blank. Finally turned back to Michael. 'Just be aware that your life depends on this. By a thread. And if it isn't what you say ...' He left the remainder unsaid, which to Michael came almost as relief, then trained his sights on Vinnie once more. 'Lard-arse, don't think this lets you off the hook. Don't think this means the end of our beautiful friendship.'

'It could be the *beginning* ... of a beautiful friendship,' Tom Quigley suggested, in a Bogart so authentic it drew laughter and grunts of approval from those who knew the context. You're such a puppet, Michael thought, glaring at

Quigley before turning away. You're anything they want you to be. When are you going to learn?

'You're dead,' Tom Quigley said matter of factly, late Friday afternoon. Michael broke from reading and looked up, hazy-eyed. It was the final period of the week again – Bartholomew's English session – and until Quigley arrived at his desk he'd been lost in Bartholomew's comments, added as a footnote to his essay. When the period began, Bartholomew had returned the marked papers. Michael should have guessed then what the subdued gasp behind him meant. In excusing himself for the toilet, Quigley had detoured past Michael's desk to deliver the message.

'You're dead, McCourt. Just watch yourself, later.'

'Why?' Michael wanted to know. 'What have I done?'

'You know what you've done. It worked out exactly as you planned. Bartholomew gave him an F because of what you did; he doesn't believe Roy wrote the essay, failed him because it was too fucking good. And now he's supposed to redo it himself during detention next week. You're dead after school, that's all I have to say to you now. The rest can wait.'

'You know, you sound just like your leader,' Michael replied, but the messenger had already turned tail.

Michael watched Quigley go, closing the classroom door soundlessly after him. During the few seconds the whispered exchange had lasted, the moisture had drained from his mouth. His heart-rate had quickened fiercely. There was no need to look behind him to gauge Sachs' reaction; he could sense the darkness accumulating at his back, the force of hatred focused towards him. At his right, Vinnie sat in a bemused stupor, unable to meet Michael's gaze. It was as if the whole class sensed what was happening; no one looked his way. Michael took a deep breath, releasing it slowly to calm himself. After counting to ten he thrust up his hand, catching Bartholomew's eye, and requested the toilet.

Bartholomew's response – a blink, a sniff – was all he needed. Without delay, Michael took to his feet. The sound of his chair scraping back broke the silence, and he sensed himself being watched to the door. It would be easy, so near the final bell, to bypass the washroom and head home instead, but that wasn't his first thought at all. It wasn't until he was striding along the corridor that he knew clearly what he intended to do.

The nearest toilets were by the main exit. Beyond the double doors at the corridor's end a short flight of stairs reached the foyer, which was flanked by dark cloakrooms. On the walls here and there were postered warnings about theft, and the rows of metal coat pegs were empty. There was an odour of wax polish and, less emphatically, faeces and disinfectant. Michael crept to the boys' washroom door, where he waited. Above the sound of flushing urinals his breath sounded rasping, loud enough to give him away. From inside came the squeak of rubber soles and an image of Tom Quigley turning, doing himself up, fixed itself in his mind. Tensing himself, Michael thrust the door open and stormed in.

As he did so his heart leapt out of control. The face staring back at him, open-mouthed, wasn't Quigley's. This, at least, was Michael's first impression. But shock had transformed Quigley's face; without the mob to support him he looked faded, reduced to nothing. Both his hands were fussily engaged with his fly buttons; his lips worked as if searching for words. He was still blinking back surprise when Michael went for his throat.

There was an instant of what felt to Michael like sheer weightlessness. The washroom flew past at great speed in the mirror above the three enamel wash basins. If Quigley was shocked then so was he, by his own momentum, crashing the messenger backwards through the half-open door of one cubicle with such force the door slammed open and shut again twice behind them. When Michael let go, Quigley tottered against the cistern and fell, landing awkwardly on the damp toilet seat. Nursing his throat, he gazed into space, unable to hold Michael's look. The cubicle smelt foul, almost poisonous.

'You're just nothing,' Michael said calmly. 'Without the others you're nothing at all. I don't even know why I'm bothering with you.'

'Then *don't* fucking bother, it won't do you any good. If

100

you think it'll help ...' Quigley broke off, perhaps less than certain where to go from there. Above the dripping, flushing washroom ambience, the final bell sounded. They listened and waited for what followed. Within seconds, distant doors could be heard thumping open along corridors, the school pouring forth its confusion of competing voices and footsteps for the weekend. The noise seemed to revitalise Quigley, who made as if to get up. Michael prodded him down again.

'Tom, how long are you going to be a whore for that pimp? You're a fool if you think you matter a damn to Roy Sachs, just because you're willing to run errands.' When Quigley failed to reply he went on. 'Don't you realise how pathetic it makes you seem, performing to order, cracking jokes and putting on voices whenever he clicks his fingers? It isn't even that you're safe − if that's what you think you are as long as you play along with him. Can't you see he's using you to get what he wants? To control everyone? Can't you see he's doing the same to Fleetwood and Jimmy Jazz?'

'Then why not tell *them* that? What makes me so special?'

Michael shrugged. 'Nothing at all, if none of this means anything to you.'

'Have you finished?'

'More or less, yes. All I want you to do is think about what I'm saying. Think about how − '

'Then I'm free to go,' Quigley concluded, this time forcing himself up and past Michael without meeting resistance. 'And maybe you should think about what *you've* been told. You're dead, Mike. Tonight. Very soon indeed.'

'What kind of talk is that for a preacher's son?' Michael sniffed, but his words were smothered by three frantic knocks at the outer door, then Vinnie's voice, raised almost to a squeak, calling his name. As Michael stepped from the cubicle he saw Vinnie's face, paler than usual, peering around the door into the washroom.

'Mikey, are you in there? They're coming, Mike! They're on their way.' Seeing Quigley, his expression clouded. 'Mikey, is everything − all right? Roy and the others ... they're coming after us.'

'You hear, Tom?' Michael challenged the messenger.

101

'Shouldn't you be doing something to help them? They're coming for us and you're still checking your flies. Wouldn't your leader expect you to detain us until − '

'He's *not* my leader,' Quigley protested, his face contorting with indignation. 'I choose the company I keep. It's nothing to do with anyone else, it's none of your business.' His look was one of belligerence: brow furrowed, hands on hips. Michael thought of a quarrelsome child, but there was more than defiance in Quigley's expression. 'You'd better get moving,' Quigley added, 'before I'm really forced to do something.'

For a moment Michael was thrown by the remark. Yes, there was more to Quigley than met the eye − did he really wish to give Michael this chance? − but Vinnie was banging the door again with rising impatience and whitening face. As he did so Michael heard the double doors thump open between the foyer and the corridor. The urinals were repeating their flush cycle as he followed Vinnie back through the cloakroom towards the exit. At the top of the short flight of stairs above the foyer stood Fleetwood. He seemed to be calling, signalling to someone far back in the corridor, but his voice was drowned by the shrieks of first and second years pushing past him. The next thing Michael knew, Sachs was arriving at Fleetwood's side, his eyes glinting like cold metal. As soon as he spotted Michael he flung himself forward to the stairs, Fleetwood and Jimmy Jazz in tow. The crowd parted here and there to make way; some went tumbling, and one small girl with blonde plaited hair fell the last three steps, twisting her right leg beneath her as she landed. Michael didn't wait for what followed.

If not for the crowds bunching between the cloakrooms and the exit doors, it might have been over there and then. As it happened, he and Vinnie managed to squeeze outdoors to the yard before the worst congestion occurred, sealing the others inside.

'Which way?' Michael said.

'Let me think,' Vinnie said.

Straight ahead were the sports fields to their right the fringe of Abbotsbridge's newest and least dilapidated estate with its bland box residences that a little purposeful vandalism would soon customise. Vinnie headed left, towards the narrow thoroughfare bisecting the science and social studies blocks. In that direction the shops were only streets away. He was heading for town, where at least they stood a chance of losing themselves amongst window gazers. Remembering that Friday was market day in the centre, Michael followed at a clip. From the shops it wouldn't be far to the edge of Parks Wood. After that it was surely plain sailing.

Chapter Twelve

He was alive. By rights, though, he shouldn't have been. At times like this it was easy to believe he'd been destined to live forever.

An hour might have passed, perhaps longer, while he lay heaped in the darkened room with its narrow vista of Earl's Court rooftops. Gradually waking from the torpor produced by Michael McCourt's assault, he winced at the stabbing mass of pain that was his face and gasped with relief. The pain was something to embrace, to be thankful for. To feel such discomfort meant everything. He was alive. The Source was very much alive.

With the large bright window above his head and the rest of the house in darkness, it was like waking inside a church. If he half-closed his eyes he might even see Jesus, escorted by angels, reaching down for him, beckoning. Common sense told him it couldn't be so, not yet. *His* time wouldn't come until the mission was complete. He'd been called o to destroy the body, to rescue the souls of the sinners. Whatever they did, however many more injuries they inflicted, they wouldn't beat him down again. They had done so once before and considered it settled. That had been their first mistake.

At long last he managed to move himself slightly. Near by was the carrier bag dropped by McCourt; the shattered glass inside shifted when he touched it. The smell of rye whiskey was everywhere. It took several minutes before he felt steady enough to get up. He stood at the window, nursing the tender face that would soon enough put itself right. That was the beauty of the blessing he'd received; to pass through this life as The Source. There was so much goodness inside him the healing was a natural by-product of being. Already he could feel his swollen left eye trying to open, the heat of his open wounds cooling by degrees.

It was raining outside. The city must be beautiful on a night like tonight, the lights blurred and sparkling like ice reflecting fire. He remembered an evening not too long ago when he'd watched the illuminated streets from a hotel room balcony above Piccadilly. On the bed were some of his belongings – a notebook, micro-cassette recorder, lipstick. The night air on his face was intoxicating, coaxing him out of himself. He could rest at long last, forget work for the evening, go out. Tonight he felt like dancing.

Now, in the darkness, he fingered his burst lower lip, which at first made him wince, then seemed to seal at his touch. At the same time an aura of total calm descended on him, a calm from the night sky itself. Suddenly he wanted to be outside on the streets, away from here. He might have grown up in darkness but that didn't mean he still thrived on it. Leaving the room, he headed downstairs to the car.

Similarly, he'd hurried outside that previous night, needing urgently to be amongst people. He had made himself especially attractive then, putting on heels and a split skirt that emphasised his hips and barely reached the knee. And his face in the mirror ... But whose memory was this? With whom was he sharing it?

In a nightclub he had met a young man who reminded him of someone he had known. This was the truth. It was also a convenient opening line as they perched elbow to elbow at the bar. 'Don't tell me your name,' he had told his pick-up at one point. 'It's better if we don't get into that. Names aren't important anyway. They're just labels.'

After more drinks – one more sloe gin fizz for himself, for the young man a Coke with ice – they had returned to the hotel. There they smoked cigarettes and talked, seated on chairs separated by ten or twelve feet. The radio was on, tuned to an MoR station. The young man asked what the equipment was for, indicating the bed, and the Source replied that he'd been working on something, a commission; he couldn't say more for the moment. Tonight he'd felt the need to escape from it, that was all. These matters got to you after a while.

Driving from Earl's Court, he shook his head at the hazy memory. The healing was at its height; every muscle of his face quivered, as if he were being baptised by fire. Everything had been fine, he reflected, until the moment the young man made his first move. The Source had returned his kisses at first, holding when held, sighing when touched. The next thing he knew, the man's fingers were at work, hastily unfastening buttons, loosening belts.

In retrospect, The Source was alarmed by this, and much more: by his own physical hunger, a single-minded urge bordering on madness; by the sight of his breasts being cupped and crushed in his suitor's eager hands. It was when this touch moved lower that he danced away, half-paralysed by a sudden fear of being found out. In a minute the young man would see exactly what he'd nearly seduced: an hermaphrodite, the most unclean of all bodies, penis and nipples erect. 'Please give me a minute,' he'd said, and ducked neatly inside the bathroom, bolting the door.

In the anaesthetic space he'd undressed, clumsy with drink, surrounded by tiled mirrors, as his panic slowly passed. Wherever he gazed the slopes and curves of a woman's form were reflected. The fear was all in his mind; her mind; their mind. Finally, naked, he stepped from the bathroom. 'Now then. I'm ready,' he said. And the knife came down.

He flicked off the wipers as Hyde Park Corner approached. The light rain was tailing off, leaving in its wake roads shiny as glass. The traffic, so late, still had the urgency and density of the rush hour about it. He drove on towards Piccadilly and his beckoning past.

He was glad, in a way, that he couldn't recall where the night not so long ago had ended. He preferred not to think of it anyway. The last thing he remembered was a feeling, not an image. But then, he wouldn't have seen anything worth remembering once his eyes had been taken, would he?

Whose memory was this? Whose recurring bad dream? Surely not his when so little of it made any sense. But the knife had come down time and time again; and then other, even more precise instruments had gone to work, removing and regrafting parts of him. There was no way of telling how long this had gone on. For a period that felt like hours his only company was a severe and unbearable pain: pain that felt like a tent rising and spreading from the bed, ever expanding, ever steepening.

At long last it came to an end, the tent was lifted, and it seemed to him that the young man, his assassin, was stooping forward over the bed to admire his handiwork. At the same time the Source felt himself rise from his own mind and body. For an instant he was composed of light, brighter than the streets below, and rushing towards the face of his killer. The next thing he knew, he was a young man gazing down on the ruined body of death.

It was a young woman's body. That much was clear, even though she had no face. There was blood everywhere. In his heart of hearts he was sorry, having shared her terror – her nightmare. At least she was safe now. He'd helped her escape the prison of flesh; he'd allowed her spirit and soul to go free. Before leaving, he went through her notebooks and diaries, laying them out for all to see. Then he called the police.

Alison, he thought, some part of him thought, as he parked near Drury Lane. How sorry I am for what I've done. But the body, you see, is a dangerous vessel. Head, heart, and four limbs that must be cut off one by one. You can't just leave it intact. There's no telling what it might do.

So far, then, he had managed to dismember it partly: he had taken two limbs. This had thrown the others into shock, which was why McCourt's defences had been down at the airport tonight. A pity McCourt had slipped through his fingers. The head of the body was a prize; too great a prize to let go. And now the body was united again for the first time – the first time since ...

He stopped the thought there. The past and the time of retribution were coming together, closing in, at last. It was enough to have that assurance. He left the car and walked south on Drury Lane until it met Russell Street, then turned right. The street was quiet, with little activity outside the hotel. He continued towards it, footsteps crackling along the wet pavement. Stopping opposite the foyer he pocketed his hands and stared up at the many small yellow rectangles of light. Another winked on as he looked. Would that be Linda's, or Bill's? Although he knew their room numbers — after all, he had booked them himself — he couldn't quite visualise where they were.

Still, he had the upper hand, the advantage. He knew their plans from now on; what they intended to do after checking out. So near to completing the mission, he could wait, he could bide his time if necessary. After waiting for fifteen long years, another few days wouldn't hurt.

Chapter Thirteen

Linda arrived in her room feeling dazed and displaced. Although she had had spent most of the day since arriving in London relaxing, her legs ached as though she'd walked for miles, and her head thumped dully. Seeing the others again — they had spent the long evening together, breaking the ice — had been more than she'd bargained for. All those emotions, the doubts and anxieties, she'd been holding inside for so long were now surfacing. So much had come back to her, so little had changed. So much had remained unsaid.

Bill had developed a businessman's paunch and a beard that reminded her vaguely of George, but she still felt nothing but affection for the man underneath. For her part, Naomi had arrived looking lost, probably daunted by a hotel that was costing as much for one night as she paid in rent for a week. In any other life, Linda had thought at one point during dinner, we would have been total strangers, and yet here we are, inextricably bound together. Forever. It didn't matter that Naomi spent much of the evening listening while Linda and Bill did the talking; she was with them, she belonged. In her eyes and relieved, generous smile it was there for anyone to see. At times they spoke only to fill the silence: a silence that tonight spelled absent friends.

Linda flopped on her bed, put on the night light and eased off her shoes. A gentle night breeze lifted and lowered the net curtains. On a whim she collected the phone and called the registration desk.

'Could you tell if a Mr Michael McCourt checked in this evening?'

'Just one moment.' The clerk's French accent sounded milder than when Linda had registered earlier. She wondered whether it might be affected. A minute or two passed before she heard it again. 'Yes, Mr McCourt did register tonight, quite late.'

'Thank you,' she said, and thought, Thank you God, thank you. In the midst of chaos there was order. Something had finally gone right. Her relief felt like a spiralling dizziness; she could breathe again, the dullness that had thickened her senses all evening seeming vanquished at once. 'Could you transfer this call to his room?' she asked, and waited again.

At long last she heard the tone. After more than twenty rings there was still no reply. Presumably he was sleeping after the flight, and couldn't or simply didn't want to answer. In any case it was late; she ought to control her eagerness until morning. Chewing her lip she hung up, disappointed. The hotel room in which she found herself was characterless, not at all the place she wanted to be. There was a cheap, self-assembly look and feel to the fitted white wardrobe, the matching dresser and mirror, the shower cubicle she'd stepped into immediately after checking in. Seeing this in a brochure or colour supplement she would have blinked and turned the page. What on earth was she doing here?

Then she considered the alternative. Earlier she had telephoned George, who had returned her explanation with grunts and silences. Didn't it matter to him what she was doing and why? Wasn't he even interested? This evening he would have returned home from college to find her gone, a short scribbled memo pinned to the bulletin-board in the kitchen. During their conversation she had tried hard not to imagine Sonia with him; but a background noise, perhaps of dishes being placed in the sink, set to drain, had alerted her. 'I only hope you won't be using our bed while I'm gone,' she had told him before hanging up.

No, she needed to put that behind her and instead face her reasons for being here. When she considered how she'd felt seeing Bill and Naomi again, she knew she had done the

110

right thing. Only Michael's absence, and the knowledge of what had happened to Alison and Vinnie, had clouded the evening. Despite everything else, now that she knew Michael had arrived she felt better, if not yet able to sleep.

Linda brushed back the net curtains from the window and gazed out across the lights of Covent Garden. Night was a spell that made cities such as this great, thriving things. After dark, true colours could be worn, secret lives lived.

Long ago this had all been a dream. London town, the bright lights – bywords for success in the small sheltered world she'd called home. At that time, the only thing that counted was escaping from Abbotsbridge; success meant denying the past. Now the first grey hairs had touched her temples, and she knew there was no denying, no escaping. If we'd only known then, she thought, and closed her eyes, which prickled with hot tears. If we'd known would we ever have joined together?

It was Alison who'd discovered the ice house first. From a distance, glimpsed through a thickness of close-planted trees, it seemed nothing more than a hump in the land, littered with thick piles of old leaves and broken branches from storm-damaged trees. Alison had found it quite by chance while tracing her labrador far from the main path; the ice house hardly called attention to itself. One afternoon during the Easter break she'd taken Linda there, proudly displaying it as if showing off a newly-bought home.

The entrance, not visible from the path, was on the far side of the mound, where the land began to slide downhill. It still retained the brown rusting hinges of a door or wrought iron gate. Squeezing inside and down a slight incline, Linda thought of an igloo overgrown by peat and dead leaves. The smell of the woods seemed trapped in the cool, dim interior.

'Well?' Alison said, 'what do you think?'

The entrance may have been small and narrow but still admitted enough light to see by. As Linda adjusted to the dimness she saw how much larger it was than she'd thought. Eight or ten people might fit inside here at a squeeze. The walls were dry stone, but had been plastered over in patches.

111

On the furthest wall, a white chalk stick man was suspended by a noose from a gallows. A noughts and crosses grid had been chalked out beneath him; a single game, which the crosses had won, had been played.

'Did two people play the game or just one?' Linda said.

'First thing I thought of when I saw the hanged man was cave drawings,' Alison said. 'It's a bit like being in a cave, don't you think?'

Linda smiled as she looked around. Now she could see signs of Alison's habitation: a cardboard box stuffed with paperback books, beside it a small pile of *NMEs*, three small cushions. This partly dispelled the sense of prehistory she'd had when she'd first stepped inside. With a little more attention the place could almost be home.

'I once read a story about boys who built themselves a tree house,' Alison said, seating herself on one cushion, patting the one beside her for Linda. 'What I liked was the idea of the shared retreat, so that anyone could use it at any time, for safety or just to be alone when they needed it; it didn't belong to any one member. And I envied them for that. I used to lock myself in my room sometimes to hold onto the feeling I got from the story, but I knew it *was* only a story — nothing on earth would make me build a tree house myself!' Alison laughed fondly, and drawing her knees to her chin stared wistfully into the dimness. 'That was so long ago I couldn't even guess when. But the day I found this I knew it belonged to me; I remembered everything, and I knew.'

'Am I the first you've shown it to?'

'Yes. And I trust it won't go any further.'

'Of course it won't. We could meet here after school in the summer, or at weekends, perhaps.'

'Talk out our problems.'

'Bring flasks and sandwiches.'

They laughed simultaneously, giddily. Outside in the woods, the shattered silence sent wings beating high in the air. From treetops several birds exchanged warning calls, then settled, as if waiting for more.

Linda said, 'It's so peaceful, though. You can almost forget where you are. How close you are to the grim village.'

Alison stretched dreamily. 'That's what I love, forgetting. It's like travelling back ten years or more, like having a second childhood or something. Linda, I never want to grow out of this.' Then, with an air of gravity, 'I never want to grow up, do you? We're different to the rest, don't you think?'

Linda blinked at her. 'Different?'

'Meaning we don't fit in; we're outcasts who think differently. There aren't so many of us, either. You could count us more or less on one hand. We deserve a place like this, where we can bitch and blow off steam.'

'Yes,' Linda said, wondering whether she understood Alison fully. There were, at school and in other walks of life, leaders and followers – those who dominated, those who were willingly dominated – and she had never belonged to either party. Perhaps what Alison meant was that even outsiders needed something to belong to, something to follow. It was true. But it had taken someone to say it before she recognised the fact.

Between April and June that year, the ice house became a home from home. Alison brought additional cushions and posters of film stars torn from magazines; Linda provided pocket chess, more books and copies of *Over 21*, a corkscrew and glasses, even an old brass oil lamp that still worked, rescued from the shadows in her father's shed.

On summer evenings after school Linda came along bringing homework, finding the silence therapeutic, relishing the cool within while the temperature outside climbed steadily. On week-nights she spent more time here than Alison, who in May had started dating Bill Anderson. There was no danger in the woods; no one would find her even if they wanted to. When daylight began to fade the birdsong multiplied, and she knew it was time to move. In the woodland sounds she began to detect subtle changes of mood, the arrival of a fox, a human passing along the nearest path. Which was why, that afternoon, she was already on her guard before the footfalls came rushing to the ice house.

Suddenly there was drama in the woods; the hush came down like a curtain. Linda stiffened. Sprawled on two cushions, she gripped the paperback novel she'd been reading

113

so firmly the spine cracked. She held her breath, unable to swallow. Someone – not Alison – was heading towards the retreat at a pace. Nearby a wood pigeon issued a warning that seemed to Linda as though it had left her own lips. Flinging down the book, she forced herself to her knees, then halted, not knowing where she was meant to go from there. Now she could hear more than one set of footfalls and heavy, ragged breathing. She looked around for something to defend herself with, but there was only the lamp, the mound of books. It was all she could do to kneel and wait.

'Where now?' someone said.

'In here. In here.'

'What's that?'

'Who cares? Come on!'

They had found the entrance; all at once the light was blocked out. A pall of shadow expanded itself to cover the stonework. Linda cowered back, doing her best to suppress a cry as the first of two figures tumbled inwards towards her. There were grunts of discomfort, whispered curses. The second followed even more clumsily, losing his footing on the incline. Then she saw the faces, which were as stricken as she felt.

'Jesus,' she said. 'It's you!'

Michael McCourt jumped, wide-eyed and open-mouthed. Behind him, Vinnie Hartley was seized by a coughing fit.

'Jesus,' Michael echoed. 'It's *you!*'

For a moment, overpowered by relief, she wanted to laugh aloud. To think she'd been afraid of these blunderers! As her own fear faded, she realised their rattled appearance wasn't necessarily her fault. It might have shocked them to find her here, but both Michael and Vinnie were plastered with sweat and soil and were breathing as if they'd been running for their lives. She was about to demand an explanation when Michael put a finger to his lips.

In the middle distance, perhaps not much further away than the path, there were voices. Vinnie, nearest the entrance, grew visibly tense, his hand suspending itself in the act of wiping his brow. Linda frowned, trying to recognise the voices, which were as yet too far away and all talking at once.

114

'Roy Sachs,' Michael whispered. 'And the others. They've been after us nearly an hour. We thought we'd given them the slip at least twice ...' He paused, for his name was being called, a rising, falling two-note melody. A second voice joined in, summoning Vinnie in much the same fashion. Together, overlapping, they sounded almost spectral, like lost souls calling from beyond. Michael turned back to Linda. 'We lost them, we thought, in the chestnut plantation, and cut through the bracken thinking we were home and dry. They were waiting on the path below as soon as we came out of there and we had to double back; they've got clubs and sticks, and Fleetwood's carrying this bloody iron bar.'

Linda grew cold at the thought. 'Those pricks! They really don't know when to stop, do they? Is that what was happening after school tonight? There was such a bad feeling in the class before we left; everyone must have sensed it. And then Vinnie rushed out as soon as the bell went, with Roy and his cronies chasing after him – '

Michael raised a hand to silence her, for the cooing and calling was nearer now. Some of the group must have left the main path and were moving this way. They were close enough for Linda to hear the soft ground beneath their feet, to imagine them inching around the retreat to the entrance. The birds sounded edgy and tentative. In the half-light Linda found Michael's eyes, and he smiled. In the lull that followed it struck her that this was the first time they'd spoken or exchanged glances without embarrassment. Why did she think of that now? Last week, their eyes had met by chance across the class and she'd turned away blushing, her heart jerking ahead of her. Was that so important that nothing else seemed to matter right now?

'Mi-chael,' a voice called outside, perhaps twenty or thirty yards from the mound. 'Mi-chael, come and get it, you fucker.'

And from further away, 'Vi-nnie, remember this: you can run ... but you can't hide.'

That was Tom Quigley, typically quoting a line from a film. Linda thought of the iron bar that Fleetwood was supposed to be carrying. Then someone else muttered, 'Bastards got away. Come on. That's it, I've had it.'

115

'What? You're off now?'

'Yeah, well. There's always next week. They'll still get what's coming to them.'

The silence began at that point. If her fears had a source, there it was. It was the waiting, the not knowing, that made Linda want to rush from the ice house, waving her arms, crying for it to be over with. By comparison the threat of violence meant little; the wait was the worst thing possible. For several minutes the three of them remained poised, rigid, listening in the half-light for human sounds. Linda became aware of her stomach wanting to grumble, though she didn't feel hungry. Michael licked his dry lips and sniffed.

At long last Vinnie took a tentative peek outside. Linda kept as still and quiet as she could until he turned back. 'They're gone,' he announced.

'Then why are you whispering?' Michael said.

'Just in case.'

But the threat had passed; the feeling was almost tangible. It was as if the pressure of a vacuum had been raised from the lair there and then. They slumped on cushions, Michael blowing air through his lips, Vinnie leaning back with closed eyes against a wall, and for a time the dim space vibrated with their breathing.

'Quite a place you have here,' Michael said to Linda, looking around. 'What is it exactly?'

'It's an ice storage house. It probably belonged to whoever owned these lands in the old days. Quite an impressive pad, don't you think?'

'Who drew the hanged man?'

'I don't know. That was here when we discovered the place.'

'You and who else?'

'Alison. It was Alison who brought me here, actually. Until now we were the only ones who knew about it.'

Vinnie coughed lightly into a fist, reminding them of his presence. 'Not even Bill Anderson? Hasn't Alison even told him?'

'As far as I know she hasn't.'

'Women!' Michael sighed emphatically. 'The things they

keep to themselves. Really, you never know what they're up to the minute your back is turned.'

Linda thrust a cushion in his general direction. Michael caught it one-handed. 'Watch out, McCourt, or there'll be others besides Roy Sachs after your blood.'

There was a moment, then, in which everyone settled; a calm which required no words. In fits and starts, the birdsong restored itself, the woodland heartbeat began again. To Linda it seemed quite reasonable that Michael and Vinnie should have broken the spell of her afternoon. She mightn't be alone any more but she still had her peace. A wild idea struck her. These boys, neither of whom she really knew, were becoming her friends; she could trust them. Though the secret of the ice house was out she was content with their company.

Michael skimmed pages of a magazine without really looking at them. Still gasping, Vinnie wiped his nose with the back of a hand. Linda studied her paperback novel, tutting at the spine she had fractured. After a time Michael clicked his tongue, shook his head and looked up.

'Strange, isn't it?' he said, and Linda said, 'Isn't what?'

'To think we've spent three years going through the system together, and we haven't really talked until now.'

'It took the promise of pain and death to bring us together,' she said, half-mocking.

Michael smiled shyly, not quite holding her gaze. 'Why do you come here?' he wondered.

'Why would anyone?'

'To escape from something, I imagine. Speaking from personal experience I'd say it's to hide.'

Vinnie said, 'That's easy enough to understand if Roy Sachs just happens to be after your balls – excuse me, Linda. But what would *you* want to hide from?'

Linda considered. 'Sometimes we just need to be some-where we can't be reached or found. This is a bit like that; it's somewhere to clear out my mind. Like the places I travel to in my head when I read.' She held up the paperback for all to see: *Lord of the Flies*, which Bartholomew had once tried – but failed dismally – to assassinate. Yet another great book had survived education to tell its own tale.

117

Michael nodded vigorously. 'Exactly, I know the feeling. There are places of my own like that in here.' He fingered a temple. 'Sometimes when there's nothing else to think about and I'm writing I can go there, draw the curtains, shut out the world. Did you know I wrote stories?'

'Yes,' Linda said. 'I think you write well. I saw something of yours in the school magazine. A story about — ' She frowned, summoning up what she'd read. 'Wasn't it about some boy who ran away from home, and then couldn't find his way back when he wanted to? I thought that was very well done.'

'You really thought so? You should have said so before. But that was nothing. You should see what I'm doing now. Just wait. One of these days I'd like to . . . ' He paused, suddenly aware how their talk had accelerated, carrying them away on its tide. His eyes were alight; in some small sense Linda felt herself touched by his fire.

'What are you working on now?' she asked.

'Something for a fantasy magazine. I'm hoping to make a first sale there.'

'That would be something!'

'It really would. But there's still such a long way to go; perhaps when it's finished — if you'd like — '

'Yes, I'd love to read it,' Linda said. And no one needed to ask where they might meet in future to discuss it. The band of outsiders — The Brotherhood — was born that late afternoon in June. How right she'd been, and how ironic it was, Linda reflected, all these years later, standing by her hotel room window, that the promise of pain and death really had thrown them together — a promise which for fifteen years had kept them apart.

She turned from the window, scowled at the bed. It was no good: the bright lights, her treasured memories, the events of recent days . . . all were conspiring to keep her awake. Perhaps one more drink — but not here, with only the TV and Mini bar for company. Searching out her shoes again, she slipped from the room.

A sleepy young couple were leaving the bar arm in arm as she arrived, and someone was slouched over a shot glass at a corner table. However, the bar was still open and Linda

118

ordered kalhua and was carrying it to a seat when the man in the corner stood up sharply. She had the vague impression, as he crossed to her table, of slept-in clothes and a drunken swagger; at this time of night it was best to avoid eye-contact, which was why the last thing she allowed herself to look at was his face. When she did she gasped aloud.

'Jesus, it's you,' she marvelled.

'Linda,' said Michael McCourt.

Chapter Fourteen

The eye-contact thing, Michael told her in passing, was very much a thing of Manhattan's streets, the first of the survival codes he'd learned there. You want to buy a watch from a suitcase? A silk scarf? A smoke or a vial of crack? To look was to invite trouble. In restaurants and bars, though, the barriers came down, the heat dispersed, people unwound and opened their hearts and mouths. In England the barriers remained firmly closed at all times. Stiffness here was a condition not only reserved for the fabled upper lip.

They relaxed, not needing even to break the ice. Linda fired questions about Manhattan life which Michael answered to the best of his limited ability, adding that he couldn't now see himself settling anywhere else. New Yorkers apologised for their city to tourists these days, but survival was an art not limited to Hell's Kitchen and the Lower East Side. The Brotherhood were here, after all, because of a dot on the map in northern England. Having survived that scenario, New York was nothing.

They ordered more drinks, then decided on a walk before turning in. A light rain had fallen during the evening, and the nightlights gleamed on the streets with an hallucinatory beauty.

They headed down Bedford Street and along The Strand. In doorways, piles of newspapers and corrugated cardboard shifted as they passed: the homeless adjusting their bedding.

'It was nothing like this when I first saw London,' Linda sighed, shaking her head. 'What's happened here in the last ten years?'

'Remember when we used to say anyone could be anything they wanted in life?' Michael said. 'Does this mean wanting isn't always enough?'

'That, or not knowing what to want. But it did work for some of us, didn't it? At least I have a roof above my head, and Bill's done so well, selling software. And there's you: Mr Success Story himself from the U.S. of A.'

'Schucks, ma'am, you're embarrassing me.'

'But seriously, you got what you wished for. I still remember the way you used to talk about wanting to write, and how impossible it seemed at the time, so much work and such a long haul without reward. And now it's all there, just as it should be.'

'And you? Did you get what you wished for?'

'Well, I got married. I suppose you heard that.'

'Yes.' He cleared his throat. 'But that isn't really answering the question. The main thing is, are you happy?'

Linda took so long in replying that it seemed she was sidestepping the question. Having waited for the traffic and crossed towards Villiers Street near Charing Cross station she said, 'Ah, but are any of us really happy? Would we be here now if we were? Happiness and having what you want don't always amount to the same thing, do they?'

'Perhaps not.'

'At a pinch I'd say that me, you and Bill are more or less where we would've liked to be. Alison certainly was. And perhaps Vinnie and Naomi never quite wished hard enough or saw clearly enough what they wanted. In the end, there's probably no difference at all between us. We're all still at the mercy of something bigger than ourselves — that's how it feels to me, anyway.'

Under the Embankment there were more groups of outcasts, either bedded down for the night or preparing themselves to do so. Further on, the Thames had trapped a firework display of lights in its matt black surface as the South Bank vibrated across the water.

Strolling towards Westminster, they linked hands, doing so almost unconsciously, between strides, though it was the first time they had ever touched this way. It seemed entirely appropriate; morever, kept them from having to speak

121

profoundly about the times they had left behind or spent apart. Tonight there was sadness and pleasure in the air, contrary feelings that seemed to swell from the city lights themselves. They walked in silence, adjusting themselves to the moment, blinking into the oncoming headlights.

'It's so good to see you again, Michael,' Linda said.

'And you.'

'I'm so glad you made it. It was such a load off my mind to find you'd arrived.'

'I almost didn't, you know.'

'How's that? You had reservations about coming?'

'Yes, of course, but so did everyone, I'm sure. When Vinnie traced me to New York I couldn't help wishing with all my heart that he hadn't. But I'd always known that if the call ever came there wouldn't be much choice about whether or not I obeyed it.' He slowed down to stare out across the glowing river, aflame with reds and whites and ambers. 'No, as I said, I almost didn't arrive. Everything was fine until I touched down in England tonight.'

Suddenly, for the first time since approaching her table tonight, he was far away, lost in himself. Retrieving his hand from Linda's he went to the barrier overlooking the Thames and leaned forward against it, frowning. In the interplay of soft lights and dark ripples under Westminster Bridge, a face seemed to be struggling to form itself. A passing tug disturbed the pattern, which quickly reverted to water and light.

Linda came up beside him, resting a hand on his shoulder. 'Is it something you need to talk about now? Or would you rather sleep on it first?'

'If I thought I could sleep,' he began, still watching the water. 'Well, I will do eventually, I'll have to. When I came through customs at the airport tonight there was someone waiting to collect me: someone I had difficulty recognising at first, he'd changed so much. If he hadn't told me he was Vinnie Hartley I might still have been guessing – '

'Vinnie? But that's impossible,' Linda said, so sharply Michael turned back to her. 'Didn't you hear about Vinnie? But then, how could you have? Bill tried to contact you; I even tried calling myself but couldn't get through.'

122

'When?'

'Just the day — it would've been the day before yesterday. We were trying to find out if the reunion was still on ... in the light of what had happened.' She inhaled deeply and steadily to control herself, ready herself for what she still had to tell him.

'I think I understand,' Michael said. 'After tonight almost nothing you say about Vinnie will surprise me.'

'Well, it certainly wasn't him at the airport, Michael. What happened to Alison ... it happened all over again. Vinnie's body — what there was of it — well, he was found by his landlord three days ago. I wouldn't have known if I hadn't been visiting; you see, Vinnie had been making the arrangements for our reunion and I was expecting to hear from him. When I couldn't reach him by phone I drove over there. The police had been and gone by then, but the landlord was still in shock, he could hardly talk. Before he managed to tell me anything I'd guessed what had happened. He invited me in and made tea — the great British remedy — and we sat in his stuffy room in front of the gas fire. He clearly needed to share what he'd seen.

'Well, I thought I could hear him out — I'm supposed to be a good listener — but what he had to describe I just didn't want to hear. Whoever murdered Vinnie had bound and tortured him first. As for his face ... In the end I was forced to leave the room, I felt sick, couldn't breathe. It was more than the smell of gas. So far I haven't been able to tell any of this to Bill or Naomi. Ridiculous as it sounds, I thought it might ruin the evening. Didn't want to face facts, I suppose.'

'After so many years of avoiding the facts old habits die hard.'

Again they joined hands and retraced their steps towards Charing Cross. Above and behind them, the night sky over Westminster groaned as Big Ben struck twice.

'Even before I checked in tonight I somehow knew Vinnie wouldn't be coming,' said Michael. 'At first, at the airport, I believed this man, whoever he was. In that state I would've swallowed anything. I was drunk and jetlagged and — well, he *could* have been Vinnie. We all change in time; some

123

of us more than others. There was still something in him I recognised.'

'Ah, but there was no mistaking the Vinnie *I* met. This Vinnie wouldn't have needed to give you his name; you would've singled him out on a crowded street, no trouble. So what happened? If your escort wasn't Vinnie, who was he?'

Michael shrugged, none the wiser for having already considered this. 'All I know is, he drove me from Heathrow to Earls Court on the pretext of picking up Tom Quigley. The next thing I knew there was no Tom Quigley and no Vinnie, just a raving maniac with a knife inside a house without lights. And a voice ...'

'Yes?' She squeezed his hand harder. 'A voice, you said.'

'It seemed altered, not the same as before.'

'How, though? Altered in what way?'

'I'm trying to think. I need time.' As they neared Embankment station a bearded man dressed in an army greatcoat came stumbling from the dark beneath the arches towards them, arms outreaching, and Michael twitched Linda towards the road. 'Just drunk,' he said, but hurried her on before the man could come closer. An emaciated girl with a crew cut, wearing only drainpipe jeans and a T-shirt chose that moment to be sick on the steps outside the station. 'Oh God,' Linda said, and hurried Michael away up Villiers Street.

For some reason the homeless on The Strand seemed more numerous than before; perhaps they were simply more active, having risen from fitful sleep to seek food and drink. Those who were still crammed in shop doorways gave no sign of movement, as though something deeper than sleep had crept over them. One prone figure still clutched to his or her chest a card that read simply, HELP ME HELP ME. To Linda, the message seemed directed at them, another unwelcome reminder reaching across the years. They hurried on, putting the scene behind them as quickly as possible. As they turned back up Bedford Street she said, 'Did you feel it too?'

'Feel what?'

'The way the night changed towards us just now. Almost

124

as if it knew who we were, knew all about us, why we were here.' Michael watched her with growing concern; her eyes were focused beyond the streets, beyond the here and now. 'To begin with by the river, it was almost idyllic. Then something – I don't know – something happened to ruin it.'

'Story of our lives,' Michael said.

'Will it always be, though? Are we ever likely to be rid of whatever – whoever's holding us back?' Within seconds her strength had been sapped, and her voice sounded cracked and weary. Linda shook her head slowly. 'Will he always be there at the centre of things, do you think?'

'That's what we're here to discover,' Michael said as they reached the hotel, stopping where the light from the lobby sparkled across the pavement. 'Linda, listen to me. We've survived this far – '

'But we haven't. Vinnie and Alison didn't. And tonight you almost didn't survive either. No one would ever have known. As far as we knew you might simply have have decided not to come, and we'd never have seen you again.'

'But I *did* come. I'm *here*.' Michael tried to make that sound lighter than he felt, even forced a smile to reassure her. The nightmare was over; the sleeper had awoken to bear witness. 'If nothing else, that should prove we can still face the beast – him or it, whichever you prefer – and survive. I might have been too late for Vinnie, but now that we're here, together, don't we have a strength that we never had alone? Doesn't that give us a chance?'

Linda exhaled and nodded, a little reluctantly. He guided her in through the doors and past reception to a waiting elevator. They both had rooms on the third floor. Michael stabbed the button and watched the doors slide shut.

'There,' he said, 'now you've walked off your anxieties you might even sleep. I know this isn't perfect, but since we're here it's a matter of making the best of a bad situation – '

'You're right, of course,' she said firmly. 'We were always better together than apart. I only wish – well, I wish we'd had more time together in the first place.'

'I know. So do I.'

125

'And I wish you could have rewritten our story.'

The elevator trembled; the doors were open. For perhaps eight or ten seconds they stood there, facing each other, not breathing, not speaking. Then Linda turned along the corridor, fumbling her key on its chunky white key-ring from her jeans pocket before stopping outside room 317. Michael waited. She leaned back against the door.

'Do you – ?' she began; but Michael, smiling dimly, was already extending a hand to her face. The backs of his fingers brushed her cheek lightly, inquiringly. Along the corridor, the elevator doors thumped shut again.

'No, I don't mind,' he said. 'In fact I was about to ask you the same.'

Linda seemed visibly to relax then; her shoulders dropped, she collected his hand between hers. This wasn't their night. Everything had its own time and place. 'Were you hurt? Did he hurt you tonight?'

'Not that you'd notice. T'was but a scratch, sire, nothing more.'

She laughed softly, her eyes holding a light warmer and brighter than anything the Thames had to offer. 'And the voice? You said something about a voice that was altered? You haven't even begun to explain.'

'It's late, it can wait till tomorrow. When everyone's together, I'll go over it then.'

'All right. Don't drink any more though, will you? You reek of whisky. We want you in one piece.'

'After all we've been through, you're worried about that?'

'You bet.' She began unlocking her door. By the time it was open Michael had half-turned away. She turned and saw him watching her as if he still couldn't take her all in. 'Goodnight,' she said, and Michael said, 'I'm in 328 if you need me. And believe me, I – '

The rest he left unsaid.

Linda stepped into her room, closing the door swiftly behind her, and kicked off her shoes for the second time tonight. She undressed in the dark, slowly, at first, then with haste as her feelings ebbed and flowed. Why did she have to be so damn correct even now, out here on

126

the edge of whatever it was she felt near to falling off? Michael must know as well as she that if the dream they'd shared was ever to be matched it would have to be later, when all else was settled ... but it was easy to think such things, more difficult to put them into practice. She could still feel his fingertips on her cheek. Before getting into bed she waited, half-expecting his knock at the door. In spite of everything she'd just been through she felt unaccountably horny. She slid into bed and was dragging the sheets across herself when the phone at the bedside rang.

If it was Michael, she would take little persuading to go to his room. Suddenly she had no doubts about that. Scrambling through the dark in the general direction of the ringing, she found the receiver and lifted it.

'Hello?' she said, and waited. And waited.

And out of the silence a voice that could only be Alison Lester's replied, 'Don't cry for me, Linda. I'm still here. Nothing can keep us apart from now on.'

Chapter Fifteen

The phone calls had begun soon after that first afternoon in the ice house. The following Monday Linda ate her packed lunch with Vinnie and Michael, who were subsequently joined by Alison and Bill. They sat on the steps outside E Block, the science department, which placed them in full view of the staff room. There – at least during break – they were safe from Roy Sachs, who instead sent cryptic messages via Quigley. Michael was not out of the fire yet. The death penalty remained; and the others were now guilty by association.

'Your sins have found you out,' Quigley informed the group, Monday lunchtime. He stood below the steps in frayed denims, his right hand raised to the heavens. 'Surely the Lord will turn his hand against you. Surely his breath will smote you – or should that be smite you?'

'Will you please grow up?' Alison pleaded. 'Really, we know your dad's a messenger of God and all that but there's no mistaking you for one.'

'The grass fades, the flower falls, but the word of our Lord stands forever,' said Quigley.

Alison gave him the finger.

'Get thee behind me,' said Michael, who was safe during Monday and Tuesday evenings while Roy Sachs' served out his detention. 'The further behind me the better, in fact.'

'McCourt, if you know what's good for you –'

'If you knew what's good for *you* you wouldn't be brown-nosing Roy Sachs,' Bill Anderson said. 'Why don't you think for yourself for once, Tom?'

It must have been Tuesday – the day itself had faded in her memory – when Linda returned from school to an empty house and a ringing phone. She'd resisted taking a detour through the woods for once and taken the school bus home. The house, with its gravel drive and adjoining garage, had been cloned into the newly built Riverside estate, miles from the nearest river. This, however, was the nearest Abbotsbridge ever came to sweet suburbia. Many of these home-owners commuted to day jobs in Leeds or Wakefield. On Sundays the men connected up hosepipes and washed their Escort Ghias while the women cooked roast beef and Yorkshire pudding. It was that kind of life in the wilderness; this was what everyone aspired to.

Why, though? Because it was easier than breaking out? Walking home through the estate Linda shuddered at the thought of consigning herself to this. There had to be an alternative. In the end she almost missed her own driveway, she was so preoccupied. From the gate she couldn't hear the telephone at all; or perhaps it didn't start ringing until she neared the front door, scrabbling for her key.

The house was in a state of half-decoration. There were white sheets on the hallway carpet and a smell of new paint wafting downstairs as she closed the front door. Her parents were still at work: her father in the office at Tesco, her mother at the Wakefield library. The phone was still ringing in the kitchen. As Linda entered, Tara sat up in her basket, bushy tail twitching back and forth like a pendulum. Dropping her book-laden bag on the table, Linda snatched up the phone in mid-ring.

Initially she thought the quiet line was a faulty connection. The Abbotsbridge exchange was still years behind the world; this was, after all, the land that time forgot. But her senses told her otherwise. She was suddenly acutely aware of something within the silence – a presence, someone listening. She should have hung up quickly, but instead she recited the number, and waited.

There was nothing; no reply. But this wasn't a technical fault because now she heard breathing, scarcely concealed, as if whoever was calling had forgotten to cover the receiver. There was nothing remarkable about the sound – nothing demonstrative, no asthmatic wheezing and groaning – but that was the worst thing of all. At least a heavy breathing routine would have signalled a sense of what was fitting, a predictable willingness to shock; but this was really unnerving – the shared silence, the void on the line. Linda closed her eyes and pictured herself as a fly might observe her, alone in the kitchen, listening.

'Haven't you anything better to do?' she said finally, calmly, and hung up. For a minute or so she remained where she was, expecting the call to come again. When it didn't she relaxed; with luck she'd forget it within half an hour. Presumably some sad sack had seized a convenient directory and was working his way through it in search of thrills. A sudden damp thump behind her right knee made her gasp and twist round to find Tara watching her expectantly.

'Haven't I told you never to do that?' Linda fell to her haunches, encircling the retriever with both arms and squeezing. Tara's metallic name tag clinked softly. 'One of these days you'll give me a heart attack, I swear.' Unlocking and opening the kitchen door she watched Tara scamper away across the unfinished scrub of back yard and through a gap in the high latticed fence. The view above it was of more identical houses, the outskirts of Riverside obscuring from sight the southernmost quarter of Parks Wood, where Tara was heading.

It was a mellow afternoon, and she left the door open as she pottered about the kitchen, munching a celery stick, spooning instant coffee into a mug. In the distance she could hear a ball being kicked, children's voices raised high in excitement. Perhaps Tara would join their game on her way to the wood. A wasp tapped the window above the sink three or four times before retiring. It was one of those days when all the world's subtle sounds seemed intended for her ears only: she ought to be at the ice house now, communing with nature, reading Michael McCourt's short story or finishing *The Lord of the Flies*.

She sat at the kitchen table with her coffee, focusing her thoughts on Michael so as not to dwell on the call she'd just taken. The local directory was propped on a shelf beside the wall-mounted phone. She was wondering whether she dared seek out his number and call him when the phone rang again, making her jump.

This time the silence on the line seemed far larger than before, as though the call were outreaching the depths of some hollow, forgotten sepulchre. Again, the sense she had of another intelligence listening was overwhelming. It was better, she knew, not to lose control. She mustn't hang up in a panic; she mustn't give the caller any insight into her feelings, mustn't reveal the fear behind her lips wanting desperately to make itself heard. Again she repeated the number, doing her best to adopt a bored, indifferent tone.

'Sooner or later you'll have to choose whose side you're on,' a voice told her. At least that broke the deadlock, though she didn't feel any better for hearing it. 'Is that understood? The choice is yours.'

It wasn't a voice she recognised. Her mind tripped from one likely suspect to another – Sachs, Quigley, Fleetwood. It sounded like none of them, unless Quigley was playing infantile games with impressions again. On the other hand someone could be calling on Sachs' behalf; his influence over others was considerable, he'd have no trouble persuading them to do anything. It could have been anyone.

'I've already chosen,' she said, and was about to hang up when the caller said, 'Linda. Linda.'

'What now?'

'If only you knew.'

'Knew what?'

'How much you meant to me. How very much.'

'I'm pleased to hear it.' She was trying to sound unflustered although her heart was palpitating, her palm growing tacky as she gripped the receiver. She inhaled to steady her voice, letting it come in an ice-cool flow. 'Well, it was nice hearing from you. But if there's nothing else – '

'Oh, but there is, you know there is. Linda, I'm concerned for your soul; I don't want to see you sign it away so soon. You've so much to contribute. I want you to know there's hope, there really is.' After a short pause the caller added, 'What I want is to help you.'

131

'You could do with a little help yourself,' Linda said. 'And now, if you'll excuse me – '

'There you are again, repelling my good intentions. A sign, if ever there was, of a soul in torment. But the soul needn't perish, you know, not if the body is purged; not if the flesh is cleansed first.'

The full implication of that didn't strike her until she'd hung up and unplugged the phone from the wall. She went to the kitchen doorway and looked out, arms slack at her sides. In the distance, Tara could be heard barking excitedly while the ball game progressed – a joyful, familiar noise that meant nothing to Linda right now. She was struggling to regulate her breathing, to shut out her swirling, darkening thoughts, when incredibly, she heard the telephone ringing again.

She stared across the kitchen at the phone: the dangling plug, the empty socket. The ringing was muted, persistent, far away . . . And then she cursed her own nervy stupidity. What she could hear was the upstairs extension in her parents' bedroom. How idiotic could you get! But her relief lasted only until she reminded herself who was calling. She'd be damned if she answered it this time.

Closing her hands over her ears, she hummed to herself tunelessly, blotting out the noise. She went to the living room and put on a record at random, turning it up loud, and trooped outside to the back yard with her cooling coffee. The record was something by Louis Armstrong, the song an instrumental she couldn't have named, which itself sealed a new memory for her as she stood there watching the peach-coloured sky.

It was, as Michael put it many years later, the story of their lives: a story of torment rising from paradise. For a moment the sky, and all the gentle sounds of the neighbourhood, were suspended, and Linda experienced something quite close to perfect peace. An aircraft, so high she could scarcely hear it, marked a trail overhead, dividing the heavens in halves. She watched until it had passed out of sight; then she heard Louis Armstrong again, and Tara's bark, and she realised she was crying.

For the next few days there were no more calls. She avoided saying anything to Alison or the others. On occasions, in

132

class, she searched faces she might have suspected. Not one appeared properly guilty. Then again, would Roy Sachs ever betray signs of a guilt he was probably incapable of feeling? It would have been easy to dismiss whoever had called as merely a crank working his way through the phone book – except that he'd known her name.

On Thursday he called again. She came in later than usual that night, having stopped at the ice house after volleyball practice. There she had lounged for an hour, recovering the peace that she seemed to need more and more lately. There were times when she didn't require the ice house for this, and times when nowhere else would do. At home she found her father stir-frying vegetables from a packet while her mother set place mats at the table with strategic precision.

Her father jabbed a thumb at the darkening horizon. 'Ah, at last. We were just about to start worrying. Will you join us?'

'No thanks, you go ahead. I'll eat later. What I need now's a long soak in the bath.'

'Yes, after all that volleyball, I imagine you would. It's to be hoped they don't keep you so late when the hours start drawing in.'

Five minutes later the bathroom was opaque with steam. Linda undressed with practised efficiency, folding and placing her clothes on the closed toilet lid. In novels, young women always paused, nude, to inspect themselves before full-length mirrors, but hers was so heavily misted her face was a smudge. Turning off the taps, she tested the temperature and stepped in. She was lowering herself into the water when she heard the phone.

The tone was cut off after three or four rings. Seconds later her mother's voice came travelling up the stairs. 'Linda? There's a young man on the line for you. Shall I tell him to call back?'

'Does he say who he is?'

'I didn't ask, but he does sound very courteous. What shall I do?'

A young man for her? And courteous with it? 'I'll take it up here, then,' she called.

Seizing a towel, she trailed fat wet footprints across the

landing, into her parents' room, over the carpet to the bedside. Lifting the receiver she said, 'All right, you can hang up, I've got it.' On cue, the downstairs phone clicked off. 'Linda speaking. Who's this?'

It was the pause, perhaps only two heartbeats in duration, that told her who she was speaking to. Oh please, not again − not when she'd almost forgotten. Deep down she'd hoped this would be Michael, but already she knew that it couldn't be. Light-headed, clutching the receiver with both hands, she sat on the bed. The smell of new paint in the room was cloying.

'What are you wearing?' the caller said.

Linda hesitated before replying. She must keep her nerves from running away with her. Was the voice pitched differently than she remembered: harsher or fractionally deeper? Self-consciously she adjusted her towel where it had tried to ride up her thighs when she sat. 'That's none of your business,' she told the waiting silence. 'And if this is another of those calls ...' She trailed off on a note of impatience, sounding far more assured than she felt. 'Any more of this and I'm going to report you.'

'To who?'

'The police.'

'Report who?'

'You. Whoever you are. Report what you're doing.'

'That'll get you nowhere. They'll only dismiss you, tell you there's nothing they can do. They'll tell you there are hundreds of complaints just like yours every day.'

'Why are you doing this? What do you want?'

'Oh Linda, you know the answer already. It's you I want. To do all I can to liberate you from the body of sin; to set your spirit free.'

'Then you're out of your tiny fucking tree,' she said quietly.

'Please tell me what you're wearing this minute,' the voice pleaded. There was a new, nervous tremor to it that made her recoil. 'Then I can imagine you taking it off.'

Linda sighed. 'If you insist ... Picture this. Jack boots and long johns, a thermal vest and three football jerseys. Layers and layers of socks. You want to hear more?' She swallowed dryly. The smell of emulsion was beginning to make the room swim. Her nose and mouth were clogged, her limbs paralysed. She couldn't hang up yet – not yet. Something within her needed to hear this call out, to endure it. If she could just do that ...

'Your mother told me you were in the bath,' the caller was saying, 'so I know you're not telling the truth. Are you still wet? Will you give me that much at least? Aren't you just a little damp between your legs?' Jesus, he was steering the exchange exactly where she'd suspected he would. The sex thing had been at the heart of it all along. She stared at her pink broad feet forming damp patches on the carpet, her knees leaning awkwardly together. The voice continued, 'I'll make you wet. Down there. You wait and see. I'll have you feeling things you never imagined you could. The body is such a dreadful thing, don't you think? All the things it puts us through ... The weaknesses. The things it makes us do. Linda, I'll fuck you and purify you if you'll let me. I'll make you feel clean inside and out. Give me the chance and I'll save you from – '

'Save yourself!' she cried, the tears coming automatically, and for the third time this week she slammed down the receiver before losing control altogether.

The next few seconds were the nearest she had ever come to passing out. For a time the room turned grey and the world was reduced to her own spasmodic sobs, rising so thickly between her ears she felt close to drowning inside them. Her heartbeat was deafening. Every part of her body felt sealed or tensed; every pore, every opening. Alone in her parents' bedroom with the curtains drawn secretly together she nevertheless felt watched.

The tears were more fluent now. Descending both cheeks, the contours of her jawline, her throat, they felt dirty, like industrial rain. Could she really be so unclean inside that even her tears left muddy trails?

It was the call that had made her feel tainted. Who wouldn't be touched by that voice, those words? She felt hollow, her insides scooped out. Worse was the faint sexual urge she felt in spite of herself. Too weary to traipse back to the bathroom, she lifted her legs and leaned back on her

135

mother's pillows. With her left hand she still held the phone. With her right she reached absently between her thighs. Across the room the curtained window became suddenly illuminated; the streetlight beyond the drive had come on. After a moment she took up the receiver, listening to the dialling tone, confused as to what to do next.

Michael, she thought. She had to call Michael. And Alison. And the others. It was no good, carrying this burden alone; the time had arrived to convene a meeting.

Years later, still pressing a telephone receiver to her ear, Linda reclined in her hotel room and felt the past increasing its presence, as if her thoughts were making it stronger. Wasn't that what it wanted, though? To let the Brotherhood multiply its power by dredging everything up again?

'What was that?' she asked the receiver. Briefly, she had been so lost in thought she'd forgotten she wasn't alone.

'Linda,' said the voice she now recognised as Alison's. 'It's so good to hear you after all this time. Words can't express how pleased I am. Just thought you should know that I know where you are; where all of you are. It won't be long before we're together again. I can promise you that.'

136

Chapter Sixteen

Michael leaned back from the table, arms folded, shaking his head slowly in disbelief. He opened his mouth to speak, then closed it again. This morning he felt animated; badly hung over, pink-eyed, tight-skinned, yet splendidly giddy. A boy once again, with young blood in his veins and firm muscles, and a cloudless, beckoning future.

'Oh shut up and eat your croissant,' said Bill, and smiled warmly, pouring more coffee.

Seated either side of him were Naomi and Linda, still marvelling between snippets of talk. They were nearing their second hour at the breakfast table, and the Heartland staff were growing visibly weary.

'He isn't the only one,' said Linda. 'Anyone would understand why he's lost for words. It shouldn't be this easy, should it, after everything that's happened? We ought to be dour and skulking, with nothing to say to each other.'

'This will pass,' Michael said. 'And we'll remember what a god-awful mess we're in. Right now I want to take it all in.

'We ought to be drinking Krug Champagne and toasting absent friends,' Linda said. 'They'd want us not to mourn, don't you think?' This morning she looked flushed and radiant, better for a good night's rest, better still for breakfast.

Naomi, who had lost the strained expression with which she'd arrived, brought out cigarettes and lit one self-consciously. 'Before you say it, I know,' she shrugged. 'I never used to, I was always the ultimate anti-smoker. Still, it would be wrong if we were all still *exactly* the same, am I right? We must all have vices the others don't know about.' At her right elbow was a well-thumbed paperback edition of *Rubber Bullets*, cracked spine, corner-kinked pages and all. Her fingertips drummed the cover as she turned to Michael. 'You, for example. Some of the things in this novel made me wonder about you, Mr McCourt.'

'Really? In what way?'

'You're depraved,' Linda told him. 'I've read that book too. I worry, Michael, whether any of that comes from experience.'

'Oh, everything I write about comes from experience. It's all authentic. It all really happened to me, I swear.'

'Then you should donate your body to medical science when this is all over.'

Michael smirked, wiped his mouth with a napkin.

'Seriously, Mike.' Naomi again. 'Did you ever know a woman like – what's her name – Isabelle, the managing director's P.A?'

'Or a man?' Linda said. 'If there are men anything like your protagonist walking round in real life I'd dearly love to be introduced.'

'That goes for me too,' Naomi said. 'In my experience, all men are ready for sleep the minute they've shot their load. You finally give in to their purring and whining and give them what they want, and then you're just on the verge of getting interested when it's over. But *this* fellow ...'

'Is this really suitable talk for the breakfast table?' Bill wondered.

'No, of course not,' Linda said. 'Let's finish it somewhere else.'

They left the restaurant still filled with this frivolous, almost juvenile spirit, and called an elevator for the first floor lounge. Away from the table, conversation faded and there were smiles and reflective glances while they stood in the foyer, waiting. They needed to be buoyant just now, to keep each other going. If they couldn't do that, there was no point in being here.

Across the lobby a gangling, narrow-linbed man in a grubby parka and drainpipes leaned against the reception desk, skulking and waving away the member of staff who was trying to attend to him. Michael noticed this only as he edged inside the elevator, though he couldn't be sure the others had.

'Going up,' Bill said, thumbing the button.

Michael watched the man closely. It could hardly be the stranger he'd mistaken for Vinnie; his face would have been quite a sight if he'd lived. In the last second before the doors closed, the man turned, expressionless, to stare after the group, and Michael relaxed.

'Something the matter?' Linda asked as they came out on the first level. A floor-plan mounted on one wall described their route to the lounge, past a sauna, more restaurants, a hairdresser's salon. They turned to their left along the corridor.

'No, nothing. Thought I recognised someone downstairs, that's all. It wasn't him.'

'Wasn't who?'

'The man who met me at the airport last night.'

She looked at him warily but said nothing.

'What was that?' asked Naomi. 'Something about last night?'

'Just discussing the man who tried to kill me,' said Michael. 'Someone's way of welcoming me home to Blighty.'

Naomi's eyes widened. While Michael related the sequence of events they sat in a corner of the spacious, overheated lounge that resembled an airport bar with its chromium trimmings and edgings, red nylon carpet and soft muzak. Waitresses ferried trays of coffee and tea back and forth. Businessmen in made-to-measure suits perched on their seats looking tense, in need of the day's first whiskey.

Naomi smoked two more cigarettes while he talked. Linda chewed a knuckle and thumbnail by turns.

Finally Bill puffed air through his lips. 'Really, this is far, far away from making sense to me. There's something about this that doesn't gel and doesn't relate to anything that happened before. Look: if the man who attacked you wasn't Vinnie — and we're fairly damn sure that he wasn't — what would he gain by pretending to be?'

Michael flung up his hands. 'Search me. Well, he gained

139

my confidence long enough to come pretty close to hacking me to pieces.'

'Oh, don't,' gasped Naomi.

'Yes, he did win you over,' Bill said. 'But how did he manage that? And why didn't he try the same tack with Linda, for example – or me?'

Michael pondered. 'Well, Linda had seen him recently; she knew him by sight, so it wouldn't have worked. And you – you and Nim. Presumably you both already knew the story. You were in contact with Linda, you'd read the newspapers.' He faltered as the truth became clearer. 'Until now I was the weakest link of all, wasn't I? Out of touch with the news, still assuming Vin was alive. I was the only one he could have chosen to play that game.'

'Dead right.' Bill nodded: Bill the tactician, assuming his rightful role almost effortlessly. If Michael had always been the passionate one, the one most capable of casting feelings into words, Bill was the master of level-headedness, helping the others to see. In any storm, Bill was the fixed point of calm. 'Thing is,' he went on, 'if you were the weak link in that sense, how did *he* know that? How did he know you hadn't been in touch with one of us?'

'He couldn't have done. Not unless – '

'Yes?'

'He knew the arrangements. Everything, that is, from my flight number to the hotel reservations to ... You name it. Somehow he found everything out; maybe he even knows where we are this minute. What?' he said to Linda, who had gasped and turned noticeably paler. 'Is it something I said?'

Linda nodded. 'You keep saying *he*, but someone else knows we're here, someone who knows even our room numbers.' She was watching Michael, though addressing the group. 'Last night? When we came back from our walk? After we'd parted I got a phone call from someone ... A woman's voice, quite definitely a woman's. Someone who claimed to be Alison. The last thing she said was that she knew our plans, knew where to find us, I forget how she phrased it exactly.'

'Was there anything else?' Bill wanted to know.

140

'Nothing of any great consequence. Except she was glad to hear me again.' Linda sighed. Suddenly the flushed, rehabilitated look she'd maintained throughout breakfast was gone, and the strain was showing. 'It was late, I was tired, it would be easy to imagine I'd dreamt this. But it wasn't a dream – not after last time.' The others listened with blank, questioning faces. In brief, she described the night at the Samantans office where, for her at least, the past had begun to close in again.

'And that was the night Alison died?' Bill asked.

'Yes, absolutely.'

'You're certain the call came *before* she was – before it happened?'

'It must have done, mustn't it? I mean, I recognised her voice. And I know this was fifteen years later, but still.' She lifted her hands, palms upwards, baffled. 'I naturally assumed . . .'

'But after hearing the voice last night, you might have assumed wrongly the first time?'

Michael frowned. 'Let's get this straight, Bill, before you lose me altogether. Are you saying Alison was dead before Linda took that first call?'

'Why shouldn't she have been? We know that she was last night. Why not both times?'

Naomi clutched herself, shivering in spite of the stuffy heat. 'I'm getting out of here. This is starting to feel like more than I can handle.'

Linda gave her arm a reassuring nudge. 'Stay put, Nim, at least until we've talked this thing out. We're better together than apart; that's what we always said.'

'What about the man who could be Vinnie?' Bill said to Michael. 'Can you cast yourself back to that time in the dark, where you heard but couldn't see him? Was it Vinnie you heard? Did it sound anything like him?'

Michael considered. After a minute he reached for one of Naomi's cigarettes and lit it. 'Truth is, it was and wasn't Vinnie. I seem to remember something kind of snapping in his voice, changing, as if he were struggling to maintain the act. Then I knew I'd walked into a trap.' Struck by a thought too large to come and go unnoticed, Michael's

141

face lit up. 'Come to think of it, there was a second –
a fraction of a second – where the voice became almost
someone else's ... a woman's, in fact. Oddly, I did think
of Alison at the time. Probably because she was my reason
for coming home. And there was something he said, the way
he described himself – ' Michael swallowed. Facing the full
implication of the message he had to deliver, he suddenly
craved a drink.

'Well?' said Linda.

'Yes?' said Bill.

Naomi, not wanting to hear, shook her head as she fitted
another smoke to her lips.

'I don't think I'll need to explain this,' he said, slowly
grinding out his own cigarette in the ashtray on the table.
'There was no mistaking what he said. He described himself
as the hanged man back from the gallows.'

Nor did he need to look up to gauge their reaction.
Linda had turned white; Bill stared into space without
seeing; Naomi drew deeply on her cigarette.

'Tom Quigley,' said Bill at long last. 'He's the only one
apart from ourselves who could know what that means. And
the voice – remember, the voice? It was always his party
trick to make himself sound like other people.'

'Was he ever that good?' Michael wondered.

'Whoever this is,' Linda said, 'they're clearly bent on
getting even. They're trying to exact some kind of terrible
retribution. Would Tom *want* to do that? Jesus, he was
part of everything that happened; why would he turn
against us?'

'He wasn't one of us to begin with,' Naomi put in. 'You
have to remember that. In the end he was acting for himself,
not for us. He wasn't a member of the body.'

'That's as maybe, but he's still unaccounted for.' Bill
looked less certain than he sounded, but uncertainty was
the order of the day here. 'What happened to him? It's a
very pertinent question. Vinnie tried and failed to track him
down. Linda tried a couple of old addresses. One way or
another he's gone to ground; that doesn't make him guilty,
but it does beg an explanation.'

Michael was dubious. 'You're forgetting the fellow at the

142

airport. I mean, we stood face to face, shook hands. And I have to say there was something of Vinnie about him, no question. That's what's so scary. It was and wasn't Vinnie Hartley. But I can't, hand on heart, tell you there was much of Tom Quigley about him. Really, I haven't a fucking clue. Tom might – just might – have been able to trot out a perfect impression of Vinnie, or even Alison. But could anyone remember someone's voice so well, all of fifteen years later? And even if Tom could, how would he know everything else – our room numbers, my arrival time at Heathrow? How would that be possible, unless – '

'Unless? Go on,' said Naomi, rigid.

'Unless Vinnie told him.'

'He would never have done that,' Linda said defensively, then seemed to think again. 'Not if he had a choice in the matter.'

'Then Vinnie was forced,' Bill said. 'The landlord told you what had been done to him. You heard it yourself.'

Linda nodded reluctantly, tight-lipped. 'Oh, this is all so horrible. Vinnie was always . . . *harmless*. Really the most harmless of us all. Why would anyone want to do *that* just to learn something from him? Jesus Christ, what they did to his face, his tongue. What kind of mind?' Her eyes brimmed with hot moisture and shock; a shock that surely stemmed from a fresh revelation no one was ready to face yet. Before she could bring herself to say the rest, Michael took her hand firmly in his. 'What kind of mind?' she repeated, dimly.

There was a lull before Michael glanced at his watch. 'Early in the day it may be. But we – that is *I* – need a drink at this juncture.' He stood, dragging Linda to her feet. 'If we've any nerves left between us, the time has come to steady them.'

Several guests turned to stare as the foursome recrossed the lounge, retracing their steps to the elevator. The light-headed pleasures of breakfast were suddenly far away. All that remained was the hotel's muzak, terrifying in its ordinariness, and the clear understanding of what lay ahead. This latest atrocity, Vinnie's last stand, was a legacy handed down from Parks Wood. It wouldn't necessarily be the last.

While the women took seats in the piano bar, Bill joined

143

Michael, who was leaning across the ornate and polished counter to order.

'Don't know about you,' Bill said, 'but it seems to me he's always one step ahead so long as we follow the agenda.'

Michael turned towards him. 'Meaning the timetable Vinnie laid out for us? Linking up here, the train-ride back home — the dates and times.'

'Uh-huh. So aren't we playing into his hands if we follow it stroke by stroke?'

Michael waited until the bartender had set down the drinks and moved out of earshot. 'Yes, I see that. It's as if everything Vinnie knew, he's acting upon. He knows what to expect from us next. So what do you have in mind? A change of hotel?'

'Only that we need to consider how to protect ourselves, take the initiative.'

'We're supposed to check out tomorrow, aren't we? Then maybe we should do it a day later, or now. Right now.' Michael sniffed the double Bushmills in his glass and took half of it down in one gulp.

'See what the others think first,' Bill said. 'Later today would probably be less obvious. Checking-out time is usually about now. Besides, we're going to need the morning for something else.'

'How's that?'

'The place in Earl's Court,' Bill said. 'Where he took you to pick up Tom Quigley. Do you think you could find it again?'

Chapter Seventeen

'Shit, man, you *serious* about that? Are you ribbing me or what? You *really* wants to go back there?' The taxi driver stared at Michael incredulously. Then, with a shake of the head, got the meter running. As chance or luck would have it, Bill, perching on the kerb outside the Heartland hotel, had flagged down the West Indian who last night had brought Michael from Earl's Court. 'Are these people friends of yours, then? Does they *know* you're crazy?' To the others he said, 'Last night, he gets in here all covered with blood and shit. Looks like death warmed up. Can't get away from there fast enough. You tell me: what's going on his white bread head?'

'Now there's a question that begs an answer,' said Linda, flinching as Michael's elbow met her ribs.

The driver laughed and turned Augustus Pablo up to boiling point. By the time they were stopping and starting on Earl's Court Road Naomi was clutching her ears. 'It was just about here,' Michael said, indicating a junction on the left. About twenty yards beyond the junction was a temporary bus stop outside a post office where a tall youth in a parka stood watching. From a distance his features were indistinct; it was the clothing that drew Michael's eye.

The driver turned, tooling between rows of small shops on both sides while Michael leaned forward, rapt with tension. 'This is the street. It was somewhere round here, I'm positive.'

Slowing, the driver shut off the reggae soundtrack. An

145

electrical spare parts shop drifted by; a greengrocer's followed. 'What kind of place you looking for? You know what the number is?'

'Hold it,' Michael said. Across the street to their right was a haberdashery, its door set back in an alcove. He recognised this, as well as what followed. Several residential houses, then a tobbaconist's, then a formidable white door that from here appeared far larger than its neighbours. That was an illusion, though. The late morning sun, slanting across the rooftops opposite, highlighted the door in such a way that its paintwork glowed brightly, seeming to overspill its frame.

'It couldn't have been any other, could it?' said Bill.

'I hope you all know what you're doing,' Naomi said in a dwindling voice.

The driver pulled over and stopped the meter. 'You want me to wait?' he asked Michael as soon as the group had unloaded. 'You looking for trouble again?'

Michael fished out a confusion of five and ten pound notes and dollar bills, stuffing a couple at random into the driver's hand. 'Here, keep the change. We'll be all right from now on. You can go.'

'You're in charge, man.'

'If only.'

The taxi sped off. Michael joined the others in front of the door, which seemed to be holding them spellbound, their shadows blotting out the sun from the doorstep. The door itself was open a fraction. Michael cleared his throat. In broad daylight it was possible to see details he'd missed last night: the upstairs windows broken but sealed with tarpaulin sheets, the suggestion of darker paint under the white, the italicized number 78 on the wall above the door.

'That isn't a house number!' Linda seized Michael's jacket sleeve fit to tear it. 'Look back along this row and ask yourself where this fits in. That's a date, not a number. That's *our* date, isn't it?'

It was Bill who stepped forward to push the door open, but Michael who led the way in. Strangely, the sunlight didn't extend much past the threshold, confining itself to the street outside. The darkness in the house seemed less

146

palpable than it had last night, as did the thick, cloying smell. There was enough light to pick out motes of dust suspended in the air. At the foot of the stairs Michael stalled. A closed door stood halfway along the hall on the left; another door, possibly an exit, beckoned at the far end. For a minute the house vibrated to the sound of an underground train, rising, climaxing, fading.

'We'll try down here first,' Michael said.

'What are we looking for anyway?' Naomi asked.

'Anything we can use.'

To an outsider there might have been something vaguely comic in the way the group inched forward, shoulder to shoulder, towards the first door. As Michael grasped the handle there was a general intake of breath.

The room was empty. It didn't look as if it had ever been lived in, except by spiders. There were cobwebs in corners and between the three arms of a bulbless light fitting. A single easy chair was stationed in the middle of the bare concrete floor, facing a cast iron stove. There was no other furniture. On the floor beside the stove was a nest of tabloid newspapers, a scattering of ashes beneath the stove suggesting the papers had been intended as fuel.

'A squat?' Linda said. 'You'd think even a pauper could do better than this.'

Bill patted the chair's seat cushion and a dusty cloud rose. 'No one's been here for an age,' he said.

The other downstairs door was securely locked, though the keyhole provided a blurred view of houses in the next street. Returning to the stairs, everyone hesitated, waiting for someone else to make the first move.

Michael stepped forward, straight-faced. 'Don't kid yourselves this has anything to do with bravery.' He started upstairs slowly. 'I could well be the first one out of this dive.'

At least he could take courage from their thumps and creaks behind him on the stairs. The steps were worn and noisy, and this gave the house, albeit briefly, an aura of hubbub and habitation. Nearing the top, Michael hesitated. The door of the room he'd been trapped in last night was open halfway. From his place on the stairs he could see the

147

familiar, framed rooftops but little else. For the first time since returning to the house he felt less than clear about what to do next. Supposing ... He twisted around, looked down at the others. Supposing his assailant was still in there, alive. What then?

'What's the problem?' Bill said.

'We didn't come prepared for this,' Michael said, and Naomi said, 'Right. Damn right. We had to wait until now to hear you say that.'

'Keep going,' Bill said. 'We're with you.'

'Right behind you all the way,' Linda added.

'There's a load off my mind.' Michael continued upstairs. 'If you hear me shout, *move*. Don't look back, don't even think.' His footfalls on the bare-boarded landing were less reassuring now; the noise could be a warning to anyone lying in wait. Instead of approaching the room directly he edged to his left until he had a view through the gap in the door. There was no sign of the man he had left inside.

Michael swallowed. At his right hand Bill whispered, 'Well, what now?'

'I think it's all clear. Can't see him in there.'

Linda glanced along the landing to their right. 'Do you think he got away? Is there any chance he's still – still here?'

'He couldn't be in a fit state to go far,' Michael said. 'No further than the nearest hopital, probably.'

'Or the nearest payphone?'

'He's alive,' Bill said. 'That's a fact. We know we can't afford to relax.' He gave the door a push and stepped in.

In the daylight the room was unremittingly grim. In some ways, Michael thought, it had been preferable by night. The walls were daubed with graffiti – swastikas in black paint, the forenames of squatters who had once slept here. Here and there, great handfuls of grey and white feathers and foam, perhaps gouged from pillows, had been stuck to the walls with great wodges of paint. On the floor against the far wall was a mattress without pillows or sheets. A dark cigar-shaped stain marked its centre.

'Charming tenants this place must have had,' said Naomi.

148

'Can't you just imagine coming home to this after a hard day's rooting and begging?'

'Home sweet home,' Michael said. He was eyeing the floor, where the boards were splashed with rye whiskey and blood. Some of the blood must be his, some his assailant's. With a forefinger he dabbed at the staining, which felt tacky. The duty-free carrier sloshed and exhaled whiskey fumes. 'Such a damn waste,' he said quietly.

When he looked up he saw Linda gazing from the window, her hand shading her eyes. For a moment he felt strangely giddy, half-expecting to be seized from behind by anonymous hands. He remembered the smell of ancient gore which had filled this room last night. Then Linda's gaze dropped as her right foot collided with something near the skirting. A small metallic object skidded across the boards towards Michael.

It was a flick knife, the blade open and patched with dried blood. Michael turned it over in his hands. The handle was plastic, the blade's edge sharp as a razor. Roy Sachs had once drawn such a knife against Vinnie, that Friday afternoon after English. As they filed from the room Michael passed the weapon to Linda.

'This is what he came at me with.'

'Ugh!' Flinching at the sharpness, she returned it quickly.

Michael folded and pocketed it. 'Just two more rooms,' he said brightly, as if everything else was now a formality.

The landing was at its brightest between the room they had left and the top of the stairs. Further along, the light became murky, the ancient musty smell more concentrated than downstairs. The first door opened into a bathroom – a travesty of one. It had been used indiscriminately without plumbing for too long, and the stench that gusted forth caused Linda to turn away, gasping, as Bill slammed the door in a hurry.

Next to the bathroom was a second bedroom, which at first glance seemed less cluttered than elsewhere. A tarpaulin sheet nailed across the window was aglow with sunlight, like a cinema screen. The walls echoed the symbols and slogans of the previous room. A scrawl of identities, another swastika, more feathers. An old stone fireplace with an

149

open grate had several glossy magazines piled before it. Michael was turning away, having seen enough, when Linda caught his arm.

'Just a minute. Over there.'

There was something stuffed into the grate, so compact it was easy to miss. Linda knelt at the hearth and began tugging it free. Standing over her, Michael saw that she was fussing with a small tan vanity case, jammed between the chimney walls.

'It feels heavy,' she said, not looking up.

While he waited, Michael picked a magazine from the pile, scanning the contents page. It was a five year old issue of *The Face*. Half-way down the list of contributors was Alison Lester's name.

This was surely more than coincidence. Alison was credited with a Lou Reed interview, beginning page 34. With trembling hands, Michael searched the magazine until he reached the three-page spread. Every word of it had been defaced, obliterated. A child with a biro might have made a similar mess, but never with such determination. Alison's paragraphs had been scored out with such vigour the paper had torn in several places. Not a word had been spared; only the photographs were untouched.

'What's that? Let me see,' said Naomi.

Michael sighed and passed her the magazine. Her mouth sagged when she digested what she was seeing. For some reason this vandalism seemed worse than anything else they might have expected to find. In the other magazines, *Elle* and *Harpers & Queen* and *Time Out*, there was more of the same. Each contained a sample of Alison's work; in every case the same treatment had been meted out.

'Jesus, he's so scrupulous,' Bill said, astonished.

'Huh? Have you found something?' Linda asked, still preoccupied.

'You'll see in a minute,' Michael said.

She'd managed to drag the case clear of the grate, and was trying to prise open the lock. When it refused to respond, Michael set to with the knife and the latch gave easily with a rusty snap. 'Well then, here goes,' Linda said, and threw back the lid.

At first Michael thought he was seeing things. The case had been packed with his books; one copy of each published edition. There was even a *Rubber Bullets* mass-market paperback, published in Britain only weeks ago.

'Scrupulous? This is goddamned *obsessive*,' he said. Even before Linda dusted off the first and handed it to him he knew what he would find inside. Every page, every word, including the dedication, had been scrawled into incoherence. This work, like Alison's, had been collected only to be destroyed. What kind of mind, indeed? What must it have taken to spend hour after hour, meticulously crossing out, erasing, vandalising?

'I don't understand,' Linda murmured. 'Why would he ... Why would anyone ...'

'I think,' Michael said, 'it's time we made ourselves scarce.'

Naomi, shivering, was already backing away to the door. Tossing the novel back in the case, Michael strode past her and along the landing, faintly nauseous. Suddenly the house seemed more oppressive than ever. It wasn't so much the walls or the thick stale air as the notion that someone with so single a purpose had lived and breathed here. Someone committed to revenge and nothing else. This spartan life — no creature comforts, no distractions — had been dedicated only to that. For fifteen years everything else had been sacrificed. In this house he had waited and hated, and erased.

Later, at a table in The Dug Out, Leicester Square, they sipped aperitifs and stared without appetite at the lunch menu. The Dug Out was one of those modern English establishments straining to evoke rustic America as-seen-on-TV, with much down-home stripped pine and an elevated bar lit up like the Superbowl. The portions, however, were also generously American, the prerecorded rock and roll music an endless loop of nostalgia that grew louder as the afternoon wore on.

They ordered Caesar salads and fresh drinks. Linda sat with her elbows on the table, face squashed between her fists. To Naomi she said, 'Did you think about any of this before? I mean, before Vinnie caught up with you?'

'Only when I let myself. There were times when all I wanted was to think about *us* – I missed you so much – but I couldn't allow it. So I had to keep myself occupied. The children helped me in that, of course, and when they were old enough for school I found work.'

'Jesus, Nim.' Linda made a face. 'To have to take pains to keep the people you love off your mind. You know, I'm only beginning to realise now how hard it's been.' She paused to study the faces watching her, the fond expressions, the eyes that shared her secrets. 'In case I don't get the chance to say so again, I want you all to know now that I love you, even after all we've been through. I'm saying that now because something's changing. We're here to be together, to celebrate being together, but there's no way we can do that yet, is there? Not until everything else is finished.'

Michael, seated on her left, was the first to reach for her hand. Bill took the other without fuss. The foursome sat, unspeaking, linking hands around the table until a waiter bearing salads cleared his throat self-consciously.

'Prepare yourselves, then,' Bill said after he'd gone. 'We're on our way home tonight. We'll check out as soon as we're finished here. If he's acting according to Vinnie's agenda he might just assume we're staying on.'

'It's our best chance of keeping one step ahead,' Michael agreed. 'Vinnie thought we should rendezvous in London to begin with, which is fine as far as it goes. But we're not solving anything here, we're not likely to until we're back home again. We know that's where this is leading.'

'Home?' Linda said. 'I'm amazed you can call it that after spending half your life trying to escape the damn dump. We must be crazy, mustn't we, going back there, now that we're all finally away from it?'

'We're going back,' Bill said, 'to stay sane.'

There was a lull. 'Green Onions' began on the sound system. Then Michael raised his glass high, like the Statue

152

of Liberty. 'To us,' he said. 'To the Brotherhood.'

Glasses were clinked, drinks downed. 'This feels like the beginning of something,' said Linda soberly.

'Or the end.' Naomi looked pensive. 'I hope to God it's the end.'

Chapter Eighteen

Mid-afternoon, while bone dry manzanillas and Canadian Clubs were being downed at the Dug Out, the Source was heading north on the motorway. It was a clear day, the clouds high, and a freshening breeze rushed in at the open window. The Source drove with his right elbow jutting out, sipping bottled Coke, taking pleasure in the journey. Praise God, he was healed. He was ready to exercise judgement. *Do you ever judge people for what they do*? he thought absently, and began humming a gospel refrain.

A short while after leaving London he had spotted a self-service petrol station and parked in a corner of the yard away from the pumps. On the back seat was the suitcase Michael McCourt had abandoned. There was nothing inside but clothing, and so he had carried the case to the men's room, where he had washed, changed and stuffed his old rags in the waste bin. Although it was good to feel clean again there was something about McCourt's things on his shoulders and back that disturbed him, that made him oddly restless. He would have felt happier, if swamped, in Vinnie's shirts and trousers. But beggars couldn't be choosers, and in any case this was only to be expected; he hadn't assimilated McCourt yet.

He had, however, given him something to think about — given them all something to think about as they whiled away the days in the metropolis. He had done all he'd set out to, reminding them he was still in circulation. By the time they reached Abbotsbridge — surely they would be compelled to return — he'd be waiting.

Soon he was mouthing turn-offs along the A1, each place name a jolt, a sharp reminder. He had felt much the same mixture of apprehension and pleasure the last time he'd returned, after saving Alison's troubled soul. A prophet was always without honour at home, and the memories, the associations were not pleasant ones. Some part of himself had died here, or been lost and left behind. Soon, by God's grace, he would put himself back together again. The body would perish and his father's words would be fulfilled.

His father had been a tall, strapping man like himself, with thick wavy brown hair and eyes − such eyes − and a voice that carried. On Sundays and Thursday evenings a modern prefabricated bungalow on the outskirts of Riverside served as a church to the charismatic fellowship over which his father presided. With flushed, joyful faces and arms held aloft, locals and worshippers from near by towns came to praise God bringing songs and applause.

On this particular Sunday − a Sunday that entered his mind as he signalled, slowed, exited the A1 at a Wakefield sign − the atmosphere in the church had been humid with the Spirit. Even the boy he had been then, picking his nose near the back of the hall, had sensed a presence he couldn't identify. There were matted brows and glazed eyes, a strange peaceful glow of well-being coming from all his immediate neighbours. People he didn't know were smiling at him; others who had seemed not to know one another when they arrived were hugging, embracing. This couldn't be bad, could it? He admired his father for letting this happen, for being the doorway to such power.

Gradually the applause died and people were seated, some still holding hands, others sobbing. His father stood, upright and inner-peaceful, at a lectern on a dais at the front. His stepmother − the second marriage was perfectly correct, having followed his mother's death by two years − twisted in her front-row seat to smile back at him. He nodded shyly and looked down, wanting suddenly to break wind. It was difficult to concentrate on anything else. His father cleared his throat, waited until silence prevailed. Then he said,

'*We* are the body of Christ, did you know that? *We* are the body of Christ.' There were mutters, a cough, a Praise

God chorus. 'We're placed in this body to serve God and each other, and as members of the body we each have a purpose, a part to play: the whole is made out of many. But how do we know – how do *you* know what your purpose should be? Are you a hand, an eye, a tongue?' The urge to fart made the boy writhe in his seat, knees jarring together. 'The Word tells us, hear this, that to each one is given the manifestation of the Spirit for the common good. Wisdom through the Spirit, knowledge through the Spirit, faith and healing and prophecy and tongues. And it tells us, furthermore, that the body is not one member but many. Because God has placed the members, each one, in the body, just as He desired. And if they were all one member, where would the body be?'

He paused there, allowing the congregation to digest the message. The boy held his breath, as if that would help. Behind him on the left, the main door stood open. Someone had just arrived there, a figure he couldn't distinguish for the brightness outside who stood, arms folded, watching. When the sermon resumed, he began edging along the row to the door. As he did so, the flatulent urge passed.

'God has so composed the body,' his father's soft but pentrative voice went on, 'that there should be no division in the body, but that members should have the same care for one another. And if one member suffers, all the members suffer with it. And if one member rejoices, all the members rejoice –'

Looking behind him once to make sure no one noticed him leaving, he continued to the door. As he reached it the figure seized him with both hands, dragging him into the light outside.

'Sometimes, Tom, I really fucking worry about you,' Roy Sachs said, buffeting the preacher's son against an outer wall, a parked car, into a privet hedge, before dumping him on the street outside the church. 'Talk about the Blank Generation! Is there any fucking wonder you have no mind of your own when you're having your brain rotted by that stuff?'

Tom sat cross-legged on the ground, dusting his jacket sleeves. 'I do have a mind of my own, Roy. I do.'

156

Sachs shook his head slowly, grimly. He was wearing a black leather vest, black cord jeans and Oxfords, which made his face and bare arms seem as white as bones. 'Then why are you here?'

'It's something to do.'

'I don't mean at church, cretin, I mean *here*, in the world. Why do you exist? What's your purpose? Have you found that out from them yet?'

Tom shrugged. He considered each member of the body in turn, each Spiritual gift. 'To serve ...'

'Come again?'

'To serve God and other people. That's what they say.' As an afterthought he added proudly, 'It's what my father says.'

'You can't always trust your father though, can you?'

'I do.'

'Well, you ought to think twice about what he's selling you first.' Sachs sniffed and spat in the gutter.

'Why would he lie about something like that?' Tom wanted to know. 'It isn't as though he's gaining anything by not being honest.'

'Isn't he, though? Isn't he gaining your heart and soul, your unthinking obedience? Look how you fall into line, Tom, come when you're called, go where you're told. At your age you should be ashamed. All *you're* gaining from this is a holy fucking lobotomy.'

There was a pause. A light breeze moved down the street, stirring hedgerows and garden shrubs. A dog barked somewhere in the distance. Sachs' sat on the low red brick wall in front of the church lip curled. He seemed, by his face, to be tasting lemons. Tom sat beside him as another song began in the church.

'This is the day ... This is the day ...
This is the day that the Lord has made.'

'Do you mean to tell me,' Sachs' brooded, 'you're still into this after all we've been through together? I thought you'd have sussed the truth by now. I credited you with being smart enough for that at least, but Jesus −'

157

'What truth?'

'Life's about serving yourself, making your own way, not selling your heart and soul to these zombies. You're on your own, Tom. You shouldn't have to depend on *this* – chasing after something you can't even see.'

Tom stared down, saying nothing. For the moment it seemed better to be mute. The singing lilted towards him on the breeze. Of course there was more to life than worship, he'd always guessed as much. Except on rare occasions, he had never truly felt the Spirit that his father insisted lived inside him. Lately, in the church – even at home – he had come to feel more and more out of place, an outsider with nowhere else to go. But wasn't life also about – well, needing to belong somewhere, to be accepted, to be part of something larger than yourself?

'You need help if you believe what your dad says about doing it all for God,' Roy Sachs' said. 'Look at your house, look at the car he drives. You think he's managed all that just by keeping his nose clean?'

'You shouldn't run him down like that,' Tom said. He felt wounded, under attack. 'He's still my dad. I do still believe him.'

'Well from now on, *I'm* your dad. Chew it over. And it's way past time for our pep talk, my son. The facts of life and all that. Will you believe what I tell you?'

'Well, I ... uhm ...'

'Come with me and you might learn something.'

Sachs got up, taking a packet Embassys and matches from his jeans pocket. Lighting a cigarette, he started away to the end of the street, a cul-de-sac, where a public footpath doglegged beyond reach of the buildings to nudge the outskirts of the woods. Without another thought, Tom followed. By the time the trees had swallowed the church out of sight behind them, the song of praise had faded.

'*What* am I going to learn?' he asked, suddenly nervous. He wanted to sound enthusiastic – better than inviting Roy's anger again – but enthusiasm was hard to sustain with someone of whom you were basically afraid.

'A secret,' Roy replied. 'One of life's greatest secrets.'

They walked on. Perhaps a quarter of a mile inside Parks

158

Wood the footpath became a fork, veering respectively north and slightly uphill, then west towards Abbotsbridge town centre. Between the two was a scrubby plantation of small, ailing birch saplings enravelled with couch-grass, and beyond this several acres of dark forest floor presided over by mature oaks whose heavy foliage denied daylight. It was through the birch and towards the oaks that Roy headed, advancing with long, sure strides. Struggling to keep up, Tom gradually became aware of a sound that didn't belong here, a sound which had sent the resident birdlife into fits. Their cries charged the air overhead with excitement and panic. Somewhere not far away a struggle was taking place: by the sound of it, a frantic, all-or-nothing struggle.

Tom paused to listen. Above his own reedy breath he heard gasping and choking, someone or something in the throes of exhaustion. Roy, oblivious, continued on. They had entered the darkness beneath the oaks, a place suddenly familiar to Tom from another time. It was the day they had chased McCourt and Vinnie Hartley for more than an hour, losing them somewhere near here. It was strange, he thought, how neatly they had vanished into thin air. There must have been an explanation. Still, now that the summer holidays were here it wouldn't be the last chase. If Roy had his way, McCourt would be paying for his sins all summer long.

Then his train of thought snapped. He was coming within range of the secret Roy had brought him here to see.

Twenty or thirty yards ahead was a clearing where an animal – nearer, he could tell it was a sizeable dog, a golden retriever – had been tied to the trunk of a tree. In trying to free itself, the dog had circled the tree several times, reducing the length of nylon rope which bound it to three or four feet. As they came closer the dog cowered down, its tail flicking back and forth.

'Well?' Roy said. 'What do you think?'

'Don't know. What should I think? Is this what you wanted me to see?'

'This ... and something more. Oh, much more.' Forgetting the dog for the moment, Roy strode away towards where a hump in the ground stood at odds with the gentle downhill slope. Along the way he gathered up a thick length of fallen branch two or three feet long and began absently snapping off twigs, waving it like a baton. 'See here, Tom? See what they've been doing behind my back? Sometimes the nerve of these people is something to behold.'

He was gesturing towards the entrance of something that might have been an oversized foxhole. For a moment he stood blocking the entrance, staring directly and darkly at Tom, 'The dog was digging around here, led me straight to it. Otherwise we might never have found them out.'

'Who are you talking about, Roy?'

'Who do you think? McCourt's lot, lard-arse and Linda Grayson and the rest, that's who. You've seen them together, you know how they are. They're the only ones who'd dare do this.'

He was seething, though for the moment it was hard for Tom to appreciate why. This anger, this loathing that Roy managed to generate out of nowhere, was the force that kept everyone, Tom included, in line. Why did he reserve so much of it for McCourt and his friends, though? Because they weren't ruled by him? Because they had each other?

Tom shrugged, nonplussed. 'What have they *done*, Roy? I still don't figure – '

'Here, come look, come fucking see for yourself.'

The lair into which Tom was led felt like a homely Aladdin's cave. Initially, before he adjusted to the dimness, he had an impression of shelved books, murals, warm rugs underfoot, treasures piled high in corners. There was a rich leaf-mouldy aroma like that from a real open fire. Eventually he saw that the treasure was mostly bric-a-brac, the furnishings makeshift. It was home from home, but no Plaza Suite. On one bare wall there were various Polaroids of Michael McCourt, Linda Grayson and the others standing arm to arm, grinning, making faces. On another, a hanged man, a game of noughts and crosses. There were copies of *The Grapes of Wrath*, which presumably they'd connived and colluded over here, and one of *Lord of the Flies*. On the floor between two bean bags were several soft drinks cans and an empty wine bottle. Tom knew nothing about wine but the label, in French, looked impressive.

He gave a low, appreciative whistle. 'What a place though,

160

eh? All these things . . . ' Then it struck him; he tried to make light of it. 'This must have been where they came that afternoon. Well, would you credit that? So that's how they vanished. Let them wait till next time, then, see if it works again.'

'There isn't going to be any next time.' Roy stood with his back to the entrance, his features patched with shadow. In the small, still space his breath sounded contricted, almost painful. He was patting his left palm with the section of broken branch like a truncheon. 'There isn't going to *be* any next time.'

Tom tried to smile, his mouth suddenly unpleasantly dry. For a moment he thought he could hear distant thunder. In a stroke, Roy had charged the atmosphere with new menace. Tom swallowed and said brightly, 'Well, it's enough that you found this place out. That'll be enough to stop them coming here, give them nowhere to hide.'

'That isn't the point, holy Joe! The point is, they shouldn't have done it in the first place.'

'But they're *friends*, Roy, they stick together. They go everywhere together.' What in the world's wrong with that? he wanted to add, but thought better of it.

'They're defying me,' Roy Sachs said. The length of wood slapped his palm. 'They do everything together just to spite me, that's what they're about.' He turned, and Tom followed him back outside. As they stood blinking into the light squeezing between the trees Sachs said, 'What they've done here is build a shrine to shut me out of. If it weren't for me they wouldn't even be together. That Linda, for instance: McCourt didn't even *look* at her until we chased him into her den. And now take a look at them. They're standing against us, against the natural order . . . the way things are.'

Tom nodded, remained silent. The hysterical bird activity of a few moments ago had dwindled to nothing. Now Roy was staring across the woods as though scanning for something to focus his hatred upon. He was primed, burning — burning in a way that was new even to Tom. His eyes were alight, the cords of his neck taut. Seeing the tethered dog, a faint gasp of laughter forced itself out of him, and Tom thought of a snapping twig, the last vestige of sanity twitching free.

'Is this the secret you meant?' he asked, suddenly desperate for Roy to be normal, to behave in a way that made sense. 'It's quite something, right? A bloody downright cheek they should do this.'

Roy Sachs didn't hear him, or preferred not to. He was already marching across the clearing towards the dog. Tom stumbled warily after him. As they came nearer, the retriever lowered itself as if ready to spring. Its teeth were bared, though its tall still wagged rhythmically. The whites of its large bovine eyes were just visible. Perhaps it trusted them, and wanted to play.

'Here's where the secret begins,' Roy whispered. He drew a deep breath, threw back his shoulders. Then, with a windmilling flourish, he brought the length of timber down on the animal's head.

At first the retriever looked stunned, nothing more. The dull blow reverberated through the clearing. Tom watched in awe as the dog's legs suddenly buckled and collapsed underneath it. Spreadeagled and panting, it gazed up with unseeing eyes, bewildered. Its heavy pink tongue lolled from one side of its mouth. Its tail no longer ticked. Roy brought the weapon down again.

Tom flinched, this time unable to look. His fists were bunched so tightly his nails were scoring the palms. The skin of his face, back and chest prickled hotly. He forced himself to inhale, exhale, evenly, thinking of other matters, spiritual matters, his father's words. This was dreadful, so very dreadful. He wanted to scramble to safety between trees and through bracken, put distance between himself and this vision. Yet some quiet, other part of him − the part that felt awed, astonished − could only admire Roy Sachs for seeing it through. What character it must take, what resolve. His father preached mercy, but he could now see the attraction, the purity of its opposite. When he looked again, Roy had discarded the broken branch and was kneeling over the soft, limp torso, his hand at its throat.

'It's still alive,' he said. 'Come here and see.'

Tom edged nearer. From a certain angle, the retriever's

wide, trusting eyes seemed to follow him. He wished, if it was really unconscious, the eyes would close. He was sweating, terrified and enthralled. As he knelt beside the dog, Roy drew his attention to the silver tag dangling from the animal's collar.

'Tara,' said Roy. 'That's her name. She belongs to Linda Grayson. One bitch owned by another.'

'How can you tell that?'

'See here. Look closer. There's an address and telephone number.' He smiled secretively. 'I'd know the number anywhere – I've dialled it often enough.'

Tom watched him uncertainly. 'You've talked to Linda? And she talked to you? About what?'

'Are you simple? What do you think?'

'You're ... Are you after her?'

'I'm after them all, Tom, every one. McCourt went to war against me and *she's* in cahoots with him, they all fucking are, which isn't something I can just let pass. It has to be dealt with before it gets out of hand. They're setting themselves against the natural order, and no one – *no one*, get me? – dares do that. One way or another they're going to have to pay for their mistake.'

There was a lull. Tara let out a deep-seated, protracted whimper, but didn't move. Bending over her, Roy gently lifted her head and began wrapping a length of the nylon rope around her neck.

'How are you going to make them pay?' Tom demanded. 'With what, Roy? With what?' He wanted to lighten the moment, perhaps by slipping conveniently into another persona, assuming the voice of a film star for Roy's amusement, making him laugh, changing the course of events. But his will felt shattered; he couldn't find the voice or the inspiration. He knew too well what was coming. For so long he had played the errand boy, but now he was out of his depth, and the taste of death filled his mouth. 'Roy?' he cried. 'What are you going to do to them?'

The Source had the answer to that. Then again, he also had the advantage of hindsight. It had taken time – all these years – to understand Roy Sachs' secret, the point he had meant to illustrate that day as he tightened his grip on the rope.

As he drove through the outskirts of Abbotsbridge, towards the council estate where Naomi still lived, the Source recommenced his gospel refrain:

'This is the day that the Lord has made ...'

And rejoiced that the secret was safe inside him, now and for all eternity.

Chapter Nineteen

As he closed his hands over his face, willing the moment to pass, Tom Quigley thought: *Everything out here's alive, everything in the woods is watching.*

He was praying for the moment to end. Praying because the last thing he saw had been Roy's face, blue with strain, eyes bulging, mouth gaping until in some grotesque fashion he resembled Tara, from whom he was choking the life. He was praying not only for the torture to stop but the silence too: the overpowering sense he had of being spied on from all corners of the woods. A breeze stirred the trees, unsettling him, as if what he'd heard overhead was a voice uttering sounds he couldn't decipher.

'Listen,' Roy hissed, 'and wait. And tell me ... what you feel.' He spoke in snatches between breaths. 'She's going. She's really going. Tell me that God ever gave you a gift ... as perfect as this!'

It was small consolation, but Tara had given up the ghost from the start. At least Tom wasn't forced to hear her struggle, resisting against the odds – at least he was spared that part. His hands, pressed to his eyes, were moist with hot tears and he was trembling uncontrollably with heat and raw nerves. Please, he thought. He was genuinely praying, sharing the animal's suffering. Hadn't he been happier before, seated near the back of the fellowship's church, surrounded by so many flushed, loving faces? Surely this, Roy's alternative, wasn't the way to go. Surely –

It was then, without warning, that the power took hold of him. At first he could think of it only in terms of electrical force: like the charge of static when he whipped off his nylon sweater too quickly. At night in the dark he could provide his own lightshow like this enjoying the way his scalp and fingertips tingled. Except that this was more than a short, passing shock. The first rush was still coming.

In fact it was spreading. Light swam and diffracted, forming dancing patterns directly in front of him; light that felt trapped in his mind. Tom automatically dropped his hands and opened his eyes. He wanted to laugh, to begin and never stop.

Roy was staring into space, grinning triumphantly. He let go of the rope and punched the air with both fists and Tara dropped, lifeless, to the ground. Like everything else in the clearing, Roy was engulfed by the light; indeed, as far as Tom could make out it seemed to be flowing from him, from his gaping mouth and dark eyes.

Tom watched, startled. Now his face, neck and chest were alive with frantic tics that multiplied by the second. He was on fire; his hands shook, his lips were thickened as if by novocaine. Through all of this he was able to think only one clear thought: it was God's work, the healing hand of the Spirit. Something had entered him, bringing him peace. This was, after all, the day that the Lord had made. How else could his fear have vanished so readily? Wasn't this the answer to his prayer for an end to the suffering?

When he finally managed to speak, his voice sounded muffled, far away. 'What's happening to us, Roy? What am I feeling?'

'You're alive,' Roy said. 'That's what it is.'

'But how? I mean, I *know* I'm alive. But this is so different, so — '

'New? Well, no wonder. It's your first time and the first time is nearly always like that.'

Tom stared at him slack-mouthed. 'The first time? The first time for what?'

'The first time you've gained a new life.' Roy glanced at the dead retriever. Though the tongue was extruded, the eyes were now closed, and she looked at peace. '*She's* what you're feeling,' Roy said. 'She's what's inside us. And everywhere round us. There's more than enough of her to go round.'

166

Tom looked at the dog. 'Her? *That*? You've got to be kidding, Roy. She's only ...' He didn't know what to say.

Roy took a moment to stretch his arms, extending and clenching his fingers. 'Everything that's alive has this power, some things more than others. This one, I'd say she had a lot of it in her. And now she's passed over, bless her heart, and she's ours.'

Jesus, Tom thought. Even though the patterns of light were beginning to fade, he felt dizzy, deprived of oxygen. 'You're talking about souls. You're telling me you strangled her for her soul. Are you serious?'

'Never more.'

Their eyes locked until Tom felt compelled to look away. He shook his head slowly in disbelief. Very gradually, out of the stillness, the birdsong resumed.

Roy got up and leaned back against the tree, arms folded. His biceps were swollen and veined. 'Something wrong, holy Joe? Is the idea all too much for your head to take? Next thing, you'll be claiming you feel worse for what happened here –'

'No, that's just it. I feel – well. I feel great. Yes, I *do* feel great, I *do* feel alive. But I always thought ...'

'Hmm?'

Tom shrugged and shut up.

'Don't worry, I know damn well what you thought.' Roy clicked his tongue disdainfully. 'You thought this was God's own territory – your dear old dad's territory. No wonder, if you've spent your life being brainwashed into believing your soul's something you save and give away to Jesus. What did I tell you, Tom, about taking what you needed from life? These things are for grabbing, not giving away or leaving to rot. When are you going to listen to me?'

Tom put up his hands. This euphoria was all the proof he needed, and he wanted to apologise. 'I *am* listening, Roy, I always listen.'

'Then hear this, my son. This gift isn't for anyone. How would your dad put it? – few are chosen. So consider yourself one of the few. Do you think you can keep this a secret?' Staring fixedly at Tom, he took out his cigarettes

167

and lit one. 'Because if you can't, I'll kill you too. I'll have your life too.'

'Yes,' Tom said. He spoke eagerly, without fear. For the first time in his life he belonged somewhere. He'd touched the beyond and sensed its power; why would he risk losing that? 'I'm with you. I won't breathe a word,' he said.

'Right then.' Roy gave a wry smile. With his left foot he nudged Tara's body gently, as if the dead were more sensitive to rough treatment than the living. 'In that case let's get started.'

It took less than half an hour to unravel the rope from the tree trunk and tie the noose, which was then slung over the firmest, thickest bough. They worked together for speed, Roy calling orders, Tom following instructions to the letter. Finally Tara was hoisted up, and the rope secured.

As they stood admiring the job, Roy dusted his hands and said quietly, 'Now do you understand?'

'About what?'

'When you asked before how McCourt and his clan were going to pay for what they'd done. Have I answered your question now?'

Tom nodded, not taking his eyes from the dog for an instant. She was heavy; the rope creaked against the woodwork, and the corpse swung very gently as a new breeze cut through the clearing. He felt that someone should say a few words, even for a dog; he knew now that dogs, like men and women, also had souls. Tom smiled to himself, remembering that dog spelt god backwards. After all these uncertain years it wasn't God's spirit but Dog's which had saved him.

Later they walked back to the Riverside estate in respectful silence. There was no need to talk. It was better not to, as long as the experience was still fresh in their minds. As they went, Tom hummed the melody the church had been singing when they left. Roy didn't seem to object – presumably his attention was elsewhere.

Soon they were nearing the edge of the wood where the bridle-path curved back to the estate. There was first a stile to negotiate, then a short stretch with hedges on both sides, then houses. At this point the church and the lower end of the street came into view. The street looked empty; the service would have ended some time ago. Suddenly Roy let out a small gasp of delight and tapped Vinnie's arm. Michael McCourt was idling down the street, past the church, towards them. He had on a tracksuit top and blue jeans with sneakers and was carrying a blue and white sports bag. By the time he reached the cul-de-sac he still hadn't seen what he was walking into.

'Got to hand it to you, Tom,' Roy Sachs said gleefully. 'Some things you can't deny. This *is* the damn day the Lord has made!'

They set off.

It happened right here, the Source marvelled. Right here. He stood beside his car on the drive outside the church, hands pocketed, gazing down the street. Concentrating hard, with half-closed eyes, he could almost see the ghosts of Tom Quigley and Roy Sachs come running from between the concrete posts where the path began – and, nearer, the ghost of Michael McCourt turning tall.

Those were the days right enough, he thought. But now ... The sun was falling, though it still had a way to go before reaching the rooftops. The windows of the disused church were stapled over with metal sheets these days, like any off-limits crack house in London. The rest of the houses in the street looked similarly neglected, but were probably inhabited. Fences and gates were either in tatters or missing completely; front doors hadn't been painted in aeons. The only cars within sight had no wheels. Twenty years ago this estate was brand new; but everything under the sun was perishable.

He had driven to Riverside first because it was only a short detour from his route to Naomi's house. Now he had seen enough; it was time to start looking forward again. In less than ten minutes he was on the other side of Abbotsbridge, where council tenants were stacked four-storeys high above streets of empty, condemned terraced houses. Dragging his parka from the back seat, he got out.

This community, where Naomi had raised her two children, had once been notorious as a sink estate, a place where the council consigned problem families. It appeared that little had changed. The walls were grey, pebble-dashed and desecrated with graffiti. There were scruffy, unsupervised children everywhere, on the stairways, blocking doors, in the forecourt outside where a group of three played tug-of-war with something that resembled a live cat. The air reeked of tinned baked beans and soiled Pampers.

Naomi's flat, on the third floor, was the first he saw as he rounded the stairwell. Thankfully the corridor was empty. From a door further down came the depressing noise of bickering adult voices. The Source knocked and waited, just in case. There was no reply, which probably meant Naomi had packed the kids off to her mother's until she returned. He tested the handle and gave a firm push. The door resisted, but wouldn't take much forcing; the council spared every expense when it came to secure doors and windows.

He thought again. If Naomi found the lock smashed she probably wouldn't even enter. To his right, past the stairwell, was a door that led outside to the balcony. He went through it and edged along until he came to Naomi's kitchen window, then drew a suitably sized chisel from the lining of his laden coat. A scream from below made him falter, but it was only the children playing. In less than a minute he had the window open and was lowering himself inside.

Now he could rest for a while. He stared from the window across Abbotsbridge, feeling pleased with himself, pleased to be one step ahead. The sky was on fire, and he thought of a painting he'd once seen of the sun going down over Hiroshima. A suitable sky for judgement day, he thought.

The drive had tired him and stimulated his appetite. From Naomi's fridge-freezer he took a family size deep pan pizza, which he ate in the lounge in front of the TV. On top of the TV there were school photo-portraits of Naomi's children: the russet-haired girl, the older, darker boy with Sachs' features.

The place was clean and comfortable, uncluttered. There were few books to read, apart from a couple of romantic novels and a couple for children by Michael McCourt.

170

But there was food, hot water, a soft double bed. He hadn't slept on a bed in years. He could live here, then, until she came home. He could rest, and prepare himself, and wait.

Chapter Twenty

There was a message from Harvey Klein waiting for Michael when they returned to the Heartland after lunch. At four thirty the others ordered a taxi for King's Cross and began checking out while Michael telephoned New York from his room. It was nothing too urgent: a producer at Lorimar was interested in *Rubber Bullets*, but saw it in terms of a bowdlerised Mini-series for television. Would Michael be interested in collaborating on a pilot script? Michael told Harvey he would think about it. Five minutes later he had packed his few remaining things and left.

It was Friday, and King's Cross was a hothouse of rush hour commuters by the time they arrived on the platform. The next InterCity service to Wakefield was already packed with stern and weary faces, and the only spare seats were in first class compartments. Michael wrote a cheque, upgrading the tickets. The journey would take two and a quarter hours.

The first few minutes dragged. London withdrew slowly, reluctantly, mile after drab residential mile. After Manhattan these brown tower blocks looked like sad, half-hearted imitations. Even the sky seemed tinged with ochre. Then came the first stretches of flat green English landscape, and Michael felt sleep crawling over him. Time and place vanished through a pinhole of light like a fading silent film and then he saw himself running, picking up speed, struggling to keep pace with the train, his breathing and movements synchronised to its rhythm. He was veering towards it, in

172

danger of falling under the wheels. His arms moved like pinwheels, his legs were a blur of motion.

At Peterborough he blinked awake at the slamming of doors and tannoy announcements. Naomi and Bill were asleep, leaning shoulder to shoulder, head to head. Beside Michael in the window seat, Linda was reading the proofs of *Pushover*. She nodded to herself as she turned a page, lost in the story, unaware he was watching. Michael wished dreamily he could capture what he saw: absorb her form, her essence, make her part of himself, to be kept and conjured up whenever needed. But we already belong to each other, he thought. We're still alive in some way inside one another. As she traced his printed words with her fingertips, Linda's wedding ring caught the light, and Michael again closed his eyes.

This time, however, he wasn't competing with the train, he was strolling through Abbotsbridge. It was a clear, comfortably warm day with a lightly cooling breeze and the smells of cut grass and orange blossom on the air, the street sleepy and peaceful.

On Wednesday night Linda Grayson had phoned him at home, saying she needed to call a Brotherhood meeting at the ice house, though she hadn't explained why. They agreed to have it at the weekend, Sunday, when there would be time to talk properly. If she hadn't sounded so distressed he would have been thrilled that she'd thought to call him at all. Now, a few minutes early for the rendezvous, he was savouring the morning while it lasted. A perfect Sunday morning in the Riverside estate; perfect, that was, until he saw who was pelting up towards him from the cul-de-sac.

It was Quigley he saw first, then Roy Sachs. Their appearance out of nowhere was like a gun going off. They were coming at him so quickly, so unexpectedly, with such eagerly hostile faces, he lost seconds before he could think what to do. Sachs was mouthing threats and promises, obscenities, waving a fist for victory; Quigley's expression was unreadable as ever. By the time Michael wheeled around and set off they were almost within arm's reach.

The street was all uphill. On the left, the church, with

173

its vacant entrance, tempted him inside, but that would be fatal. If they trapped him in there he'd never see daylight again. He continued past it, up the rise, and three houses along dodged sharp left along a loose gravel drive.

This was a gamble. It was a longish haul to the top of the street but he might instead, with luck, shake them off between the gardens. He dashed past the house and across its back lawn, where baby clothes flapped on a washing line and a sprinkler rotated lazily. An Alpine rockery and low stone wall divided this garden from the next. Michael scrambled up the rockery, at the same time slinging his bag over his shoulder for convenience. The dry summer soil flaked away underfoot as he went, the bag thumping the top of his back like a lazy second head. He didn't look back, but behind him the air carried breathless chants of '*Bastard ... get you ... this time ...*'

Then he was over the wall and across the next lawn while Sachs was still tackling the rockery. As far he could see there were no killer dogs standing guard and there was daylight ahead: the next street. He flung himself towards it, not knowing where he was going, not slowing until he reached a miniature roundabout around which the estate roads fanned out in five directions.

Faced with so many choices he felt cornered, unable to think. All the roads looked the same. If he hesitated Sachs and Quigley would be on him, tasting blood. One backward glance and he saw Sachs come tumbling over the stone wall and into his stride across the lawn. In sheer desperation he glanced at the street names: Park View, Gunn Lane ... To his right there was one − Willow Close − that he recognised from somewhere. He was already sprinting towards it when he made the connection. The address went with a phone number he had looked up one evening before nerves stopped him dialling. Willow Close was where Linda Grayson lived.

All he had to do now was summon up the house number. As he crossed the narrow road to the Close a large stone whistled past him. Sachs was shouting something he couldn't hear for the wind at his ears − not that he needed it repeating.

174

Her house number was either 23 or 32 Willow Close, he was convinced. Which, though? Whichever was nearer, he hoped, as another projectile skimmed the back of his calf; they were gaining, he was slowing. As he turned in the gate outside 23 he saw a large soft teddy bear lolling in an upper room window as if surveying the street. It looked the kind of childhood sleeping partner Linda might have kept and treasured. It had better be. If he'd made a wrong choice –

His heart skipped a beat as he reached the front door, pounding the solid wood with both fists. Suppose no one was in? There was no sign of a family car in the spacious open-doored garage. What if Linda had done what he'd meant to, leaving early for the meeting, making the most of the weather?

He hammered again. Then, as an afterthought, lifted the letter-flap and called Linda's name, two, three times. It was too dark to see anything inside. Certainly there was no sign or sound of movement. At the periphery of his vision he saw Sachs and Quigley charging along the Close, gradually slowing as they came nearer. There was no need to hurry now; there was no answer, no one at home. Their charge was cornered and the game was up.

'*Linda*!' he cried, one last desperate time.

Then, from somewhere deep inside the house, from upstairs or behind a closed door, 'Just a *minute*, I'm coming ...'

Seconds spun out in agonising slow motion. Sachs and Quigley strolled up the Close, regaining their breath, hands in pockets. They wanted to take their time. Michael swallowed and licked his parched lips. From indoors he could hear Linda thumping haphazardly downstairs. Come *on*, please come *on*, he thought, shouldering the heavy varnished door, not daring to look behind him. Of course, Sachs and Quigley weren't near enough to hear what he heard. They were no doubt as shocked as he was relieved when the latch clicked solidly and the door eased open.

Linda saw only Michael at first. She had come straight from washing her hair, which was plastered in straggles to her forehead and cheeks. She was wearing a yellow

175

T-shirt and faded blue denim shorts, and had a bath towel draped around her shoulders. She was about to speak when Michael threw himself forward, almost knocking her down as he blundered inside.

Linda turned on him. 'Well, I *must* say! There's me on the verge of saying good day and and how goes it and inviting you in, and see how my hospitality gets thrown in my face! It's a damn good job my folks aren't here. They'd think — '

'Never mind that.' He took hold of the door and pushed it shut with a firmness that shook the building's structure. As he did so they both caught a glimpse of the twosome heading up the drive, Quigley impassive as ever, Sachs' lips contorting around fresh obscenities.

'Great,' Linda said. 'That's just great. The one thing we need right now. How did this happen?'

'You know the entrance to Parks Wood, where the path skirts around below the new church? They were coming up from there when I ... Well, I was halfway down the street before I saw them: too late to do anything but run. I'm sorry I led them right here but I didn't know where else — '

He was cut short as the door was bombarded from the other side. What sounded like a concentration of fists, feet and clubs went on for ten or fifteen seconds. Linda jumped and reached instinctively for Michael, who caught both her wrists to steady her. When the assault on the door tailed off he let go. She turned away, hugging herself.

'Let us in,' Roy Sachs pleaded through the door. Then his mouth, pinkly wet, appeared at the letter-flap. 'Please, please let us in.' His voice was pitched high in a purposely grating whine. 'You'll only make things worse for yourself if you don't.'

'Don't answer him,' Linda said. 'It's better to ignore than provoke him. Let's go through here.'

She gestured along the hall to the kitchen. Michael went ahead of her. Behind them, the crashing and banging erupted again, more protracted and intense than before. As Linda pushed the kitchen door to, the letter-flap clunked again and Sachs called, 'That's right! Hide where you think you can't be seen. Where you think I can't *reach* you.'

176

Linda glanced across the kitchen at the telephone. She leaned back against the door as if that would shut out the noise, but Sachs' voice was pervasive.

'There's no getting away from it, sooner or later you'll have to face facts. Go on, hide, lock yourselves away where no one can find you. *I'll* find you. *I'll* know what you're up to together.' He was whispering now, yet sounded nearer than before: a presence inside the kitchen, like a voice on the phone or the radio turned low. A brief burst of laughter sounded like static. 'Go on then, McCourt, we know what you *really* want from the bitch. Whip it out and put it in her hands. See if she knows what to do with it, see how she likes it when you give her the old mouth to cunt resuscitation routine. Fuck it stupid, go on, eat it, you know what she wants, we know what you're all about, all of you.'

Linda and Michael stood facing each other while Sachs went on. Linda looked near to tears; her features had tightened. She averted her eyes from his, and Michael felt the embarrassment and hurt, and wanted to hold her. But he wouldn't dare touch her now. The next thing he knew, the hurt and the fear had turned to something else: a rage in the pit of his stomach that he could only project outwards.

'Sachs, you're not going to have the last word,' he shouted at the top of his voice. 'Don't ask me how or when or where, but you're going to get *yours* too. You're going to know what this feels like, you shithead!'

There was a lull, an interval during which he began to think his words had had some effect. Then, very softly, Sachs spoke again.

'Hey, McCourt. Spitting in the wind comes back at you twice as hard. Remember that. And Linda? See you when you least expect it, whore.'

The clunk of the letter-flap. Then a time of silence and uncertainty, as if the punchline had yet to come. It took Michael a minute before he could bring himself to look at Linda again. Flushing, she forced a smile, doing her best to shrug off what she must feel. Seeing her like this, damp-haired and moist-eyed, without make-up, with a strength and poise she was struggling to maintain, filled him with loving sadness and pride. They had broken the mould when they made her. She wasn't like others; didn't need artificial means, perfume and paint, to make herself special. He recognised this; therefore she was his. And always would be. He wanted to tell her so, though he knew how ridiculous it would sound spoken aloud. Then Linda brushed past him, and the moment was gone.

'Would you like coffee?' she asked. She put two mugs ready, plugged in the kettle, spooned coffee from the jar, found milk in the fridge.

Michael watched, transfixed, by the way she performed these domestic tasks. Too briefly, he was a fly on her wall, privileged to see her as no one else in the world could.

'Do you think they'll come back?' she wondered. 'I'm going to feel bad about setting foot outside the door after this.'

Michael took a seat at the table, where a plump mound of Sunday papers waited to be read. 'If they really meant business they'd still be outside. As far as Roy Sachs is concerned, this was just something to do on a dull Sunday morning.'

'What's *wrong* with the boy, is what I'd like to know. Why is there so much hate inside him?' Linda stood watching the kettle; shivering, she rubbed her hands together. 'Where does it come from? What does he want?'

'In my case, he wants to get even.'

'Huh? Because of some silly essay? You're kidding yourself, Mike, if you think that's anything more than an excuse he's making.'

'How so?'

'Because it isn't *enough*. He wants to hurt you for that, yes, of course he does; but any run-of-the-mill school bully would have blacked your eye and had the matter settled by now. Not Roy Sachs, though, it goes deeper than that with him. There's some other reason behind what he's trying to do, as if –'

Michael waited. 'Yes?' he said.

The kettle was steaming, the window above the sink misting over. Linda poured boiling water into the mugs and brought them to the table.

'Well,' she said. Her voice was muted and hesitant, and

she was avoiding his gaze. 'It's to do with everything he said just now. Sick stuff, agreed, but there's more to it than Roy trying to shock or upset us. There's something – God knows what – some kind of sexual jealousy thing going on with him. He resents us, all of us, I swear, because we have one another and he's not included. And you and me he hates most of all because, well, I imagine he sees us as ringleaders.' She paused to let Michael take stock of this. Steam and the aroma of coffee permeated the air. After a while she said, 'Isn't it a shame how coffee always smells better than it tastes? You expect so much more. This isn't the first time Roy Sachs has talked dirty to me,' she went on. 'In fact that's the reason I'd called this meeting.'

Michael was alarmed. '*When*? When did this happen before?'

'It's been on and off for weeks now. Always by telephone.' She waved a hand at the phone on the wall. 'Lately it's reached the point where I can't face answering the damn thing when it rings. I can tell who it is before he speaks. There's a silence, a particular *kind* of silence. I hang up now straight away when I hear it . . . At first I hadn't the good sense to do that.'

'You said this began weeks ago. Why didn't you mention it before now?'

'I really don't know. Maybe at first I thought, how-ever horrible it was, it would pass. He'd give up, try someone else for size. If I'd been able to see straight at the time I would've known it was better to share the burden.'

'So while we were together, laughing and joking, you were keeping all this to yourself? Every time we met at the ice-house? That rainy Saturday afternoon watching *King's Row* and drinking beer? You were dealing with this in private?'

Linda nodded and nursed her mug in both hands. 'There were times when he didn't call for days and I began to think it was finished. I'd even run to the phone when it rang, not thinking about him. Then I'd hear the silence, and that would set off the alarm bells again. Besides, I

179

couldn't be sure who was calling. I couldn't be certain it was Roy Sachs. Not until today.'

'You didn't recognise his voice on the phone?'

'Well, yes and no. I had my suspicions but ... It was almost like now: there was something else in his voice when he whispered, like another part of him, another personality.' She shook her head, twitched her hands in bewilderment. 'Which sounds like lunacy, right? Here's someone we *know* is a bastard through and through. It reads all the way through him, like Blackpool rock. No one I know would claim to have found any redeeming features there. But, Mike, there's something even worse underneath. That's what we heard, and that's what scares me − the idea that all that hatred doesn't know when to stop.'

Michael contemplated his coffee. 'You make it sound like − like he really wants blood. *Our* blood.' Linda regarded him levelly but said nothing. 'Like he won't be satisfied with anything less.'

'That's what I feel. When you've heard the silence, and the things he has to say, when you've listened and he's put these godawful thoughts in your head, you just *know*.' There was a pause. Then she said, 'What are we going to do, Mike?'

For a moment he seemed to be drifting, not seeing her. Then he snapped to attention, brought her back into focus. 'You know what we are? The Brotherhood, whatever you want to call us? We're a body, that's what. Four limbs, one head and one heart. We look after ourselves, we're self-reliant, and none of us can drop out without being noticed. We're stronger together than apart − we can do things together we couldn't ever do alone − and that's the whole point, that's what he wants to take away from us. But it's also how we're going to stand up to him. If he calls you on the phone, we're *all* involved, we're *all* under fire. It's our problem too. We'll share the burdens, not keep them bottled up inside; we'll ... Why are you looking at me that way?'

There was something dawning in her eyes as he talked, like a light coming on, a light suddenly blossoming with colours, that had stopped him from continuing.

'What?' he said, and Linda smiled.

180

'I love to hear you talk like that,' she said. 'You really are a wordman.'

'Better than a birdman.'

They exchanged a long, fond look across the table until the air itself seemed to shimmer and the wall-clock chimed one o'clock. That released them; and at last, a little reluctantly, Linda pushed back her chair and stood up.

'God, the meeting,' she said. 'The others will be there by now. We'd better not keep them waiting. I'll just get the dog in first.' She opened the back door, called for Tara, and waited. When there was no response she shrugged it off. 'Trust her. She'd spend all her days in the woods if we'd let her. Come on, Mike. You can bet she'll be waiting for us there.'

Chapter Twenty-One

The train was nearing Grantham when Linda looked up from the proofs, cleared her throat and gave Michael a nudge. He jumped out of his reverie with a start.

'Sorry. Were you dozing? It's just that this is so close to the bone, it brings so much back. The scene where they string what's-his-name, Shaun, up by his ankles in the gym and leave him there, and then later the staff discover him. The way you've caught the villain, for want of a better word. It makes you feel you're reliving it all.'

'Don't read on if it bothers you. I'll understand why.'

'No, I want to. I can see how you must have gone through the mill, making yourself face it again. Doesn't it hurt to do that, day after day?'

'That's the nature of the game.' Michael gave a wan smile. 'Besides which, it's the only way I know how to make a buck.'

'There are easier ways to do that, aren't there? You don't have to expose yourself like this.' She patted the wad of proofs. 'Give so much of yourself away.'

'But I do,' Michael said. 'It's a case of having no say on the matter. The subject chooses me, not the other way around — it's a case of being haunted until the spirit's properly exorcised. See this?' He began rooting through his flight bag until he located the artists's rough: the hanged man and gallows chalked on a blackboard. 'It doesn't make me feel better to see the image conjured up again, but it's the right one for this book. The story's incomplete without it.'

Linda shook her head at the rough, as if it were too much to behold. 'To think this was written, and this was sketched, weeks, even months before Vinnie caught up with you . . .'

'Yes, exactly. The further we are from it in time, the nearer we are to it in other ways.'

The train was slowing for Grantham. On the intercom the guard was announcing arrival times for Doncaster, Wakefield, Leeds.

'And now look where we are,' Linda said.

Almost there, is where, Michael thought. Almost back at the moment in time that changed everything, a moment we've spent all our lives regretting, re-writing in our heads and in books to no avail.

At his desk he had learned how easy it was to make the wrong turn, to plot a chosen course and divert from it, thus ruining everything that lay ahead. He had discovered how great a difference one stray detail, one deleted scene could make. Plots were houses of cards, finely stacked. Words not spoken, thoughts not given voice to, actions not taken – these were matters which shaped the story, and the world.

If only became his incantation, a key to unlock any door, give him access to any boudoir or bedsit. *If only* this happened instead of this; *if only* such and such could be avoided; *if only* X had never been born. What then?

This was fiction in the making, and this was why he fled to that world, where even chaos could be ordered and facts rearranged for convenience. In New York particularly he had seen how impossible it was to control events. The real world could not be made to measure; it did not forget or forgive. In the real world, *if only* made the difference between living in and being a fugitive.

There was something he could not re-write no matter how many times he tried: a fact that nothing could alter. In the real world there was a time and a place for everything; a moment when anyone, really anyone, was capable of murder.

He didn't feel murderous at first. He didn't, it occurred to

183

him later, feel anything much at all. The sight that met him as he led the way into the clearing that afternoon struck him numb; it was an image that seemed to belong somewhere else, in classical art, in a time-darkened painting of the crucifixion. It belonged on a gallery wall, not here. All at once his legs refused to carry him forward. He pulled up so sharply Linda, at his heel, bumped into him.

'Don't look,' Michael urged. 'Let's go back.' He turned towards her, lifting his hands to block the view.

It was seconds too late. Linda had already seen for herself. She looked stunned, deliberating whether or not to believe her eyes. Then she tried to speak, but no words came, no words that made sense, nothing more than a muttered confusion of breathless gasps. Her whole face became pinched and reddened. Slowly, absently, she lifted both hands to cover her mouth.

Across the clearing, two figures – Alison and Naomi – stood on tiptoe at the base of the oak tree from which Tara hung. They were reaching at full stretch to support the limp body as Bill gently lowered it from above. Bill sat astride the bough, guiding the rope that Vinnie was slowly unravelling and feeding upwards from the trunk. The terse grunts and groans the group made as they worked sounded like bursts of grief; perhaps they were. The muted creak of the bough, the slackening rope, the buzzing of insects in the trees: Michael, watching, felt these details burn themselves into his memory for ever.

As Tara was lowered to the ground, Bill made an utterance that didn't quite carry as far as Michael and Linda. He had spotted them, and the others were turning to look. Alison came marching across, knuckling tears from her blackened eyes, wiping her nose and mouth with the back of her hand. As soon as she came within reach of Linda they fell into each other's arms.

'Those bastards,' Alison said quietly. 'Oh, Linda, Linda, I wish I knew what to say.'

Michael looked again at the tree. Bill had now finished shinning down from the bough. For a moment he knelt beside Tara, ruffled her thick mane of hair, slowly shook his head at the senseless waste. Naomi had turned away, hugging herself, unable to look. Vinnie swayed between his feet, torn between staying where he was and crossing the clearing to Michael.

'Let's get you out of here,' Alison said quietly to Linda. 'You've seen it now. There's nothing you can do.'

Linda couldn't reply at first. She was struggling to swallow, to breathe, the tears she was suppressing almost choking her. Then she said, 'I'll stay where I am. I want – want to see her properly buried. I'm not going to leave her again.' Detaching herself from Alison, she went to where Tara was lying and fell over her.

Her cries came freely now, from somewhere deep down inside, from a part of herself she hardly even knew, a well where grief never ran dry. For minutes she lay with her head against Tara's, a hand on the spot where a heart used to beat. 'Why?' she demanded. 'What *for*? Oh Christ, Tara, where are you? Can you see what they've done?'

There was a note of anger in her voice, Michael thought. That could only be healthy; anger was positive; anger would help lift her out of this.

At long last, Linda sat up. She lifted one of Tara's forepaws, considered it for a moment, then let it flop. She wiped her eyes with a handkerchief and blew her nose. 'She was my fourth birthday present,' she said quietly. 'A pup I could hold in one hand, who peed in every room in the house. She was almost twelve, all trust and faith and love, and look at her now. Look what they've done. To a member of my *family*. Look what those bastards have *done*.'

The others surrounded her, consoling, not speaking. Naomi laid a hand on her shoulder. 'I'd like us to bury her here,' Linda sniffed, 'in this clearing near the ice-house, because then it'll mean something – not only for her, for all of us. Tara was part of us too, she wouldn't have been here otherwise. She came because we came. That's why ...' She faltered. 'That's why they did this, why *he* did this.'

She meant Roy Sachs, of course. They all understood that, but this was an escalation out of all proportion. To resent the body, to despise its members for being outside his control, was one thing. But this kind of barbarism was new and unprecedented. It could only mean –

185

'Fucking hell,' Vinnie said. 'What you're getting at is, he did this to Tara because he saw her as one of the group? Because this is how he'd like to treat all of us?'

'Chances are,' Michael said, 'as much as anything else, it's a warning.'

'A promise,' said Linda.

'Enough is enough,' Naomi said. We *know* who's responsible here. Isn't it time someone called the police?'

Linda shook her head. 'This is more than we should waste on the police. This is personal.' She was watching Michael as she spoke, and he knew from her face she was thinking about Roy Sachs' mouth at the letterbox, the phone calls, the threats that for weeks had been part of her life.

'Then what's next?' Bill was anxious. 'We take matters into our own hands?'

'She's distraught,' Alison said. 'This is no time for discussing what Linda thinks we should or shouldn't do.'

'Why not?' Linda was furious, her eyes wild, her voice raw and fragile, on the verge of shattering like glass. 'Why shouldn't he get what's coming to him? We've suffered enough from the likes of him; everyone has, for far too long, and he still isn't satisfied. It's *blood* he's after.' She flattened a hand to her breast. 'It's something inside here he can't touch that he wants. And it's high time someone – ' She stopped herself there and drew a deep breath.

Vinnie cleared his throat. There were uncertain shuffles and sniffs amongst the others; an awkward minute spun out. Then Bill said, 'Perhaps ... Well, perhaps we should talk this through later, another time. When we're clearer about what we're saying.'

Linda glanced at him sharply, then down at her hands in her lap. On top of everything else she now looked ashamed by what she had nearly said. To Michael, it felt as though catastrophe – a car crash, a fatal fall – had been narrowly averted.

'Linda,' he said. But when she looked at him he realised he had nothing to add.

'It's going to be all right,' Vinnie told her. 'We're *all* going to be all right.'

Linda nodded, playing her fingers through Tara's fur one

last time. Her bare legs and elbows were bonily white and trembling, despite the warm breeze. 'Can we put her near the ice-house?' she said.

Because Linda's house was nearest, it was agreed they would bring the necessary tools from there. They were kept, Linda said, in the shed, which was often unlocked. Michael and Bill set off while the others remained with Tara, listening as Linda described the phone calls.

'Guess what?' she said when Michael returned, pitchfork in hand. Bill was just behind him, spade slung over his shoulder like a Disneyland dwarf. 'Guess what I've just been told? Those heavy breathing routines on the telephone? I wasn't the only recipient − *or* the only one to keep it to myself.'

'Who else?' Michael said.

Naomi lifted a hand, as if pleading guilty.

'Why these two and not me?' Alison demanded. 'I'm beginning to wonder whether I shouldn't feel insulted.'

'What did he say, Nim?' Michael asked.

'More or less the same, by the sounds of it. He wanted − well, this isn't the time or place to go into it, but I'd agree with Linda − there's no doubt about who he was. And I'd say his ideas about sex, like his ideas about everything else, are pretty twisted.'

'Doesn't he realise he's forcing us together, not further apart, with these tactics?' Michael surveyed the others and saw the nods and looks of resolve. 'Even *this* isn't enough!' He indicated Tara. 'What he can't see, because he's either too fucking stupid or insensitive, is that we're unique. We belong together because we don't belong anywhere else, that's why we'll never come under his thumb. Roy Sachs is the old guard, a member of the fucking *system*. He's nothing if he's not in complete control. All he's done here is make the Brotherhood mean something more than it did. What Linda says is true: Tara was part of us, part of our body. We're going to bury ourselves with her right now, and come up fighting.'

This was Michael the wordman, the breeze in his face and hair, trying − but failing, he thought − to explain what everyone sensed deep down. The others − he could see, he could feel, he *knew* − were with him one hundred percent, even if he was overdoing it. This, he thought later, on the train between Doncaster and Wakefield, this was the stuff of swashbuckling fiction – all for one and one for all – with himself crying liberty, pitchfork in hand.

It now all seemed rather artificial. But then, with the breeze stirring leaves and drying grubby tears on Linda's cheeks, and the respectful hush throughout Parks Wood while Tara lay lifeless at the foot of the oak, it had made perfect sense. They were fifteen and very much alive, with death at their feet, and God knew what the future was about, but it was something to be fought for, grasped and held onto. Surviving was everything.

They took their time, all six of them, working a rota as the soft peaty earth was cut, dug deep, then deeper. Insects buzzed in their faces. The air became warmer, more humid. Vinnie grew scarlet and perspired, dark patches marking the armpits and back of his T-shirt. Then Tara was placed in the hole, a rectangle deep enough for a coffin. A few words were muttered and Linda dried her tears as the hole was refilled. Death lay in the ground then. The first shot had been fired and the air still resounded.

Linda gathered a handful of brushwood and scattered it over the grave to mark the place where Tara laid.

Chapter Twenty-Two

The waste land between Doncaster and Wakefield: a handful of small towns where the train didn't bother to stop, several grey miles of mineworkings, slag-heaps, allotments, scattered lights that might have been isolated houses beyond the sidings. Linda raised her eyes from the stack of proofs on her knee and caught a glimpse of herself in the window looking out at the dark swollen landscape beyond.

'Where are we?' Bill wondered, thick with sleep, heavy-lidded.

'Almost there,' she replied.

'Thought as much. Thought I could feel it. Can you?'

She could, though she couldn't explain why. She had travelled the line a thousand times on local trains without this sensation, the clear sensation of being called home, as if the train's patter, the clusters of lights, the evening itself were part of some seductive conspiracy. Jesus, she lived not so far from here. She still did her Sams stint in Abbotsbridge. It wasn't as though returning to the scene of the crime, remembering as she did so, was something she hadn't been through before. It was different this time, was all she understood. It was because they were together again.

Naomi giggled, but from nerves, and touched her lips by way of apology. Familiar landmarks − an automobile graveyard, the Double Two factory − eased past the window, and then, in the distance, the cathedral spire rose between the rooftops and evening sky. Linda frowned at Michael's proofs, unable to recall what she'd just finished reading. Her mind had emptied. The text looked mysteriously like runes holding secrets she would never unseal. When she looked up she saw Michael staring, not at her but the townscape, with fear and wonder. His wide eyes were filled with a boyishness, an openness that immediately transported her back fifteen years.

'Shall we catch the next train?' she said hopefully. 'That is, the next one to London? Then a stand-by flight to the furthest, remotest island on the globe?'

'Count me in,' Bill said, and began plucking luggage from the overhead rack. 'Anything that'll get us out of *this* shit.'

Linda's Mini was marooned in a long-stay car park not two minutes' walk from Westgate station. It had already been agreed that she would drop Bill and Michael at their hotel in town before driving Naomi home to her Abbotsbridge flat. With the four grown-up bodies and their bags crammed inside the car the windows quickly misted over. Linda tried the ignition, which needed encouragement at first. She spoke to it calmly, kindly, stroking the wheel as she did so. At the third attempt the engine responded. Linda patted the dash. 'There! The little engine that could really *can*.' As the clutch bit and she pulled out she turned to Naomi. 'Are you sure you don't want to stay over at my place, Nim? Open a bottle and see out the night through a drunken haze? There's a spare room where you can crash when you really can't take any more.'

'Really, I'd love to, but I'm ready to crash right this minute. As you know, happiness is a warm bed.'

'Party pooper.'

'Will I ever live it down?'

But Linda was yawning in sympathy as she turned into traffic. 'Well, an early night's something we all could do with. God knows what we've let ourselves in for by coming here — as if we had any choice. But we're going to need clear heads if we're to stay in control. Last night wasn't exactly the restful experience it should have been.'

'Hope you can sleep, is all,' said Michael. 'In my case, a light supper and a large Scotch or three ought to get the job done.'

'So much for clear heads,' Linda said.

'Damn right, but don't knock it. If it weren't for booze

190

I doubt very much I'd be here at all. Just one thing: don't let me get sober, folks, or you'll lose me for sure. I'll be the first one in line for that stand-by flight to nowhere.'

The hotel was a small one in St Johns, not far from the centre of town, with a bar and a restaurant that had closed more than an hour ago. The entrance hall was moodily dark, wood-panelled, smelling of silicone polish. Tiny dim electric flambeaux studded the downstairs walls. Michael and Bill approached the reception counter while Linda waited to make sure the reservations would be good one night early.

The hotel was half-empty, however. Bill collected his overnight bag and his key, pecked Linda's cheek, and started upstairs. 'Goodnight,' Linda called after him, and was almost out the door when Michael touched her elbow.

'You could stay, you know. We could all stay here tonight.'

She smiled; her eyes sparkled. 'Nim really does want her own bed tonight; she won't rest otherwise.'

'And you?'

'Well, I live so near, it seems almost . . .' She hunched her shoulders. 'Not pointless exactly, it's just that I need time to think and be clear.'

'About what?'

'Well, everything. Us. Things at home. Everything.'

Michael nodded and touched her face, hesitating briefly before kissing her. It was last night outside her room all over again, but she didn't kiss back, and withdrew before he did. 'If you change your mind you know where you'll find us,' he said, and Linda said lightly, 'Yeah, getting blitzed in the bar.'

She felt him staring after her even as she turned outside and made a beeline for the car, where Naomi sat waiting. There was an aura − of what? Desperation or sadness, perhaps − coming from him in waves. She could sense how urgently he wanted her. She wouldn't look back though, she told herself. If she saw him at the entrance, still watching, she would have to go back and to hell with every other responsibility. It still wasn't their time, not yet. She had George to consider. And Quigley: Tom Quigley, the key to it all. There was so much to deal with before she dared think of Michael.

At least Naomi would help keep her mind off him. They could gossip their way to Abbotsbridge. It was only the return journey she needed to worry about.

'Are you sure about this?' she asked, somewhere on the road out of Wakefield. Darkness had swarmed over the land out here; for several miles there was nothing before her but the Mini's dipped headlights on the road and the pattern of dead insects stippling the windscreen. 'Don't you mind being alone tonight so far from town − and so near ...' She didn't finish.

Naomi yawned at length, fingers reaching at the end of a stretch. 'Once I'm asleep I'll never notice. In any case we've all been alone for so long.'

'Yes. Even those of us who *haven't* been alone.'

'Did you ever tell George?' Naomi said.

'About us? No, I couldn't. There were times when I came very close.'

'Do you think it made any difference? Did it come between you?'

'It's hard to be sure, but I suppose it must have done. I always had this doubt that when it came to it, he wouldn't understand, wouldn't be able to. Maybe you'd have to be one of us to really know. You?'

'After two broken marriages I'd say something got in the way all right. It's bound to, isn't it, when you can't give yourself over to someone because of all you're holding back? Then again,' Naomi added on the edge of a laugh laced with bitterness, 'I doubt it would have made much difference with bastards like those.'

There was a pause. Then Linda said, 'None of us grew up to be entirely happy, did we?'

'Bill, perhaps.' Naomi shrugged. 'He seems the most settled, the closest to being there. Then again, he doesn't wear his heart on his sleeve,'

'Do you feel angry?' Linda said.

'About what? The fact that nothing worked out the way I'd hoped? Not angry, no. I'm the one who made the mistakes; I'm the one who pays.'

'The children must be some consolation.'

'Oh yes, you can't take that away from me. They're the

only damn worthwhile thing I've ever had. So sometimes good does come out of bad. The problem is − everything else.' She was wringing her hands in her lap, gazing from the window at the blackened fields. 'You should see them: Sean's fourteen, Ali's seven. I named her after *our* Alison. You really should see them, Linda. The spitting image of −' She faltered, seemed to lose herself.

'Of their father,' Linda said. 'Of their fathers.'

Naomi shook her head faintly. 'Ali is so much like me, but with Frank's colouring, the fair hair and blue eyes; Frank was my second mistake. I wonder what you'd say if you ever saw Sean, though. I wonder how you'd react.'

Linda said nothing. There was a punchline, she was certain, that Naomi would deliver any minute. What was she hinting at? Not knowing made Linda feel strangely uncomfortable. Distracted, she found herself staring into the pall of oncoming headlights too long, and her vision flared. When she blinked into darkness again, the lights were still there, imprinted behind her eyes.

As Linda slowed for a bend, Naomi fished out a cigarette and said heavily, 'There's something you ought to know that I couldn't get out in front of the others.' She seemed to be waiting for Linda to respond. Lighting her cigarette she rolled down the window.

'You know we've always been able to discuss anything with them,' Linda said. 'That's one of the things that made what we had so special.'

'Sure, I accept that. It's just that some things ... You'll know how it is. Sometimes it's easier to confess one-to-one.'

'Something about me seems to bring out the confiding instinct in people. Even teaching makes me feel like some agony aunt trapped in the wrong profession. If it isn't the students, it's the staff.'

'You were always so easy to talk to,' Naomi said fondly, then took a deep draw from her cigarette. 'I wish I could have told you about this at the time ... But that was after we'd made our pact never to communicate again.' In the dark she made a sound that might have been a laugh or a sigh. 'Crazy to think of it now, but at the time it seemed the only solution.'

193

There was a lull. Then Linda said, 'Go on.'

'I'm thinking how best to put this. You remember how it was before − before that day? How Quigley was always outside the group, not one of us, before he redeemed himself?'

'He was easily led. It wasn't easy for him to shrug off Roy Sachs. I'm sure he would've been fine if he'd mixed with the right kinds of people. But he was such a chameleon.'

'I thought so too. I recognised that at the time. He was never one of the Brotherhood, but now and again you'd catch a look from him, as if deep down he wanted to be with us, not Sachs.'

Linda waited, wondering where this was leading. On a clear stretch of road she flicked the headlights to full beam. In the distance a hare or a rabbit scurried smartly across the road for cover.

'I broke the pact,' Naomi said. 'The summer after we all left school − that was when it really came home to me that we'd never see each other again; never speak, never write. It was hardest at first, before some of you went off to colleges and other schools. It was like ... I had everyone's number fixed in my head, I knew how easy it would be to pick up the phone.

'Even after you and Mike and Alison and Bill cleared out, Vinnie was close, he never left home. Neither did Tom Quigley. In the end it was Tom I contacted; God knows what made me, unless it was because he was such an outsider, and that seemed to make him safe, almost a stranger.'

'What did you say to him?'

'Only that I'd go stark staring mad if I couldn't talk through what had happened with someone, even him. Funnily, he didn't take much persuading to see me. He said he'd been half-expecting it. We took a long summer evening walk together. Drank beer that Tom had filched earlier from some off-licence. He seemed − ' she studied the orange-glowing tip of her cigarette ' − *different* from how I remembered him. Perhaps, I thought, that was because he had the burden off his back. There was a confidence about him, almost a cockiness, I'd never seen before in Tom. At the end of the night we decided there was

194

no harm in meeting again. It kind of developed from there.'

Linda took a moment to accomodate this. '*You* and Tom Quigley? The two of you were – '

'It sounds so cynical, but yes, and not because I liked him particularly. He was available, convenient, and there were things I didn't need to explain or hold back from him. You see what I'm saying? Right then, all I needed was to feel free about what we'd been through. Tom was my way of letting go. He was also Sean's father.'

A silence of several minutes extended along the road to Abbotsbridge. Linda tried hard not to break it: she couldn't be sure what she'd say if she opened her mouth. Eventually a signpost loomed out of darkness and she slowed the Mini, indicated and turned right along an uneven track road past the fringe of Parks Wood.

'You can't be mistaken?' she said at long last.

'There was no one else,' Naomi returned. 'Not at that time. We slept together twice, and I can't really say it was anything special. I was almost seventeen, a little bit wary. Scared, I suppose. And Tom was – how can I put this? – more experienced than I'd expected him to be. He was also very demanding. He hurt me and seemed to take pleasure in that. In the dark it was easy to believe I was fucking someone other than Tom – someone who hated me, body and soul. Both times he left me feeling dirty and used, there's no need to go into details; the second time was when I came to my senses and told him there couldn't be anything more between us. Of course then there was the baby. By the time I found out, though, Tom was nowhere to be found. That was the last I ever saw or heard of him.'

'You didn't have any qualms about having the baby?'

'At first, My folks practically disowned me when they heard. They didn't throw me out but they didn't support me when I needed them to, and if anything that decided me to have it, made me more determined. I said to myself, why shouldn't I get something out of this, why shouldn't I do this for *me*? Sean was almost a year old when I met Terry, my first husband.'

The outskirts of Abbotsbridge were now within view –

the disused railway bridge, the half-constructed tower blocks, the few remaining redbrick terraces, amongst them the Samaritans' Centre. It wasn't so many days since Linda had taken these rubbled streets for granted; now the mere sight of them caused her to stiffen. Her skin felt alive, crawling with nerves as her mind crawled with unanswerable questions. They were home, and home would never − *could* never − be the same again.

'Now I see what you meant about Sean,' she said. 'I'd gasp when I saw how much like his father he was. How like Tom Quigley.'

Naomi inhaled smoke, shook her head gravely. 'You'd keel over more than gasp. You'd probably pass off what you'd seen as a trick of the light. Because Sean doesn't look much like Quigley at all, or me, or anyone else − except *him*. Don't ask me how that could be. Don't ask me what put the idea in my head; but in all this time I haven't been able to shake it.'

'Shake what? What idea?'

'That Roy Sachs was the father, not Tom.'

Chapter Twenty-Three

If Naomi said anything after that, it failed to register. Linda drove on in a daze that felt like the town's lights flaring at the edge of her vision. Naomi's brief fling with Tom Quigley was a hard act to follow – but *this*, after all they'd been through, was a patent impossibility. Images, faces, rushed at her out of the night and the past: Quigley, Roy Sachs, Naomi at fifteen; a dark-eyed child with leering lips and black hair. Not even genetic mutation, not even magic or chance . . . The road ahead rolled in and out of focus as Linda tooled through the streets. In the end she was so preoccupied that Naomi had to nudge her before she drove past the estate.

They sat in the dark, not speaking, while the engine trembled and turned over in the forecourt beneath the crumbling council high rises. Three floors above them, a figure stepped back from a window, a light went out. Elsewhere, a child cried and glass broke.

Linda sighed. 'But he *couldn't* be, could he? There's no physical way on earth he could be the father. Apart from the fact that it's Tom you were sleeping with, apart from the obvious, Nim, where *did* you get the idea?'

Naomi gave the slightest of shrugs. 'When you're carrying a child, you come to understand certain things that just can't be explained or put into words. The way you feel about what's inside you – the being *acquainted*. Even after Sean was born, there was more to it than just how he looked. I *knew* him, and he knew me. Linda, if you saw him you'd jump; but to live with him, to see his moods shift and hear the things he comes out with . . .'

'Why didn't you mention this before?' Linda asked. 'Didn't you think it had any bearing on why we're here now?'

'I don't know. It might have. But believe me, there've been times when none of this has seemed relevant at all. It's just that coming home, thinking it through, being forced to remember how everything happened ... It makes me afraid, Linda. Afraid for all of us.'

'You're not alone.'

'To think that Tom's still out there. And Roy – '

'Ssshh.'

'Are we making it happen all over again? Is that why we came back, to start a new cycle?'

'Maybe. I don't know. Maybe we have to.'

'Linda ...'

'I'm here, Nim. We all are.'

'Will you always be there, though, when I need you?'

Linda said nothing, but offered her hands. They exchanged a long, firm hug while the night closed in, cheeks touching, breath faltering, parting almost reluctantly, as if the embrace might allow the threat time to pass. But it hadn't passed yet: not in all these years. They were holding on now in weakness, with all they had left.

At last Linda said, 'You're going to be all right until tomorrow? You still want to spend the night here?'

'Yes.'

'Tomorrow we'll talk. Call me. Or call Mike or Bill at the hotel.' As an afterthought she added, 'We'll take bread and wine to the park, if the weather's fine.'

'Yeah, I'd like that.' Naomi began easing herself from the car. 'That could be just what I need.'

'See you tomorrow, then.'

'Tomorrow.'

Linda remained poised over the steering wheel, watching while Naomi marched away towards the flats. The forecourt was well lit, but at a distance of twenty paces Naomi became no more than a featureless shape with a shadow several times her own size. Near the entrance to her block she stopped, turned, and waved vigorously at Linda before continuing. It was a moment like any other, fond and sad and unresolved;

198

but like memories of all the best and worst moments, the farewell was instantly fixed in Linda's mind. She couldn't be certain why. When Naomi disappeared from view, Linda released the handbrake and eased the Mini forward, suddenly anxious to put Abbotsbridge far behind her.

Tomorrow would take care of itself, she thought, somewhere on the road back to Wakefield. Until then she didn't want to consider the implications of what she'd just learned; not least because the more she deliberated, the more convoluted things seemed. Clarity was vital now, and there was precious little chance of that if she followed the course she most wanted to take – returning to the hotel and Michael. No, first she needed to feel at ease with herself. George would be wondering about her, possibly calling the Heartland in London. There was so much to deal with, at home and in her heart.

Half an hour later she was turning up the drive and through the open door of the double garage. George's Sierra was parked and silent; the housing estate slumbered in an amber haze. At the front door, key poised in the lock, Linda stopped and listened. There was nothing to hear, but the silence was such that the day's events – her very thoughts – had become trapped between her ears, like tinnitus. Her legs ached, her shoulders and back felt clenched with tension. Anticipating hot running water and clean sheets, she unlocked the door and stepped in.

The hall was warmly welcoming, with a lingering smell of Italian cuisine. She could hear George pottering in the kitchen, opening and closing the fridge, padding about barefooted. He was probably tidying up before taking an early night. Suddenly she was glad to be home, to be hearing and smelling this familiar domesticity. Removing her coat, Linda passed down the hall to the kitchen door and pushed it aside.

It was Sonia, not George, who spun round to greet her. Linda stopped dead in her tracks. Sonia's first expression was playful, mischievous, as if she thought she had caught George creeping up behind her. Then she saw Linda, and the muscles of her face seemed to sag. She raised a hand to her lips and the robe she was wearing – Linda's robe –

199

fell open. To Linda a full minute seemed to pass before she made sense of what she was seeing; it was longer still before Sonia managed to fumble her even-tanned belly and tawny pubic bush out of sight as she struggled to close the robe. In the sink was a heap of dirty pans, on the kitchen table, an unopened bottle of Laurent Perrier Rosé; beside it two glasses. Sonia stared fixedly at the table in an effort to avoid Linda's eyes.

'Whose idea was the champagne?' Linda said. 'Yours or his?' At the moment she could think of nothing more constructive, more direct, to ask. The shock of finding Sonia here had numbed her.

'George picked it up,' Sonia said. Now she was studying the floor at her feet; even her feet looked tanned. 'It wasn't entirely his idea.'

'It was yours, then.'

'Well ...'

'That's something, at least.' Linda rested against the door-jamb, arms folded, blocking Sonia's way. Let her try to make an escape, squirm her way out of this! 'Then whose idea was it to use my bed?'

Sonia managed to raise her chin defiantly, though her gaze still avoided Linda's. 'We didn't. We – George suggested the spare room.'

'Oh. The spare room. That was considerate.' Linda fought to swallow as a hard painful lump blocked her throat. 'Good old George, doing his best to spare my feelings.'

She had barely finished speaking when she heard the soft tread on the stairs behind her. Turning to look back along the hall, she saw George rounding the foot of the stairs. He must have been drawn by Linda's voice; he didn't look particularly surprised to see her. He was wearing white boxer shorts and nothing else. A penetrative smell of aftershave accompanied him. The pale skin of his chest and stomach looked reddened; by Sonia's hands, Sonia's mouth. About halfway along the hall, he stopped and cleared his throat.

'I suppose you'll expect me to say I can explain this, and it isn't what it appears.'

'I don't expect you to say anything.' She was doing her utmost to keep her voice low, to keep in the anger and hurt

200

that threatened to rise from her heart in a wave. 'The less you say now, the better.'

'You're early,' he said. 'You're not supposed to be back until tomorrow.'

'Evidently.'

'Can I?' Sonia muttered as she tried to edge past Linda at the door. She sounded desperate, almost tearful. Linda stepped aside to let her pass. 'Better get dressed,' Sonia said, looking down, not looking back, as she fled along the hall and upstairs.

'We'd better talk,' George said quietly.

'Damn right, but not now.' She doubted she'd maintain her composure much longer. 'There's a *lot* to discuss, but I haven't the strength or the inclination tonight.' She started along the hall towards him, suddenly aware that she still clutched the front door key in her hand, held it so tightly her fingers felt welded to it. For an instant she was sorely tempted to jab it towards George's face, but he looked so pathetic, so stranded, she instead strode past him to the door.

'It wouldn't be so bad if you didn't take my comings and goings for granted,' she said. 'But *this*, George, it's so grab-what-you-can-when-you-can obvious I'm amazed she has any respect for you.'

'I think she's in love with me,' he admitted through a sigh, as if that was the worst news of all, a burden he was forced to bear. 'I'm not so sure she respects me.'

'Jesus wept, it's love now! As if I haven't already seen and heard enough for one night. And you − do you love *her*, George?'

But she didn't wait to hear his reply. She was outside in seconds with the door slamming behind her, the whining between her ears like a distant siren. She stood on the doorstep, inhaling, exhaling, until the threat of dizziness passed. She wanted to scream, but who would care? Who out there would understand?

The emotional blockage in her chest and throat was unbearably painful as she reversed the Mini, glanced once at the house and accelerated away through the estate. She knew it would be easy − because she had been through this before − to release the hurt through tears and screams, mollify herself for a short while; but of course that was no solution. The thing was not to cry, not to submit. In her heart of hearts she had always given George one more chance, but something had silently snapped in her now, something she only partly understood. To get on, to make things work as they must, it was sometimes necessary not to feel anything, to discipline oneself not to feel.

As she sped from Park View she wound down her window to let in the air and keep herself fully alert. She junctioned left, then right, not caring where she drove. Her eyes burned, her throat worked as she strained to hold back the tears. She was free to go anywhere, do anything. The world was her ashtray. She needed to stay awake, almost as badly as she needed to sleep. Most of all she needed to let herself go, let everything inside herself go, but how she did that depended on where she was heading, and just now she considered herself lost.

Chapter Twenty-Four

The first thing Michael saw on retiring and switching on the colour TV in his room was a black and white still of Alison Lester. He turned up the volume until someone in the next room began pounding the wall, lowered it slightly, then perched on the edge of his bed to watch.

The news report had already assumed a clear connection between Alison's death in London and Vinnie's in Stanley, Wakefield. A police source was quoted as saying there were reasons to treat the two murders as linked, in style at least. In reference to the killings, words like 'sadistic' and 'gratuitous' were bandied about without qualification. There were no graphic details and, as yet, no proven links between the victims.

The report concluded, he switched off the TV, overwhelmed by a feeling of crushing inevitability which swallowed his every thought, which cast the spectre of Parks Wood and September rain over everything. His mind racing – one more nightcap downstairs would have helped – he hauled himself back on the bed, kicking off his shoes as he did so. One thumped harmlessly to the floor, the other ricocheted off the wall where, after a beat, the irate pounding recommenced.

'Fuck you too,' he murmured, closing his eyes.

Some time later, the hammering brought him back from the verge of a sleep he desperately wanted to dissolve into. It took him a moment to recover his senses; another half-minute to realise that a small, fragile knock had roused him, not the pounding next door.

He managed to sit up, throw his legs out of bed, grope for the bedside light-switch. As he did so the knock at his door repeated itself; three slight, timid taps. Knuckling his eyes, he shuffled to the door.

'Just a minute! Just coming.'

When he'd fumbled the door open he saw Linda, looking as dishevelled as he felt. Michael glanced at her twice to make sure he wasn't hallucinating. There was a darkness about her complexion, as though she'd been crying or was about to begin, and something in her manner − a helplessness, a silent pleading − that made him want to reach out for her at once.

'Mind if I come in?' she said softly.

Closing the door after her he leaned back against it while Linda removed her coat and flung it on the nearest chair. She hadn't changed since the journey from London, and was still wearing her white crochet sweater and cropped khaki trousers.

'Is there anything to drink here?' she wondered, surveying the room.

'Not here. Downstairs at the bar, though. They'll be open for a while yet.'

'Later, then. It'll keep. I ...' She spun round, gesturing at the furnishings. 'Nice room. Not spacious exactly, not quite to American standard, but cosy.'

'Linda, what's wrong?'

'Wrong? Nothing's *wrong*. I just changed my mind, that's all. Is there a law against that?'

She stood, slack-limbed, hands at her sides, forcing herself not to look at him. The room seemed to swim out of focus for a second. Then their eyes met, and hers were alive, all water and light, and her lips formed the faintest of smiles.

'Did you go home?' he asked. 'Is there something you want to talk about?'

Linda shook her head and stepped nearer. Michael, like a mirror image, advanced towards her. Something in his stomach slowly tightened as he did.

'Do you remember the time we lolled around drinking beer and watching *King's Row*?' she said.

'Sure, the afternoon it was raining. And Vinnie couldn't

204

make it. We drank beer and howled at the screen. Ronald Reagan lost both his legs and screamed – '

'Where's the rest of me?'

'Sure, I remember it well.'

She nodded. 'Me too.'

'Why?'

'That was the first time I remember really *seeing* you; you follow my drift – looking at you and feeling ...' She pressed a hand to her stomach and shivered, visibly glowing. ' – *You* know.'

'Horny?'

Linda laughed drily. 'Realising I had quite a crush on you, and liking it, liking the way it made me feel.'

Michael reached absently for her face. She was just within range, and he let his fingers skirt across her cheek and beneath her chin, framing her jawline, absorbing her. The air, he realised, had turned electric in an instant. In Linda's eyes he saw reflected the charge he could feel in his bones, at his nerve-ends.

'Does it still feel like that?' he asked, and she nodded and broadened her smile. 'Remember how we used to gaze at each other in class and look away with embarrassment?'

'Mmmm. Silly us.'

'To think, if things had been different, it would never have gone any further. Just mooning and moping.' He sighed. They drew closer. 'And now look.'

'Just look.'

'How are we able to talk like this now, tonight, when everything – '

'Sometimes it's better not to think,' she said. 'Sometimes it's better just to do.'

The next thing he knew, the next thing that mattered, they were together, cheek to cheek, and the weight and warmth of her against him was a relevation he was forced to remind himself was real. Suddenly all the things he'd wanted to discuss when the time came – George, especially – were irrelevant. So was whatever change of heart had brought her here tonight. In fifteen years he had only been able to imagine this physical closeness; now he could feel her breath leaving her body, moistening his neck, her softness rising and falling against him. He wanted to pause now and describe what he felt, this jumble, to etch the moment in words. But Linda managed that first.

'Jesus, it's been a long time,' she said.

Her face was inclined towards his, eyes closed, lips fractionally parted. He kissed her cheeks first, a dab here, a dab there like touches of colour, then allowed the tip of his tongue to seek out her lips, her teeth, her own tongue flicking a moist welcome. Briefly he drew back, caught the glazed look of abandon in her half-conscious eyes, and kissed her again.

All these years, he thought; all the secret messages couched in sentences and paragraphs, written and published and sent out to find her, wherever she was. All the secret messages of love. This time the embrace was so forceful he was helpless to prevent her from stumbling backwards as he pressed himself closer. Linda held on, dragging him with her, laughing through the kiss until he was laughing too and their mouths were apart, joined wetly, and her hips jarred into the dresser. The oval mirror tilted; some object − a glass or a tea mug − skittled over and fell harmlessly to the carpet.

'Wait,' Linda said. Already her face looked pinkly smudged. She took a quick breath. 'For Chrissakes, let's do this properly.'

Yes, he thought; please let's, he thought. The room was gyrating, and with it, the hotel, the world outside, Tom Quigley, the threat that had manoeuvered them into this moment. Everything was out of focus: everything except Linda, lifting her arms, sweeping her sweater over her head. She cast it aside and looked at him, half-questioning. She stepped from her shoes and her trousers to stand in white briefs and a peach-pink camisole top.

'You should see your face,' she said lightly. 'Your jaw just hit the floor.'

'You don't shave your armpits,' he said. 'Why does that drive me wild?'

She shrugged. 'That's your problem, boy, not mine.'

Not daring to take his eyes from her, Michael began to undress: shirt, trousers, socks, pants, These he cast

206

randomly, almost frantically, aside. After a moment he reached for her hand, edging her with him towards the bed. As they went she let her free hand slowly descend his chest, his belly, to enclose his rising penis.

'Hello,' she said quietly.

Michael caught his breath, then relaxed. Even now he was searching for something to say – something poignant, a phrase they might both remember and quote to each other in future times. Again the author's need for words at all times passed, and Linda was beside him on the bed, with the sheets drawn half over them and her hand gently stroking his hardness.

'You want the light on or off?' he said.

'On. I want to be able to see your face.'

'Yours is beautiful,' he whispered.

'Yours too.'

'Remember the time we – '

'Ssshh,' she said, straddling him, drawing each of his hands in turn towards her face, taking each separate finger into her mouth. He felt the gentle pressure of her teeth and tongue. He loved the sound her lips made. Then he was allowed to touch her, his fingertips tracing the contours of her face, shoulders, her conical breasts through the silk top. Her nipples hardened quickly at his touch. With growing urgency he forced the top upwards to her throat. There was a small brown birthmark the shape of a pear beneath her left breast; a fine dark hair about half an inch long grew from the nipple. These were the things that made her real to him, a personality: far more than a body.

There was a lull; a silence. Michael felt the first warm caress of pressure from above as Linda eased herself downwards, over him, onto him.

'You're wet,' he said.

'Mmmm. And willing.' She eased herself up again, down again.

'Don't stop that. Don't ever stop.'

'Not for the next fifteen years.'

'And after that? Is that all I'm good for?'

'We'll have to see how you stand up to the punishment.'

'Remember the time we ...?' he began to say, then let it

207

ride as Linda put a finger to his lips, stroked his chest. They could talk about future and past times in a while, throughout the night; not now.

Suddenly he was inside her. Michael sensed Linda's breath give for a second; she arched her back and he let his hands retrace their course down her ribcage, her hips, to enclose the rounds of her thighs.

'Got you,' she said.

'Where you want me?'

'Where I always, always wanted you.'

Something in her tone, her expression, the feel and lightly scented smell of her exploded in him them, and he lurched upwards, into her, fully and almost violently, at the same time dragging her aside and over and onto her back. Linda gasped, half laughing, half sobbing. The headboard creaked, thumped the wall. He was still inside her, and her hips willed him deeper, as deep as he could physically go. Her fingers scraped his shoulders and back, seized fistfuls of hair. They were moving and breathing together, first in slow, then quickening time, adjusting to each other, perfectly synchronised.

For a matter of seconds he was aware of almost nothing, his mind blank, his body alive with pure feeling. He was joined to her, part of her, physically inseparable from her now. With each successive thrust he sensed her response, the ebbing and flowing, the sigh of breath. He could feel how wet she was inside, how aroused and alive and in need, but he mustn't dwell on that; it would be over too soon if he did.

Then he lost sight of her: there was a point, as always, when he no longer knew the woman or what she meant to him, why her legs were enfolding him, why her body rocked in sympathy with his or her voice stroked and soothed him.

Her sobs and sighs brought him back to himself. Through dazzled eyes he glimpsed her face, Linda's face, and realised this must be her, the same Linda, after all. Lacking signs of strain and stress, she was almost unrecognisable; her lips were parted, her eyes still half-closed. She was everything he wanted. Yes, this was Linda — *really* her — and she was his, and she wanted this as much as he did, and knowing that was too much, so much that he came while still lost in her eyes, with a numberless succession of uncontrollable stabs, like the stabs of a blade, like a sheer gleaming blade that cut deeper and deeper, until he lost sight of everything.

At length he returned to himself and she was calmly nibbling his shoulder and stroking the nape of his neck. Her breath was slowing: 'Was it good?' she asked. When he tried to move he realised his body was gummed naturally to hers. He gave in, subsided over her, gasping. 'Was it good?' she repeated sleepily, and he felt himself shrink and then the inevitable small comic plop as he withdrew from her.

Perhaps ten minutes elapsed before anything more was said. Then Linda announced, in a new tone of voice, 'I've used you. I'm sorry.'

'That's all right. I used you too.'

'No, I mean . . . This was what I wanted. But it was also to punish George.'

'You shouldn't let him off so lightly.'

'I'm serious, Michael.' She sounded it. 'This is rotten of me. It should've been just for *us*.'

'Well, it was, in a way.' At last he rolled clear of her, fixing her gaze across the pillow. 'Wasn't it?'

They lay, face to face, fingers and legs interlaced. Occasionally they kissed, lightly, and smiled and compared hand spans, palm to palm. The room, the hotel seemed to settle around them. 'Do you smell that?' Linda said after a while, and Michael said, 'Mmmm, I think so.'

'That's us,' she said. 'That's the smell of us together, the smell we make.'

'Better get used to it, then.'

'Dare we?' She added sadly, 'George doesn't know who I am. Not the way you do. After all our time together he still doesn't know who I am.'

'Ssshh.' He touched her lips with a finger.

'Ssshh yourself, McCourt.' She sought out his penis, angry again already. 'You're supposed to be keeping my mind *off* all that stuff.'

'Suit yourself. Just show me how.'

Later, they drifted in and out of sleep. More than once

209

Michael woke with the weight of Linda's head against his chest. The night passed slowly, morning appeared through a crack in the curtains.

The telephone rang. Drugged and spent, Michael buried his face in the pillow and willed it to stop, but was vaguely aware of Linda lifting the receiver. Her voice was a low murmur, and he couldn't make out the words; didn't care. There was a dream closing over him, a dream in which he and Linda and possibly the others were the chief protagonists: perhaps not so much a dream as a distortion of reality, of the truth. In any case he was letting it happen, he wanted to see what secret the dream contained, and he hardly registered Linda's parting kiss as she eased herself from the bed and began to dress.

Chapter Twenty-five

Halfway across the forecourt, Naomi stopped and turned to wave at the waiting car. Although the area in front of the flats was well lit she couldn't see anything inside the Mini; if Linda waved back, Naomi never knew. Continuing indoors she heard, behind her, the Mini manoevering, pulling out, and her heart lurched. Suddenly she wanted to run, flailing her arms until Linda noticed; she wanted to catch up, jump in, drive from this place forever. She turned back again, but the vehicle's taillights were already shrinking away from her along the main road.

She was home, trapped where she belonged. Linda had offered her an escape route and instead she'd chosen this prison, this urban hell, in which three suicides had taken place already this year: no wonder.

But what choice did she really have? Hadn't they all, in their own ways, faced one kind or another of solitary confinement since that day – a day when rain fell from a clear September sky? Even Michael, buoyed by success; even Linda. That was the awful truth which had dawned on her, seeing everyone together again; no one had really survived, no one slept peacefully these nights. She wasn't the only outsider, nor the only one whose life story seemed a mess, a drab soap opera. Perhaps she needed isolation tonight to be clear about what it meant for the body to be together again. Was there a slim hope the spell could be broken now, the curse lifted? If this was the start of a new cycle, could they make it work this time – could they make it permanent?

The tiled floors, the bare scrawled-on walls, the echo of her heels climbing the cool concrete stairs. How many more times? It had to end; not just this grey existence but the emptiness filled with fear. At times, up there on the third level, the screams of unwanted children down here on the stairwell had seemed to emanate from inside her head. Tonight, the vacant stairwell made the whole building feel deserted, her footsteps the steps of an intruder. Almost half the lightbulbs on the stairs were out. It was cold here too, as if windows and doors were wide open all through the place. By the time she reached her door her fingers were so numb she could barely hold her key.

Was it too late for second thoughts? Shouldn't she be making the most of Linda's company tonight instead of brooding alone in bed? Perhaps she'd call Linda later; a friendly voice on the phone might be all the reassurance she needed. Shouldering the door open − it had a tendency to stick − she stepped inside.

As soon as the door was closed after her she could tell how much cooler her flat was than the stairs she'd just climbed. More than cold: freezing. It stole her breath. The place was not well insulated, but this was ridiculous; it felt less like the place she called home than −

She stopped, a hand at the light switch, the flat in total darkness before her. There was something too familiar in the dark, in the cold, perhaps in a scent or an atmosphere she sensed. She put on the light, and the lounge with its spartan furnishings was almost a shock to her. Why, for an instant, had she expected to see something else? − the bare stone walls inside the ice house, the chalked hanged man, a white-fingered hand beginning its slow trajectory towards her face?

Naomi, shuddering, hurried to put on the gas fire. It was the cold air that brought the image swimming back: that, and the exhaustion she felt throughout her body. Now, from the centre of the room, she detected a draught. The source seemed to be the kitchen, where a gale was blowing, by the feel of it. No wonder the flat felt like a crypt if she'd left a window wide open while away. It was a wonder no one had broken in. She was passing the

212

bedroom, which adjoined the lounge, when she realised that someone had.

Unless she was wildly mistaken, the someone was reclining in there, on her bed. The door was half open, and from where she'd paused she could just distinguish the prone shape atop the sheets. As she watched, the figure – a man's, she was certain – turned sleepily over on its side, then began to ease itself upright. Heart racing, Naomi took a step nearer the threshold. Any further and she'd never have time to escape. She ought to be running right now, not loitering, but her need to identify the face was overpowering.

It was a dream, she thought; a dream without danger, without reason, and until her curiosity was satisfied she couldn't even begin to feel afraid. And here it came – the revelation. As the figure rose to a sitting position, his face broke the column of light from the open door. He seemed to be still half-asleep, his eyes unclosed, both arms stretching. Then he blinked and saw Naomi, and smiled.

As he did so, she heard herself gasp. The man's features seemed to contort for a second, struggling to rearrange themselves, to assemble an identity. *Roy*, she thought. Oh, Jesus. But the long jaw and bovine eyes and dishevelled hair couldn't have been his. Rising shirtless from the bed, rubbing his face awake, Tom Quigley gathered up his clothes and came stumbling towards her.

Naomi drew back as he did, casting one anxious glance at the telephone on its table beside the TV. Tom kept his distance, however. His smile had broadened, and she saw his gleaming lips and unclean teeth and marvelled that she'd ever suspected him – or, for that matter, slept with him. He was such an imbecile, what harm could he do? Time hadn't changed him; if anything he'd regressed. She watched him dress – first the shirt, then the parka, so heavy it made his shoulders sag. She could run from him easily, he was so ungainly, but she no longer felt that she needed to.

'Haven't you anything to say for yourself?' he asked, still beaming. 'After all this time?'

'I was about to ask you that,' she said.

'But I asked first.'

'I've been looking – we've *all* been looking for you.'

'And now you've found me.'

'But I didn't expect it would be like this. Maybe I should ask what you're doing here.'

'What I'm doing?'

'How you found me.'

Tom shrugged and gestured towards the phone. 'You're in the book like everyone else. Even without your maiden name you were easy enough to trace. You haven't exactly gone to ground, have you?'

'No.' She regarded him levelly. 'Unlike you. We saw where you were living in London. *How* you were living. Like a rat amongst garbage.'

Quigley's inscrutable smile was fading. 'Times are hard. Sometimes you have to make the best of a bad lot.'

'Is that what you had?'

'The worst, Nim, the fucking worst.'

'Really? And what do you suppose *I* was left with?'

She sat on a chair-arm, arms folded, back straight as a board, while Quigley idled on the couch. As he shifted his jacket clanked metallically. He stared at her, then at Sean and Ali's photographs on the TV.

'That's strange,' he said.

'What is?'

'Is that your boy? He looks so – '

'Yes, he does, doesn't he? Why do you suppose that is?'

Quigley shrugged.

'Why did you disappear?' Naomi asked. 'You had what you wanted, then threw me away. When I came looking you weren't there. You were such an irresponsible louse, Tom, you didn't think about anyone but – ' She stopped herself there, before she began ranting.

Quigley sat forward, his features concentrated to a point. There was a silence before he said, 'Whatever happened then, I'll apologise for now. Whatever you think of me – things aren't always what they seem. They weren't then, I mean. I didn't just run out because I didn't care. I had to disappear before I . . .' His eyes were glazed, his lips puckering, as if the effort of speaking was almost too much. His gaze was on the photo of Sean as he finished. 'I got out before I could hurt you.'

Naomi waited, swallowed drily. An image came to mind: of herself, in a tangle of bedsheets in a darkened room, nursing her aches and pains as Tom rolled away from her. She was sixteen years old. She could smell, almost taste his stale breath, his sweat. Her breasts were so sore they felt bruised, lacerated. There were tiny dull sore points in all the places he had bitten her, and worse, a deep-seated pressure in her ribs where his fist had struck.

'If memory serves, you hurt me anyway.' She was watching him critically; now he'd reverted to the old, dull, expressionless look she loathed. 'That was the only way you liked it. Maybe it was the only way you could get it up.'

'It wasn't me! That wasn't my way.' Now he was aggrieved, offended. 'You can't understand what I was going through. If I'd hurt you the way I thought I might have to, that would've been much, much worse than −'

'What do you mean, it wasn't *you*? If you didn't hurt me, who did?'

'It was hard after what we'd all seen and done,' he said. 'There were times when I − I forgot who I was. Lost control of everything.'

'Yeah, Tom, I follow. *You* weren't responsible, just your body.'

He looked at her, slighted. He seemed to be grappling with some private, intractable problem. His facial muscles seemed to be trying to shift their expression again, which for some reason made her remember his gift of mimicry.

'Why London?' she said. 'What on earth sent you there? Living like *that*, like some animal?'

'I could lose myself there. It was easy to blend in without being noticed. I thought that would help postpone the day.'

She scowled at him. 'Day? What day? What are you talking about?'

'You know. The day of judement. You all know about it; you've all felt it coming. Otherwise why were you looking for me?'

'Because,' she began − but Quigley was right. That *was* why they had needed to locate him. 'You were the missing link, the only one who could explain what happened to Alison and Vinnie.'

'Is that what you think? You're trying to make me responsible for them?'

'Aren't you?' She waited a moment, but Quigley was silent. 'If you aren't, who is?'

'I think you know,' he said, and at once his gaze darkened, became someone else's. 'Deep down, I think you've all known all along.'

This time it was Naomi who fell silent. A moment ago she'd been in control here; now she was less confident. In an instant, Quigley had changed his manner and tone of voice, and her flesh crawled with coldness again. The gas fire hissed, but she sensed no warmth from it. And the building sounded unusually empty: suddenly there were no arguing voices or blaring TVs.

'Why would I – me – Tom Quigley – want to do what was done to them?' Quigley protested, at the same time pummelling his chest with a fist. 'What would possess me to obliterate their faces, carve up their bodies? Don't think I don't know what they looked like when it was over. Don't think I don't know about that.'

'But how *would* you know, Tom? Who told you? You didn't learn that from the papers.' She tried not to glance at the door as she stood. In spite of herself she must appear casual, unwary. If she'd misjudged him she needed to move before he could react. Half a dozen paces would do it. She said, 'At the place where you'd stayed in London, we saw the collection of magazines. And the books; Michael's books. We saw what had been done to the pages.'

'Oh? And what did that tell you?'

'That only someone completely obsessed could do a thing like that. Someone must have been *living* for revenge, just marking time until – '

'Until?'

'Well, until – judgement day.'

'Yeah, that sounds about right.' Quigley grinned. Now he was up on his feet also. Naomi edged slightly towards the door, readying herself to run if she had to. 'Yeah, I'd say someone was marking time. But not me, not Tom Quigley, you're all wrong about that.'

'Then who, Tom? Who?'

216

'Really, Nim, who do you think? Be serious now.'

'Not Roy. You can't mean Roy –'

'Why not?' he replied, Roy Sachs replied, for it was Sachs' leer that greeted her now. The suddenness of the transformation froze her where she was, delayed her dash for the door by seconds – long enough for Quigley to reach inside his jacket, drag out whichever instrument he touched first, then flash it towards her face.

It was a knife of some sort, travelling too fast for her to see clearly. Instinctively she put out a hand, her left, then gasped at the illusion he'd conjured: as the blade came down between the third and fourth fingers, the flesh parted like butter halfway to the heel of her hand.

Naomi yelped, not yet from pain but the sheer shock of the vision. But this was no vision – she realised that as soon as the blood showed. So much blood, at first a thin trickle, then a growing, endless stream. She tried to cry out, make herself heard, but her breath was sucked inwards and no sound came.

For a moment the man with Quigley's body and Roy Sachs' features stood watching her, saying nothing. His head was cocked to one side, like a dog, she thought, a dog that was captivated by a sound or scent. There was a faint, almost rueful smile on his lips, as if he regretted what he'd done. For some reason she imagined he was about to apologise when, casually, he retrieved the heavy cook's knife from the wedge he'd made in her hand and brought it angling down across her face.

Naomi reeled backwards, knocking aside a standing lamp as she went. There was no pain yet, only cold and numbness. The room was swirling. Even now she was much less afraid than disorientated. Who was this murderer and why had he singled her out? Of course she knew the answer, perhaps always had; perhaps that was why life had been such a grey drudge all these years. What was happening to her now had always been inevitable. She'd waited out her life for punishment, just as Sachs had waited out his for revenge.

Now, with all her resolve, she flung herself towards the door, yanked the handle with one hand, flat-palmed the wall beside it with the other. The door stuck, refusing to budge.

217

As Quigley took her under both arms to drag her further back inside the room she saw the smeared red hand-print she'd left on the wall. From a distance it looked decorative, as if painted there, a cheap design detail, the last thing she was likely to see.

'Why?' she said. She wanted to cry but she hadn't the strength. It was the only question that occurred to her; in the end, the one it all came down to. '*Why*, Tom, *why*?'

'The body must perish. The spirit must soar.'

Slowly, she sank to her knees while Quigley delved into the recesses of his jacket once more and drew out the hammer and nails he required to finish the job.

Chapter Twenty-Six

Linda was already awake when the phone call came. It was just after six, a golden morning, first light at the curtains. She was at peace with herself, staring up in contented silence at the high white ceiling, turning over last night in her head again. The smell of Michael, the sound of his breathing, the look of him — she liked the idea of watching him sleep while he was oblivious. It warmed her; she felt she was where she was meant to be.

The phone was on his side of the bed. As soon as it rang, Linda jumped like a trapped nerve, clamoured across the bedspread, over Michael's sleeping body and snatched up the receiver before the noise roused him.

'Yes? Hello?' She was whispering. 'Who's that?'

'Linda, it's me. Naomi.'

'Nim?'

'Yeah. You're in Michael's room? That figures.' She sounded drowsy, distant, but then it was early. 'When I couldn't get you at home I guessed you must have doubled back there.'

'Well, you know how it is.'

'I know. Is Michael there?'

'Still asleep. Do you want him?'

'No, don't — don't disturb him.'

There was a brief burst of static on the line. Feeling a chill, Linda seized what she could of the bedclothes to cover herself. 'So what's happening, Nim? You're calling so early. Did you have a bad night?'

'An enlightening one. In fact it's a good thing I came

home alone. So many things became clear to me, Linda. I understand everything now.'

Linda waited, expecting Naomi to elaborate. When she didn't she said, 'Is this something you can talk about here and now, or would you rather I came over?'

'I know it's early, but could you come right away? It'd mean so much to me, honestly.'

'Fine. Just give me time to wake Michael and – '

'Really, don't bother the others.' Naomi's voice was suddenly laced with anxiety, as if she couldn't bear to be kept waiting. Whatever this was must be more important than she'd first made it sound. 'Just get yourself over here, Linda. Remember last night what we said about some things being easier to deal with one to one?'

'I follow,' Linda told her. 'I'll be over as soon as I can.'

She hung up, replacing the receiver quietly to avoid waking Michael. Still dead to the world, he unburied his face from the pillow and turned, sighing, onto his back. Linda planted a kiss on his brow before collecting her clothes from the four corners of the room and dressing in a hurry on auto-pilot. In the soft light Michael looked almost childlike, the sheets dragged to his chin, his face clear of every adult worry. How often had she stood over George and marvelled like this? There must have been occasions in the past, though they seemed impossibly distant now.

Finished dressing, she stooped over the night-table to scrawl a message on the blotter beside the phone. *Mike – had to rush off to Naomi's. Thought you could use the rest. Will be in touch Later. Love, L.* She ought to be rushing, but her instinct was to loiter, watch until Michael came round. She wanted to see his eyes open. There was so much to be said that she wanted to say now – right now – before it faded. On the other hand, had anything really faded in fifteen years? In the end she had to force herself from the room, as if she were seeing him for the very last time.

Who was she kidding? No doubt she'd be back here before breakfast, Naomi in tow, and Michael would still be asleep – the old lush. That, she thought, was the one thing she'd have to work on: his drinking. She wouldn't let him destroy himself, not when he had so much to offer.

Closing the door, trooping down the stairs, it struck her that she hadn't mentioned Naomi's involvement with Tom Quigley to him. No doubt Naomi would want to do this herself, on her own terms; perhaps that was part of what she wanted to discuss.

Linda shuddered as she stepped outdoors. There was something in the air this morning, or maybe she was still intoxicated by the events of last night. Either way, she felt rejuvenated, ready for anything. The air was bracing, the dawn sky awash with gold. Her car, parked a two-minute walk around the junction from the hotel, started first time without a fuss. Something had changed overnight; she felt it in her bones. It was as if today was the day she'd been waiting for. The more she considered Naomi's call, the more important it seemed, however vague. 'I understand everything now,' Nim had said and, driving from Wakefield, Linda sensed that, for her too, understanding was just around the corner.

Chapter Twenty-Seven

This is the day, the Source told himself, *the day the Lord has made*. Naomi assimilated without a hitch, and now Linda on her way over. It was going so smoothly, he hardly dared breathe. He wanted to – to rejoice right away, give thanks and praise for his good fortune.

All flesh is grass, he thought, surveying his handiwork. Naomi moaned softly from her upside-down position on the wall. Although she was still alive, her soul had departed hours ago, as if anxious to leave. Now she belonged to him, like the others, and the part of him that was Naomi said quietly into the telephone,

'Linda, come quickly. I'll wait for you here.'

The voice was almost there. At the far end of the line, Linda didn't sound remotely suspicious. The call concluded, he hung up and went through to the kitchen for a view of the sky over Abbotsbridge. The morning was clear and cloudless, with a mellow golden glow. But this was September: there would be rain soon, he was sure. It would be just like before.

As he stood there, forgetting himself for a minute, his thoughts returned to that day again, the day the rain came from nowhere. It had been warmer then than now; a slow September afternoon, the last week of the summer vacation.

He was at home, alone, spreadeagled without shirt and socks on his bed by the open window, listening to the flies. His left hand lolled lifelessly at his crotch, his right behind his head like a pillow. He was thinking about bodies – not the physical kind, his own or anyone else's, but the kind his father had told him were invincible if their members worked together, loving and serving each other. Perhaps if he belonged to a body like that he wouldn't be where he was now; but his father's – the one at the church – meant less to him each time he attended. Lately, it was the body the *others* belonged to he couldn't get out of his mind: McCourt's lot, Alison and Naomi and the rest, with their once secret hide-out in the woods.

Why, when he thought of them, did he burn with envy? After all Roy had shown him – the mystery of life and death itself – what more could he desire? He imagined he knew. He wanted to belong. If they'd only accept him, see him for what he was, they might be pleasantly surprised. But excluded like this, shut out, he could almost understand why Roy despised them.

Closing his eyes, he managed to invoke Naomi's face – the full, sensual lips, the dusky compexion. His free hand tensed at his groin. She couldn't have an inkling how he felt at heart. If only he had the opportunity to speak to her properly, without being judged by her. But that was the issue, wasn't it? The Brotherhood *judged* him, considered him unworthy. He was guilty by association.

As the picture of Naomi in his head grew clearer, Tom rolled from the bed and stood up. At first he couldn't be sure what made him; it took a moment to be certain. There were no two ways about it, he was going to have to call her. Even if it killed him, he would make himself go through with it. She wouldn't necessarily believe him – after all, he'd been Roy Sachs' messenger boy for too long – but what could he lose by asking?

Then a better idea came to mind. If he simply pleaded to meet her, it would be easy on the phone for Naomi to refuse point blank. But if he somehow manufactured a situation whereby she could see for herself how sincere he was ...

He idled downstairs, pondering. In the living room, where the phone was, the walls were covered with glass-framed psalms; there were no books, except several editions of the Bible, ancient and modern. Tom sat touching the phone, steadying himself, working the muscles of his mouth.

'Naomi, it's me,' he rehearsed in a voice he had never attempted before but which sounded – to his own ears – incredibly accurate. There was a high, fragile quality about Vinnie Hartley's voice that was easy to reproduce. With luck, he might just pull it off.

By the time he'd finished dialling his mouth had run dry. After the first few rings he considered hanging up. Then Naomi answered dreamily, as if she'd just woken.

'How are you? It's me,' he said, and waited.

There was a nervous interval. Then, 'Vinnie? That's odd, I was just this minute thinking about you.'

'Nothing bad, I hope.'

'Of course not. Just wondering how you were.' She cleared her throat, and he sensed her settling into the call. 'Strange, isn't it, how you can think about someone and the next minute – there they are right in front of you.'

'Yeah. Yeah, it is strange.'

'So what're you up to? Have you seen Mikey?'

'Not since –' Tom considered; the ploy was working, but he was now into unknown territory. 'Not since we were all together last.'

'Seems like an age. That was – Jesus – the night after we buried Tara. I've seen Linda and Ali and Bill since then, but I'm sure that's when we were last all together. Do you know something, Vinnie? I still have nightmares about Tara. I don't think that'll ever leave me. *Ever*. Those lowlifes.'

'Yeah, that Roy Sachs. There's no telling what makes them tick, people like him.'

Naomi was silent for a minute. Then she said, 'It changed us, didn't it?'

'What did?'

'That time, finding Tara strung up like that; knowing who'd done it, and why. And what Linda said about not letting it go, not forgetting or forgiving. I've been thinking it over since then, what she was really getting at. I'm still kind of scared, because you *can't* help but be affected, you're forced to be changed by something like that, aren't you?' She forced a hoarse laugh. 'I'm sorry, Vin. This isn't the time or the place. This was only a social call, right?'

'Well, yes and no. I mean, I think about it too. Most of

224

the time lately. Now and then it's good to be able to share these things. That's what makes the body so special.'

'The body?'

'You know. *Us*. And the way we fit together, arms and legs and all, and help each other.'

'Sure. Didn't Michael say something like that once? Tell you the truth, it was over my head at the time, but the way you put it, maybe I understand now. The body ... It's a nice way of seeing things.'

'I was calling,' Tom said, rushing ahead before his doubts made him fumble, 'because I've this free afternoon, and I thought if you'd time to talk we could meet. That's if you're not busy.'

Naomi took a moment, and he tried to imagine what she must be thinking. Was Vinnie on the pick-up, or was this a purely platonic request? Either way, she was in for a surprise. Then she said, 'You'll be pleased to hear there's a three o'clock gap in this painfully packed schedule of mine. Shall I round up the others?'

'That's okay. You leave that to me.' A nervous reaction clenched his fist around the receiver. His own voice tried to intrude, and he feigned a cough before continuing. 'Would you like to meet me in town, for coffee or something?'

'Let's make it the ice-house,' she said. 'I need some books I left there last week.'

It wasn't ideal – the instant she saw him, the mere fact of his being there would dredge up her worst memories – but at least he'd be hard to avoid in the woods. She'd have no choice but to hear him out, and if Naomi would listen, perhaps the others would too. The trick was to catch them without Roy's influence colouring the way they saw him, to prove – to himself as much as anyone – that he thought for himself and could act alone. The Brotherhood saw him as an empty vessel, a mindless zombie, and it was time the image cracked.

After the call, hurrying upstairs for his shirt and socks, Tom Quigley marvelled at his talent, the wonders he could work with his voice. If he could be Vinnie Hartley, if only for five minutes on the phone, was there any limit to his gift?

225

Chapter Twenty-Eight

The Source remembered an idyllic day, the air warm but fresh, Parks Wood coloured tawny and gold with the leaves readying themselves for the fall to earth. Picturing the scene now, he grew confused, seeing too much at once. Naomi and Tom had taken different routes to the clearing. He remembered both clearly, as if two stray thoughts were converging to form a cohesive whole in his mind. He saw through two pairs of eyes; his senses were doubled. From the south-west came a mellow cross-country breeze that secretly stirred the trees overhead. To the north the faint susurration of town traffic could be heard. Entering the clearing, it was as if all other sounds became suddenly muted, and the rest of the world was left behind.

Naomi walked steadily towards the tree from which Tara had hung. Some short distance beyond was the slight mound marking the grave. The clearing was dappled with natural light, and a patch of sunshine brightened the grave like a spray of flowers. She stopped for a moment, shielding her eyes, the sunlight warming her hand. As she did, movements near the ice-house caught her attention. She turned, expecting to see Vinnie unwinding himself from the entrance. Instead, it was Quigley, his mouth open but speechless, his hands raised defensively.

'*You*?' she said. 'What are you doing here?'

'Looking, that's all. I came upon this place some time ago and came back to see if anyone else knew about it.' He approached slowly up the gradient. The air hummed faintly with insects. 'Have you seen inside? It's like someone's pad.

Books and papers, and posters up on the walls, and bottles and cans left over from some party.' Seeing Naomi withdraw, he stopped several feet short of her. 'Do you know anything about this?' he said.

He was feeding her a line. Surely he knew more than he was letting on. Naomi waved a wasp away from her face, glared at him until he squirmed and looked down. 'What are you doing here?' she repeated.

'Like I said, just looking. I wanted to see – '

'Well, if you've finished, you won't mind excusing me. I'm supposed to be meeting someone here.'

'It's a free country, isn't it? I can stay if I want to, can't I?'

'You can stay but don't expect my undivided attention. You're hardly my idea of a good time.'

Tom Quigley smiled as if the remark was wasted on him. Hands pocketed, he strode to the tree in that inimitable long, lazy fashion and leaned back against it. 'So who's it you're meeting, then?'

'Just a friend. He'll be here any minute. You'd better get going, Tom.'

'In a minute I will. When I'm ready.' He raised his eyes to the trees, the cloudless sky, a kestrel gliding in mid-flight. 'This is where you all meet, I'll bet. That stuff in the ice-house is yours.' Naomi said nothing. 'I remember one time I was with Roy and we chased your friends out here – Michael and Vinnie, it was – and they kind of vanished when we got near this point. We couldn't figure it at all. Lost track of 'em altogether.' He rubbed his long chin and grinned at her. 'Still, if we'd looked a bit closer we'd have found them, wouldn't we?'

'You must be dead pleased with yourself,' she said.

'Not really. There's more to me than meets the eye.'

'That's something then.' She was growing more impatient by the second. 'Now if you'll excuse me – '

'He isn't coming,' Tom Quigley announced.

'What's that?'

'He's not coming. The friend you're expecting isn't coming.'

She stared at him, fish-mouthed.

227

'Believe me, I'm sorry,' he said. 'I know who you're supposed to be meeting. But I had to do something. It's the only way I could work this.'

'Tom, what the *fuck* are you talking about?'

'Vinnie,' he said, and was about to elaborate when something across the clearing drew his attention. In the trees to his left there was sudden activity: the sound of bracken being trodden down, twigs splintering underfoot. Several birds fluttered into the open, panicking. Someone out walking the dog, most likely.

'What *about* Vinnie?' Naomi demanded. 'How did you know about him?'

'That was me,' he began, but she was watching the trees beyond him. 'The phone call, I mean. It was my way of trying to − '

'Nonsense! I heard his voice; I'd know Vinnie anywhere. There,' she insisted as a gap in the trees opened up and a figure emerged. 'So much for your bullshit. I knew he was coming.' She took a defiant step forward, meaning to greet Vinnie, then faltered. The figure jogging into the clearing from the trees was not Vinnie Hartley but Sachs.

Several paces nearer, Sachs stopped, noticing Tom and Naomi for the first time. For a moment his face was blank, the cogs turning somewhere behind his eyes; then his gaze fell on Tom, and he smiled gleefully.

'Nice work, holy Joe. How did you manage this catch?'

There was a beat before Naomi made the connection. In a flourish, she hurled herself at Quigley, slapping his face so hard his head rocked back against the tree. She struck him twice, both times with her right, and stood seething, clutching herself. Nursing his singing cheek, Quigley regarded her stupidly.

'Bastard,' she said. 'It *was* you. You lured me out here for *him*. You set the whole thing up and I − God, how stupid!'

'No, it wasn't like that.' But how could he explain himself now? Even in the unlikely event she'd believe him, in front of Roy Sachs he was powerless. As far as Sachs was concerned, this was another free shot at the Brotherhood. The body must perish. 'It wasn't what you think,' he managed quietly before Sachs came within earshot.

There was a moment, then, of dead calm; the three of them forming a loosely defined circle in the tree's shadow, around them the woodland hush. Naomi had heard this silence before, the moment she entered the clearing to find Tara swinging above the very spot she occupied now. What was it about this place? Why on earth had she fallen for Quigley's ploy?

'Nice thinking, my son,' Sachs said to Quigley. 'Such things you find in the woods these days, I swear. Here's me, all set to trash that fucking hidey-hole of theirs, torch the fucking place to the sky, and see what I find instead! Were you keeping her all to yourself or what?'

'No, Roy. That is – ' He caught Naomi's eye, but her expression made him falter. 'I was just killing time here, we met by chance.'

'Chance? There's no such thing.' Sachs was watching Naomi. 'There's destiny, there's learning what's meant to be and making sure it takes place. There's punishment for wrongdoers who refuse to stay in line.'

'I'm out of here,' Naomi said brightly.

'Not yet you're not.' Sachs broadened his shoulders, jerked aside to block her escape route.

'Roy, please ...' Quigley's voice was a whimper, faint as the breeze.

Sachs ignored it, addressing himself to Naomi. 'Where are they now then, your friends, when you need them? See how much use they are?'

'Listen,' she said. 'They'll be here soon, we've a meeting here. It's arranged. I spoke ...' Her voice was cracking, her confidence expiring. She flashed a quick glance at Quigley. 'After I spoke to Vinnie I called Linda and Michael right away. They know where I am. They're all coming over. We arranged it, see? You'd better believe me.' This was more than a desperate lie; perhaps even Tom Quigley sensed that. It was a vain attempt to summon the others, to will them to appear. She waited to see what impression she'd made on Sachs. When he didn't react she strode forward, intending to rush past him. With both hands he seized her

229

and flung her to the ground, then dropped his full weight on her shoulders, pinning her there.

'Then we'd better settle this quickly,' he said.

At first she was too dazed, too displaced to react. She was sprawled underneath him, dragging his face into focus: that familiar Sachs leer. Then she understood what this meant. He had crossed the line once; he had killed once already. If she'd learned anything about Sachs, it was that the thin line between good and evil had no meaning for him. He didn't care. She tried to struggle, but her arms were useless, flattened and numb, her breathing reduced to gasps and snorts of air that burned her sinuses. She kicked out, brought her right knee up against his spine with all the force she could gather. She saw his stunned look as he rocked forward, felt the gradual adjustment in his posture. Then he said casually, 'Tom, hold her legs.'

'But Roy — what she said about the others ...' Perhaps Tom had swallowed the lie; or was this his way of helping her?

'Never mind the others,' Sachs hissed. 'Hold her legs!'

'God, no,' Naomi heard herself mutter. It was a voice she hardly recognised, forced from her lungs as it was by the pressure bearing down from above. His knees on her shoulders felt like knives and his open mouth hovered inches above her face. She nearly blacked out from the effort of kicking out a second time; then a dull blow at the side of her head extinguished the lights, and Sachs and the clearing faded to grey.

Chapter Twenty-Nine

There was something too familiar, Linda thought, about her approach to Abbotsbridge this morning. It wasn't just the place or the time, but a feeling of *déja vu* so strong she could taste it. On the outskirts of town the first commuters to Sheffield and Leeds were backing from their drives, milk floats rattled from street to empty street – but little of this diverted her. It was as though even now, especially now, some nameless dark thing she'd presumed dead and buried was luring her irresistibly onwards. The feeling of anticipation she'd set out with this morning had subtly become trepidation: what had been solved by coming home? Had the years of distance and doubt been so much worse than anything they might have to face now?

She needed to seize control. Her whole constitution felt fragile. Drawing into the forecourt below the council flats, she took a moment to compose herself, gazing up to see if Naomi had spotted her. There was a flicker of movement at a third floor window, but the balcony obscured her view. She'd give Naomi a minute before heading up.

Now she had time to think, Naomi's confession last night seemed like something she'd imagined or dreamt: even less credible in the daylight. The idea of Tom Quigley fathering Naomi's first-born was bad enough – but *Sachs*? It was patently impossible. Naomi must be living on her overwrought nerves, unless ...

Linda frowned, trying to picture the day in September again, her first impression as she came within sight of the clearing with the petrified hush all around her and the muffled cries just ahead; but the time-scale was wrong, everything about it was wrong. There was something she'd overlooked, something that held the key she required. An HGV rushed past, along the main road. Tapping the steering wheel, Linda sat watching the dust rise in its wake.

The phone was ringing. It was fifteen years earlier and the phone was ringing. As the dust settled over the road Linda half-closed her eyes to focus the memory. At first she couldn't quite hear the phone − in her room Joy Division were playing full-volume on her radio.

Then the song faded out, and Linda sat listening to the phone. There had been no more of the calls since Tara − which, if anything, proved Sachs was guilty − but she nevertheless anticipated that unbearable absence of sound whenever she lifted the receiver. At last she tore herself from the room, thumped across the landing, arrested the phone in mid-ring.

It was Michael, much to her relief. She sat on the bed to talk. It was a warm afternoon, the right side of humid, and to stand seemed like too much effort.

As ever he sounded nervous with her, more so than with the others, which she found stangely thrilling: proof that she mattered. 'Linda, are you free now? I'm calling a Brotherhood meeting on spec. Nothing urgent, just who-ever's available can come.'

'Count me in,' she told him. 'But what for?'

'There's good news at last. It won't change the world, but the summer's been such a fuck-up − excuse me − I thought it might brighten your day. Remember the story I submitted to *Fantasy and Science Fiction*? Well, I'm holding a letter of acceptance right here in my hand.'

'That's wonderful! Congratulations!' The achievement felt like hers too. 'Oh Mike, I'm so proud. The first of many sales, I just know it! How are you planning to celebrate?'

'*We*, you mean. Wait and find out.' He sounded full to overflowing, scarcely able to contain himself. 'It's been too long since we did something together. They say they'll be publishing it the issue after next. I'll bring the letter along.'

232

'And the story, don't forget. Bring that as well.'

'Even though you've read it?'

'Once is not enough. Will you call the others or shall I?'

'See if you can round up Naomi; I'm already at Vinnie's, and I bumped into Ali and Bill in town on my way over here. They'll meet us at the ice-house at three. Wait where you are – we'll be over right away.'

'I won't move a muscle.'

When Michael hung up she dialled Naomi's number. There was no reply. Five minutes later she tried again, without success.

In the bathroom she washed and put on clean jeans and a lemon yellow sweatshirt baggy as a tent, checked her complexion in the mirror. With all this preening she should have been preparing for a night on the town, but Michael's call had refreshed her and suddenly she was awake and alive again. It was nearly two weeks, she realised with disbelief, since she'd seen him. A chance encounter on the high street one market day; another nervous *au revoir* just when he'd seemed on the verge of inviting her out. If this went on much longer she'd have to follow Alison's advice and do the asking herself.

Unearthing her shoes from under her bed, she remembered a congratulations card she'd bought for some family occasion or another and never used. Perhaps Michael wouldn't appreciate the spray of red roses, but the thought was what counted. By the time she'd scribbled *with love from Linda* below the sickly verse she could hear him downstairs at the door.

'Well, *thanks*,' he told her when he'd prised open the envelope, still moist where she'd sealed it. 'It's truly disgusting! I love it!'

'You earned it. It's the least you deserve.'

He grinned at her. Vinnie held aloft a bottle of Australian fizz and said, 'Well, it ain't champagne, but so what? We're going to get soused while McCourt reads aloud. We even brought paper cups for the toast.'

'I'll get my keys,' Linda said.

Five minutes later, passing Tom Quigley's father's church

233

at the foot of Riverside, Michael became noticeably subdued.

Linda nudged him. 'Something wrong?'

'Aftershock, that's all. I was remembering when Sachs and Quigley came tearing up the street after me ... How easily I could've been dogmeat. There's a blind spot down there, see? You only need to drop your guard for a second and – '

'Then we've a duty to look out for each other.' Linda turned from him to Vinnie. 'Isn't that the point? The body fending for itself? We can't stop living because of what might be round the next corner, can we? We won't let those freaks dictate what we do or which route we take.'

'You're right,' he agreed feebly, though the tension didn't drain from his face until they had entered the trees, the blind spot safely behind them.

They walked a little way without speaking. Linda understood exactly how he felt – how the bad experiences left deep scars, like stigmata. Even returning to the ice-house was something she'd rather not do, given the choice. What had happened there was too painful; the image of Tara strung up like some carcass in a butcher's shop and the Brotherhood grouped about the tree was too fresh in her mind. But alone in her room she'd convinced herself that facing the horror was the only alternative to being consumed by it. Take the phone call, revisit the scene: don't let the bastards dictate.

Overhead, the sky was blue and as impossibly high as English skies ever got. We're here to celebrate being together, Linda thought absently; one success like Michael's is everyone's success, and one loss is everyone's also. It seemed silly, pretentious, to put into words what the Brotherhood meant; and yet everyone instinctively understood, always had.

A few minutes later they turned from the main path, through a patch of young birch saplings crowding with root suckers. Vinnie went ahead, black t-shirt riding up his broad white back, wine bottle patting his hip. Linda cringed, half-expecting the cork to blow. Apart from their movements, Parks Wood was silent.

'The trees are on guard,' Michael whispered behind her. 'You can hear the birds listening.'

That might have amused her, if it hadn't been so uncannily apt.

Beyond the birch plantation was a shaded grove of pine trees with a ground cover of overgrown rhododendrons. A little-used track wound, somewhat obscurely, south. At points here the sky was virtually excluded, the only light some distance ahead, where the clearing began. It wasn't until they were pushing through the scrub at the edge of the clearing that Linda heard anything at all: sounds which had silenced the woods. Suddenly Vinnie stopped dead, flung out an arm to prevent both Linda and Michael from rushing ahead.

'Listen,' he said.

Even before she identified the voices, Linda knew from their tone that something was seriously wrong. Here, the rhododendrons were bunching so thickly between the trees that her only view was of the distant fields above and beyond the clearing. Two voices were ranting, one then another in harsh, quick succession. Then a third gave a muffled cry, and Linda felt the blood drain from her body.

'That's Nim. What's going on?'

'What's she saying?' said Vinnie.

But at once it was strikingly, horribly plain what Naomi was saying: '*Please ... no ... please ...*' Then silence again.

'She needs help,' Michael said, almost casually, and then he was threshing his way forward through the undergrowth. Vinnie stumbled after him, shadowed by Linda. A branch snapped back into her face, across her right cheek, but she hardly felt it. As she stumbled on, the clearing opened up before her, and then she had an uninterrupted view of the figures sprawled on the ground near the foot of the tree.

They couldn't have known they were being watched, she thought. They were lost in what they were doing. Perhaps it was the shock of seeing them like that which made her feel minutes had passed before anything more could happen. There was Naomi, a barely recognisable mess with her hair plastered over her face and her bare legs extending straight out. Sachs was on top of her, pushing her skirt up her body

235

with one hand, unbuckling his trousers with the other. At the same time he was ranting – the words were unclear – and Tom Quigley, who until then had been standing above them, came around to take hold of Naomi's ankles.

There was no misinterpreting the scene, no way Linda's eyes were deceiving her, though she wished with all her heart she could be wrong. This place, she thought; this place must be cursed, it isn't meant for us to be happy here, happy anywhere. She had perhaps two or three seconds to think this, to see things for what they were. Then everything happened so quickly she was simply swept along by the tide, unable to think at all.

Michael was already moving. She was jostled aside, and then Michael and Vinnie were both running, Michael screaming at the top of his lungs, Vinnie suddenly imposing himself in a way she had never imagined he could. Vinnie was making a bee-line for Sachs, who was already up on his feet. The bottle of wine was held high, like a nightstick, and Sachs was grinning on all sides of his face at once while Naomi rolled clear, covering herself, to the foot of the tree.

Linda had several impressions all at once. There was so much to take in. She too was sprinting involuntarily towards the action. It has to end, she was vaguely aware of thinking; here and now and once and for all. On the ground she saw, trampled underfoot, the envelope containing Michael's letter and the scattered, smeared folios of his story. Then the bottle came down in the same instant Sachs' arm came up, and as the bottle went spinning aside it was Vinnie, not Sachs, who went down groaning, hands pressed to his groin.

Then Sachs was wielding a knife, a switchblade with the blade out, swishing it this way and that while Michael screamed 'Bastard, bastard,' and hurled himself forward, one arm hooked round Sachs' neck, both feet clearing the ground.

Together they hit the deck. This moment had been years in the making. Tom Quigley stood by Naomi, hands outspread, absolving himself. And Naomi was screaming, 'Stop this, stop this *now*,' while Sachs, teeth bared like an animal's, jabbed the knife backwards and up against

Michael's shoulder. There was blood now, blood seeping through Michael's grey grandad shirt, but Michael's response was to lever himself forward, biting deeply into the hand that held the knife. Sachs yelped, dropped the blade, reached blindly towards Michael's face. As his hands closed around Michael's throat, Linda stepped smartly across to take up the discarded bottle.

She didn't think twice about using it. They had all reached a point of no return, where only actions counted for anything, and she swung the bottle down at an angle. It caught Sachs heavily across the right shoulder. There was a dull, solid resonance that she felt all the way up her arm, and then Sachs fell aside, clutching himself.

Now, she thought. She held the bottle in readiness. But now *what*? There was still time to stop. If this went no further – if Sachs would allow it to end here – but she knew that he couldn't the instant she caught the look in his eyes. He was pushing this to the limit, to the logical conclusion. That was what he wanted from her.

'No,' she said under her breath. 'You can't have it. You can't fucking have it!' Gasping with the effort, she flung the bottle as far as she could away to her right.

Sachs was unmoved, however. 'I'll have you all, take you all down with me.' His gaze was black, filled with murder, with the pleasure of giving and receiving pain. He smiled at her – how could he smile? how could he *want* this? – and the next thing she knew, he was moving through space towards her.

He came at her quickly, without any warning. Behind him, the others were still licking their wounds. *Why doesn't he stop?* she barely had time to think, before she felt the full weight of his fist in her face.

The pain she felt was quite incredible, a hot and cold swelling that began somewhere beneath her left eye and quickly seemed to expand to fill her whole head. For an instant she couldn't be sure whether she was standing or falling, whether what she was experiencing was unconsciousness or something worse, something terminal. She felt her eyes filling with water. The trees, the daylight seemed to swim and cave in for a second. She was alone

237

here, there was no one else, the pain was just an illusion, a dream. Then he hit her again, harder still, this time between her breasts with a force that choked, almost crippled her, and he hit her again and then again until she remembered and cried out – cried something; she didn't know what – and managed to claw her fingernails down both sides of his face at once. After that she felt him being dragged clear of her.

When she came to, a minute or two later, she was on her knees and Vinnie and Michael were struggling to hold Sachs at bay, eight or ten feet away. There were bright red track marks on his temples and cheeks; he was drooling uncontrollably from the mouth. This was how rabid dogs were supposed to behave, she thought. He was throwing himself about like something possessed, mouthing words she couldn't hear, didn't want to – promises, threats, everything he wanted to do to her, dismemberment, rape – and she remembered the phone calls and the terrible silences, and suddenly, out of nowhere, made sense of what she was seeing.

It wasn't just about control. He was sent to destroy us, destroy what we had and he couldn't have, she thought, quite clearly. And the worst of it is, one way or another he's going to have his heart's desire. It had always been so much easier to tear down than build up, life was like that, and Sachs was determined to tear everything down. With seemingly little effort, he pushed Vinnie aside, squirmed from the hold Michael was trying to put on him, and began scrambling back towards Linda.

Perhaps it was the effect of his assault on her and she really was seeing things, but just as he reached her he seemed for a moment to shift and change, as if his features were straining to become someone else's. His hands reached for her, clawing the air, frantically, blindly. Then he was turning blue, his eyes bulging – which was when she saw Quigley standing behind him, and understood what was happening.

There was a length of nylon rope wrapped tautly around Sachs' throat. He was choking because Tom Quigley was strangling him. Quigley had retrieved from the ice-house the length of rope Sachs had used against Tara, and was pulling

238

it so tightly his knuckles bled white. There was a air of intense concentration about him. While Sachs struggled, Quigley's face remained impassive − not the hollow, expressionless gaze she'd come to expect from him, but the gaze of a man at peace with himself, at peace and very much in control.

Already Sachs looked numb, as much with shock as anything else. Somewhere, seemingly far distant, Naomi moaned. Linda glanced quickly away towards Michael. He didn't see her; his attention was fixed on the struggle now taking place. He was chanting something under his breath: kill him, kill him −

'No ...' Naomi murmured, but the protest seemed feeble because Sachs' eyes were rolling skywards, his tongue was distended and protruding, even the movements of his hands seemed involuntary. His fingers plucked uselessly at the rope. Quigley was dragging him away now, away from Linda, backwards and away towards where Michael and Vinnie were standing as if hypnotised. The day was completely silent, waiting, the sky ovehead a serene blue.

'Go on, go on, finish the fucker,' Vinnie said quietly.

Linda looked up for a moment, away from the scene. As she did she felt something prickle her face: the first tiny, speculative spots of rain. She looked back at the others, heart pounding. Michael was watching her now, seeing her and yet − this was dreadful − not seeing her at all. Suddenly it was like old times again, like the very beginning. On cue, they looked away from each other in shame. She knew then it was over, the dream the Brotherhood was meant to bring to life. She knew because Quigley was pulling Sachs, limp and submissive, towards the ice-house, and no one had raised a hand to prevent him. In an instant, in Michael's gaze, she had seen it all: the whole crushing inevitability of it all.

'It's the only way ...' someone said, Vinnie perhaps, even Quigley. 'Got to end this now. Got to stop it now, forever.'

She had thought the same dark wishful thoughts herself at times, but this was hard reality, and it burned. Sachs kicked out despairingly; but his hands fell limp at his sides, trailing along the ground as Quigley dragged him. The rain was quickening, streaming into her eyes, and she wiped the back of one hand across her matted brow as she stumbled across the clearing to Naomi.

'Let's go, Nim,' she said. But Naomi had retreated into herself. She was leaning back against the tree trunk, watching the proceedings empty-eyed, no longer protesting. Now Tom Quigley stopped, just where the ground dipped down the slope towards the ice-house entrance. He let go of the rope and Sachs fell slackly to the floor and lay still.

Perhaps a minute passed before anyone moved. Then Vinnie and Michael, Michael clutching his redly damp shirt-sleeve, edged nearer. Quigley regarded them levelly. Folding his arms, he stared down at Sachs without expression.

'Jesus,' said Vinnie.

'You fucking well killed him,' said Michael in awe.

'Now what?' said Vinnie.

Tom Quigley said nothing at first. Instead, he turned smartly and vanished inside the ice-house. No one followed. Presently he reappeared carrying the garden spade that had been used, not so long ago, for Tara's burial. 'God help us,' Linda said under her breath. 'It never ends, does it?'

Beside her, Naomi was weeping. Drawing her knees up to her chin, burying her face between them, she said, 'Make it go away, someone please. Make it all go away.'

Suddenly, off to Linda's left, there was movement. Bill and Alison, arm in arm, had just entered the clearing. Linda glanced their way in time to see the look of eager anticipation fade from their faces, Alison cup a hand to her mouth, Bill's silent exclamation as they registered what they were seeing. At another time, in another place, their reaction might have seemed comical, but then Vinnie was shrieking, 'He's moving! He's breathing! Jesus, he's alive – he's alive!'

All too briefly Linda felt greater relief than she'd ever imagined she could for Sachs. It didn't end here, then; there was more to follow, they were going to be allowed one more chance. Life would go on after this.

Then someone screamed – maybe Alison or Naomi or both – and it was over again, just as it had been a moment ago, just as quickly as her hopes had been raised. In one fluent stroke, Tom Quigley raised the spade to the sky – a clear, cloudless sky, from which the rain still fell – and brought it down over Sachs' face.

Chapter Thirty

Michael McCourt awoke with a start, the dream still fresh in his mind. The image of Roy Sachs' flattened, smashed face with the rain beating down on it, the open eyes and mouth wide and gaping and streaming with blood and rain, had never been more vivid to him. At times – certainly since the move to New York – he'd been able to suppress the image, let the city overwhelm his deeds and thoughts, but now he was close to the source, emotionally and geograpically closer than for fifteen years and more.

At some point, some dark hidden part of himself had urged Quigley on, wanted and longed for Quigley to follow through what he'd started. There was a moment, just before Quigley let go of the rope, where he might have been able to intervene. Then he saw Linda, the bruise already swelling one side of her face, and he saw the fear and horror in her eyes, and remembered who had put those feelings there in the first place.

Seconds later he caught sight of Bill Anderson and Alison Lester as they entered the clearing. He couldn't even make himself acknowledge them. Then the weapon came down, the garden spade that Tom Quigley had brought from the den, and Sachs' face was immediately a pulped broken mess, and Quigley was utterly lost as he lifted and brought down the weapon again, this time at an angle, the blade splitting Sachs' head in two.

'There now,' Quigley spat, and dropped the spade, and fell back several paces, dusting his hands. 'That's for *you*. Finally got what you wanted, what you had coming. What you deserved. Stay dead, you sick fucker.'

For a moment he looked set to launch himself forward at the body once more, as if what he'd accomplished was only the beginning; then he subsided, breathing raggedly, shoulders gradually drooping as he surveyed the damage.

'Jesus Christ ... Jesus fucking Christ.' This was Bill, hands clasped at his mouth. He didn't need to demand an explanation: what he and Alison had missed was self-evident.

'The body must perish,' said Quigley finally, perhaps to himself, and forced a short, brittle laugh touched with lunacy.

This, Michael later concluded, was the point where the Silence really began – where the course of their lives changed forever. When he finally raised his eyes from Sachs' corpse he saw the others forming a vague semi-circle about him. Even Naomi and Linda were on their feet, though Naomi looked ready to keel over at any moment, and Linda too dazed to account for what she was seeing. That must be why she seemed to be forcing herself to avoid Michael's gaze. He longed to reach out for her, give her what small reassurance he could, but what good could that do now? Perhaps Linda knew it was usless; that all they'd dreamed of and wished for was over.

Then Vinnie said quietly, 'Maybe ... Maybe we should put him ... ' He fingered his mouth nervously. 'Maybe we should put him somewhere.'

Michael cast a glance at the garden spade. They were standing just feet from where Tara lay. He said nothing, felt the day swim around him, the rain patting down, the sound of the rain and the prying feel of it on his shoulders and neck.

Bill said, 'The minute any of us touch him we're *all* involved – you do realise that, Vin.'

'Then what do you call this? *Un*involved? Does it look like we're just passing through?'

Quigley was down on his haunches, staring blankly at the ground, saying nothing.

'We can't let him answer for this alone,' Linda said. 'It isn't only his responsibility. He was trying to keep Sachs away from me – '

'That's not what it looks like,' Bill said. 'To me it looks like he was trying to cave his fucking skull in, and I'd say he near as damn it succeeded.'

'*Damn* him,' said Alison. Her jaw was set, her gaze indignant. 'Damn him right to hell, the spoiler. He couldn't let anything alone, he had to smash whatever he couldn't control. He had to destroy – '

'He's destroyed us, hasn't he?' Linda said then. Her words forced a lull in the gathering. No birds sang; the rain, easing slightly, was the only sound. 'Well then, hasn't he?'

Yes, Michael thought. That's exactly what he's achieved; that was his mission, it was all he was good for. 'At least we should get him out of sight for now,' he said.

'Let's just be clear about what you're doing,' Bill said, then amended, 'All right, what *we're* doing. There's no going back once we're started.'

'We started a long time ago,' said Naomi. 'Please let's make certain it finishes here.'

In his hotel bedroom, so many years later, Michael turned over, reaching blindly for Linda, then remembered her flitting about, dressing, in the early hours. He stared bleary-eyed at her pillow, the impression her sleeping head had made, and thought vaguely: where did she go?

She couldn't hack it, in all probability. She'd arrived at his door last night because, let's face it, she needed to get this out of her system once and for all; perhaps to prove something to herself, who knows? He would always remember last night, but perhaps last night was all there would be.

After a time he forced himself up, squinted between the curtains at the bright new day. There was a note from Linda beside the phone. She would be with Naomi by now.

Michael showered and dressed and then pushed back the curtains so the light could flood through the room. It was just before eight: perhaps time to rouse Bill for breakfast. Dialling the switchboard he asked for Bill's room. After ten or twelve rings Bill answered sounding distant, still half-asleep.

'How long do you need?' Michael asked.

'How long do I get?'

'See you downstairs over coffee and croissants. Last one there settles the taxi fare to Abbotsbridge.'

Bill cursed placidly through a yawn and hung up. As an afterthought, Michael summoned the switchboard again, this time requesting an outside line. Perhaps it was nothing; but hadn't Naomi's dawn call been just a little abrupt? Surely if whatever it was she needed to see Linda about was so urgent it couldn't exclude himself and Bill − in which case why had Linda set out alone?

Somewhere he had Naomi's home number. A short search led him to jacket pockets stuffed with crumpled memos and subway tokens, amongst them the scrap of paper he needed. Having clattered out the number, the wait for the ringing tone seemed impossibly long. Then the connection was made. Michael sat on the bed, hypnotised by the tone, watching the sky framed by the window of his room. Perhaps two minutes ground by before he hung up. Naomi and Linda must have left, perhaps were even on their way to the hotel.

Collecting his jacket, he headed downstairs for breakfast. Probably there was nothing to worry about: but the sullen waitress who attended his table in the empty dining room had to ask three times what he wanted before he realised he didn't feel hungry. Shrugging, he ordered the croissants and coffee and she scowled and turned away with a whisper of cheap perfume, and he remembered then how badly he'd needed to escape all of this; the sullen northern Englishness; the cheapness; the smallness. It had been hard enough to leave behind − the attempt had taken years − and now he felt cheated.

For a second he felt a directionless rage, an impulse to turn over the table and walk out, to flee for the next available Transatalantic flight. He could be home in less than twelve hours, arriving at JFK before the evening gridlock took hold. He picked up a knife and put it down, considering his various options. Then he saw Bill at the doorway, dishevelled and stretching, the sun in his eyes. He grinned and sat back, waiting for the coffee to arrive.

'What's *her* problem?' Bill said after the waitress had dumped plates and a basket of croissants on the table,

245

clattered the cups and saucers, slammed down the coffee pot. 'Isn't she happy in her work?'

'Would you be if you were her? If you woke up one day to find you'd gone as far as you were going to, ever? That this was what you were pinning your hopes on?'

'Christ, you sound on a downer this morning. She probably doesn't see it like that at all. She's probably just doing this until something better comes along. For all you know she has a remarkable future in store.'

'It isn't just her,' Michael said, 'that isn't what I'm getting at. It's the whole damn thing, everything we left behind, the way people here reach a point where they just, I don't know, give *up*. The look that comes over them − you've seen it − the resignation.'

'But *you* got away. In our different ways we *all* got away from it − well, most of us did.' Bill made a nonchalant gesture, a flick of the fingers, as if to prove how painless and easy the transition had been. His composure only made Michael feel more fraught.

'Then what are we doing here?' Michael demanded, glaring. 'If we really left it all behind why did we need to return?' He sighed and reached for the coffee. 'Look, I'm sorry. It's just that ... I'm worried, that's all. I'm afraid, like everyone else.'

'Always suspected you were human underneath,' Bill said. 'In spite of appearances.' Buttering a croissant he blinked into the light. Beyond the windows, St Johns vibrated with early morning traffic. 'Did it ever occur to you that it isn't really their fault? These people, I mean, the ones you say have resigned themselves to making do with a second-rate lot. Don't you ever feel grateful that you had the talent to break out? It takes more than will-power alone, you know.'

Michael poured coffee, gazed soberly into space. He couldn't explain his irascibility, his volatile mood. It was more than confusion, more than just not knowing what to believe − whether Sachs had somehow found a way back; whether Quigley provided the key. If anything, he supposed what he really feared was a *dénouement* he could not control. The finale was out of his hands; events could not be cropped conveniently to fit. There was no poetic justice here; how could there be? What could replace the lives of Alison and Vinnie, or pay back the lost years?

Nothing ever could; he had realised as much at the time. He had felt hope slipping away while together – Bill and Vinnie, himself – they manoeuvered Sachs' body inside the ice-house, through the concealed entrace, into the dark. Bill took the legs, Vinnie the midriff, Michael supported the shoulders and head. Adjusting his hold as they twisted towards the entrance, he couldn't prevent Sachs' ruined head pressing damply against his midriff. He tried to push it away; recoiled as his fingers sank inwards. By the time they were inside his hands felt slippery with gore, which he wiped off hastily, without thinking, on the thighs of his jeans. 'There there,' someone said, and Michael glanced up to hear someone crying and someone else – Vinnie, he thought, though his eyes were still adjusting to the dark – doubled up in a corner of the ice-house, retching.

Everyone was here. Even Quigley, at the entrance, had followed. No one was running from this – yet running was all that remained to be done. There was a long uncertain moment, then the six indistinct members of the body huddled together in the gloom, not daring to speak or breathe, afraid to touch or draw closer, the sound of rain drumming down, the water flowing, never-ending, and outside the sky, bright and clear, fused with warmth.

Not looking at the others, instinctively not wanting to see what was in their eyes, Michael cleared his throat. 'Well. Does anyone want to say it?'

'No,' Linda replied faintly. 'No one wants to; maybe you'd better. You're the wordman.'

He nodded, waited until he could bear the silence no longer. 'We leave here today and that's that,' he began. 'We have to put this behind us, deal with it now and forget it. That's easy to say, I accept that, but what it really comes down to is, once we're all finished here today – *it's* finished. We're finished. If we're walking away from this then we're going to have to protect ourselves, which means ...' He paused; no one stirred. 'It means that from now on we don't know one another. This never happened. We never shared it. If we – if we try to deal with this together it'll

247

make things worse, we'll drag each other down, and so we *have* to let it go. There isn't any choice.'

There were no dissenting voices. Alison and Bill clung to each other, heads bowed, Bill calmly stroking the nape of her neck; Linda was shaking her head, eyes glazed. Naomi said almost timidly, 'But this is all I've got. You're my *family*, practically. We can't let him take everything away from us, not like this, not like this . . . ' She tailed off.

Linda rested a hand on Naomi's arm. 'Yes, I know, but think how it would be if we came here again after this.'

'Not here, then. Somewhere else. It isn't the place that matters, you know that yourself.'

'Then name a place, any place, where what we've just been through won't be eating away at us,' Linda said calmly. 'It'll be hard enough just seeing each other around, at school, and *knowing*, without having to face this over and over again.'

'Yes, but . . . ' Naomi murmured. 'Yes, but . . . '

It seemed a long time before anything further was added. It was much like a dream, Michael thought; a dream he would gladly have woken from but which seemed to be trying to etch itself permanently into his memory; the half-light, the clammy taste of peat in his mouth and nose, the tacky feel of his palms.

At last it was Bill who said, 'Then what are we going to do with him? Leave him here? Just clear out our things and leave him to it?'

Michael drew a deep breath. Propped against the bare wall beside him was the garden fork he had used to help make Tara's grave. 'You know full well what's next. I don't see why all of you have to stay. Linda?' She nodded on cue, gravely, not looking at him. 'Nim? Go home, why don't you? Bill, why don't you take Alison?' He wanted this to end, if it had to, in orderly fashion, without further tears. He and Vinnie would conclude the dirty-work, cut the earth, bury the evidence, shake hands as if sealing some contract, thereafter departing forever.

What in the fucking world was he *thinking* of? How could he allow this, *accept* this? But he could sense the same numb, astonished resignation in the others as they reclined, unmoving, uncertain what to do next. Then someone – Tom Quigley, still blocking the light from the entrance – cleared his throat and straightened himself.

'What you're saying, Mike, it's right, it's the only way, but . . . Suddenly you're trying to make it sound like *you're* all to blame, all of *you*, when . . . ' He paused. 'This is between me and him, understand? What happened just now is private. You got that?' He fingered his brow with long, pale fingers, fumbling for words. 'Private between all of you, sure, but between me and him too, and I can't let you take it all on yourselves. I've played my part and there's more to do yet before I'm finished, like it or not.'

They watched him in stony silence, the sound of rain fading slightly, the light at Tom's back brightening sharply, dramatically.

'What are you saying, Tom?' Michael asked.

'That you're to leave this to me; this is my doing and I don't want any interference.' His face was little more than a blackened, backlighted oval but from his tone of voice it was clear that Quigley meant business. 'If I'd come to my senses sooner, well, chances are none of this would have had to happen. One thing – you might not all accept me, but I got a mind of my own, there's more to me than you'd know and I can make my own decisions. You're not to interfere, is that clear?' He licked his lips. 'Mike's right about you forgetting now, putting it behind you, and you've already more than enough to take with you when you go, so go now, let me settle this. This is between him and me.'

'Why, though?' There was a softness in Naomi's voice, a rising musical melancholy. 'Why did you turn against him?'

'It was time,' Quigley said.

'It was . . . ?'

'When I knew he wanted to make me *like* him, a part of him. He would've done the same to you if you'd given him the chance.'

Michael shook his head, saying nothing. Every part of his mind and body felt numb, artificially suspended. Tom Quigley was all at once an unknown quantity, someone – something – he'd assumed he understood but had misjudged

249

completely. He was a victim like the rest: another outsider.

'Are you sure you want leaving alone with this?' Bill said weakly, but the answer was already self-evident.

Squinting into the daylight over breakfast, Bill shook his head and stirred his coffee with a look of fixed apprehension. 'We really shouldn't have let him, you know.'

'How's that?'

'There was something about him that afternoon – how can I put this? – something *other*. There's no way I recognised any such thing at the time, and no wonder; can't even remember when it first struck me, probably not for years. I mean, when you're staring oblivion in the face you don't see so clearly, do you?'

Michael pulled a face. 'What are you getting at, Bill? Is this some intractible new programmer's language you're speaking or what?'

'What bothered me – still does – was the feeling that Tom was just beginning. After what we'd witnessed, well, wasn't that enough? Wasn't that the end? But he spoke as if Sachs was still alive: "*This is between him and me*", remember, like Sachs was alive, like there was still unfinished business between them. And Sachs lying there with his face mashed to pieces.' With a sigh, he pushed his breakfast plate away from him, two buttered croissants untouched. 'Answer me this, Mike. Why do I sometimes get the feeling that what happened after we left Quigley was so much worse than what we saw for ourselves at the time? Why should I feel we're paying for something *else*, something we never took part in? Mikey, we should never have left Quigley alone.'

Michael stared at him, bewildered. After a moment he shrugged, returned to his coffee.

'Where are the others?' Bill said wearily.

'Linda went over to Nim's,' Michael said less than confidently. The hair at the back of his neck was bristling. 'They should be here any moment.'

250

Chapter Thirty-One

The brown dust rose, the HGV shrank from view, but as yet there was no sign of Naomi, who presumably hadn't sighted the Mini. Taking a deep, controlling breath, Linda threw her bag across her shoulder and started towards the tower block, which so early in the morning seemed a silent, sleeping grey monolith.

Her own echoing footsteps followed her through the main doors to a grimly unwelcoming foyer: concrete floors, regulation lime-green walls. Should human beings really be expected to live like this? It depressed her to think that Naomi had accepted such a fate. Surely two failed marriages couldn't be entirely to blame, given that Naomi had always been smart enough, able enough, to rise above small-town insignificance. It was as if she'd accepted her punishment, choosing her fate willingly; perhaps in the end that had been the reasonable, realistic thing to do. Perhaps no one really rose above their circumstances. Even Michael, shipped off to America, hadn't managed so much.

Taking the stairs to her right, she climbed the stairwell. As she reached the first floor a puddle of vomit blocked her path, and she sidestepped, trying not to inhale. Jesus – what was the difference between choosing to live here and allowing oneself to be abused by the likes of Quigley? Last night Naomi had described what he had done to her in bed; if she'd refused to tolerate him, why opt for this instead?

As she turned up the stairwell from the second floor Linda noticed a rapid fall in temperature, sharp enough to make her shiver. A door stood open to her right; at the threshold stood a dumpy mid-fortyish woman with a rat's maze of dark hair and distended, bruised lips and jaw. She wore only a white slip and punk fluffy slippers. Who would buy slippers like those, even when times were hard? Just as Linda passed by, a man's blunt, beery voice called out from somewhere behind the woman, summoning her inside. For a moment Linda sensed the woman's hunted, pleading stare following her; but she hurried up six or eight steps, and by the time she looked down the woman had vanished.

Oh Nim, she thought, this is such a sad, sorry place. Let's get you out of it, you and the children, once and for all.

The third floor was cooler even than the stairs, although the door giving access to the balcony was firmly closed. There was a moment, before she knocked at Naomi's door, when it seemed to Linda the cold was inside, preparing to unleash itself; but what she felt was most probably apprehension, the gnawing uncertainty Naomi's early morning call had set off in her. She knocked and waited, and presently Naomi's voice answered.

'Linda, is that you?'

'Yes, Nim. I made good time. Open up now.'

After a lull there was sudden muffled activity close behind the door, a scramble of movement, as if Naomi had decided there was no time to lose. The latch clicked, the handle turned; then Tom Quigley was at the door and, before she could act, or react, Linda was being dragged inside the room.

Once over the threshold Quigley stopped, grinned broadly, his whole face alive with muscular tics, and let go of her arm. She had no trouble in recognising him, though she couldn't think what to say; then she registered his shirt, the blood — surely it was blood — and saw his hands twitching from recent labours, and she half-turned away and it was then, with the room subsiding from her, that she saw Naomi upside down on the wall.

She had been nailed there. Quigley had nailed her there, though not before — she couldn't make herself look away — not before he had cut off her feet and hands. Or perhaps he had done that afterwards; it must have been easier once she had given up the struggle. With what must have been

252

a complete set of butcher's tools — knifes and bone-saws, skewers, all laid out on sheets of newspaper beneath her — he had literally taken Naomi to pieces: slashed her throat, gutted her, criss-crossed her face with lightning strokes of some terrible blade until there was no face left at all.

She was dead at least. Thank God she was dead, even though her eyes were still open. But that was because the lids had been cut off; presumably he'd made sure she would witness even her own farewell.

'It didn't last as long as you'd think,' he said softly, in a voice that, at another time, she might have mistaken for Naomi's. Weak with shock, Linda stumbled, recoiling, away from him, until the backs of her knees jarred against something solid, a chair or low table. In the same gentle feminine voice he said, 'All in all, she didn't suffer too badly. In fact she died very well: a martyr's death, practically.'

Her mind was reeling; she felt on the verge of falling, endlessly. Her lips worked with impossible questions, questions she had conjured up before, alone, many times: *Tom? Why? Why did any of this have to happen*? But all she heard was the despairing sigh somewhere deep within herself. It was worse, far worse, than her wildest dreams had led her to fear: this was more than mere butchery. In an instant, the blink of an eye, she caught sight of Naomi rippling through his features; the faintest hint of Naomi's gaze in his; and she knew. Then Quigley licked his lips, and she thought, perversely, of a cat caught red-handed, having swallowed the prize canary. Naomi was *inside* him, part of him, just as Alison Lester had been the night that call came through.

'It was *you* that I spoke to, Tom, wasn't it? You're the one who made those calls: not Alison, not Vinnie. There was always something else — something I couldn't define. It was those voices of yours, those tricks — '

'No tricks. Something more than tricks,' he said, sounding slighted, as though she'd missed the point. 'Good God, is that all you think it is?' Even now, his face, Naomi's voice, was fading, shifting, as if the flesh were grappling with itself. There was a wildness surfacing in his eyes now, more than the madness that must have driven him through the act of barbarism. Much worse, there was a quality she recognised, the life-spark of a new personality.

'There's a difference,' he began, 'a whole *world* of difference between *doing* somebody and *being* somebody. If it was down to me and me alone – Tom Quigley, the butt of your jokes, the loser – ' He was beating his chest – 'there's no way on earth we'd be here now, trying to finish this. If it had been up to me there wouldn't have been any comeback. I was to blame more than you.'

'Then how, Tom, how ...' But she already knew, and this was a question for which there could be no answer she wanted to hear. Quigley moved his lips a fraction, perhaps even spoke, but she was too numb to hear or feel anything but the screaming silent fear that felt layered, one level of terror beneath another. There was something in his features now that reminded her of Sachs. Was this, she thought frantically, something Alison had witnessed at the last? And Vinnie? And Naomi?

'Linda.' He smiled, and the last of her strength seemed to ebb. 'Yeah, you're right. It was me all along. I'm here again. All of us are.'

This was worse still, not least because the voice somehow failed to match the features. What she heard sounded trapped, half-formed; a mockery of Vinnie Hartley's whine, Alison Lester's clipped, street-smart patter. No, he wasn't quite Sachs, not yet. Could she make the door in the time it took him to adjust? He looked so alive, unconfused; in between characters he might have been, but they were *his* now, they were *him*. They were residents.

'It's been such a long time since we were together,' he said.

Something snapped.

Linda breathed in, and the next thing she knew she was flinging herself, involuntarily, towards the closed door, in an act of sheer desperation. The odds were impossible. Even as she hit the woodwork she knew it was too late to grapple it open. The door refused her first weak tug, and in any case he was right there behind her, yanking her back, then thrusting her forward so hard the door smashed her nose.

At first the pain felt too small, too ethereal to be pain; but this was only the first layer of many, and her senses sang, and briefly she floated, high then higher, out of herself. *'Please,'* she cried out, slamming the door with both palmed hands. Even then she couldn't hear the noise she was surely creating. She tasted the dull metallic taste of blood, saw the first redness from her nose smeared across the white gloss paintwork. Then Quigley was turning her around to face himself, Sachs had his hands on her shoulders and was turning her, forcing her to look into those eyes, the windows of captive souls, and she tasted more blood and clasped a hand to her face and saw red on her palm; then beyond it, Sachs smiling levelly.

'But we killed you ...' she murmured. 'We laid you to *rest* ...'

'No rest for the wicked,' he replied with a laugh, and licked his lips emphatically, reminding her of the moment — brought it rushing back, every unwelcome detail — when he had spoken to her through the letter-flap, assaulting her with his words. He wanted to do that again now, she could see, for the lips were the same lips and his posture was such that more violence seemed likely, but this time he wanted really and truly to fuck her without wasting words on the fantasy. Dead or alive hardly mattered. *Please*, she repeated, but her mouth was dry, there was no sound, only terror and terrible impressions of the room: Naomi, a dark red patch on the wall directly in her field of vision; the weapons displayed on the floor beneath her; the parts of her anatomy he'd removed placed strategically on sideboards and shelves like ornaments.

She gagged as his hand found her throat. She closed her eyes and thought briefly, longingly, of last night in Michael's hotel room. She wanted that to be the last thing on her mind when she died. Instead she was alone with her killer, no one listening. She had no voice, and this was the end. Her eyes were closed and she saw only grey.

Although she was ready, death didn't come. Quigley's fingers remained at her throat, but relaxed, didn't strengthen their grip. *Please*, she thought, or said, or screamed. There was blood everywhere, all through the room, flooding her mind. Then Quigley said softly, 'You're special, you know.

255

And this isn't good enough; you deserve something better than this.'

She swallowed and opened her eyes. There was at least as much of Quigley as Sachs about him now; he was crying, his eyes moist and pink, lips puckering.

'Let me . . .' she began, 'Tom, let me go. You don't want this to continue. It's so much easier to put an end to it.'

'Really?' He had her in focus again.

'Really, honestly. You're not responsible, *he* is, Roy *Sachs* is, no one else.' She was striving for something beyond reach, casting reason before lunacy. 'Don't let him make you think *you* were the one. Tom, if you ever – '

But his smile quickly silenced her. 'You see, we're all in this together, all of us who belong to the body. That was the master plan, Linda. I woke up one morning and understood everything. If the body wouldn't accept me, I'd just have to accomodate *it*. Do you know how it feels to be locked outside, never wanted, never welcome? You didn't have to face that; you were always on the inside looking out.'

'Bullshit! We were never like that. The Brotherhood came about because *none* of us belonged, because everyone who was included wanted something more, something new and unusual – God knows what. We were different then in some ways: we were dreamers, but we change, Tom, we change. Is it really right to punish us now for the way we were all that time ago?'

'It's the will of God,' said the Source, without a flicker. 'It doesn't involve right or wrong. It's His will, is all.'

'It's what?'

'I asked you once if you judged others by their actions, remember?'

She remembered: Alison Lester, a voice from nowhere, the first shattering night of this journey through the past. Alison must have been there, carved to pieces, in the room when he called.

'Well, it's difficult not to,' he said. 'Especially when you can't imagine the outcome. What you don't understand, you who judge, is the *good* that comes with suffering.'

'Good?' She took in the room, the blood, Naomi's remains. 'What good?'

'We're perfected through suffering. That's how He makes us like Himself. Purge the body and the spirit will flourish, and believe me, *this* body needs purging, this gold refining by fire.'

He was close to the edge, a flicker of madness in his eyes, and she was acutely conscious without having to look of his hands clenching; unclenching. She tried to buy time.

'You'll have to help me out, I don't follow,' she said. 'You'll have to explain what you mean.'

'That's fine, there's time. And I want you to understand everything. What's important is that we can be together again, this time forever, without being separated. Isn't that remarkable?' Now he was searching his jacket for something. As he did so the telephone rang, though he seemed not to notice or care as he dragged out a coiled mass of rope, the same kind he had used against Tara — and against Vinnie, years later. 'Don't worry. This is for your own good — to make sure you don't try anything foolish.' On the thirteenth ring, the telephone went quiet.

She had nothing left to fight with; when he asked to bind her wrists she offered no resistance, kept still as he tightened the knot. At least when he pushed her outside the flat, she experienced a flood of relief to be leaving the bloody vision of Naomi behind. At least he wouldn't kill her in there, like that. *She* deserved better, he'd told her — whatever that meant.

On the second floor, while he guided her downstairs by an elbow, she saw the woman with the bruised face again. She was back at her doorway in her ridiculous slippers, smoking a cigarette. Behind her, so loud it distorted, the breakfast television news.

'Please help,' Linda said as the Source drew her past, towards the next flight of the stairs. 'Please! He's going to kill me.'

The woman exhaled smoke from her nostrils and fingered her bruises, smiling sadly, appreciatively. 'Yes, dear. Don't think I don't know how that feels.'

Chapter Thirty-Two

They had been driving for perhaps ten minutes when Quigley said, without prompting, 'It was something more than killing for the sake of it. You'll need to understand that much before you'll see why I did what I did.'

He was at the wheel, idling through the dust-brown streets that were only now coming alive with traffic. Linda, whose ankles he had bound once they'd reached the car in the forecourt outside the flats, lay huddled on the floor in the back. 'It's fair to say he taught me everything I know, so I can't really hate him. We're too much a part of each other for that. What I learned from him has helped me survive.'

At least he hadn't gagged her as well, but she had nothing to say. She was too preoccupied, not only with the blooming mass of numbness in her face but the thought that he planned much worse for her than this.

'Is there anything you'd like to ask?' he wondered, and went on regardless. 'It really began with the dog. Was it yours? He had a thing about the dog *because* it was yours: it must have meant something to him, I couldn't guess what, or maybe he was using it to demonstrate something.' She sensed the car slowing for a junction before turning left, then sharp right. 'There was a power came out of it − a life-force, you follow? It felt like a light coming on in my head, and the power was in my veins, my blood. It felt like coming, only not so urgent, and not over so soon, but going on and on and on. Roy explained how it worked at the time, but it took me days to really see for myself. Then I knew the dog was inside me – the body was dead and gone but everything else was right there, in me. And I guess there was something deep inside that I couldn't contain, that drove me, well, *wild*.' He managed a mirthless laugh. 'So that dog gave me something – Roy helped it give me something I'd been trying for all my life. My dad used to tell me I had the gift anyway – even used to warn me I'd lose it if I didn't watch out – but he was wrong; I had nothing inside me until then.'

Linda dry-swallowed. The car was travelling too slowly, as if she were part of some grand and sombre funeral procession. She closed her eyes and saw Naomi plastered to the wall, saw what Vinnie Hartley's landlord had seen, and for one unbearable moment pictured Quigley there too, lost in the act he was perpetrating, his arms slickly red to the elbows. She was too numb to weep now, too broken to mourn, even for friends with whom she had shared so much. The Mini cornered again, and she heard the town fade and then the familiar countryside hush, the traffic on distant roads like a muted, fast-flowing stream.

'And is that what you did to the others?' she asked, forcing the words from her aching throat 'You destroyed their bodies and stole what was left? That night at Sams when I heard Alison's voice on the phone – I was still hearing Alison? You weren't just playing games?'

'All I am,' he replied, 'is a vessel – an empty vessel. And that's all I ever was to your lot, something that Roy brought along for the laughs, a dummy he could speak through; push the right button and I'd perform for kicks. But now it's for real; I am *me*, and the voices aren't jokes anymore. I can be filled with anything, anyone, and these characters – these people – are my family. You'll be part of us soon, Linda, and we'll all be together, the way it was meant.'

She could smell the trees, sweet scented pine, and knew instinctively where he was taking her. 'But there's Michael ...' she began; she was clutching at straws, striving for anything that might hold him off. 'I left him a note to say where to meet. Just like old times. I'd planned to take Nim there; we'd arranged it last thing last night ... Michael will be on his way over now.' She waited for his judgement.

'Do you really think I wouldn't *know* if we'd planned for that?' he replied in a voice that was suddenly softly feminine, too familiar, chillingly reminiscent of Naomi. 'She's inside my head, Linda; her thoughts are mine, my memories are hers, we share everything. Of course I know what we discussed last night.'

'We?'

'You and I.'

'You *can't* know that.'

'Everything Naomi was, I am now.'

'Then you both need help,' she said quietly.

'No, Linda. *You're* the one needing help. Just look at yourself — who's there for you when you really need it? Where are they *now*?'

Alive and well and living somewhere inside you, she thought. 'But you, Tom, you were the one who finally killed Sachs — so why turn against us now? Haven't we been punished enough?'

'You'd better ask him that.'

'Who? Roy Sachs'?'

'Who else? After all, *he* knows the secret. Roy was the one who showed me that strength is perfected through weakness.'

'What happened, Tom?' she wanted to know; to her own amazement she genuinely wanted to know. 'What went on between you and him?'

'Ah, now *there's* a long story,' he said, and she sensed him softening, wanting to confess, and the car slowing further as if its speed were governed by his concentration.

It was a very long story, many scenes from which she had already lived through. But until now she hadn't known what had lived in Tom Quigley's heart. She hadn't known about the deadness in there; the passion; the hunger. 'It began with the dog that day,' he began. 'What we received from her made me realise how much more life there was out there; how much power just crying out to be — assimilated. Once, there was a newsreel ...'

A newsreel in which the brown starving victims of some bloody civil war in a dark and neglected backward continent were seen piled together, twisted and broken and swollen;

and staring, transfixed, into the cathode ray tube, he had sensed the life escaping them, still hovering perceptibly above the unfed bellies and jutting, bony arms, the wasted power rushing out to fill the world, from the world. All this horror from the world, so much of it. The dead were everywhere; and soon every life stopped short before its time began, suddenly, to mean something to him as he sat there, mesmerised by the TV screen: potential. From every ending there could be a great beginning. Life must go on ... and on. And he remembered the light that rushed forth from Tara, and how it filled him to overflowing, and knew that he'd discovered the secret. Each time he took a new life for himself, he could access that source of power. With a garden spade he struck Roy Sachs down in a moment of rage, thinking only of being free, breaking the bond once and for all. The crowd were screaming, he sensed their cries charged with hunger for blood, and in that moment he knew only one thing: the bastard must perish. This *has* to end. After the rains came he breathed the sweet new air and saw the redness washed away by the rain, his spirit stirring. *Potential*, he thought. *It mustn't become wasted potential. The body must perish but the spirit will soar.*

'Why you, though?' Linda demanded now. 'How come only you know the secret? Why can't the rest of us see what you've seen?'

Others do constantly, he told her. Many are called but few are chosen. There were countless others out there somewhere: undernourished scavengers, empty vessels longing to be filled, to claim life where they found it. Perhaps *you* are one of us, he shrugged, his voice never wavering.

Once, there had been a newsreel ...

And he had witnessed the secret for himself and understood.

'Leave this to me,' he had told the others. 'This is my responsibility now.' Slowly, reluctantly, they gathered themselves together in the dark and filed slowly from the ice-house, backing from the clearing while he stood near the entrance, unable to tear themselves away. 'Go *on*,' he cried. 'It's *over*, this is him and me now.' Two

261

of the girls, Naomi and Linda, were in tears, the others were either mortified or numb. That was the last time he had seen them all together.

The rain had relented and the woods sounded clean and new as a breeze stirred the branches overhead and droplets of water cascaded down. The birdsong was here and there, speculative, stopping and starting. Above the ice-house, just before the land inclined down the slope, he found heaps of dead bracken and splintered branches, crackling drily. These he manoeuvred to the entrance, arranging them so that even the remains of the old, rust-hinged gate were concealed. The nearest footpaths were some distance away, and it was unlikely that supervised dogs would stray this far afield. Even for someone knowing the den's whereabouts, the entrance would be difficult to locate now. From above and below it, all that was visible was the scrub. Satisfied, he turned away towards home, leaving Sachs, still enshrined in the dark, to the birdsong. It was wiser, he felt, to finish the task once the light had begun to fade. In the meantime, Sachs wasn't likely to go walkabout.

At home, alone in the lounge with the framed psalms on the walls, he quickly grew restless, wringing his hands, wishing there were someone he could explain himself to, share the burden with. There was no one, of course, only Roy – and Roy was out of reach for the moment. One thing especially troubled him: where was the life-force, the equivalent of what he'd felt when the dog passed away? Shouldn't there have been at least some flicker, some sign, when he struck the second blow that killed Roy? He couldn't still be alive, could he? – not with his face in pieces like that. Then maybe there was something more, another dimension to the secret: maybe some lives lay dormant for a time, not rushing out at the moment of death. Perhaps even – and this thought astonished him – perhaps Roy understood what was meant to happen next, and was waiting. Waiting for Tom to return.

As if to spite him the light seemed to last indefinitely. By seven, his nerves were fraying, he couldn't keep still. Before leaving he strayed to his father's shed, with its solid workbench and racks of polished tools – his father

262

had always encouraged physical work, claiming it helped cleanse the soul. From here he collected the equipment he needed, loading it into an empty kit-bag which he found draped from a nail behind the door. There were shovels and spades at the ice-house already, so he needn't worry about hauling those too. Taking care to throw the bolt on the door, he set off.

There wasn't a great distance between home and Parks Wood — no more than a fifteen minute stroll through two back-to-back housing estates — but it felt like miles, the time passing in protracted slow motion, his steps leaden and weary. Worse, each face in the street seemed familiar. Neighbours stared as he passed, scowling and chuntering when he failed to return their acknowledgements. 'Hey, Tom,' gushed someone he knew from school; adding sharply to his back, 'Bugger you then, don't speak.' But if they saw his face, he calculated, they were likely to read his intentions; he couldn't afford to reveal his guilt, not so close to the prize. He hurried along, head down, nervous heat pricking his skin.

At least there was no sign of the Brotherhood, which was what he'd most feared. His route took him close to Linda Hartley's house and, regardless of what had been said about splitting up, never meeting again, it was hard to imagine them keeping to such an agenda. Surely they needed each other now more than ever, at least until the memory of the nightmare became manageable. Everyone needed someone — besides which, Sachs had died trying to split them apart. Wasn't it self-defeating, allowing his death to achieve everything he'd wanted in life?

To his relief there was no sign of anyone at Linda's, though the curtains were drawn as if to block out the whole sordid experience. Did she really believe running for cover would make any difference? At the gate he hesitated, half-expecting the curtains to move; if Linda had shown her face he wouldn't have known what to do. Finally, the work-tools growing heavier at his side, he moved on.

Above him the rooftops were now lapsing into silhouette against a cloudless sky as red as coagulated blood. Somewhere in the distance he heard the snarls and yelps of a dog-fight

263

and neighbours screaming in panic to stop it. His senses were heightened, as if everything out there in the dusk felt his presence. By the time he reached the church, where several cars were parked for the evening service, he was able to imagine Roy lying in state, willing Tom to hurry, to claim the prize. He passed the church without incident, without being spotted, picked up his step to the thoroughfare, and was free.

Entering the woods he heard, briefly − before he broke into a run and the sound dissolved behind him − the first of the evening's hymns on the night air. Although the song was new and unfamiliar to his ears, and he didn't know the words, he picked out the melody, humming it as he went, repeating and repeating the same cycle of notes until the song became an incantation that carried him forward, through deeper woods, along darker pathways, towards his finest hour.

The clearing was like a vision, he thought, a vision of an idyllic world cast in blood. Fringed by the trembling upper reaches of the trees, the sky seemed haemorrhaged, its redness spreading outwards like a veil, intensifying to colour everything in sight. This world was, he marvelled, his mirror. Its brightness was light guiding the way, directing his steps to the den. In seconds he had worked loose the foliage that clogged the entrance, casting it aside, here and there, no longer caring to hold himself back. A weird incandescent light blurred his vision; everything appeared fringed with blood. Perspiring, he knelt at the entrance for long minutes, gazing into the waiting dark, breathing deeply, letting his senses drift. The smell of death filled his mouth. The kit-bag of work-tools lay on the ground near by. He looked at his hands: small, pale, fragile hands which indolence had kept from labour until now. But there were times when blisters were gained for a purpose, when lesions could be worn with pride. This was his moment, and the darkening sky seemed to know it, and at long last, dragging Roy Sachs outdoors into the wash of red light, he set to work.

The car was idling, pulling over, which meant they had either arrived or Quigley wanted to finish his account at leisure.

Linda, unable to block out the slow, insistent drone of his voice, screwed her eyes tight, willing him not to go on. Her hands were fixed, immobile, and she could not cover her ears; her shoulders and limbs ached with cramp. 'Please, Tom,' she managed, but Quigley proceeded as though she had never spoken, almost as though he'd forgotten she was there.

He was lost again – as he'd needed to be in order to see the task through. The flesh, he explained, was just an obstacle, not something he could let distract him. Crouching low over Sachs, inhaling death, he saw that both eyes were glazed and wide open, bisected by the deep gash which had finished him. Even halved like this the face was still clearly Sachs', the gaze darkly penetrating, a gaze impossible to hold for too long. Because he was no longer a physical being, because this body like all bodies must eventually perish, Quigley decided to work on the face first of all. Using a heavy bone-handled hunting knife he cross-hatched the brow, cheeks and shattered nose with thirty or forty strategic sharp downward blows and angled swipes until Sachs' was no longer recognisably himself. All flesh was like this, he marvelled: malleable, easily transformed, appalling in its mortal condition. Look at it now; see what it all amounted to. Once a leader, living and feeling and breathing, spreading fear and unease amongst peers; now dead meat.

Having re-drawn the face, Quigley then set about removing the head from the torso. For this he employed a hacksaw from his father's workshop with a new twelve-inch stainless steel blade that kinked twice as he worked but never broke. This all took time, however. The dense knot of superficial neck muscle proved tougher, more resilient than he'd anticipated; then twice he struck bone and was forced to reapply the blade, adjusting the angle of incision. Everything now was bathed in red; his hands were quickly coated to the wrists, like slick gloves. He decided it would be preferable, all things considered, to keep the head intact, without further subdivision. Pausing for breath, he imagined, wistfully, hanging it from the tree like a trophy – it would have been so appropriate for Sachs, an exhibitionist to the last – but really the point was to bury him here so that no one would find or identify him.

But surely there was nothing so wrong about planting the head in the shade beneath the tree, or arranging the limbs some distance apart from it, the right arm twenty metres due south, the left the same distance due north, the trunk somewhere central, the legs –

Tom Quigley wiped his brow, smearing it crimson, as the half-formed thought took hold. Something about the idea appealed to him, as if separating the body while maintaining its structure was the most respectful way to put Sachs to rest. This way, it would be as if the body were a larger, more considerable force than could ever have been possible in life. Its power was dispersed, sent far afield across the earth, yet in pieces it remained identifiably whole.

Straining to cut loose the first arm where the bone was weakest, at the clavicle, Quigley had the strangest sensation that what he was really doing was making history – planting history. Under a brooding night sky as deeply red as his fingers he was summoning something greater than himself, greater even than the life-force he craved.

Adrenaline carried him forward now. Sweat beaded the tip of his nose and drenched his back. As the blade jerked sharply beneath him and the limb gave with a muffled damp splintering noise and came free, he sensed he was being watched. Glancing up, he noticed that Sachs' lips had formed a vacant smile, that his eyes glared accusingly from the stippled mess of his face. Sachs wasn't still alive; it was only an impression created by his own hyped-up nerves. Yet anything was possible now, wasn't it? He'd crossed the line, broken many worldly laws in these past few hours: mightn't he have broken several *un*worldly laws too? But this was no time for contemplation. Licking his cracked dry lips, he lifted and placed the head face down to the ground so that he wouldn't see the eyes and made ready to continue. Then he shifted the blade neatly across to the right shoulder. As he drew the hacksaw steadily towards him, particles of light seemed to leap from the wound he was opening.

No, Sachs wasn't alive; but this was a sign that his power was still here for the taking. He *had* been waiting for Quigley after all. Quigley was jubilant. The light diffracting in front of his face, white and yellow and blue, was at least as intense as it had been before. Without thinking, unable to think, he let the saw fall and clasped his hands firmly, prayerfully together. Then he gasped as the force of a hand – at least, it felt like a hand – seized his stomach and twisted. At the same time the red-tainted light seemed to deepen, grow thicker, as if a curtain of blood had been drawn across the clearing.

This was not as before. He sensed no euphoria, in spite of the lights. Whatever he'd tapped into was affecting his breathing as well as his vision, and for a second he was suffocating, his mouth clammy with the rusty taste of old blood. At the same time he knew it would be pointless to run. This was only a moment, a bridge to cross, a final nervous flutter before he claimed what he'd come for.

He tried to stand, thinking that to stretch his legs and clear his head would be all that was necessary, but something held him rigid, every muscle tensed: a surge of blind hatred and anger that came from nowhere, that made him want to strike out, destroy, tear to pieces. The feeling shook his whole body. The invisible hand grasping his stomach twisted sharply again. Firmly fixed in his mind was a graphic image of Michael McCourt, the head of the so-called body, stripped and gutted and strung from the bough of the tree one bright golden dawn. Then further pictures came to mind, one after another, a flood of barbaric details: other members of The Brotherhood flayed and burnt and eyeless, turned inside out, dissected and scalped and left for the birds. So much horror, he thought bitterly, from the world. So much horror from within.

Then he understood where the images came from – and worse, what he'd really accomplished by killing Roy Sachs. These mercenary thoughts, this will to pay back the debt, were all Sachs'; so too was this teeming red vision of the world, glimpsed through a curtain of blood, through a smokescreen of burning flesh. No wonder he felt no euphoria; this was as good as it got. Sachs was inside him, and there would be no more light shows, no giddy spiritual highs, because this was the inside of Roy's soul.

267

Not yet sixteen, Tom Quigley had inherited the secret, and for the first time could see his life mapped out before him in a way that made sense. If nothing else, this gift would raise him above the mediocrity of small-town small mindedness; in one stroke he'd become a man with a mission. A mission to search and destroy: even if it took months; a year; fifteen years. Since life had conspired to make him an outsider, that was what he would be.

For a time he saw and understood and considered this. Nothing stirred in the woods outside his brief reverie. He was alone here, and insane. *This is my body*, he thought, gazing down on the various severed parts of the now anonymous corpse. If any man's body is a temple then it must be torn down, in order to be rebuilt, made new again.

'So now,' Tom Quigley said to Linda Walker, 'you'll appreciate what's been achieved. So much has come together since then, and now, well, the body is almost complete.' He spoke, as if to demonstrate the point, in a voice that sounded like a fusion of souls: Vinnie, Naomi, himself.

'What now, then?' she asked. 'Me? Then Michael? Then Bill? Won't you rest until you have all of us?'

The Source licked his lips.

'Michael will be here soon,' she said, but the lack of conviction in her voice made her cringe.

'It's late,' he said dreamily. 'Later than I would've preferred.' He sat for several minutes, breathing so faintly she wondered if he had fallen asleep. Then, opening the car door, he flipped the seat forward, reaching into the rear towards Linda. Past him, outside, she could see rickety wooden fencing, a stile and a flourish of trees just beyond.

How long since she'd been here? Unfolding herself from the Mini, she wished she could draw reassurance from such a familiar sight; but with her last visit here the endless, waking nightmare had begun, and while Quigley untied her ankles so that she could walk with him back to the ice-house she wondered whether this was where, finally, it was going to end.

Chapter Thirty-Three

They arrived at the flat to find the door unlocked and Naomi
as her assassin had left her. Bill set eyes on her first: he was
standing in silence at the door when Michael floundered to
the top of the stairwell behind him.

'Are they in?' Michael asked, edging nearer.

'Naomi's here. If it is her. Maybe you'd better see for
yourself.'

It took Michael several seconds to take in the vision,
to make sense of it; then he was sagging involuntarily
against the door-jamb, overwhelmed, his mind swimming.
The room subsided, narrowing itself to a convex pinhole
image. He had seen works of art of this kind on gallery
walls, portraits by Francis Bacon which seemed torn from
bleak dreams; vivid, splashy action paintings by de Kooning
and Pollock and their protegées. But this was flesh and blood
he was staring at, once warm and vibrant, once alive, now
fit for nothing. What sort of mind would want to distort
and transform the human body to this degree? How ugly
we are once the mask's off, he thought, how terrible under
the surface.

'Please let this stop,' Bill murmured, his voice faintly
cracking.

Outside, their taxi was waiting. Falling into it, they reclined
on the rear seat, neither speaking, neither knowing what to
say. Michael's mouth felt thick and clammy; the warmth
and smell of leather in the taxi was suffocating.

'Where to?' the driver asked.

For long moments there was no reply. 'Jesus,' Michael

said at last, wiping his brow. 'The man has a point. Where to? Where the fuck are we supposed to go now?'

The driver shook his head slowly; the meter clunked up another unit.

Finally Bill said, 'If you were Quigley, where would you go?'

Michael considered, then gave a nod. 'Parks Wood,' he told the driver. 'The south side, just outside town. Quick as you can.'

It was still before nine, and the roads were clogged with traffic using the town for a thoroughfare. This was not a place people journeyed to but one they passed through, or avoided altogether. 'Spend enough time here,' Michael said sourly, 'and see what becomes of you.'

Safer in New York, he thought; safer on any sleazy sidestreet in Alphabet City after dark than here, in this nondescript no-man's-land. Now, in slow motion, he saw the small town once again for what it really was: the littered streets, the overstuffed lidless dustbins through which underfed dogs were foraging; the unwanted infants put out first thing in the morning, taken in last thing at night like cats; row upon row of brown terraces crippled by vandalism, subsidence, neglect. Rubbled housing estates, demolished, never rebuilt. All of this could be found in Manhattan, simply by walking a few blocks in any direction – the difference being that here this was *all* there was. Here, there were no glittering symbols, no aspirations just around the next corner.

'If the bastard harms one hair of her head,' Michael began, and tailed off, his breath forming mist on the window.

'Yes, I know,' Bill whispered. 'Yes, I know.'

'Is this where he's been leading us, do you think? Is this part of his plan, to take us apart one by one until no one is left? Finish it there, where it started? Where's the sense in that? Where's the reason?'

'There never was any reason,' Bill said.

Soon they were stop-starting along the market streets, where with heavy eyes Michael saw the ghosts of yesterday's traders still preparing their stalls before business hours. Crates of damaged goods, ripped and torn garments, bruised fruit, blocked the road; a handful of early shoppers fidgeted, browsed.

He blinked at the empty town centre, the dark mouth of the alley he and Vinnie had dodged through, and thought abstractedly: we're almost there again ... back at that time where we first discovered each other, became one body. For a moment he could taste the aromatic peat, picture the day he and Vinnie tumbled into the ice-house to find Linda reclining there, no less startled than themselves.

'What are we going to do?' he said. Bill fingered his beard and gazed without a flicker of expression from the window. 'More to the point, what's Quigley going to do?'

'Do you think she's still alive?' Bill wondered.

'Linda? God, we have to believe so. If not, how come he didn't finish her there, like Naomi? She has to be alive. Otherwise we've – ' Come so far for nothing, he almost concluded, as if his and her survival were all that truly mattered. Even now, at the dark heart of his panic there was selfishness, the simple fear of losing what he wanted to keep, and he hated himself for it.

'Then why?' Bill frowned. 'If all he wants is to tear us apart one by one, why is he bothering to keep *her* alive?'

The taxi driver coughed, and Michael met his gaze in the rear-view mirror. His stare told the driver: just keep going and mind your own business.

'Your guess is as good as mine,' he replied in a whisper. 'Perhaps he *knows* ...'

'Knows what?'

'That we're on our way. That after us, there's no one else. Perhaps this really is as far as he wants it to go and it really does end here.'

He was about to go on when Bill sat forward sharply. 'Pull over, right here, right here.' He was already fumbling cash from a pocket with one hand while battling the door with the other when the taxi shrieked to a standstill, whiplashing both passengers back in their seats.

They had stopped, Michael saw at once, directly behind Linda's Mini, abandoned askew in a passing place on the edge of the woods. The door on the driver's side stood wide open; there was no sign of anyone inside. He was out of the

271

taxi and striding towards the rickety wooden stile before Bill had finished paying the driver.

'You want me to wait?' the driver asked, and Bill shook his head.

'Don't bother. Chances are we won't make it back alive anyway. Here, keep the change.'

With a crash of gears the driver fled at speed towards safety and sanity.

Chapter Thirty-Four

As he blundered her into the clearing, yanking her wrists so firmly the rope burned her skin, it seemed to Linda that nothing had changed in her absence: time had frozen since she'd last set foot in these woods. Even the silence was the same: the bated-breath atmosphere that made the undergrowth crackle with tension, the leaves return the wind's whisper as if the dead were conspiring against all-comers. Grey squirrels scattered for cover, skirting rapidly up convenient trees as they passed; blackbirds took flight, clucking frantic warnings. She was gasping involuntarily now. Though she wanted to scream, her panic was a firm hand gagging her mouth. Across the clearing the tree which had haunted her days and nights these fifteen years had changed only slightly, its pitted trunk now a rich mossy green. At first she was convinced that this was where he was guiding her, intending to string her up from the bough as he'd done to Tara — and then he was veering past, past the overgrown mound that marked the dog's grave, down the slight incline to the ice-house. As they reached the entrance he stopped, so abruptly the rope snared her wrist, and looked at her.

She knew he wasn't seeing her. She glared back at him, but he didn't react. He had heard a sound she couldn't begin to imagine. 'What?' she said; and then Quigley put a finger to his lips, shushing her.

'There's someone inside,' he announced quietly. Then, turning his attention to the ice-house entrance, his voice became a snarl, sheer Sachs. 'Get *out*! Get fucking *out* of there before I'm forced to come in and fucking well drag you out! Do you hear me?' His face was contorting, a malleable mask of rubber. 'You don't belong here. Find your *own* place. This is *ours*, understand? It's always been ours.'

There was a long, uncertain moment before his threat filtered through to whoever was holed up inside. Then there was activity, at first gradual and cautious, somewhere down in the dark recess beyond the opening.

Linda drew breath, felt her stomach contract. Her heartbeat seemed impossibly rapid, violent enough to split her apart. Quigley gave a fierce quick tug at the rope binding her wrists and she flinched. Her first inclination was to cry for help, and then she recoiled, struck by the sudden heart-stopping thought that some half-human thing was about to crawl forth from the earth, a body stitched together from the disparate severed parts of Quigley's victims, a limb hacked from Vinnie, a face flayed from Alison, an incomplete body crying out to be finished.

But the first face she sighted, pale-skinned and lightly freckled, squinting, deprived of daylight, was distorted by fear, not the butcher's knife. She was staring into the narrowed eyes of a boy at least half her own age. As he scrambled forward through the entrance he glanced anxiously at Linda, then at Quigley, all the while mouthing a silent apology. Close behind him came two others, a second teenage boy, bedenimed and long-haired, and a girl whose intense dark features Naomi had shared. *Oh no*, Linda thought, Not again.

'Get out of my sight,' Tom Quigley said.

The first boy nodded, backed away. 'We're sorry if we ... Is this really your place?' he said to Linda, guilty, half-pleading.

'It used to be,' she told him. 'Please do as he says. Don't get involved, don't ask questions.'

With a nod the boy half-turned, backed off. The others followed, their eyes on Linda's wrists, which were bleeding. 'All we were doing,' the girl said, 'was sitting there, talking. That's all we've ever done in there, so you see this was always *our* place, ever since we found it. You've no cause to do this.' Her gaze found Quigley's for a second, and she faltered. 'What are you ... What are you going to do?'

'Ask no questions,' Quigley replied evenly, in a single sweep drawing from his jacket lining a kitchen knife with a gleaming six-inch blade, 'and I'll tell you no lies. Now out of my sight before I answer you less politely.'

'Sure, no problem, right away.' But the girl, though retreating, was addressing Linda. 'Is there something we can do? Get help?'

'Just go,' Linda said. 'Stay out of it.' Then the threesome were sprinting across the clearing, legs pinwheeling, in and out the dappled shadows, finally vanishing from sight through a flourish of dark undergrowth, taking her last hopes with them. What now? she thought, but the clearing, the tree, the ice-house offered no reprieve. Once, this place had spelled liberation; now ...

'Get down on your knees,' the Source told her.

'No way.'

He brandished the knife, its blade lovingly, no doubt painstakingly sharpened. She heard it slice the air as he wafted it back and forth, imagined how easily it would slice anything else. She musn't give in though, not as long as her ankles remained untied. She backed up slowly, considering the odds, whether her legs would support her if she made for the woods. But then he was at her, so suddenly he must have been reading her mind, and the blade was poised at her throat while his free hand forced her down by the shoulder.

Her knees buckled easily. The ground underneath her was a soft morass of dead leaves and dry bark, and the pressure of his hand was too much for her.

'Is this what you're about, Sachs?' she spat. It made sense, she reasoned, to call him by his true name. 'Is this all you're good for? Bullying, brutalising anyone who gets in your way? No wonder you were never accepted, no wonder we kept you outside – '

'Shut up, shut up!' To her surprise he looked confused by her words, her naming of Sachs, and momentarily the knife lolled slack in his hand. Perhaps anger was the best chance she had right now: no matter how distressed she felt she musn't let him see, for terror only encouraged him, fuelled his appetite for more. 'One more word out of you and ...'

'Yes?' Linda challenged him. 'One more word and you'll what?'

His eyes narrowed; a glimmer of bewilderment, surely significant.

'Is it tough?' she wondered, 'carrying so many others around inside your head? That is, when you don't see eye to eye – when you want to go your separate ways?'

'We don't!' His voice trembled with hostility and resentment: and, perhaps, fear. 'We don't go separate ways. We are one.'

She was on the right track, she sensed it in her bones. Bound and forced to her knees, submissive at the point of the knife, she nevertheless held the initiative.

'But are you all agreed this time?' She said, 'Or does Sachs do all your thinking for you? *Alison*,' she said abruptly, so apruptly her attacker flinched, 'are you really happy to have some man – this man, this *thing* – dictate everything on your behalf? You were always so strong in yourself, such an outlaw, never taking orders. So what happened? And *Vinnie* –' Call them each by name, she thought; bring them forward, draw them out one by one. 'Vinnie, tell me, how did it feel when he carved you up? When the knife went in and he took you apart piece by piece? Don't you resent being held prisoner by someone who made such a mess of you?'

'Fuck you,' he said, livid, the knife poised at shoulder height for the downstroke. 'You're such a sly bitch. I'll fuck you with this knife just for that; fuck you and gut you with it. Christ, you're not even worth –' His eyes rolled skywards, and briefly he was lost, his thoughts scattered, his mouth working noiselessly.

'Who are you now?' she said, still baiting.

He gazed at her, still undecided.

'*Tom*,' she insisted. 'Didn't it ever strike you that what you've become is worse than the showroom dummy, the empty vessel, you used to be? When you killed Sachs, didn't you mean to leave him behind, to stop him controlling you? So what are you now, Tom? Who are you now?'

His lips and nostrils were quivering like those of a petulant schoolboy. Linda half-closed her eyes, convinced the blade was about to flash down, punish her for her taunting. Then, at the far side of the clearing, she saw Michael and Bill, red-faced from running, slowing as they entered the frame-frozen scene. Yet for the moment she felt no hope, no relief; she had gone too far for that.

'Who are you, Tom, really? Who are you underneath all this show?'

She might die for these words. But all that she had in the end was her ability to reason, to help others see themselves for what they were. If she possessed any gift it was this.

'See, Tom?' she exclaimed, flinging a hand towards Michael and Bill. 'Everyone's here now, it's almost complete. Isn't this what you wanted, the whole body together again? Brothers and sisters — Vinnie, Ali, Nim — we're here, can you see us?'

Perhaps the homecoming was all too much, or he'd taken as much as he could from her. The knife slipped from Quigley's hand, skimming her shoulder as it fell, rooting itself in the ground.

'Who are you, Tom?' she repeated. 'Underneath?'

Empty-eyed, he shook his head. He was almost in tears. There was a momentary lull, a terrible silence. At the periphery of her vision she saw Michael edge nearer, though she couldn't distinguish his face and didn't want to lose sight of Quigley, who was stooping to the ground, falling to his knees directly in front of her, as if begging for absolution. 'Let them go,' she whispered. 'Go ahead Tom, be a true Brother; let our friends go free. You wanted to be one of us once; maybe this is the your chance to prove yourself.' She tried to find his gaze, but he no longer saw her. All the muscles of his face were at work, the cords of his neck stood out sharply. Choking, he fought to loosen his collar.

'Linda?' said Michael.

She shook her head, signalling him to be quiet. Somewhere beyond the trees to her left a broad expanse of golden-yellow rape shimmered in the sun. A handful of crows rose and hovered above it. Somewhere in this world there was peace, she thought, but not here, not until this was concluded. Still gagging, Quigley tugged at his shirt collar with such force the buttons flew; then he was frenziedly pulling off his coat for

277

air. He was sobbing, taking great hollow gasps of air. As the coat was cast aside, scalpels, pliers, a claw hammer scattered. Linda glimpsed the lining, all the instruments of torture he'd carried for so long stitched into it, saws and knives and can openers. Then he was tearing loose his shirt from neck to navel, and she heard herself draw breath, not believing what she saw, perhaps for one moment hallucinating that his torso was covered with dark eyes, gaping mouths, a confusion of faces not yet fully formed, which he could no longer hold inside. She twisted away, willing the illusion to pass; then caught sight of Michael's expression, one of sheer horror, which could only confirm her own worst fears.

'Oh please God, please – '

She smelt the burning seconds before she dared make herself look at Quigley again. When she did he was still on his knees, crossing himself, raising both arms to the sky as the flames stormed up his body to engulf his face and hair. At the same time she heard what could only be several voices crying at once, a chorus of captive souls emerging from one mouth somewhere at the heart of the fire. Was this all her doing – this release of so many souls in conflict? Was this what she'd willed to come out of him? If this was her wish fulfilled – the end of the endless retribution – she had it and then some. She stood alone now, lost to the fire, unable to think. Before she knew what she was doing she had stretched a hand to the flames, the hairs on the back of her hand singing black, just as Michael rushed in to sweep her clear.

'Is it over?' she wondered, though Michael didn't – couldn't – answer. Perhaps he was mesmerised by the lights that seemed to dance, diffracting, multicoloured, from the source of the fire to the sky, to all corners of the woodland clearing; she sensed him grow tense for a second, his fingers firming their grip on her shoulder. After that he relaxed, and the smoke rose steadily in plumes. It seemed to her there was nothing to add – no questions to ask – at least until the flames had had their say.

278

Chapter Thirty-five

The calls had been so infrequent tonight she was beginning to drift towards sleep at the desk when her telephone rang, startling her. The receiver was right at her fingertips, as it had been since the last call, forty minutes ago. On the third ring she lifted it, taking a deep breath as she did so.

'Samaritans, can I help you?'

The delay was fractionally too long; long enough to fill her mind with thoughts about quitting, never answering another telephone again. But the cavernous noise on the line was neither static nor the heavy breathing she'd anticipated.

'I'm at Heathrow,' Michael said. 'I promised to let you know when the time came. Flight leaves in just under an hour. Are you sure – just a minute – ' Thunder as an aircraft took off or landed. 'Are you sure I can't persuade you to drop everything and come with me? You'll not make this flight, but I'll wait and we'll take the next.'

She forced a laugh, though she felt no more frivolous than Michael was attempting to make himself sound. 'It would be so easy,' she said.

'Precisely why I'm asking. Could I make it any plainer? Do I need to? Like it or not, we're part of each other; I want you to share this with me, I want you move to New York and live with me there for as long as we're able to stand each other.'

'This line is supposed to be for genuine distress calls,' she informed him. 'You shouldn't be ringing me here.'

'What's this, if not a genuine distress call? I'm on my way to fucking *America*, dummy. Remember the other night?'

'Of course I do, I remember everything. Don't think I don't.'

'So what's keeping you?'

'There's so much to consider, there's George and – ' Little else, but she needed peace of mind above all. 'Even if we've been having a hard time lately it's wrong of me to opt out; we've seen bad times before. Mike, I still have *responsibilities*. To George – to both of us.'

'Why?'

'You're incorrigible. Please go now. Call again when I feel less vulnerable.'

'When will that be?'

She shrugged and frowned through the window at her car, trapped in a patch of orange sodium light. The street, like the Centre, was very peaceful tonight. 'When I know I can come to you freely.'

'You're mine,' he reminded her in an arch, adopted tone. 'You always will be. You shouldn't waste time, yours or mine or George's, because it's inevitable. Don't you see? Remember that line – what was it in now? – *Educating Rita?* That classic line: "It would be nice to leave a country that's ending for one that's just beginning." Remember that?'

'Yes,' she said. 'I remember that too.'

'So here's your chance to put everything behind you; everything we've waited for. We didn't go through the fire for nothing, did we? What good would it be if we had?'

'Just give me time. Time to speak with George, see how things are between us, look at this from all sides. Right now that's the most I can manage, Mike.' She waited for another blast of aircraft noise to subside. 'Please don't think I don't desperately want to be on the next plane with you. I do, really I do. There's nothing I'd rather – '

'Sure,' he said, sounding snubbed, as if he hadn't believed a word she'd spoken. 'It's clearly not an easy decision for you.'

'Michael,' she began – but this was not the time or place to hack out the rest of their lives. Surely he recognised that?

280

'People who need me might be trying to get through on this line.'

'People who need you?' he said, and hung up so sharply she wondered at first if the line had been cut.

Epilogue
TriBeCa Blues

'So out with it, Michael,' Harvey Klein said. 'How did you find the old country?'

A question which left Michael, the wordman, temporarily stranded. Frowning at the bowl of crispy noodles on the table between them, he seized one, ate it, and considered the fortune cookie on his side-plate which he hadn't yet opened. They were seated upstairs at the Peking Duck House on Mott Street, restfully quiet at this hour and still serving set lunches, though as usual Harvey was flaunting expenses, insisting on the house speciality. The slivers of duck on his plate were golden, glistening, photogenic.

'Didn't I tell you Ed Koch used to eat here?' Harvey wondered. 'Maybe still does. Or was it that place on the Bowery?' He considered this for a moment, then shrugged, undecided. 'So England: how was it?'

'The same,' Michael said. 'Always and forever the same.'

'Really? You sound about up to here with it. Why bother making the trip if that's how it grabs you?'

'It was kind of unfinished business.' He sighed and fingered his temple.

'Unfinished business? You don't give much away, do you?'

'You wouldn't want to hear the whole story, Harv, frankly. This was just me and a few old friends journeying through the past darkly.'

'And not so damn enthusiastically, right? Did the others share your feelings?'

'The ones who survived it did, yes.'

282

Harvey didn't take this literally, He nodded and poured himself tea, gazing back at Michael with an air of compassion. 'If it's any consolation, you've returned to a work-load that should at least stop you dwelling on merry old England. Yesterday I had lunch with this producer at Lorimar, who apparently are deadly serious about *Rubber Bullets*; not only that but they want you to write the pilot script, which at least should allow you *some* degree of control, even if their requirements – ' He speared a new sliver of duck. 'Well, remember that we're talking American prime time TV here, You'll gather the level they're aiming for.'

'No F-words, no nipples?'

'You're getting there.'

'In which case count me out. *Rubber Bullets* without sleaze is simply unthinkable.'

Harvey was grinning broadly. 'Of course I'm aware of your preferences, but I know what's best for you also. In a couple of weeks we're likely to see some very advantageous terms on the table, better than anything we're able to secure by waiting.' He cleared his throat. 'In my opinion.'

Michael nodded, fingered his unopened fortune cookie. His plate of chillied baby shrimp was still half uneaten, cooling by the minute. He was miles away again. All he could see was Tom Quigley collapsing forward in slo-mo, a burnt-out husk from which black smoke spiralled. They had, this time, buried the evidence together, at a point not far from where Tara lay, tearing up the earth with bare hands until their fingers grew raw and painful. It was Bill who unearthed the bones – humerus and scapula, several spare ribs – which Quigley himself had buried there.

There was nothing to scream at any longer, no terror to share; all they had left was tears. 'This is such a fucking tragedy,' Bill mourned, and when the ground was covered over and trodden down they had walked the familiar mile through the woods back to where Linda's Mini waited at the roadside.

' – more care of yourself,' Harvey Klein was saying.

'How's that?' Michael blinked back to the present. A fog of noise swirled in his mind.

'You seem weary and overwrought, Mike. Your eyes are so heavy, and you've been overdoing the booze again by the looks of it. Tell me honestly, is it becoming a *problem?* It shouldn't be, is all: you're on the upward curve and without meaning to tempt fate I'd hazard a guess it'll keep getting better. What I *said* was you should take more care of yourself.'

'I will, Harvey. I will from now on.' Nevertheless he craved a large Bushmills on the rocks, packed with ice the American way, maybe with a beer for a chaser. He still felt on edge, driven by nerves; the temptation to look over his shoulder was almost irresistible. *Security*, he thought. The key word henceforth is security. He remembered Linda's plaintive, hopeful voice at the last – *'Is it over?'* – and understood why he hadn't been able to answer her. Nothing was over; nothing could ever be fully resolved. Perhaps he had sensed as much before ever flying to London.

'Did something happen over there?' Harvey inquired now, poised and frowning. He was wearing a favoured charcoal Brooks Brothers suit, the red silk tie immaculately knotted with machine precision. As a rule Harvey inspired confidence in Michael. But today –

'I'm sorry, Harv.' Michael shook his head. 'This wasn't such a good idea after all. Maybe we'll do this again in a week or so, once you've talked business with Lorimar and I've had time to rehydrate.'

'Did something happen?' Harvey asked again. 'Something it might help you to talk over?'

'If it did you'll no doubt read all about it in the next manuscript,' Michael said, then relented. 'Yes, something *did*, Harv, but right now it's all inside me. Here.' He thumped his chest. 'Still taking shape. Now is too soon for me to make sense of it.'

Harvey Klein nodded, took a sip of his tea. 'So what does it say? It's obvious you're just dying to find out.'

'What does what say?'

Harvey waved at the fortune-cookie.

'Oh, that.' With a flourish Michael tore the cookie

284

in halves and read the slip of paper it contained twice through, finally managing a laugh as he set the message face-down on the table. '*You are independent politically,*' he said.

Chapter Thirty-Seven

After lunch with Harvey he walked the twelve blocks to a place he knew in the East Village where he had an appointment to see a man about a gun. It was one of those idyllic late September New York days where the climate suddenly relented, the punishing heat and humidity of summer were forgotten, and the neighbourhood streets took on a happy-go-lucky carnival atmosphere. On St Mark's Place the doorways vibrated with crosscurrents of jazz, rap, late 70s punk; even the street hustlers grinned amiably when he told them where to get off. Michael had always felt inexplicably at home in this vibrant Bohemia as he had never done in England; taxiing back to his apartment in TriBeCa, .38 snub-nose tucked in his pocket, he knew he had found his place in the world.

There was a message waiting from Bill Anderson on his answerphone when he got in. It was brief, breathless and to the point: 'Mikey, I'm in town for the week, would you believe? There's this important PC exhibition that IBM and Microsoft are sponsoring, and that I managed to blag tickets for. I'm staying at the Days Inn, if you'd like to get back to me. Are you in New York right now? I really do hope so. There's something we need to discuss, re Tom Quigley. Do get back to me if you're able ...'

In a matter of minutes he was through to Bill's hotel room. Bill, who must have been rushing to answer the call, sounded not only out of breath but also, Michael sensed, almost artificially pleased to be hearing from him.

'Well, I didn't think we should leave it fifteen more years

before we hooked up again!' he said brightly. 'Thank God that's all behind us now.'

'Still, it *is* very soon,' Michael said, 'all things considered.'

'It's just that this came up at short notice.'

'You're here on business, then.'

'Yeah, well. Unfinished business more like.'

'So I gather. You said there was something we ought to talk over.'

'That's right. What I mean is ... Even though it *is* all behind us, what happened, at the time we never really had the chance to – this sounds crazy – *appraise* what we'd been through. There's so much I still don't understand.'

'Me too.'

'You don't think I'm being presumptuous, do you?' It was beginning to sound as though his breathlessness had been brought on by anxiety: unusual for Bill, who had always been the level-headed member of the body. 'Well, I happen to have your address down in TriBeCa. I could be there in an hour, once I've eaten.'

'Make it in less and eat here,' Michael told him. 'Frozen pizza and beer's as exotic as it gets, though. Be warned.' Then, as an afterthought before hanging up, 'Bill, it'll be something to see you again. Really it will.'

Within twenty minutes, rather sooner than he'd anticipated, the buzzer in his apartment sounded. Bill was standing in the hall outside, still recognisably himself in a herringbone jacket and black necktie, his beard carefully trimmed and hair tidily combed, but as Michael let him in his eyes didn't quite match his broad, forced smile.

Security is the word, Michael thought. He knows something, knows it isn't over quite yet. The computer show isn't the reason he's here.

But Bill was taking in the apartment, waving his arms at the generous loft space. 'Some retreat you have here. And some view. Not at all bad, Mike. I approve.'

'Well, it fits, even if the rent is climbing again. Rather here than anywhere else, I suppose.'

Bill seized his bearded chin like Rodin's Thinker. 'Who knows, though? One day it could be Fifth Avenue facing the park? It's good to see where you've landed. You deserve all you've worked for, Michael, I mean that.'

'Thank you.'

Wringing his hands restlessly, Bill moved now to the window, which overlooked West Broadway. Near and far, Manhattan's lights were clicking on in a mesmeric, complex formation. 'Yes, it's really something,' he mooned, and then turned to face Michael. 'Linda would love it here.'

'Linda? Have you seen her since? To talk to?'

'Not really, though we decided we'd be keeping in touch this time.' His words sounded strained, coerced from himself under pressure. For a moment he didn't seem able to meet Michael's gaze.

'Where's this leading?' Michael wanted to know.

'Do you need me to tell *you* that?' Bill looked so flushed, agitated. 'Then again, perhaps I'm mistaken. Christ knows, after all we've witnessed anyone would be hard-put to see straight.' He paused for a moment, crossing his arms on his chest, his breathing ragged and harsh. 'Mikey, what we need to discuss – what I need to know – is exactly what you saw. Whether you saw anything *else*, anything *other* when Quigley ... burnt out.'

'Anything other than what?'

All at once the mask was off. 'Something tells me you know more than you're confessing. Something came out of him, didn't it? Something came out of Quigley that lit up the clearing. More than smoke, more than fire. You saw it, Mikey. You must have done.' Bill's eyes, suddenly piercing and dark, alight with twin flames, found Michael's at long last. 'Our *friends* came out of him, didn't they? Our fellow-sufferers. You must have seen them and heard them too. Those sounds – were they voices? – like prayers being spoken, so many voices speaking in tongues. You must have heard. He'd been holding them prisoner inside himself, and for a second you could hear them, hear how elated they were to be free of him. Don't ask me to believe you didn't share the experience. I *know* you did, Michael.' He was perspiring, wiping his face with the back of his hand, standing flush against the window as if suddenly desperate to retreat further. 'You were standing behind Linda, your hands kind of perched on her shoulders, and you were watching the fire. Me? I couldn't make myself look any more; it was all too much to bear, and the light burned my eyes. And at some point I looked over at you and it was then that I saw how your face changed, the look that came over you, your eyes lighting up and your mouth ... Jesus, Mikey, how you licked your lips! You can't imagine how it felt to me, seeing that. Then the look passed off, almost as quickly as it came, but it left me feeling ... '

'Go on,' said Michael, stepping nearer.

'Gave me the feeling you'd – swallowed something. You'd seen the light and – I don't know – absorbed something inside it. Believe me, I haven't been able to think of anything other than that since. I haven't been able to picture anything but the way your face changed, just for that moment.'

'Sure. I can see why that would disturb you, but there's nothing to worry about, Bill, really nothing. It's nearly over.' Michael smiled, at the same time whipping out the .38 snub-nose he had purchased on Avenue B from his pocket. *The body must perish*, he thought with a clarity that felt like a rush of adrenaline, *but the spirit, yes, the spirit will soar*. 'Here's retribution the American way,' he said. In the space of three seconds he had raised the gun to Bill's mouth, his free hand clasping his necktie for purchase, and fired twice, blowing out the back of Bill's head and the window behind him.

Outside, a police siren ascended and dipped several blocks away; early evening traffic waged war on their horns, still gridlocked from the rush hour. The sound of the gun shot was just another stray detail, washed away on an endless tide of city noise pollution. No one knew, no one heard. The primitive was at large in the mean streets, and utterly anonymous for all that. For a moment or two Michael held Bill upright, by the tie, just until he sensed the life-force evaporate and enter himself, this time softly and languidly, without fanfare, and at last he let the hollow body slide to the floor.

Later he reclined in an armchair across the room, sipping Maker's Mark and smoking one more stale cigarette from his desk, watching the smoke rise against the darkness in a cool blue lambent spiral. Night slowly, very gradually enclosed the room while the city lights blossomed beyond. He would dispose of Bill Anderson later and at leisure, he decided, and call a man about the window first thing in the morning.

Around nine-fifteen the telephone rang. It was Linda Walker, and though he hadn't heard her voice in several weeks − not since the night he had called her from the airport − he wasn't surprised in the slightest to hear her.

'Michael?' The Transatlantic line seemed agonisingly clear. He could practically feel her, smell her. He remembered the smell of her sex. 'Everything's fine. Or will be in time. I just wanted you to know that; couldn't keep it to myself any longer. Actually I didn't even manage to speak to George before I discovered *he* was leaving *me*. Isn't that bloody ironic? − though I'm hardly surprised, I guess if I'd been able to see things for what they were I would've seen it coming long ago. In fairness I had really intended to make another effort with him; after all, we were married for so long, who'd treat that lightly? But there's nothing to hold me now. The bastard walked out a fortnight ago. So since then I've been holding off this call and trying very hard to be clear about what I want − and if you still want me I can be there as soon as the loose ends are tied up here.'

'And you still want *me*?'

'More than ever.' She paused. 'Especially now that I'm free to give myself to you without looking back. It's been a nightmare, Mikey, an endless and unbearable nightmare − but we made it, didn't we?'

'It's been so long,' he mused, and took a swallow of Bourbon and leisurely carted the phone to the shattered window where he could stand with Bill Anderson at his feet and an uninterrupted view of West Broadway and the cool night air in his face. 'So long I can hardly believe it's true. Together at last. Just think of that.'

'Yes,' she said dreamily. 'Just think.'